# VALIANT LADIES

MELISSA GREY

# VALIANT LADIES

FEIWEL AND FRIENDS

New York

A Feiwel and Friends Book
An imprint of Macmillan Publishing Group, LLC
120 Broadway, New York, NY 10271 • fiercereads.com

Our books may be purchased in bulk for promotional, educational, or business use.
Please contact your local bookseller or the Macmillan Corporate and Premium Sales
Department at (800) 221-7945 ext. 5442 or by email at
MacmillanSpecialMarkets@macmillan.com.

Library of Congress Cataloging-in-Publication Data

Names: Grey, Melissa, author.
Title: Valiant ladies / Melissa Grey.
Description: First edition. | New York : Feiwel and Friends, 2022. |
Summary: In Potosí, a silver mining city in the new Spanish viceroyalty
of Peru, two teen vigilantes set out to expose corruption and deliver
justice after Kiki's brother is murdered and the prostitute he loved
disappears. Includes author's note.
Identifiers: LCCN 2021047576 | ISBN 9781250622204 (hardcover)
Subjects: CYAC: Vigilantes—Fiction. | Murder—Fiction. |
Corruption—Fiction. | Lesbians—Fiction. | Potosí (Bolivia)—Fiction. |
Peru (Viceroyalty)—History—17th century—Fiction. | LCGFT: Novels. |
Historical fiction.
Classification: LCC PZ7.1.G75 Val 2022 | DDC [Fic]—dc23
LC record available at https://lccn.loc.gov/2021047576

First edition, 2022
Book design by Veronica Mang
Feiwel and Friends logo designed by Filomena Tuosto
Printed in the United States

ISBN 9781250622204 (hardcover)
1  3  5  7  9  10  8  6  4  2

To the girls
with steel in their bones
and fire in their blood

Let him who calls me wild beast and basilisk, leave
me alone as something noxious and evil; let him who
calls me ungrateful, withhold his service; who calls me
wayward, seek not my acquaintance; who calls me cruel,
pursue me not; for this wild beast, this basilisk,
this ungrateful, cruel, wayward being has no kind
of desire to seek, serve, know, or follow them.

—Marcella, Miguel de Cervantes's *Don Quixote*

# CHAPTER 1

*Kiki*

It's a shame what we're about to do to this tavern. Admittedly, it's already a bit of a shithole, but it's our shithole. Mine and Ana's. The proprietor, Santiago, always keeps barrels of his best booze aside for us and makes sure to save the very best gossip for our ears only. But alas, some confrontations simply cannot be avoided.

The tip of the knife digs into my skin as the man holding the blade sneers at me. He's standing and I'm sitting, which would theoretically put him at an advantage, but if I had to put money on someone, it wouldn't be him. He's an ugly bastard with the personality to match. A ragged scar runs from his hairline to his chin, and he's missing several teeth. I'd wager most of them were victims of bar fights.

Much like the one about to break out now.

I tilt my head back to look the man in the eye.

Never take your eyes off your opponent. That is the first rule of swordplay.

We aren't playing, and this isn't a game, but the rules still apply.

• • •

I don't need to look down at the cards in my hand. I memorized them as soon as they were dealt. It is an excellent hand. A shame, really, that I'll have to hasten this fool's shuffle off this mortal coil before I get to play it.

I set my cards down on the table as the corners of my lips tick upward. It isn't a pleasant smile. It isn't meant to be. "I wouldn't do that if I were you."

"Why not?" The man's words are slightly slurred, but he isn't swaying on his feet, and the hand holding the knife is steady. So he isn't fully drunk, not yet. Just drunk enough to feel brave.

And that will be his undoing.

I may or may not be entirely sober myself, but that is beside the point. I know my limits. I don't think this pendejo does.

"Because these are my favorite boots." I reach for my cup. It's a solid wooden thing, mostly full of a passable vintage. "I would hate to get your blood on them."

From the corner of my eye, I spy movement in the tavern. The man's friends, no doubt, slinking about to flank us.

The urge to glance at them is so strong it's almost like an itch. But I refuse to give in to it. I trust the woman sitting to my right to watch my back so I don't have to.

Ana throws her cards down with a disgusted snort. "I fold."

Without breaking eye contact with the knife-wielding simpleton before me, I ask, "So soon? But we've barely even begun."

"Oh, I don't know, Kiki. I can think of better ways to pass the time."

Something warm and dangerous blossoms in my gut. I love it when Ana calls me Kiki. I love the way the hard consonants sound bouncing around on her tongue.

Only a select few people in the entire Viceroyalty of Peru are allowed to call me Kiki. Ana is one. The other is my older brother, who began to do so when my full name, Eustaquia, proved too much of a mouthful for a three-year-old. My father thought it was cute, so he started using it as well. The usage of that name is a sacred privilege, bestowed only upon the worthy.

Ana leans backs in her chair. I can't see her hand moving, but I can feel the rustle of fabric beside me. The man's eyes dart toward her.

I don't need to see her to know exactly what she looks like in that moment. Her hair a wild tangle of auburn waves. Her skin kissed by the sun and dotted with the most charming freckles I've ever come across. Her honey-brown eyes gleaming with the promise of a little good old-fashioned bloodshed.

"Don't move," he barks at her.

"Sorry." Her voice is sweet but not the least bit sorry. "I don't take orders from gutter scum who entertain themselves by robbing defenseless women. Though I suppose they put up the only fight you stand of winning."

Rage flits across his face. He pulls the knife away from my throat to brandish it at her.

He realizes the error of his ways as soon as he does it, but that split second of distraction is all the time I need.

I lob my cup at his head, angling it so the wine splashes him right in the eyes.

And just like that, the fight is on.

Ana kicks the table hard. The man is just the right height to take the sharp corner to the crotch. He collapses, howling in agony, as the knife drops from his suddenly nerveless fingers.

His friends attempt to stumble into action, but it's soon clear they are woefully unmatched. One catches my elbow to his nose. The cartilage gives a satisfying crack under the force of the blow. Another gets well acquainted with the heavy sole of my riding boot when I slam it into his groin. I grab the back of my chair and swing it into his face when he tries to get up. The wood smashes against his skull; my arms tremble with the impact.

With them down, I have the slimmest moment to admire the girl beside me. Ana whirls as she slips two daggers from the sheaths strapped to her forearms. The sleeves of the masculine frock coat she's wearing—a deep emerald that complements her coloring—are perfect for hiding them but wide enough to make it easy to pull them when needed.

We both have swords, but knives are often far better suited to close-quarters combat like this. It's a smart move on her part. Sometimes though . . . I prefer the flash of a sword to anything else, even if it's not the most utilitarian choice. I draw the saber at my hip, baring my teeth in a snarling smile.

One of the man's friends skids to a halt, his eyes darting from the gleaming steel to me and back again.

"Having second thoughts?" I ask. "Can't say I blame you."

The taunt makes something snap inside him. You'd be surprised how many men can't handle a pretty young woman making fun of them.

With a pathetic excuse for a battle cry, he all but drives himself into the tip of my saber. I pull back so the blade doesn't get lodged in his ribs. It takes only one time to learn how costly a mistake that can be.

I have the scars across my own back to show for it.

He melts to the ground as his legs go out from under him, the shock of the pain and blood loss rendering him completely useless.

Behind me, a faint whoosh of air disturbs the hair at the back of my neck. I duck, just in time to see a clay wine jug smash against the wall behind me.

"Oh, come now," Ana calls over the fray. "That's no way to treat perfectly good wine!"

Her shouting distracts this new foe long enough for me to sweep his legs out from under him with a well-timed kick. My foot snaps out as he tumbles to the ground to smash his kneecap as hard as I can.

That should keep him down for a good long while.

I glance up just in time to see Ana clock one of the last men standing with her elbow. He falls back onto the hearth, nearly setting himself on fire.

How any of these witless men survived into adulthood in a city as notoriously unkind as Potosí, I haven't the foggiest.

In the time it's taken for Ana and me to dispatch his friends, the first man, the one with the sneer and the missing teeth, has pulled himself up with the help of a nearby table.

He looks worse for wear, though I hardly touched him.

"Back for more?" I twirl my sword, flicking the blood off the tip onto the ground.

The man spits roughly in the direction of my feet. His spittle lands a safe distance away, as he seems too afraid to get any closer. "You'll regret this."

I smile sweetly at him. "Doubtful."

He mutters a curse I don't quite catch, but then he stumbles out of the tavern, dragging one leg behind him in a noticeable limp.

A resigned sigh escapes me as I survey the damage. The patrons with sense fled at the first sign of trouble—one doesn't survive in Potosí for long without learning to sniff it out—but there are a few stragglers left huddling against the walls. One absolute legend of a drunk hasn't budged from his perch at the bar. He's still nursing the same cup of fermented chicha he was when the fight began.

"You all right, Kiki?" Ana asks. She's kneeling, going through the pockets of one of the men she took down. There's blood masking most of his face, and I would bet my father's entire villa that he won't ever be getting up again. When she finds what she's looking for, she stands with a triumphant shout. "Got it."

In her hands is a purse of crimson velvet, tied together with a garish golden rope. Not the sort of thing these men would call their own. And it isn't. They stole it. And we've now retrieved it. We meant to track them down later tonight, but luck brought them to us first.

Santiago might not feel so lucky when he sees the state of his fine establishment now. Blood drips from the tip of my sword onto the packed dirt of the tavern floor. The toes of my boots are already dark with it. Disaster surrounds us in the form of overturned tables, two smashed barrels of chicha, and a perfectly good roast pig dumped on the ground, its sightless eyes seeming to stare at me in accusation.

I distract myself from the sight of how fetching Ana looks with droplets of blood smeared across her freckles by focusing on the dead man at my feet. The one who all but gutted himself on my blade.

Fool.

He is not my first kill. And he will not be my last. No one survives long in this town without cracking a few eggs.

"Ana," I say, "must you always make such a mess wherever you go?"

Ana shoots me a mischievous grin. With sweat beading on her brow and plastering her shirt to her skin, she has never looked more beautiful to me. Her hair began the day bound back in a green ribbon of the finest silk. Now it flows around her shoulders, as free and wild as she is. My hands twitch with the urge to run my fingers through those auburn tresses, to feel that silken softness against my skin. The kicker is that I don't have to imagine the sensation. I know what it feels like. I've brushed and braided it more times than I can count. I know exactly what it looks like spread against crisp white sheets. I know these things, but I wish to know them even better and in very different ways. I clutch the hilt of my sword a little tighter, grateful to have something solid to hold.

"Oh, come now, Kiki." Ana winks at me. My heart sputters in my chest, like a bird fighting against a too small cage. "Don't tell me you didn't enjoy yourself."

At my feet, the man I mistook for dead groans. Ana arches a thick eyebrow at me. I roll my eyes and flick the blood from my sword again. It's a pointless gesture. It will need a thorough cleaning once we get home. "I would but . . ." I shoot her a grin. "We both know it would be a lie."

I draw in a breath—through my mouth, not my nose, as the man's stench is quite atrocious and will only worsen with death—and drive the finely sharpened steel through his heart. I make it look easy, but it's not. There's a certain trick to sliding a thin blade into the space between a man's ribs. It took me quite a few tries to get it right, but now that I have it down to an art, it's a mercy really. A direct blow to the heart kills a man quicker than anything else. It would have taken him an hour to bleed out from his stomach wound.

I may be ruthless, but I am not cruel. I think it's one of the things Ana likes about me. I do bad things when I must, but I try to do good when I can.

Today, we have done a public service in more ways than one.

These men were the worst of the worst. I'd call them bandits, but that would be an insult to proper bandits everywhere. No, these men preyed on the most vulnerable denizens of this sprawling city. Young women. Children. The elderly. They'd tried to pick a fight with us after clocking the quality of our weapons. It was the last thing they'd ever do, and the world was slightly better off for it.

"You're making that face," Ana says, wiping the blood off her own blades before sliding them back into their hidden scabbards.

"What face? I'm not making a face."

"You are." She furrows her brow and tilts the corners of her lips down just a hair. "This face. Your thinking face."

I roll my eyes. "I do not have a thinking face."

"You so do. You have a face for everything. It's why you're so bad at cards."

"I am not bad at cards. I was about to beat you just now."

Ana makes an indelicate sound. "That's only because I let you win."

I open my mouth to challenge her to a rematch, but a gruff voice cuts me off before I can make another peep.

"I hope you know you'll be paying for this mess."

I turn to find Santiago standing in the doorway with his hands on his hips. A crate of bottles—several now smashed—lies at his feet, right beside the prone form of a man I distinctly remember assaulting with a chair. Looks like Santiago barely missed getting hit by the man as he fell. His bottles of what might be wine, judging from the deep burgundy color spilled across the floor, weren't so lucky.

I wish I could say it was the first time we'd trashed Santiago's place, but that too would be a lie.

I point to the dead man at my feet. "He started it."

It's almost not a lie. And therefore not really a sin, in the grand scheme of things.

Ana tosses her arm around my shoulders. My heart does a fractured waltz in my chest. "Yeah," she says. "We just finished it."

"And you couldn't have finished it outside?" Santiago sighs before bending down to retrieve the salvageable bottles of wine.

"Relax," I say, extricating myself from Ana's hold. I want to stay close to her, but I want it so badly it frightens me. I need distance. "We'll cover the damages."

I fish a generous handful of coins from the pouch tucked into the waistband of my breeches. I lay them down on the nearest table, one by one so Santiago can see that I'm good for it.

His eyes widen at the pieces of eight I place on the table. It's worth far more than the cost of a few broken tables and some spilled booze. It's good to keep one's friends happy. Especially friends like Santiago, who've proven more than once to be an excellent source of both information and ale.

"A little extra for labor," I say with a smile. It's the smile that's smoothed over more than one sticky situation at the society parties my father insists on hosting. It works only half as well on a man like Santiago, but it works all the same.

The fight goes out of him as he huffs a defeated sigh. "I take it you're not sticking around to help clean up."

"Not really our style," Ana chimes in as she all but skips toward the door.

"We do have a reputation to maintain," I add, sheathing my own blade.

Santiago mutters something about street rats and hooligans, but once I cross the threshold, the sounds of the busy thoroughfare drown out his complaint.

It's late, but Potosí is as alive as ever. Torchlight floods the road like spilled honey, leaving only the alleys in darkness. I can hear bodies shifting in some of them with the telltale sound of fabric sliding out of the way. It's honest work, I suppose, but those women won't earn nearly as much as the ones in the brothels down the road.

People spill out of taverns. Some to fight, some to drink, some because they've run out of coin to pay for their habits. There's a place nearby that hosts the most vicious card game this side of the Atlantic, but I'm not sure I have enough left on me for the buy-in.

"Where to next?" Ana asks, slipping her hat on her head. She's tucked her hair up under it, but there's nothing she could do to make herself look like anything less than the beautiful young woman she is. She throws her arms out to her sides and spins as she walks. "The city is our oyster. Where shall we hunt for our pearl?"

"Aren't you tired?" I ask.

"Tired?" Ana's smile is more like a baring of fangs than anything else. "You know I'm never tired after a fight. I could take on another ten men, easy. Twenty maybe."

"I envy you your vitality," I say. It's a lie. A small one, but still. I'm not tired. Not in the least.

Nothing makes me feel more alive than a good fight. Blood pumps through my veins, so hot and hard I can almost taste it. It all but roars in my ears. But I know that if we don't return to the villa soon, we'll regret it later. Twice already this month, a servant has caught us sneaking back in well after we've allegedly retired to our beds. I am under no delusions that my bribes can continue to buy their silence. The servants are loyal to one person at the Sonza estate, and it's not me. My father is a good master, generous and kind. They'll hold off on ratting us out but only for so long.

"We should head to Esmeralda's, return the purse, and then head home," I say. "If we stay out much longer, the rising sun will usher us home."

Ana pouts at me. "Must we go home so soon?"

I offer her a small smile. "I fear we must."

Ana stops so abruptly I almost walk into her. I stop, mere inches away.

"Are you sure I can't tempt you?" Ana's voice is low enough that only I can hear her. Her words seep into my skin like warm oil.

A drunk stumbles past us, patting what I'm sure are empty pockets. A lack of sobriety is just asking for a pocket to be picked.

From this close, I can see that Ana's lips are chapped. She has a tendency to worry her bottom lip with her teeth. The urge to smooth that harried skin with my own lips is so strong I almost reel where I stand.

She cocks her head to the side. "Kiki? You all right?"

"What?" How long had I been staring at her in silence like some lovestruck fool?

Before I can try to cover my own idiocy, Ana reaches for me. Her hand is cool against my forehead. It's a battle with my own baser urges not to lean into her touch. A flush works its way across my skin.

"You feel a bit warm," Ana observes. "Are you coming down with something?"

*Buffoonery*, I think, and wisely do not say.

But she's granted me an out, and I would be a fool not to take it. "Maybe," I lie. "I think I just need to sleep it off."

"Well, we can't have you getting sick before the ball," Ana says with an insincere flourish. She twirls into a truly abysmal curtsy. She's capable of a better one—I made sure of it—but she seems to delight in flouting the habits of high society whenever possible.

I groan. "Don't remind me."

The viceroy is hosting another one of his parties in a week's time. Normally, the parties don't bother me. I almost enjoy them, but my father seems unduly preoccupied with this one. So far, my father hasn't said a word about it, but he likes to keep his own counsel.

Ana slips her hand into mine. My palm is sweaty, but I can blame that on the fight if I have to. Or the illness I'm apparently faking now.

"Come on," Ana says, giving my hand a little tug as she pulls me down the street. "Let's get this over with so we can get you home."

I let her lead me onward, away from the heart of the city and all its violent delights. And if I hold her hand longer than is strictly necessary, well . . . let that be between me and God.

# CHAPTER 2

*Ana*

Kiki's hand in mine is worth killing for. I'd slay a thousand men to keep us in this moment, gilded by the torchlight that illuminates the cobbled streets of Potosí. In these stolen fragments of time, we are our truest selves. We bring that out in each other. Or at least she brings that out in me. I can only assume she feels the same.

I've always been a good judge of character, and I know what I see in Kiki. When she's out here with me, swords at our sides, our coats trailing behind us as we stride through the twisting labyrinth of the city's alleyways like we own them, she is so wonderfully alive.

I steal a glance at her as we walk, and just like the first time I saw her, I feel something unfurl in my chest, like a spring blossom fighting through the crust of a winter's chill.

A small contented smile plays at the corners of her lips. The color is high in her cheeks from the fight, and it's sinful how much willpower it takes me to not entertain other activities that might leave her with that flush on her face.

Her hair is so smooth, the reflected firelight of nearby torches dances on it as if it were water.

I am not a poetic person by nature, but there is something about Kiki that inspires in me a truly nauseating verbosity.

I'm saved from my profane thoughts by Kiki tugging on my hand. She's frowning now, a little wrinkle marring the skin between her brows.

"Ana, look." Kiki points to something over my shoulder.

I pivot in place, ready to be annoyed by whatever put that look on her face, but dread chases the thought away when I spy the crowd gathering at the end of the alley.

*　◉　*

There is a certain flavor to tragedy. One you can taste on the air if you're close enough. I learned it well and too early. I can feel it now, cloying and strong on my tongue. Something bad happened here. Something worse, perhaps, than the usual sort of bad that happens in Potosí.

A gaggle of onlookers cluster around some central point. Latecomers crowd around them, popping up onto their toes for a better look.

People stream by us in ones and twos, each soul keen to see what the commotion is.

"Hey." I grab the sleeve of a boy trotting by us. He can't be a day older than thirteen, but he has that look in his eyes that makes him seem far, far older. He wrenches his arm out of my grasp before he recognizes me. His gaze darts from me to Kiki and back again. I can't quite place his name, but he knows us. Most people in this neighborhood do. We're a bit of a fixture, Kiki and me.

"Oh, it's you." He smooths the rumpled fabric of his sleeve.

I jerk my chin in the direction of the crowd. "What's all that about?"

"Haven't you heard?" Morbid glee tinges the boy's voice. "There's a cutthroat on the loose."

Kiki steps up beside me, her shoulder brushing mine. "A cut-throat? You mean like . . ."

"Like a madman with a knife and a taste for the ladies, yeah." The boy glances back at the growing crowd, his expression a touch too keen for my tastes. Some people like gawking at dead bodies. I am not among their number. I have seen enough to last me a lifetime. Death is common in this city. It's common in every city, I suppose, but it feels especially common here.

It takes a bit of elbowing, but Kiki and I force our way through the crowd. When we get to the front, I regret giving in to the siren song of curiosity.

There is a dead girl in the alley.

She lies flat on her stomach, which is a small mercy considering the blood peeking out from under her belly. Her skirt's rucked up around her knees, exposing her pale silk stockings. They're fine, finer than her dress, which is odd. Normally, it's the other way around, a pretty shell with threadbare underthings lurking beneath. She's wearing but a single shoe. The other is nowhere to be found, at least as far as I can see. Her face is turned to the side toward us, one unseeing eye open and pale as if to confront us for staring. Smudged rouge stands in lurid contrast to the death pall of her skin. An open wound, fresh and angry, trails along her neck like a scarlet ribbon.

I frown. "There's not enough blood."

"What?" Kiki asks.

She's gone a bit pale. Kiki may be no stranger to violence, but she's not as well acquainted with this side of it as the rest of us. Her life was far more sheltered all the way up on that hill. It's one thing to take a man's life in defense of your own. It's another to see an inno-cent life stolen when you know it wasn't well deserved.

"Her throat's been slit," I say. It's easier to focus on that than on the deliberate cruelty of the display.

"Yes, I can see that." Kiki gets testy when she's uncomfortable. Can't say I blame her really.

"If she was killed here, there'd be more blood. A cut like that would have hit a vein. A big one. So . . . more blood."

Kiki nods, paler still. "Come on. We should go."

Kiki tugs at my sleeve, but my feet are rooted in place. There's something about the way she's been left here. It's almost as though she's been displayed like this on purpose. Like someone wanted her to be found, exactly like this.

"We can't save everyone." Kiki pulls me harder. "And it's too late to save her."

I walk backward, trusting she won't let me stumble. But I can't take my eyes away from the girl's legs. From the splash of blood on her white stocking. The shoe hanging off one foot, its mate lost.

This is Potosí. The richest city in the New World. And the poorest. Every coin of Spanish silver in the Empire begins its sordid life here. In our mountain. In our mines. Wrenched from the earth and pounded into submission by those who will never have the luxury of spending it. People live. People die. People gamble with their souls, and sometimes they come out on top. But sometimes, they don't. Sometimes they wind up facedown in an alley, dumped and forgotten like so much garbage.

Kiki slips her hand in mine, as if she can read my thoughts. I shoot her a grateful shadow of a smile. I don't need a mirror to know it doesn't reach my eyes. I let her lead the way as a single thought chases me, all the way from the alley to our next destination.

*There but for the grace of God go I.*

That could have been me. If I had stayed on these streets, that could have been me. But Kiki saved me. She was right in one regard. We can't save everyone, but she did save me.

I'm so lost in my thoughts that I don't even realize we've arrived at Doña Esmeralda's place until Kiki says, "We're here."

She exchanges a nod with a man standing by a nondescript door in a curiously clean alley. If you didn't know what you were looking for, you would never know that we were entering one of the better brothels in the city, the sort that catered to men of means who demanded discretion and cleanliness almost as much as they demanded loose women with questionable morals. They liked to slum it with the poor but only so long as it didn't soil their pretty garments.

As we enter, the coins jingle pleasantly against my side as the purse bounces against my hip. That sensation alone feels like a luxury.

Some people, like Kiki, are born with silver spoons in their mouth.

I am not one of those people.

I was born with nothing. Not silver. Not a spoon. Not even a name. It wasn't until the señora of the brothel in which I was born—this very one—realized my natural mother had no intention of christening me that I was given one.

Doña Esmeralda gave me a name and a roof over my head and just enough food to survive, which was more than what most get. At least in this part of the city. It was more than a brothel-born bastard could ask for.

The smell of the brothel hits me before my eyes adjust to the candlelit interior. It's not a bad smell. Pipe smoke, scented powders, and competing fragrances the women wear to set themselves apart from one another. Once upon a time, that smell meant home to me.

The smoke blurs my vision as it permeates the air, sweetened with the palo santo Doña Esmeralda burns. She swears by its invigorating powers and its ability to stimulate the senses.

The brothel is packed to the rafters tonight. Girls spill out into the foyer much like the décolletage spilling out of the tops of their dresses. I tip my hat at them when they see me. I may not live here anymore—and haven't for years—but they know me. They know I'm not a mark or client. To them, I'm not business. I'm practically family.

Esmeralda's voice booms over the heads of her girls.

"Ana, mija!" She approaches me, arms open. I plant my feet and brace myself. Her arms wrap around me, crushing me to her ample bosom. I turn my face to the side. *Mija.* It's a term of affection but it's also a sham, like so much else about her. She'd barely looked at me the day I'd packed up my meager belongings—a cracked mirror with a painted backing one of the girls had given to me on my tenth birthday, a thin stiletto blade I'd lifted from a patron too drunk to keep track of his weapons, and a small brass locket I guarded with my life. Esmeralda had probably assumed she'd never see me again.

But I have not forgotten where I come from. I don't want to. I have seen what wealth can do to people. It has the power to make them callous and cruel. It renders them unable—or unwilling—to know the suffering of others. It can make their worlds so unbearably small. And besides, even if I did want to forget my humble origins, no one would let me.

Kiki shoots me a wry grin as Esmeralda does her level best to suffocate me in her cleavage. To her, Esmeralda is a benevolent force of a woman. The truth is less rosy. Doña Esmeralda may consider herself a maternal figure to me, but she is not. She allowed me to sleep in a nice warm corner of the kitchen so long as I brought in my share. I was too young to work the brothel like the rest of her girls, but I had other usable skills. Nimble fingers that could slip into pockets or empty a purse without anyone being a single bit the wiser. I was useful to her then. I'm less useful to her now, but my meteoric rise in station makes her treat me with a kindness she never showed when I lived under her roof, sleeping in a shivering huddle by the dying embers of a kitchen hearth and eating scraps.

I extricate myself from Esmeralda's arms. The cloying scent of her perfume clings to my nostrils. "Is Rosalita here?" I hold up the purse. "I have something that belongs to her."

Doña Esmeralda's fingers twitch with the repressed desire to snatch the purse right out of my hand. It's such a fleeting gesture, I wonder if Kiki's even caught it. She's come a long way from the naive, brave little girl I met all those years ago, but she's still as much a product of her environment as I am of mine. We are what we are, and a change of clothes can't alter that simple fact.

Esmeralda gestures behind her to the dimly lit salon where the girls who aren't currently engaged in the rooms upstairs are entertaining prospective clients. "Her last suitor just left. She's free for a few moments at least."

I snort.

*Suitor.*

It's a lovely name for a man who pays for sex. It's not exactly courting, is it?

When we enter the salon, a few men glance our way, but their gazes slide away once they take in our appearance. Our garb makes it abundantly clear we are not merchandise. All of Esmeralda's girls wear dresses. None would be caught wearing men's clothing, especially not with conspicuous bloodstains on the sleeves.

It'll be a bitch trying to get *that* out of the wool.

Heavy brocade drapes cover the windows as effectively as they help retain the heat of the massive hearth at the center of the far wall. The carpeting is plush enough that my boots sink into it. Esmeralda must have replaced it recently. Business must be booming for her to invest in improving the decor underfoot. For as long as I can remember, the salon had boasted the same threadbare woven rugs that were once fine but had been worn thin by years of scuffling boots and silk slippers.

I pop up onto my toes to scan the crowd. Few of Esmeralda's girls are what I'd call truly beautiful. Pretty, yes, and with most of their teeth, which is impressive, but not beautiful. Rosalita in the exception.

She's easy to find. A gaggle of well-dressed men cluster around the hearth, where Rosalita is holding court. They're all leaning in, hanging on every word of some story she's telling. I recognize a few of them from the society parties Kiki drags me to, but I don't acknowledge them and they don't acknowledge me. At the end of the night, when the horizon threatens to spill over with sunlight, we will all retreat to our sprawling villas overlooking the city and pretend none of this ever happened.

I wave my hand as I call out. "Rosalita!"

Her eyes dart to me, and I am reminded of just how powerful they are. They're the deepest, richest, loveliest shade of brown I have ever seen. There is a warmth to her eyes that few in this brothel—maybe even in this entire city—possess. It was she who made me realize my tastes might run toward the fairer sex, and for that, I will always love her just a tiny bit.

Her smile transforms when she sees me. It's not the perfect one she flashes at men to loosen their hold on their precious coin. It widens just enough to reveal the slightly crooked canine tooth she always goes to great pains to hide.

With more grace than I could ever hope to embody, Rosalita muscles her way through her crowd of admirers. My heart may belong to Kiki now, but I am not dead. You'd have to be to ignore Rosalita's charms.

"Ana! So lovely to see you." She leans in to kiss the air beside each of my cheeks. I wonder, frantically, if I missed wiping all the blood away, but she doesn't seem to mind. "And Kiki!"

She treats Kiki to the same greeting. Something small and venomous coils in my stomach at the sight of Rosalita's delicate hand resting against Kiki's sleeve. I adore them both, but for some reason, I do not like the thought of Rosalita touching Kiki.

A thought best abandoned, naturally.

"Did you find it?" Rosalita asks, her painted lips a perfect pout of annoyance that her belongings were stolen in the first place.

"Have I ever let you down?" I ask as I toss her the purse. She catches it with a delighted laugh.

"My dashing heroes," she says, clutching the purse to her chest. "What would I do without you?"

"You'd manage, I'm sure." Kiki smiles at Rosalita, and that little venomous snake rears its head again.

I put a hand on Kiki's sleeve, at the very same spot Rosalita touched. "We have to run, but let us know if anyone else bothers you, okay?"

I'm already steering Kiki toward the door when Rosalita calls out. "Wait."

I pause.

Rosalita steps closer to me so that no one can hear her hushed words. "It might be nothing but . . ." Her eyes slide to the side. Nervous.

My jealousy disappears like smoke on the wind. "What is it? What's wrong?"

"It's just something I've heard. There are girls going missing from some of the brothels. First it was the ones who work the street, so no one really noticed but . . ."

"Has anyone gone missing from Esmeralda's?" Kiki asks.

Rosalita shakes her head. "No, thank God, but . . . I just thought you should know. I know you two are more than capable of taking care of yourself but . . . be careful. Please."

After a moment's hesitation, I pull Rosalita into a firm hug. Shame bubbles thick inside me. Rosalita is my friend, and I've known her since we were children. It's wretched, letting myself feel jealous of her.

"We'll be careful," Kiki assures her. "We always are."

Rosalita steps back with a laugh that sounds like the chime of bells. "Now that I do *not* believe." She twirls around in a swirl of skirts to return to her flock of drooling men.

I watch her go, a frown creasing my brow. Kiki takes my arm, tucking it against her side.

"Come on." She guides me out of the salon. "If we don't get back home soon, Papa will have both our hides."

I nod, but my gaze is pulled back to the salon. I try to steal one last glance back at Rosalita but she's already lost to my sight.

*Kiki*

Dawn pushes at the edges of the horizon, smearing dusky purple light against the stars. The imposing bulk of the Sonza estate rises up against the moonlit sky, a bulwark against the chaos and the fire and the life of the city.

It is beautiful and imposing and impressive. Its luxury shrouds the truth of what it is.

A gilded prison.

There are worse ways to come into the world, I know. I have never wanted for anything in my life (almost anything). I have never known hunger or the cold cruelty of a winter's night without warm bricks placed at the foot of my bed. But even so, the bars of that cage hold me in, like the stays of a whalebone corset digging into my sensitive flesh.

Down in the city, with a sword at my hip and Ana's hand in mine, I feel like myself. My truest self.

I stop as we reach the crest of the hill that will lead down into the orange grove that surrounds the property. The land here isn't really suited to oranges—they prefer much lower altitudes than Potosí—but that is one of the many things that gold can buy. Inappropriate extravagance.

*See how rich our owners are*, those orange trees seem to say. *They have enough money and influence to grow fruit that can barely survive in this climate.*

Ana's presence in my life has made me see things that my privilege had prevented me from noticing. Before her, I had never questioned my place in this world. In this villa. In this city. In this land that belonged to others once, not to the crown. Seeing my world through her eyes has been illuminating. The orange grove is a prime example of this. I had never questioned its presence until the first time she saw it. Her eyes had widened, as if I'd opened a magical door into a world beyond her wildest imaginings.

It's a silly thing to do. Growing oranges in the mountains. I know this. But I also know that I relished the sight of Ana taking her first sip of freshly squeezed juice. I would not have traded that sight for anything. Her eyes shone as if someone had lit a candle inside her skull. And then she'd wrinkled her nose as the tartness hit, screwing up her lips as she worked her way through the flavor. Sweet, and a little sour. Just like her.

As I am rather fond of having all my limbs attached to my body, I kept that thought to myself.

Ana draws up beside me. I squint at her in the half-light of the late hour.

"Something on your mind?"

Her voice carries on the crisp night air like birdsong, clear and resonant. Her vowels are nice and round, her consonants perfectly enunciated. If you didn't know any better, she would sound almost as refined as I do. Over the past five years, she has worn down her street urchin accent, but it's still there, hiding beneath the surface. It peeks out every now and then, when she's angry or drunk or simply unfettered, enjoying herself without restraint. She wears that society accent, but it is not hers. It is not truth. It is a mask.

That is why we're out here, skulking around in the dead of night instead of tucked into our beds like good girls. Neither of us fits quite right in the home we've been given, so we sneak out, searching for the things that feel right and true and good.

What I don't tell her—what I can never ever tell her—is that the only home I know, the only home I ever want to know, is her. Not this house or its finery or its wealth. Just her.

I shrug and opt for something that's not even a lie. "Just thinking about what Rosalita said. About girls going missing."

I wasn't, but now that I've said it, I am.

Ana nods. "I wish I could say I was surprised but . . ."

"But this is Potosí." I sigh. "That sort of thing just happens, I know."

"We'll check in with Rosalita tomorrow. I'm sure she'll be fine. But for now . . ." Ana grins at me. It's a tired grin and a little ragged at the edges, but it's still good. "Race you home."

With that, she takes off, her boots sliding against the dew. I follow her, letting the rush of wind in my hair distract me from my thoughts.

She beats me to the villa, but just barely.

I'm faster than her, and we both know it. That's why she had to cheat.

Without missing a beat, I kneel down to give her a leg up to the window we've left open for precisely this purpose. I hoist her up, and she climbs in. She reaches her hands out to help pull me up after her.

I collide against her as my boots slip against the marble floor, and we nearly collapse in a fit of giggles.

I'm about to shush her when a sound from outside silences me. I clap a hand over Ana's mouth. Her breath is warm and moist against my palm.

"Did you hear that?" I whisper.

She shakes her head.

Then I hear it again.

A rustling, like there's someone in the bushes outside. I put a finger to my lips with one hand and draw my sword with the other.

Hands appear on the window ledge a second before the bulk of a shadowy figure attempts to hoist himself up.

My blade is at the man's throat before he can set foot inside.

"One more move and I slice your throat open like a bag of rice."

His features are hidden, but I'd recognize his voice anywhere. "Honestly, Kiki, rice? Is that the best you've got?"

I have barely enough time to pull back my sword before he tumbles through the window and onto the floor in front of us. It would be remarkably bad form to gut my older brother like a pig in his own home.

Alejandro pushes himself up on unsteady legs. His dark hair tumbles across his forehead in a way I've heard the kitchen girls call "rakishly handsome." His eyes gleam in the dim light as a crooked smile graces his lips. Ana says he looks a lot like me when he smiles like that, but I am convinced that it's less charming on his face. I'm just prettier.

"You're drunk," I say with a sneer, as if Ana and I haven't stumbled through that window in exactly that state more times than either of us care to admit. But if you can't be undeservedly superior with your siblings, then, pray tell, who?

Alejandro's lips tilt into a cheeky, sideways grin. He holds up a finger to his lips as his eyes crinkle with mirth. "I won't tell if you won't." He pushes himself up off his knees, brushing dirt from his breeches. "Besides, let he who is without sin cast the first stone. I'm fairly certain that's in the Bible."

"I'm shocked you could open the good book without bursting into flame." There's no fire in my words though. I don't mean them. Alejandro is a decent man and an even better brother. Even if he does like to indulge a touch too much in the fine arts of spirits and wine. Stones. Sin. He's not wrong.

Alejandro starts walking down the hallway toward his own rooms in what couldn't be called a straight line even if you squinted in absolute darkness. His shoulder bumps into a vase that he only just barely manages to catch before it shatters on the ground, alerting every soul in the house to our presence. He sets it right, shooting me a sanctimonious look. "I'll have you know I take the word of God very seriously."

He hiccups before disappearing around a corner.

"And to think," Ana mutters, "that's the man who's going to inherit all of this."

The words sting though I know she didn't mean for them to. As a woman, I am only entitled to what my father's generosity grants me. And after him, my husband.

With a weary sigh, Ana begins tugging me toward our own rooms. *I will never marry.*

The thought flits through my mind, an erratic little fly, buzzing about, begging for my attention. I'm tempted to let it stay, but it's too dangerous. Too seductive. I swat it away.

"Oh, to have been born a man," I say, though I don't really mean it. Life is what you make of it, and I happen to like the one I've made for myself with Ana. That's the thought I think I'll let warm me as I crawl into my own bed, with nothing but a wall between us.

# CHAPTER 3

*Ana*

Normally, when I've had a generous amount of wine—which I have had, thank you very much—I don't dream. My sleep is solid and thick. Undisturbed. I like it better that way. I like it when I close my eyes with the moon in the sky and open them with the sun in its place.

But tonight is different. Tonight, dreams come to me in the form of memories. At least it's one of my favorite memories.

The memory of the first time Kiki and I met.

The dream has that fuzzy quality all dreams do. Some details are crisp, but others are hazy around the edges, half-forgotten.

I remember the taste of the apple—stolen, of course—as I bit into it, watching the display before me, partially hidden by an alcove in one of the seedier alleys in Potosí. I had swiped the apple from a stall in the market. The man who owned it was an asshole who beat his family, so I didn't feel any guilt about the theft. I tried to only steal from people who deserved it. Not people who were down on their luck. I knew what it felt like to go hungry. I wouldn't wish that on anyone.

But the clearest detail in the dream was what Kiki looked like.

A shorter version of the young woman she was now, but no less grand for it.

Thick as a brick considering the mess she got herself into, but a pretty little thing. Glossy hair as black as tar. Skin the color of cream. And dressed like she wanted to skip through town screaming, "Steal it all! Everything must go!"

Rich girls. More money than sense, the lot of 'em.

"You lost?" The words came out around a mouthful of masticated apple.

The girl jumped at the sound of my voice. She hadn't noticed me standing there, not five feet away from her.

Like I said, thick as a brick. She wouldn't last long in this town. I gave her an hour, tops.

She blinked at me, visibly wrestling back her composure from wherever it had fled. "No."

I snorted. I knew a lie when I smelled one. "You sure about that? Because you look lost."

She frowned. I took another bite of the apple, the sound of the crunch loud despite the ambient din of Potosí at night.

The girl stiffened. "What's wrong with the way I look?"

I'm sure she thought she looked like she'd blend in down here. Black riding boots. A pair of thick woolen breeches. A dark cloak the same blue of the sky at midnight. But it was all too new. Too shiny. Too rich.

"Nothing, princesa. Just can't believe you made it this far without someone killing you for those boots. Or that cloak. Or that sword. Or that pouch of coin at your hip."

Her hand shot toward the pouch tucked into the waistband of her breeches. It was concealed by the cloak, but I knew it was there all the same.

"How did you—?"

"You jingle like the carts rolling away from the mint."

Her frown deepened as she studied me. "Are you going to rob me?"

Maybe she was cleverer than she looked.

I shrugged. "Haven't decided yet."

"I would rather you didn't."

That made me laugh. It was the first time she'd done so, but it wouldn't be the last. "What on earth brings a girl like you to a place like this?"

I gestured at our surroundings. The alley we were in was sandwiched between a brothel and a gambling hall, neither of which catered to the sort of person who could afford even a single thing she was wearing.

She shrugged one shoulder, and I could tell that she wanted it to come across as casual. It didn't. "I wanted to see Potosí. The real Potosí."

I quirked an eyebrow at her. "Is it everything you dreamed?"

She opened her mouth to answer, but she didn't get the chance. Another voice sounded from the mouth of the alley. Male. Dark. Uneven. Colored with drink. And with crueler intentions than mine. I remember the sound of that voice well, too. In a way, he was responsible for everything that came after.

"Well, well, look what we have here."

I chucked the remainder of the apple over my shoulder and turned to see the man—no, men—standing behind us, blocking the end of the street. They were not the sort of people you wanted to run into in a dark alley, that was for damn sure. Even from a distance, I could smell the man who had spoken. Sweat and stale beer. That smell stayed with me too.

He smiled, revealing a mouth with more teeth missing than present. "Looks like we got two for one, boys."

The men at his back chuckled in that way of men who mean no good.

I kicked away from the wall and reached for my knife. It was a simple kitchen tool, a world apart from the shiny new sword the girl who did not belong here carried, too dull even to gleam in the moonlight, but sharp. And sharp is what does the trick.

I shot the girl a look. I thought I knew what I would see in her face. Fear. But instead I saw something that surprised me. Glee. Anticipation. And a steely determination I hadn't expected. Her hands shook as she reached for her sword, but only slightly. It made her more interesting than she had been seconds ago.

The men came toward us, moving as an undisciplined unit. I spared her a quick glance. "Hope you know how to use that pigsticker, princesa."

She shot me a look that was as sharp as that sword. "Baronesa, technically. Well, almost."

"Huh." I twirled my knife as I watched the man approach. He thought we were easy prey. Two girls. Children, really. She might have been, but I damn well wasn't. "If we live through this, you'll have to tell me how the daughter of a baron wound up in a place like this."

"Deal."

"What's your name, by the way? Just in case I have to inform your loved ones of your sudden death at the hand of drunken assholes."

She smiled, sharp and vicious. "My name is Eustaquia de Sonza, daughter of the Barón de Sonza. First of her name."

With that, she charged, sword aloft, straight at them. Straight at four men twice her size and drunk as rats drowning in a barrel of ale. Straight into the arms of certain death.

And somehow, she did not die.

The fight goes fuzzy in the dream. The details of it aren't important.

What was important were the nights that followed. I waited for her in the same spot, in that alcove. Without fail, she came by again and again. We would run amok, looking for trouble and causing it when we didn't find it. On one such night, she invited me to her house. And then, I never left.

The dream fades as I roll over in bed, mostly still asleep, but with a smile on my lips. I liked that memory because that was it, really. The moment I knew.

I, Ana Lezama de Urinza, was in love.

The rest, as they say, is history.

## Kiki

My head aches only a little when I wake up, but it's enough to make me wish I was still asleep.

I wasn't drunk. If it weren't a sin, I would swear to the Lord on high that I wasn't. (Let us not begin an accounting of my sins; I fear the list would be far too long to get through in one sitting.) It's just that my love for wine is woefully unrequited. The slightest bit of it and my body rebels. The cup—or two—I had at Santiago's is enough to make me regret ever having taken a single sip.

The tiny headache nestled at the back of my skull isn't so bad until the maid pulls open the curtains. The sunlight pouring into my room feels like an attack of the most vicious kind. I squeeze my eyelids shut and burrow deeper down in my sheets.

"Ten more minutes," I whine into my pillow. Already I can feel the tendrils of sleep pulling at me, beseeching me to return to my peaceful slumber. Swords and silk and steel danced in my dreams, and I would love nothing more than to return to them.

"Your father is waiting."

The words are like a splash of cold water on my face. My muscles tense, no longer languid with sleep. I pop myself up on to my elbows and frown at her, my hair falling half in front of my face in a manner most unbecoming a lady of my stature. "What the hell did you just say?"

She meets my gaze with a cool stare. Magdalena isn't new here. My mercurial moods do not cow her in the least.

"Don Carlos de Sonza will take breakfast with you in the solarium." She putters about the room, tidying up after the mess I left in my wake last night. My dirty boots, bloodstained shirt, and torn breeches paint quite the vivid image of what I was up to last night. But Magdalena doesn't bat an eyelash. A good maid never judges her mistress's nighttime activities, no matter how salacious they may be.

My father. Waiting. I cannot remember the last time he joined us for the morning meal. Only, on the rarest and most special of occasions, does he ever break his fast with us. It is simply not done. His gout gives him such terrible grief in the mornings, it's too painful for him to rise early, his joints too stiff and inflamed. Usually, it's just me, Ana, and Alejandro, if he can bring himself to rise before noon.

"Why?"

Magdalena scoffs as she folds my dirty clothes across her arm. She will mend them and remove the stains if possible. They will find their way back into my closet with nary a comment. "I do not make a habit of interrogating the master of the house about his motivations, my lady."

With a groan, I let myself flop back down onto the mattress.

This cannot be good.

I have a feeling I know what it is, but I don't want to talk about it. Not now. Not ever.

Like a coward, I hide under my sheets, listening to the sound of Magdalena flitting through my room. The doors of the wardrobe creak open—the hinges will need oiling soon—and a rustle of heavy fabrics follows.

"If I were you, I wouldn't keep him waiting." Magdalena's voice is not the least bit sympathetic.

I pull the sheet down just enough to glare at her. She's holding a dress up, one suitable for daytime but still frillier then I would like. They're all frillier than I would like. Delicate white lace spills from the sleeves. The deep yellow silk complements my complexion, or so I am told. In that moment, I hate that dress more than I have ever hated anything in my life.

"Now, will you get up or will I have to drag you from the bed like a petulant child?"

I mutter something unkind under my breath, not so quiet that she can't hear it. Magdalena merely smiles in reply. But I do as she says, sliding out from between my nice, warm sheets like a convict on her way to the scaffold.

The water she pours into the copper basin at my vanity is nice and cool. I scrub at my face as Magdalena pulls my hair back into some semblance of respectability. Her deft fingers braid it into an elaborate style I would never be able to accomplish myself.

When she holds up the corset, I cringe.

"Must I?" Another futile question.

"You are a *lady*," Magdalena reminds me. As if I need reminding.

With a sigh, I let her slip the corset over my head. I hold on to the bedposts as she pulls it tight. A bruise I don't remember acquiring reminds me of its existence, eliciting a pained hiss from my lips. Magdalena loosens the corset, just a hair. That is all the sympathy I know I am going to get from her today.

Once my elaborate frock is on—the yellow does little to complement the bruise on my collarbone—Magdalena tsks as we both take in my reflection in the mirror. I meet her eyes in the mirror and quirk a single eyebrow up, daring her to comment on it. Her lips press into a hard, displeased line, but she keeps her thoughts to herself.

My father, I know, will be less inclined to do the same, and I like to conserve the amount of lies I am forced to tell in a single day. For the betterment of my immortal soul, of course. Nothing a few recitations of the Lord's Prayer won't fix. Such is the beauty of the confessional.

My skirts whisper against the floor as I make my way to breakfast. I am no stranger to finery, but after a night spent in breeches and boots, the dress feels heavier than it truly is. Like it comes with a weight that cannot be seen, only felt.

I try to ignore the pounding in my head, but when I get to the solarium, the sun pouring in through the massive windows is an affront to every single one of my senses. It's a battle not to squint.

My stomach roils at the smell of rich fried meats with which my father prefers to break his fast. He's seated at the head of the table, poring over a stack of letters. His left leg is propped up on a low stool. I try not to look too closely at the ankle joint. It is swollen and red with gout. The illness has sapped the life out of him these past two years. He seems smaller, somehow. Not in size, but in presence.

It is hard to believe that this is the same man who would play at being knights with me, muddying his fine boots as he swung a wooden sword about. He greets me with a jovial grunt as I slide into my seat, resisting the urge to place my head down on the table and fall back asleep.

I am not quite the last to arrive at the breakfast table. Alejandro greets me with a wave that's entirely too cheerful considering the late hour we both arrived home and his level of inebriation. It's unforgivable, honestly.

Ana meets my gaze across the table as I shift in my seat, trying in vain to find a comfortable position. The stays of my corset dig into those hard-won bruises from last night's scrap at the tavern. She's also in a dress—slightly less extravagant than mine, not because my father provides her with any less but because she can get away with it—but her hair falls in loose waves around her shoulders. There's always something a little wild about her. A length of silk isn't nearly enough to steal that from her. I wonder if beneath her dress her skin is as speckled with bruises as mine. And then I immediately try to think of anything else besides what's under Ana's dress.

Down that road lies madness.

She squints her eyes at me, tilting her head slightly in the direction of my father. Her expression asks the question her silence withholds.

*What is going on? Why is he here?*

I cannot answer her directly—and I do not know—so I do the next best thing.

"You wanted to see me, Papa," I say as I reach toward the basket of bread rolls at the center of the table. They're still soft and warm from the oven. I cradle one in my palms before breaking it in half. The soothing scent of freshly baked bread is far kinder than anything else in the room. Ana politely shoves a plate of sliced fruit toward me. I accept it with as much grace as I can muster, though I fear digesting anything more challenging than an apple.

My father clears his throat, shifting in his seat as he places the letter on top of the stack. There's something slightly unsettled about him, and it puts me on edge.

"Is everything all right?" I ask, glancing between Ana and my father.

Alejandro shrugs as if he hasn't a care in the world, but it's not the effortless gesture he means for it to be. It's a little too stiff. A little too deliberate. Ana drops her gaze to the tablecloth as she toys with one of the tassels hanging off it. They both know something I do not. That cannot be good. "Has something happened?"

"Only good things," my father says. There's something in his voice that reminds me of how he talks to the skittish mare in our stables. "You are aware, I presume, of the viceroy's upcoming ball?"

I take a tentative bite of my roll. It smells divine, but the bread sits in my mouth like soggy wood. When I swallow, it goes down in an uncomfortable congealed lump. "How can I not be? It's the social event of the season."

Ana snorts. I recognize it for the unkind sound it is.

I put down my roll. "Father, something's going on, and I'm not terribly fond of being the last to know anything, so can we please just skip the preamble and get to what it is you want to discuss?"

"Always too clever for your own good." His tone is softer than his words. "But fine. Have it your way." He smooths his hands over the tablecloth in what few people besides me would recognize as a nervous gesture. "I have spoken to the viceroy and we have decided to announce your engagement to his son at the ball. It's a fitting place for it, I believe."

The roar in my ears has nothing to do with my hangover. I stare at my father as thoughts slosh around in my skull. A clatter of silver on china pulls my attention from his steady gaze to Ana. She's thrown her fork down on her plate. With a disgusted sound, she pushes away from the table and stalks out of the room, her hair flowing behind her.

I watch her go because it's easier than looking back at my father.

I knew this moment was coming. I thought I would be ready for it. I thought I would be able to fend it off with sly words and steely determination, but now that I am confronted with it, I know that I had been a fool. A little girl, letting dreams get the best of her.

I want to throw up. I want to scream. I want to pick up the porcelain plate in front of me and smash it to the ground. I want to stand my ground the way I always do.

But I don't do any of those things. I stare down at my plate and hate how small I feel. How helpless.

"I'm not ready," I mumble. I am never going to be ready. Sebastian and I have been betrothed since I was all of six years old, but I have given marriage nary a passing thought since then. And at that age, I hadn't the foggiest idea of what that word even meant. I just thought it was another occasion to wear an unreasonable dress and eat cake. I didn't know what came after. That wives and husbands were meant to . . . do things.

My father reaches a hand across the table to settle on mine. I hadn't even realized I'd made a fist until he gently starts to pry my tense fingers open.

"My dear . . . you are a woman grown now." Yes, that is most certainly the voice he uses with his mare, Estrella, when he can sense she's about to bolt. "I have given you all the time I can, but the future cannot be held at bay forever."

I nod, a little too rapidly. The movement makes my mostly empty stomach churn. I can imagine that single unhappy lump of bread roiling on the waves of my bile. I dab at the corners of my mouth—rather unnecessarily—before pushing myself to stand. My hands smooth over my skirts, needing something else to do lest they curl into fists and begin beating at the walls of the villa until it crumbles down around us.

"Kiki . . ." Alejandro's voice is kind and soft and in that moment, I hate him for it.

I do not want his kindness. I do not want his softness. I do not want his pity.

He will marry for business or politics or whatever reason our father can concoct, but it'll be different for him. It's different for men. It always is. They don't understand. They will never understand.

"If you'll excuse me . . ." I clear my throat noisily. I can see one of the servants in the corner of the room wrinkle her nose at how indelicate the sound is. "I have to . . ."

I don't bother finishing that sentence. There's no excuse good enough to cover what is very obviously a desperate retreat. My skin feels hot, like my blood is boiling and if I don't get out of here soon, each and every one of my veins will rupture. The seams of the dress dig into my skin like knives.

Alejandro rises from his chair, but Papa stops him with a hand on his arm. "Let her go, son. She simply needs a moment to herself."

A hysterical giggle claws at my throat, but I grind my teeth to keep it inside. I don't know what I need. It is greater than a moment to myself, far greater, but I know I will not find it here, not in that room. Not with them. They mean well, my father and brother. They do, honestly. But they will never know what it is like to navigate this world as a woman. To know society will always see you as a pawn to play, a commodity to trade. The thought makes me sick.

I stumble away from the table, knocking down my chair in my

haste with these ridiculous voluminous skirts. I want to tear them off. I want to fling the silk and lace to the side and run far, far away. I want to be someone else besides who I am in this moment.

A girl trapped in a future that was written for her by someone else. A girl who is brave enough to saunter into the darkest corners of the city and fight anyone who would dare try her but isn't brave enough to stand up to her own father.

# CHAPTER 4

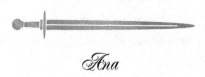

*Ana*

My emotions are a mess. It's like I'm feeling every bad thing possible, all at the same time. Sadness. Despair. Fear. Confusion. Loss. But one emotion stands above the rest: anger. It is so thick and palpable, I feel like I'm choking on it. It's like I've swallowed a mouthful of rage and it's slowly killing me from within.

I knew this was coming. But now that it is here, I want to scream into the gilded corridors of this godforsaken villa and never ever stop. My surroundings pass me by in a blur as I make my way out of the villa through the door in the kitchens. The servants will not try to stop me. They will hold their silence just as they hold it every time they see me and Kiki sneaking in near dawn, or catch us trying to hide the dirt and blood crusting under our fingernails, or spy us sparring in the gardens when we're supposed to learning embroidery or something equally useless.

A poisonous voice whispers through my skull. *Kiki is going to marry the viceroy's son and move into his house and leave you here.*

*She is going to lie down in his bed and spread her legs and bear his children and never think of you again.*

*You will be left to rot in this empty cage, alone and forgotten.*

Sunlight warms my cheeks as I stalk across the grounds. It's only when I scrub at them with the sleeve of my dress that I realize they are wet.

I pause, staring down the tearstained fabric.

"I'm a damn fool," I whisper.

A bird chirps at me from a nearby hedge as if in agreement.

"Oh, fuck you, too."

The bird flies away, leaving me perilously alone with my thoughts. If I'm feeling like this . . . I cannot imagine what Kiki is feeling.

Worry cuts through my anger, sharp as a knife. She doesn't want this. I know she doesn't. Marrying Sebastian, moving into the viceroy's villa—that is not the life she imagined. It is not the life *we* imagined. When we spoke of our future, it was always one in which we're together. I cannot picture my life without her. I don't want to. I don't know what that would even look like. Would the baron still want me here, after she left? Would I still be welcome? Would this still be my home?

I glance back at the villa. It looks so different during the day. The walls are a soft shade of pale yellow, like sand. The red shingles on the roof make it look a bit like a stonework sunset. In the courtyard, a servant beats out a rug, sending clouds of dust puffing up into the air.

I cannot go back in there. Not after storming away from the table like a child who hasn't gotten their way.

*You are a fool*, I tell myself. *A shameless, selfish fool.*

All I could think of was myself when I should have been thinking of *her*. My feet feel welded to the paved stone of the courtyard. I have to find Kiki. This much I know. But if I do, we will talk about what has just transpired and what will transpire, and I do not know if I am strong enough for that.

A world without Kiki in it is not a world I have any interest in inhabiting.

*Go,* that tiny, nigh imperceptible voice nestled at the back of my skull whispers. It's my voice of reason. I've done a fair fine job of ignoring it for the past seventeen years, but maybe there's a first time for everything. *Find her.*

I pause, my feet at the very edge of the cobbles of the courtyard.

It's not that I don't know where she is.

I know exactly where to find her.

I just don't know if I should.

*Go, you fool,* says that voice. *You absolute buffoon.*

And so . . . I go.

There are several places on the grounds of the estate where Kiki likes to go when she wants to be left alone.

The first is usually the library. No one uses it much but her. Don Carlos de Sonza will occasionally show off the room, with its high ceilings and sun-drenched leather tomes seated neatly on mahogany shelves, but for the most part it is Kiki's domain. She has always loved books. When she realized how completely illiterate I was when her family first welcomed me into their home, she took it upon herself to teach me how to read. It took countless painstaking hours, but she never gave up, and so, neither could I. Now, I can comfortably stumble through her favorite Cervantes, which I do only to humor her.

But she won't be in the library today. It would be too easy for her father or her brother or her maid to find her. And if I know her at all, she wouldn't want to be found. Not by them. Not right now.

I walk farther away from the villa, deeper into the grounds. The orange trees rise up around me in sweet citrus columns, blocking me from the brunt of the sun's glare. They aren't very tall trees, but as a child, they felt massive. Now, they barely rise above my head.

The hem of my skirt drags along the dirt. I'd pick it up but that would be fighting a losing battle.

In the distance, I spot a figure seated beneath one of the older orange trees. It is still humble in height, but it is wide and lush with growth. Fat heavy fruits hang from its limbs, bending them down with their weight.

Her head is bowed over her lap as she fiddles with something in her hands. Her dark hair is halfway out of its elaborate braids, like she'd started to pull it out and gave up halfway through, leaving it to tumble around her face in soft waves. Her voluminous skirts pool around her like bubbles on bathwater.

She is lovely, as she always is. The yellow of her dress complements the oranges in the trees so well, she looks as though she's stumbled from a painting of some artist's idyllic notion of perfection.

A twig snaps under my foot. Kiki's head jerks up, her brow furrowed in consternation, her mouth open slightly as if she was readying to hurl invectives at whosoever dared to intrude. But when she sees me, her mouth snaps shut.

"Hello." I didn't come here with a plan. That seems as safe a word as any.

She tosses the orange in her hands to the side. As it rolls away, I see that half of its skin has been picked at, messily and without much care.

A waste of food, I think, but then such is life among the aristocracy.

"Did Father send you?" Without something to hold, Kiki's hands start in on each other. If left to her own devices, she'd worry the fragile skin around her cuticles to shreds. Any other day, and I would reach out and take her hand in mine to keep her from hurting herself. But today, I keep my hands to myself. It will be good practice, I think, for the future, when she will not be so near for me to touch.

I kneel by her side before rocking back onto my rear in the dirt next to her. My skirt will no doubt be terrifically soiled, but I can't find it in me to care.

"No," I reply.

"Then why did you come?"

"Where else would I be?" It's not an answer, not really. She deserves more than that, certainly, but we are both dancing around truths we dare not share. We have been for years. It's a dance we both know so well that the steps are emblazoned in our memories. We don't even have to think about doing it. We just do.

She hums softly in the back of her throat. I open my mouth. Shut it again.

I feel like the whole world is holding its breath. The birds go silent in the trees. The leaves cease their quiet susurration. All I hear is the too loud sound of my own heartbeat.

I ask her the very question I don't want to. But I have to. I must. My tongue darts over my suddenly dry lips, moistening them just enough for them to release the words.

"Do you want to marry him?"

The look Kiki shoots me breaks my heart. Her brow pinches as her fingers cease their restless tangling.

"How can you ask me that?"

It's preposterous now that I think about it. Of course she doesn't want to marry him. Sebastian is an ass. An utter, unrepentant ass. I know it. She knows it. Her father knows it. Hell, even the viceroy probably knows it. But none of that matters in the face of centuries of traditions and bloodlines and the crushing weight of expectation.

I shrug, aiming for something light. "I don't know. You did get hit pretty hard on the head last night. Thought it might have addled your senses."

The sound she makes isn't quite a laugh, but it's not so terribly removed from one that I cannot accept it as the tiniest of victories.

"No. I don't want to marry him. I never have." She reaches for a twig and begins to pick off the drying leaves that stubbornly cling to the bark. Her hands do so loathe to be idle.

*Oh, mother of God.*

Exasperated, I reach out and take one of her hands in my own. Her movements cease. There is a slight tremor in her fingers, like a rabbit waiting in a bush for a wolf to pass it by. I feel foolish for having let my anger consume me. For letting my own fear win. Now, Kiki needs me to be brave. If not for myself, then for her.

I take the stick from her and set it aside. I don't want her fidgeting with something to take her mind off this moment, for I am about to say something incredibly chaotic, and I would like to have her full attention when I do.

"Just say the word, Kiki." My hands retreat and curl into the fabric of my skirt because I don't trust what I'd do with them otherwise. Touch her, probably, in all the ways I'm not supposed to crave. "Say the word, and I'll get you out of here."

That pulls a startled laugh out of her. A real one. She brushes the hair back from her face and looks at me, really looks at me, for the first time since I sat down.

"Get me out of here? What will you do? Whisk me away on your trusty steed? Shall we journey into the world as Don Quixote did, seeking out adventure?"

"Depends," I ask, aiming for jest and falling several miles east of it. "In this scenario, which one of us is Sancho Panza?"

My voice may waver, but the words work.

Kiki exhales a sniffling laugh. "So you did read that book after all."

"It only took three years of cajoling. I was rather fond of the horse."

"Rocinante," Kiki says softly, toying with the fringe of lace spilling from her sleeve. She looks up then, but not at me. Her eyes settle on something in the distance, something far, far away. "Let's say we did it. Let's say we ran. Would we ride into the sunset together like . . ."

*Like star-crossed lovers*, she doesn't say. But I hear the words all the same.

"And why not? We don't need this." I fling my arm wide, hoping the gesture encapsulates the entirety of this world that's trapped her so. The silly, impractical orange grove, and the ridiculous dresses I know she hates, and the painfully small life she's being forced to live. "We can make it on our own. I know we can."

But Kiki just shakes her head. There is something mournful in the set of her slumping shoulders. I have never seen her like this. Withdrawn. Worn. Defeated.

I cannot stand it. It isn't right. She shouldn't be feeling any of those things.

My hand, entirely of its own accord, reaches out so that I can trace the loosened plaits of her braid. Her hair is so soft. It looks like black silk and feels even softer. I wish her hair was completely free and unbound. She is so beautiful when her hair is loose around her shoulders, framing her face.

I wish I had told her that before.

I wish I could tell her that now.

But I can't. It is just one item on the long list of things I cannot do. Not now. Not ever.

I cannot close the space between us, breathing in that mixture of scents that is both uniquely hers and unique to this moment. The floral perk of the rosewater she dabs behind her ears. The sharp citrus tang of the oranges around us. The warm vanilla of the oil she works into the ends of her hair.

I cannot place my hand on her face. I cannot delight in how perfectly the curve of her cheek fits against my palm. I cannot run my thumb over the sharp jut of her cheekbone. I cannot trace the line of her lips with reverent fingers.

I cannot do the thing I want most.

I cannot kiss her.

But . . .

I do it anyway.

Our noses collide before our lips do. I almost laugh right into her mouth. Her lips open in a gasp of surprise against mine. I lean in, crowding her against the trunk of the tree.

My hands. I don't know what to do with my hands. They open and close at my sides, useless. I have imagined this scenario so many times, but now that it's happening, I scarcely know what to do with myself.

Kiki's hands come up to cup my face, her palms curving against the line of my jaw like they were made for precisely that purpose.

The feeling of her lips against mine is downright sinful. Now I know why priests don't want us to do this. If everyone knew how good this was, they would never do anything else.

A soft sigh escapes her, and I think it's maybe a pleased sound, but then I realize her lips are as still as stone. She isn't moving.

She isn't kissing me back.

Kiki presses against my face, pushing me away gently but firmly.

My soul begins to shatter, piece by piece, like a pane of glass fracturing into a thousand tiny shards.

"Ana . . ."

We stare at each other for a long moment, our chests rising and falling with too rapid breaths, like we've just come running from a fight.

Her thumb traces my lower lip, and by God, if that isn't the most divine sensation I have ever experienced. It feels so good that I know I must be condemned to the fiery pits of eternal damnation because nothing in the world is supposed to feel like that.

When Kiki pulls her hand back, it's as though she takes a part of me with her, a little piece of my heart suspended on a string.

"We cannot." Her words are quiet but firm enough to crush me under their weight.

I wait for her to say something else, but she doesn't.

She blurs as I look at her. I blink, and the blurring only gets worse.

I'm crying. I don't know when I started, but I'm afraid that now that I have, I won't ever be able to stop.

Without another word, I push myself away from her. It's too much. It is all too goddamn much.

I stumble to my feet, trying not to see the way she peers up at me. She looks so lost. So confused. So hurt.

She has no right to look that way. Not when she was the one who pushed me away.

I try not to run as I escape the grove. Branches whip at my face, but the pain is nothing to me. I welcome it. I crave it. I deserve it.

I like to think of myself as brave, but in this moment, I run from her like a coward.

Kiki is not mine to have.

And now, she never will be.

# CHAPTER 5

*Kiki*

I don't know how long I sit there beneath the orange tree. Hours, certainly. The sun continued its trek along the sky, slow, inexorable. It peeked through the leaves, growing in strength with every silent minute. By the time I stand, brushing moist dirt off my soiled skirts, it is high, beating down on the villa's grounds as if to scourge the earth off all impurity.

My lips still burn. I wonder, briefly, illogically, if that was what hell feels like. Good and bad all at the same time. I am a soul haunted by pleasures I know I cannot have. Not now. Not in this life. The rest of my body is woefully numb as I force one foot in front of the other and make my way out of the grove.

The wind picks up once I am no longer protected by lines of trees, whipping my hair around my face and my skirts around my legs. A small, feral part of me wants to rip the heavy fabric off my body and throw it to the ground and stomp on it like a child throwing a tantrum. I don't, of course, but the thought is there. I feel something I rarely—nay, never—do: powerless. Like I am a fallen leaf being carried away by a tempestuous river, my fate determined by forces beyond my control. That is what marriage—specifically, mine—will be. A fate determined by people who are not me. By men who never thought to ask my opinion on the subject.

The villa looks bleaker than it normally does as I walk back. Its bulk stands against the cloudless sky, foreboding. The thought of heading back into that house, of seeing my brother and father again, makes my stomach churn. I don't know what I'll find on their faces. Disappointment at my childish antics? Or worse, pity? Either way, I want no part of it.

Catching the curious glance of a pair of maids beating a carpet out on the courtyard behind the kitchens, I ball fistfuls of skirt in my hands and change course, slippers pounding against the dry earth. My attire is incredibly ill-suited for the stables, but that is where I'm heading. I need to remind myself what freedom feels like, and there is no greater approximation than the sensation of wind in my hair as a horse gallops beneath me.

I smell the stables before I round the corner and see them. The scent of hay and horse fills my nostrils like a balm to my soul. The stables are mercifully devoid of anyone who would dare bring up the subject of my marriage. A groom dips his head in acknowledgment as I enter. He eyes my gown and my inadequate footwear.

Voice dubious, he asks, "Would you like me to tack up your horse, mistress?"

I shake my head. "No, thank you. I'll handle it myself. A moment alone, if you don't mind."

And of course, he does not mind. With another dip of his head, he sets down the leather saddle he was carefully conditioning and departs, slinging the oil-stained rag over his shoulder. Once he's gone, I sag. I hadn't even realized my posture straightened when I caught sight of him.

*A lady of the house must always carry herself with dignity.*

The words belong to my old governess, the one who raised me in the absence of my mother, God rest her soul. She died when I was a mere infant, carted away by an illness that had rampaged through Potosí, claiming the lives of peasants and gentry alike. I was too young to have formed my own memories of her. All I have are the ones passed down to me by my father. Spirited was the word he most often used to describe her. *Just like you, mija.* I wonder what she would say now. If she would push me into Sebastian's waiting arms or laugh at the thought of marrying her only daughter off to a boy with more money than sense. But none of that matters, I suppose. She is long dead, having taken her opinions on the subject of a woman's fate with her to the grave.

My horse neighs as I approach his stall. Rocinante is a stallion, tall and proud. He throws his ivory mane and stamps his hoof against the ground. Always ready to run, this one. His light gray coat gleams, nearly white. The groom must have just brushed him.

"Hello, my sweet." I raise my hand to pet the short, bristly hair between his eyes. He angles his snout to sniff my hand, huffing out a discontented protest when he realizes it is absent of the apple with which I usually greet him.

"My sincerest apologies." He nuzzles me, the soft skin of his nose bringing a smile to my face. It is impossible to be upset in the presence of a good-natured beast. Of this, I am certain. My worries don't exactly fade, but for the moment, at least, they subside. I rest my forehead against Rocinante's cheek, lips ticking upward as he moves his lips against my hair, wondering perhaps if that is where I have hidden his apple.

An impatient whinny rises from the stall beside his. I turn my head to meet the dark brown eyes of Ana's horse, Tornado. Those eyes are nearly as dark as his midnight-black coat, interrupted only by a single white blaze on his face. Standing next to Rocinante—as light as Tornado is dark—they make a beautiful pair. Neighing, Tornado paws at the ground, as if to ask, *Where is my mistress?*

No apple. No Ana. I have disrupted their entire routine.

"It'll only be me and Rocinante going out today, I'm afraid."

Tornado tosses his head before turning away and lifting his tail. He defecates. Well, I suppose that's how he feels about that.

"Your father was right. You do have a deft hand with the horses."

The sound of that voice makes me start, which in turn, makes Rocinante start. He knocks his heavy head against mine as we both catch sight of the intruder.

Sebastian stands in the open doorway, riding gloves in hand, the sun haloing his golden hair. He smiles at me, his blue eyes crinkling at the corners. "My apologies. I didn't mean to startle you."

And just like that, my plans to saddle up Rocinante and gallop until I felt only the wind in my hair dissipate. I rest my hand against Rocinante's shoulder, calming him. "What are you doing here?"

If my rudeness bothers Sebastian, he does not show it.

The heels of his riding boots click over the stone of the stable floor as he approaches me. My muscles tense entirely of their own volition. He pauses a few feet away, brow furrowing.

"Are you all right?"

I blink at him, steadying my breath. Rocinante's skin twitches as he shifts his weight with agitation. He is responding to my emotions. I have raised him since he was a skinny-legged foal. He can read me better than almost anyone can, but my disquiet is obvious enough for even Sebastian to notice.

"I'm fine." A scratch behind the ears calms Rocinante. "I simply wasn't expecting you."

The divot between Sebastian's brows deepens. "Did your father not tell you we were coming?"

"We?"

Before Sebastian can answer, the clop of hooves and the tread of boots provides an answer for me. My father enters the stables with two men in tow, the reins of their horses in the hands of the groom I had dismissed earlier.

I recognize one of the men with Papa—Sebastian's father, the Viceroy of Peru. The other man, however, is new to me. His hair is light, but not golden the way Sebastian's is. It is a cool blond, almost ashen. His gray eyes take me in as if measuring me. I don't like the way he looks at me. Not one bit.

My father's affable smile dims when he catches sight of me. "Mija, what on earth—"

Only then do I remember that I look quite the mess.

Sebastian's chuckle is soft and low and too familiar for my taste. He reaches toward me, his hand moving slowly as if I am a skittish mare wary of his touch. I go still as he plucks something from my hair. A mild flush of embarrassment sings through me when I see the dirty leaf he grips between his fingers. From the orange tree.

"Enjoying the natural splendor, I see." The viceroy's voice is gruff and disapproving. His jowls quiver as he harrumphs. This is not how he expected to find his future daughter-in-law, I am certain. He's always been a judgmental man, seemingly preoccupied with appearances on a near constant basis. Rumor has it his rise to viceroy was nothing short of meteoric. He went from the second son of a minor noble house to one of the most powerful men in the Spanish Empire in a matter of years. His skill at forging beneficial connections was the stuff of legend. I suppose that is what I represent to him: a fruitful alliance, very nearly cemented.

My father hustles to my side, his eyes sharper than they normally are. "I was going to inform you of our guests' arrival earlier, but we missed you at breakfast."

Not *You threw a tantrum and stormed away from said breakfast in a fit of righteous pique.* No. Never that, not in polite company. Simply *We missed you.*

"Ah" is all I manage to say. My eyes are drawn to the stranger among them. My father follows my gaze and sighs, realizing he has no option but to introduce his utterly unkempt daughter to this new person.

"May I present Cristobal Téllez-Girón, the Marquis of Peñafiel."

Sebastian leans in to whisper in my ear. "A close friend of the family." It takes everything I have to not squirm away.

The man strides forward, capturing my hand in his. With his eyes on mine, he raises my hand to his lips to brush a kiss along the ridge of my knuckles, unbothered by the dirt under my fingernails. Beside me, Sebastian stiffens. Jealous, perhaps. I fight the urge to scoff. Already acting as though I were his property, ruffled by the sight of another man touching me.

"A pleasure," the marquis says as he straightens.

"Likewise." I say it because it's polite. I resolutely do not mean it.

My father clears his throat and shoots me one of those quintessential paternal looks. The kind that says, *Please, dear Lord, behave yourself according to both your station in life and the mores of polite society.*

"They're here to discuss matters of business. Shipping. Trade.

That sort of thing." My father says this as if it is nothing to concern my feminine little head over. It's unlike him. Normally, he treats me as no less inferior than my brother. It's entirely possible he's simply trying to bring this impromptu meeting to a quick and painless end. "The marquis has recently arrived from Spain and has a tremendous amount of work to do here."

Sebastian offers me a warm smile. "We'll also discuss our impending nuptials, naturally. There is much to plan."

On the inside, I gag. On the outside, I merely blink. "I see."

My father makes a gesture that is clearly meant to shoo me along. "Why don't you go clean up? I will send for you for dinner once we've finished."

Though I am not presently pleased with my father, I am grateful for the excuse to escape this wretched moment.

I cut a quick curtsy and mumble my apologies before I make my way out of the stables. I have no intention of joining them for dinner. I'll have Magdalena claim I'm ill or something.

I'm halfway across the yard when my father catches up to me, huffing slightly, his hand gripping the head of his cane tightly. "Mija, wait."

I pause. I'm not so spiteful that I will make my ailing father run to catch up with me. The gout causes him terrible pain, and he can no longer move with the alacrity of a younger man.

"What is it?" My voice is still sharp though.

He frowns, but there is no recrimination in it. "Mija, please. Give him a chance."

"Do I have much of a choice?"

"There is always a choice."

"It really doesn't feel that way."

Another heavy sigh. He rubs at his temples with his free hand. "You're so like your mother sometimes. She could hardly stand the sight of me when we were wed."

I blink at him. This is news to me. The older members of our household still reminisce about the love between my father and mother.

"Love is a seed, Eustaquia. To grow, it must be nurtured."

I sink my teeth into the skin of my cheek. "What if I don't want to?"

His eyes are so kind, I want to scream. "Keep your heart open. That is all I suggest. It's not easy for a woman alone in this world."

"I just—" I bite off my words in frustration. "You raised me to wield a sword, and now you're expecting me to drop it to become someone's wife."

He shakes his head. "Wield your sword all you like, mija. But maybe, just maybe, *he* can be your shield."

With that, he turns back toward the stables, the thud of his cane echoing in the courtyard with every step.

I bristle at the words all the way back to my rooms. The thought that Sebastian would be pleased with a wife who dons men's clothing and gambles and fights her way through the rough streets of Potosí is laughable. He may seem kinder, more accepting of my eccentricities than his father, but he is cut from the same block. I stomp up the stairs, displeased with how soft my footfalls sound in these godforsaken slippers.

There is a sound coming from the opposite side of my door that gives me pause. I wait, my hand on the gilded knob, listening.

Sobs. Deep and wretched.

"Ana?" I'm through the door before I get a reply. I have never heard Ana cry like that. I don't know if she has it in her. And even if she did, why would she be doing it in my room?

Magdalena's head shoots up as I barrel into the room. Magdalena. Not Ana.

She is sitting at my vanity—peculiar in and of itself for a maid— and clutching a crumpled piece of paper in her hands.

"Mistress." She wipes hastily at her tears, her fists white-knuckled around the note. "I'm so sorry. I thought—I didn't realize—"

"Magdalena, what on earth happened?"

She is so distraught, it knocks every other thought out of my head. I rush to her side, taking her slim shoulders in my hands. Though she's trying valiantly not to cry, her arms tremble with the weight of her tears. She tries to stand, to brush me off, but I hold her tight. She sags against me, another sob racking her body. We stay like that until her sobs subside. As she pulls away from me, her eyes widen when she sees the state I'm in. Dress soiled. Hair askew.

"Your dress—"

"Never mind the dress. What happened?"

With a wet sniffle, she holds the letter out to me. "I've just received word. My cousin—she—"

Another sob, more powerful than the last. Poor Magdalena doubles over in agony, her forehead falling into her hands. The letter drifts to the floor. I snatch it up and read it, keeping one hand on Magdalena's shoulder.

It is written in an unrefined hand, the letters sharp and jagged.

> *My dear Magdalena, I wish I was writing to you with*
> *happier news, but it pains me to tell you that your*
> *cousin Juana was found dead last night . . .*

Magdalena keens, low and terrible. "Murdered. Left to rot in the street like a dog—" Her cries overwhelm the rest of her words.

I go still, the note half-read, half-forgotten.

A girl in the streets, left to die. The memory of the unfortunate soul Ana and I encountered near Esmeralda's returns, as vivid as if she were laid out right in front of me, here at the feet of my bed-chamber.

Magdalena hiccups, trying to speak. "She wasn't—she wasn't a bad person. She'd just lost her way, she didn't deserve—"

"What do you mean, lost her way?"

The sharpness of my tone takes Magdalena aback. "What?"

"Juana. Your cousin. How did she lose her way?"

Magdalena blinks at me, her already ruddy cheeks turning redder still.

"She was a God-fearing woman," Magdalena says. "She just . . ."

"Was she a prostitute?"

The bluntness of the question makes Magdalena start. "I—"

"I'm not going to judge her or you. That is not my place. Just answer me plainly."

Magdalena seems to consider my question, brow furrowing. Then, she nods. "Yes. But, mistress, you must understand, life is hard in the city. I'm lucky, so lucky to have a place in this house but—"

She hiccups again, her body catching on a sob. "Poor Juana. I tried to find her work, I swear it. But she was never good at serving others. She just—Who would do such a thing?"

Magdalena looks at me, as if I might have an answer.

I don't. Not now. Not yet.

I rise, already making to shed my skirts in favor of breeches and steel. Magdalena watches, fresh tears falling from her eyes, as I fetch the sword she'd dutifully tucked away in my wardrobe.

My father was wrong. I do not need a man to be my shield. I am my own. And now, I will be one for the women like Juana. The ones who cannot protect themselves.

"I don't know. But I promise, I will find out."

# CHAPTER 6

*Ana*

If there is one thing I've learned in my short but illustrious life, it's that you can't feel sad if you're too goddamned drunk to feel anything at all.

I'm not quite there yet tonight, but, thanks to the bottle of something old and expensive I swiped from Don de Sonza's wine cellar, by the time I arrive at Esmeralda's I'm well on my way. My desire is simple. I want to erase the memory of that afternoon. The kiss in the orange grove. The sensation of my lips against *hers*. It happened hours ago, but I can still feel them. Warm, soft, and a little dry. If I don't destroy that memory, I will carry it around with me, haunted by it. Enough wine should do the trick. Or at least, that's what I keep telling myself.

The fuzziness of my thoughts is why I don't immediately recognize the person I slam into as I make my way inside.

"Watch it, ass—"

"Ana?"

The familiarity of that voice makes me stop dead in my tracks. It's masculine, but there's something about it that makes me think of Kiki. I blink, my vision already starting to blur a bit at the man who said my name.

"Alejandro?"

He's staring down at me, brow pinched. There's a smudge of what looks like rouge on his cheek. Not really surprising. After all, this is a brothel. I spot a few of his friends behind him, tugging on their coats as they prepare to depart, looking for a new place to sully with their presence.

"What the hell are you doing here?" I ask.

It's a silly question. Again, brothel.

He waves his hand as if swatting my question right out of the air. "What are *you* doing here? I haven't seen you at home all day."

I shrug. Behind me, some lout who can't hold his drink retches into a ditch. It's true. I threw on a pair of boots and breeches and hightailed it away from home right after making a complete fool of myself. But then, was it ever really my home? Or was I just sleeping under a borrowed roof until the rich family who owned it got bored of me? Everything in it reminds me of Kiki. Every corridor, every corner.

"What can I say? I've had better things to do." I peer around Alejandro's bulk, looking for Rosalita, but there are too many people blocking my view of the inside of the house.

Ale makes a sound deep in his throat. Exactly the sort of sound Kiki makes when she disapproves of something I've done. Usually, something uncouth, like eating meat with my bare hands. Why dirty a perfectly good fork when you don't have to?

"Kiki loves you, you know."

It is the wrong thing to say.

Everything I've been avoiding slams back into me. It's like falling off a horse into a pile of wooden spikes. The orange grove. The kiss. The way she looked at me and I knew. We both knew. I could never have the one thing I wanted most of all.

"Kiki can go to hell."

I brush past Alejandro, stumbling a bit as I dodge the hand he reaches out to me with. I meant what I said. She can go to hell. Alejandro can go to hell. That entire family can go to hell. They were never mine anyway. None of it ever will be mine.

"Ana!"

My feet are not as nimble as they are when I'm sober. I trip over my own boots and nearly fall right into the roaring fireplace. It is only Alejandro's strong hands that save me. He pulls me away from the fire and steers me toward a seat currently occupied by one of Esmeralda's girls and the two lovestruck buffoons fawning all over her.

"Move," Ale tells them.

They look disgruntled, but there is something in Alejandro's voice that makes them obey. He sits me down and follows, patting my knee as I wait for the room to stop spinning.

"I wouldn't fret too much about this whole Sebastian thing," he says.

*This whole Sebastian thing.* That's a hell of a way to sum up the worst thing to happen to me.

I scoff, which is maybe a mistake, since it makes bile rise up in my throat. If I throw up on Esmeralda's carpet, I will never hear the end of it. I swallow. "I'll fret if I damn well please."

"I'm just saying." Alejandro holds up his hands in a beseeching gesture. "I think it'll take wild horses to drag my sister down that aisle to marry someone she doesn't love."

"But she has to."

He shrugs. "Maybe. Maybe not."

I squint at him. Partially to focus my blurry vision but also to show my suspicion. "What do you know that I don't?"

Alejandro presses his lips together, as if weighing his next words.

But then he huffs a determined little breath and says, "For one, I know that her heart belongs to someone else."

"Yeah? Who?"

"You." He knocks his shoulder into mine in a brotherly gesture.

I look away sharply. He is saying things out loud that were never meant to be said. "We Sonzas are a stubborn lot. When we love, we love with our whole hearts. And when we make up our minds about who we love, that's it. No one can convince us otherwise."

In his words, I sense an opportunity to shift the focus onto him. "Are you saying there's someone *you* love? And who actually loves you back?"

He presses his finger against his lips. "A gentleman doesn't kiss and tell."

"Yeah, but we're not talking about a gentleman. We're talking about you."

His hand flies to his heart as if to clutch it. "You wound me, dear Ana."

"You make it so easy."

This banter between us is comfortable. Familiar. Almost like breathing. Kiki may occupy the central place in my heart, but Ale inhabits a not insignificant portion of it.

Before he can respond with his own barb, we are interrupted by a group of his friends. One of them shouts over the din of the brothel. "Ale! Come on!"

Ale pats my knee once more before pushing to stand. He offers his hand to help me up. I take it, grateful. I don't trust my feet, not after they just betrayed me.

He taps the underside of my chin softly. "Keep your head up. Everything will work out. I promise."

Heat tickles at the backs of my eyeballs. Before I can say or do anything embarrassing, he's pulled into the crowd by his friends. He shoots me a soft smile. It chips away at the stone I want my heart to be so that it doesn't hurt so much. One of his friends throws an arm over Alejandro's shoulders, tugging him farther away. I dive into the crowd, hoping to lose that kind gaze. I don't want him to be so nice to me right now. It'll just make me soft.

Rosalita finds me before I find her. Sweet, kind Rosalita takes one look at my face and pulls me away from the bustling, boisterous crowds. Esmeralda is none too pleased to have her top earner take a break when the night is young, but Rosalita can be very persuasive when she wants to be. The girl could sell silver to a miner sitting on a juicy mountain of ore if she so chose.

We don't go far. I snag a bottle of a wine from the pantry—swill compared to the Sonza stash—and follow Rosalita up to the roof of the brothel. How she navigates that ladder in a gown is a mystery for the ages.

I waste no time putting a sizable dent in the bottle. I don't want to think. I don't want to feel. I don't want to consider the look on Alejandro's face as I ran from him. I don't want to remember the look on Kiki's when I ran from her.

*They can all go to hell.*

Rosalita contents herself with dainty, polite sips. One of us should have their wits about them so long as we're on a roof, I suppose. The last thing I need is to take a spill off the shingles and crack my skull open against the cobblestone below. Or maybe that's exactly what I need. I remain undecided.

Potosí stretches out before us, but not in the distant way it does when viewed from the villa. We are not so high up that we cannot smell the acrid woodsmoke rising into the air or the cloying sweetness of cheap perfume or the tang of meat cooking over open flames, juices dripping onto coals. There are no orange blossoms here to mask the life of the city. No high-born lies to cover up a messy, beautiful, chaotic truth.

Rosalita takes a swig of wine straight from the bottle. I watch as her throat bobs with the motion of swallowing. When she's done, she wipes her lips with the back of her arm. I've spent the better part of the week hating everyone and everything around me, but now, I can't help but smile.

"Doña Esmeralda would have you over her knee if she saw you drinking like that," I say as I accept the bottle Rosalita offers me.

"What she doesn't know won't scandalize her," Rosalita says, stretching her legs out and rolling her ankles, her bare feet pale against the darkened tiles of the roof. "I trust you won't tell her."

"Your secret is safe with me." I swirl the wine around in the bottle, the red liquid sloshing up the sides. I wonder if it would taste less sour if I were in a better mood.

Rosalita sighs, wiggling her toes. "I don't like the thought of you wandering the streets alone, Ana."

"I'm not alone. I have you."

She rolls her eyes. Deservedly so. "You have me *now*. But what good will that do you when you're walking home? The villa's a long way off and in case you've forgotten, there's a rampaging madman on the loose."

"Rampaging madmen are welcome to take a stab at me." The wine burns all the way down as I knock back a generous mouthful. "Slaying them might put me in a better mood."

Rosalita snorts. "Still . . . promise me you'll be careful?"

"I'm always careful."

She levels me with a very pointed look, eyebrow arched, lips pursed in a disbelieving little smirk.

"Okay, fine," I sigh. "I am rarely careful. But for you, I will try."

"Thank you. That's all I ask."

A breeze lifts the hem of her skirt, making the light material flutter in the wind. Leaves skitter through the gutters, chittering against one another. Something drifts through the air, a pale speck of who knows what, lifted up from the ground below.

A feather. White. Probably from some doomed chickens slaughtered in the yard for last night's supper. It lands on Rosalita's head, looking for all the world like an ornament she chose to put in exactly that spot. Such is her radiance. It can elevate even the humblest of chicken detritus.

I swallow my mouthful of wine and gesture vaguely at Rosalita's face. "There's something in your hair."

Rosalita pats at her head, missing the feather by miles. "What? Where?"

"Here, let me." I set the bottle down and roll onto my knees. The edges of the shingles are uneven, and they dig into my bones as I crawl toward her. I'm not quite as steady as I would like to be, considering we are on a roof and a fall would mean a good crippling at the very least. I brush the feather from her hair. "There. All gone."

"Thank you," Rosalita says.

Now that I'm kneeling before her, I am reminded of just how beautiful she is. My fingers travel through her hair, down and down and down, until they reach the smooth skin of her cheek.

*No*, I tell them. *Stop.*

They do not listen.

I lean in, so close our lips would brush if one of us were to speak.

*Kiss her*, my brain cajoles. *You want to. You've always wanted to.*

But then, she leans back.

"No." Her voice is quiet but firm. Devoid of judgment, but unwavering.

I sit back on my heels, swaying a little from the wine and the sting of rejection and the well of sadness that's been simmering in me all day. I am but a simple creature, and it's more feeling than I'm used to experiencing all at once.

"I'm sorry." It seems like the right thing to say.

Rosalita shakes her head, a sad smile touching the corners of her mouth.

A mouth that *my* mouth will never know.

"I'm flattered, Ana. Truly."

I suspect this might be a lie, but she's trying to be nice when I've been such a selfish ass, so I decide to allow it.

"But I know it isn't *me* you want."

The thought of flinging myself off the roof seems not quite so terrible in that moment.

My sitting back down is more of an artful collapse, but neither one of us comments on it. I grab the wine bottle and take a large swig from it.

"Don't know what you're talking about."

Rosalita merely pats my knee. "Of course not. You're just sad and drunk on a rooftop, miles from home for no reason at all."

I slump to the shingles, banging my head a little too hard against them. "I need a distraction. Tell me something good."

"Like what?"

"Anything," I say. "Make something up if you must."

Rosalita hums thoughtfully as she considers her answer. Voices drift from below, bawdy and loud and thick with drink. Glasses chime faintly from the parlor on the ground floor, the clink of cup against cup ringing through the night. Rosalita's perfume masks the pungent scents of the street. It's soft and familiar, a smell I wouldn't mind wrapping around myself and having a nap in.

After a lengthy moment of contemplative silence she says, "I have a new beau."

This piques my interest. "Oh?"

She blushes. Rosalita. Blushing. Perish the thought.

In that moment, she's the picture of girlish innocence, no matter what she does for coin. "He isn't like the other men I see, Ana. He's smart and kind and gentle."

She sighs, leaning back to lay beside me, her eyes resting on the heavens like she's looking at something more magnificent than the stars. "I never thought I would find a man like him."

"He sounds like a catch." I try to keep the skepticism out of my voice, honestly, I do, but from the way Rosalita huffs indignantly, I can tell that I have failed.

"And you sound like an awful cynic."

What can I say to that? *Love is a painful illusion, and we're all going to die alone?* Probably not what she wants to hear in the moment. So I settle on a truth I can support: "I'm happy for you. I mean it."

She smiles softly, toying with the thin golden chain around her neck. I hadn't noticed it earlier but it's new. Not a part of her normal work wardrobe. A fragile golden locket rests in the valley of her bosom as if she's deliberating hiding it from view.

"Did he give you that?" I ask.

Her hand flies to the locket, her fist closing around it. "He did."

There's such tenderness in her voice that I almost relinquish the death grasp I have on my skepticism. Almost. Not quite, but I flirt with the notion.

"Will you tell me his name?"

She shakes her head, pulling her lower lip between her teeth as she smiles. "Someday. But not today."

I don't push. I simply nod, and lace my fingers together atop my stomach and gaze at the stars.

*At least one of us is happy*, I think.

For now, that will have to be enough.

# CHAPTER 7

*Kiki*

The wind in my hair as my horse gallops toward the golden glow of the city's lanterns is almost enough to make me feel like myself for the first time in days. The reins feel natural in my hands, as if the horse was not another being but an extension of myself. I am not a girl, chained to a fate written by an author who knows not my wants or my needs or my truth.

I am a woman of action.

We slow as we reach the city gates, Rocinante's hooves crunching over gravel roads instead of hard-packed dirt. The city guards barely glance at me. I am a familiar sight. A noble girl in a men's frock coat, sitting astride a stallion finer than any they will ever ride. I tend to my business, and they tend to theirs. Normally, I would pass by without uttering a single word. Today, I alter that pattern, tipping my hat in the direction of the nearest guard.

"Sir," I say, trying to inject both sweetness and authority into my voice. It is a tricky—nay, impossible—balance to strike.

The guard lifts his chin to meet my gaze. He takes in my attire. The fine boots. The plush dyed wool of the coat. The shining coat of my steed.

"What do you want?"

"A moment of your time, if you can spare it."

He glances at his partner. Spits on the ground. Shrugs. "Make it quick."

"Is the city guard investigating the recent murders of young women?"

His facial expression fails to change in the slightest. "Murders? In Potosí? You don't say."

His partner chuckles as they knock elbows together. It takes every ounce of my God-given strength not to roll my eyes.

"Is that a no, then?"

He snorts. "Girls die every day in Potosí. Who cares?"

My hands tighten on the reins. The leather digs into my palms. The pain grounds me. "I do."

The guard waves me off as a cart rolls up to the gates behind me. "Don't know what you're on about. Now get moving. We've got a job to do."

"Not guarding the city evidently." I dig my heels into Rocinante's sides before the guard has a chance to respond. What is the death of another poor soul? What is the life of a woman born in poverty worth? To them, nothing.

The city path diverges before me. Rocinante snorts, tossing his head and tugging on the reins in his impatience. His is not a beast for standing still.

If I turn Rocinante's head to the left, the road will lead us to the brothel district. If I am investigating the murder of a woman of the night, it would be the most logical place to start.

But it is also where I am nearly positive Ana would be. We haven't spoken since the orange grove. Have not even locked eyes.

Rocinante paws at the ground, shuffling his weight.

"Fine," I tell him, patting the side of his neck. I turn his head to the right, away from the brothels and Esmeralda's and Ana and toward Santiago.

It's not a cowardly decision.

(It is.)

If there is anyone in Potosí who knows the latest news and gossip, it is Santiago. And so, Rocinante and I make our way to his tavern.

It is as bustling as it ever is. I leave Rocinante with the stable boy. I know him, and he knows me. I toss him an extra coin because I'm feeling generous.

It's strange, being here without Ana. I cannot recall if I ever have. She and I are a pair. A team. A set. Santiago's eyebrows inch upward as I take a seat at the long counter that separates his realm from his rabble-rousing customers. "No Ana tonight?"

The intonation of his voice tells me that he knows something is not right between us. "Has she been here?"

It's a pointless question, but I ask it anyway. The pursuit of futility is such a peculiarly human pastime. "Haven't seen her since she was last here with you." His brow furrows. He looks like he's seeing right through me, sussing out emotions I would rather not share with him. Or with anyone. "Why do you ask? Something going on with the two of you?" His knowing look turns wry. Bemused even. "Lovers' quarrel, perhaps?"

The word *lovers* makes something in my chest curl up into a spiked ball in the corner of my chest.

I shake my head, accepting with gratitude the flagon of wine he puts before me. "I'm not here about Ana."

"Then what brings you to my humble establishment?"

"Information."

He cocks his head to the side, his eyes roving over the crowded tavern behind me as if scouting for any stray ears. "What is it you want to know?"

"A friend of mine received some unfortunate news. Her cousin has been murdered."

He wipes at the counter, his hands sure and steady. But there's a twitch in his eye. "Truly, a shame. What can I do to help?"

"Tell me anything you know. Anything you might have heard."

He sighs, resting the heels of his palms against the wooden countertop. "I hear lots of things. Most of them bad." He lowers his voice. "Stay out of it. For your own good."

If he was trying to quell my curiosity, that was the wrong thing to say. "Why?" I lean over the bar. "What do you know?"

With a weary sigh, he meets my gaze. "You're not going to leave it alone, are you?"

I simply hold his gaze, letting him read the truth on my face.

"Fine." He tosses the rag to the side. "Girls are going missing. Dying. Usually, it's the sort of girl no one cares too much about. The kind of girl who comes and goes without many taking notice. This city eats people up and spits them out, and life goes on."

"So what makes these deaths different?"

Santiago shakes his head. "There's something about the way they're being left behind. The bodies, I mean. It's almost like someone wants them found."

"Like whoever's doing it is showing off?"

He nods. "It's like they have no fear of being found out. Like they want us to know they're untouchable."

I drum my fingers against the table. "Have your little shadows heard anything?"

As if summoned by the words, a small child appears at my side. I hadn't heard him approach. He emerged from the crowd, squeezing between men who tower over him, unobtrusive and silent.

"Paolo." I greet him with a nod. He is one of Santiago's shadows. Santiago puts a roof over their heads and food in their bellies, and in exchange, they bring him information they glean from the darkest corners of the city. There's a reason Santiago knows everything that happens in Potosí.

He looks at me, silent. There's a smudge of dirt on his cheek. I reach into my purse and pull out another coin. The shine of it catches his eye as I turn it over in my hand.

"Call it," I say, "and it's yours."

I flick my thumb, sending the coin spinning upward.

"Crowns up," Paolo says.

I snatch the coin out of the air and turn my closed fist over. My fingers uncurl revealing the visage of the king. "Looks like it's your lucky day."

Paolo plucks the coin out of my open palm, a smile cracking across his face. It makes him look younger. Almost like the child he actually is.

"What have you brought for me today, Paolo?" Santiago asks.

Paolo heaves himself up on the stool beside me as Santiago slides a wooden tray of food across the counter. Bread and cheese and a chunk of dried meat. The boy digs in, speaking with his mouth full.

"The magistrate's gambling is catching up with him again. The collectors were talking about sending a man to his house to remind him of the money he owes."

The magistrate? Interesting. The man used to go riding with my father before the gout made horses a distant memory for him.

Paolo shoves half the cheese into his mouth despite Santiago's protestations. "Saw the viceroy's son heading into Tati's."

Tati's. A brothel not too far from Esmeralda's. They're rivals of sorts. The mention of the viceroy's son—Sebastian—makes me stiffen. Santiago's eyes flit toward me. I keep my face as still as stone, which is probably revealing in its own way.

"Have you heard anything about the murdered girls?" I ask Paolo, mostly to skirt around the subject of Sebastian in its entirety.

Paolo nods, biting off a chunk of bread. I'm faintly shocked that he hasn't choked to death already. "Only that another one got dead last night."

Magdalena's cousin.

"Was there anything unusual about it? Did you see the body?"

Paolo smirks. "I got almost close enough to touch it."

The callousness sits poorly with me. I remind myself that death is a normal part of life for the street urchins of Potosí. "And?"

"And she was as dead as a doornail. Just like the rest." He swallows his mouthful of bread, his mouth puckering. "There was something . . ."

"What?"

He blinks owlishly at me. With an impatient sigh, I fish out another coin and slap it on the table.

"He'll bleed you dry if you let him," Santiago says. I ignore him.

"Talk," I tell Paolo.

"There was something on her hand," Paolo says. "Like a drawing. 'Cept it was all bloody."

Santiago and I share a look. "What do you mean?" I ask.

"It was like someone had drawn on her hand but with a knife." He picks up the knife on the plate he had heretofore ignored. He cuts into the remaining piece of cheese, but not to eat. He traces a symbol of some sort into the rind. A circle with what looks like snakes or vines inside.

Santiago and I lean closer, peering at it. "What is it? Some kind of sigil?"

"Don't know what a sigil is," Paolo says. Before I can study the symbol further, he hacks into the cheese with the knife, bisecting the hastily carved circle. "Told you everything I know. If you want to know more, go to Tati's."

I nod, sliding yet another coin across the table. Santiago snatches it up before Paolo's grubby hands can get it.

"Be careful," Santiago calls as I slide off the stool and stride toward the door.

"I'm always careful," I call back.

We both know it's a lie.

# CHAPTER 8

*Ana*

Eventually, Rosalita has to return to work. I keep drinking, but before I know it, the bottle is empty. I tilt my head all the way back and shake it, but all that hits my tongue is a single sad droplet of something that's closer to vinegar than wine. I stare at the empty bottle as if it has betrayed me.

"Can't trust anything these days, can I?"

With an angry grunt, I lob the bottle away from me. Unfortunately for whomever is standing below, I have forgotten that I was sitting on a roof.

Glass shatters in impact. Something heavy and meaty thuds against the cobblestones. I wince.

On my hands and knees, I crawl to the edge of the roof to peer over the side. A man is lying on the ground with his friends arranged in a worried circle around him. Mercifully, he still seems to be breathing. There's a gash on his forehead, but he's clutching his head and alive enough to moan about it.

I call out, "Sorry!"

"Fuck you!"

I lean back before I, too, sail right off the edge of the roof. "Fair enough."

I wish I could stay up here all night. I wish there wasn't a world outside this stolen pocket of time, but it's just that. Stolen. This isn't my home. Not anymore. I'm not even sure I have one anymore. Not after what I did.

(The kiss.)

Groaning, I push myself up to stand. I wobble only slightly as I make my way back downstairs. It's a minor miracle I make it downstairs without dying. I'm sure there's some quote about God smiling on the reckless. Probably something Kiki read to me once.

*Don't think about Kiki.*

When I reach the crowded salon, I spy Rosalita's dark hair as she throws back her head to laugh at something some asshole nobleman just said.

I huff, indignant. "All think they're comedians, don't—"

The words die in my throat when my eyes land on the man Rosalita is speaking to.

*Sebastian.*

Under my breath, I mutter, "Son of a bitch."

The last person I want to see. Especially now, in my current state. On a good day, my inhibitions are flimsy at best. Today is not a good day. Kiki is always the one to hold me back when I need holding.

Now, the only thing stopping me from slaying this worthless, entitled prick is my own self-control.

So, basically, there's absolutely nothing stopping me.

The next few moments I would blame on the wine if I didn't know myself better. Unfortunately, I do, and it's exactly the kind of shit I would do stone-cold sober.

My feet move forward, one right after the other through the crowd. My elbows shove aside perfumed women and simpering men without a single care. My eyes have a solitary target, and he is all I can see.

One of Sebastian's cronies catches my eye and nudges him in the side with his elbow.

*He doesn't have friends,* Kiki once told me. *He has sycophants.*

(I still don't know what the hell a sycophant is, and I don't much care. Also, I should *not* be thinking of Kiki, and yet, somehow, she is always there.)

Sebastian turns to me, his handsome face catching the light of the fire roaring merrily in the hearth. His jawline is frustratingly solid. He looks like he might be playing some tragic hero in a stage play.

He holds up his cup in a mocking salute as I approach.

We do not have the best history, Sebastian and I. The first-ever society ball Don Carlos forced me to attend ended with me tripping very badly over my feet in a dance I barely knew and Sebastian laughing. I kicked his chair out from under him later that evening and was banished to my room for six weeks for the crime. I was so sure that Don Carlos would kick me out of his home for the sin of assaulting one of my betters. But he hadn't. He'd simply arranged for me to be given several months' worth of etiquette lessons and a stern talking-to about keeping my violent impulses on the inside. And I do—for the most part.

I really wish I didn't have to now.

"Ah, Ana," Sebastian says, as if we are old friends and he is happy to see me. "I'm surprised to see you out here without your other half." He glances at his friends before he delivers his next words. "Though I suppose she must be busy, planning our nuptials and all."

They titter, the way only people of their breeding do. It's such a useless sound. A titter.

A seething wave of rage hits me so hard, it nearly knocks me off my feet. Rosalita senses something shift in me. Over Sebastian's shoulder, she shakes her head frantically, her eyes wide, her smile plastered to her face like it's stuck there.

I should listen to her silent warning. I should behave myself better in her place of business. I do not. Instead, I do the one thing I've been wanted to do for days. Months. Years, really.

I spit in Sebastian's handsome, rotten face.

Time slows down as I watch my glob of spittle arc through the air, elegant almost. It lands high on his cheek with a satisfying *plop*.

I smile, deeply at peace for the first time this week.

Sebastian raises a hand to his cheek. His eyes widen, then narrow when his fingers make contact with the saliva, leaving a slug trail of slime on his face. "Did you just—?"

"Spit on your face?" The hint of a laugh works its way into my voice. "Yes, it was great. I would definitely do it again."

With the sleeve of his very fine coat, Sebastian wipes at his cheek. His eyes never leave mine. There's something dark in them. Something vicious. Something cold.

"Now," he says, his own voice curiously calm, "is that any way to treat your betters?"

I make an exaggerated show of looking around me, my eyes alighting on each of the young nobleman around us. A pall of silence has fallen around the room. Doña Esmeralda is going to kill me. But what a death it will be. "Don't see any here."

Sebastian snorts. "Why don't we teach her a lesson, boys?"

It is at this point that I begin to realize how monumentally witless I've been. The odds of this confrontation were never in my favor. There are five friends with him, now that I bother to count. Six against one was never going to be a fair fight. And it was never going to be anything but a fight. And not to mention the enforcers Doña Esmeralda has on hand to deal with unruly folk like yours truly.

Oh well. We're here now. Might as well commit.

I throw the first punch. Sebastian, in all of his shining arrogance, doesn't even attempt to sidestep it. Perhaps he assumes I'm too drunk to hit my mark. Oh, little does he know. My fist connects with his face, and the shock of it trembles up my arm. A thrill runs through me at this victory—however minor—until the reality of my situation sets in. I put my entire weight behind that punch. All of it. Every morsel of my person. And there's nothing left to hold me upright. My feet scramble for purchase on the rug but it's no use. I pitch forward, heading right toward Rosalita. She looks like she's going to try to catch me (God bless her) but someone beats her to the punch. A man grabs my sleeve, whirling me about. A fist slams against my face. I don't see who that fist is attached to. I don't need to. It doesn't matter.

The blow lands heavy and hard. Sparks burst across my vision right before everything goes hazy. The second blow hurts just as bad. So does the third. And the fourth. The fifth one less so but I think that's just because I'm slowly losing consciousness. Or maybe dying.

Really, who can tell these days?

Sebastian himself never lays a finger on me. I catch a glimpse of him between his two friends. He's leaning back against the mantel, one leg crossed over the other at the ankles, a bemused look on his face despite the bruise I *know* is forming on it. The type to let others do his dirty work, then. I see how it is.

I'm spared by one of Esmeralda's burly guards. He pulls the noble prick off me (I didn't catch who it was, not that it matters really, if you've met one, you've met 'em all), and I lie there for a moment, dazed. The pain is there, persistent. It'll hurt worse when I'm sober, that's for damn sure. But that's not the feeling that dominates my thoughts in this particular moment.

I wish I was a better person than I am. I wish I wasn't such a mess. I wish I wasn't so selfish.

But I'm not a better person. I wanted the fight. I wanted the pain. I wanted the blood.

I wanted to feel something—anything—that was strong enough to eclipse the hurt I'd been nursing like a bad drink.

Rosalita falls to her knees beside me. "Are you okay?"

Something odd and uncomfortable scratches at my throat.

I slam my jaw shut to hold it back but it fights to be free.

A laugh, dark and bitter and broken, tumbles from my lips.

It's better than crying, but not by much.

"I'm great, thanks."

All of a sudden, a whirlwind enters the room in the shape of a woman. Doña Esmeralda is tripping over herself with apologies to her clientele, promising them all sorts of bullshit to smooth their ruffled feathers.

When her feet come level with my head, the thought that she might kick me flitters through my mind. Wouldn't be the first time.

"Get her out of here," Esmeralda hisses. The burly guard bends down to grab my arm and haul me up, but Rosalita stills him with a hand on his arm.

"Please."

I don't know who she's speaking to. The guard or Esmeralda. But whoever it is listens. My arm is released, flopping to the ground like a dead fish.

"Come on, up you get." Rosalita's hands slide beneath my shoulders.

I am more of a hindrance than a help as she struggles to get me to my feet. She's stronger than she looks.

I don't know how she gets me upstairs, but somehow she does. Maybe the guard helps. All I know is that the combination of too much wine and too many blows to the head is starting to hit me very, very hard. My limbs refuse to work and my brain is a fogged mess. I think I actually faint upright more than once on the way to Rosalita's bedroom.

She lays me down in her bed—her real one, not the one in which she *entertains*—and putters about, gathering supplies for God knows what.

The room is spinning, so I close my eyes. That only makes it worse. I open them and settle my gaze to a fixed point on the wall. A small painting of the Virgin Mary stares down at me, as if in judgment.

"Oh, fuck off," I mumble.

"What was that?" Rosalita asks, her voice muffled like she's got her face in a cupboard.

*I just cursed out the mother of God.* I swallow past the foul taste of cheap liquor and my own blood. "Nothing."

I flinch when she presses a wet cloth to my face. Rosalita is gentle as she cleans my wounds. A part of me relishes the pain, knows I deserve that and so much more.

"This will pass." Rosalita's voice is pitched low and careful, the same tone she used to use when she told me bedtime stories at night, the times I'd crawl into her cramped cot when it was too cold to sleep in the kitchens after the embers finally died in the hearth. "You'll recover from this. You'll heal."

It's a lie, and we both know it. But it's a nice lie. A comforting one. And for that, I'm grateful.

I turn my battered face into the pillow and breathe. It smells like Rosalita. Like jasmine and perfume and a faint hint of Doña Esmeralda's palo santo. It smells like a home I left, a long time ago. I squeeze my eyes shut and pray for death. In lieu of that, I settle for sleep.

# CHAPTER 9

*Kiki*

Tati's was a dead end.

It's all I've been able to think about since I got back to the villa. It's been three days since I went into town to ask after Magdalena's cousin, but I am none the wiser about what happened to Juana than I was three days ago.

I worried the question of what happened to her and why between my teeth during every meal. My father stopped calling out my distraction after realizing all he was getting in return were wordless grunts. I mulled it over as Magdalena selected a dress for me to wear tonight when I showed complete and utter disinterest in doing so myself.

"It's too important an evening for you to be so disinterested." She clucked. She had thrown herself into her duties as her own method of distraction from Juana's fate. In a way, she was right. Tonight was the viceroy's ball. Tonight, Sebastian and I would be formally presented as a soon-to-be married couple to the movers and shakers of Potosí. But none of it seemed to matter. People—women—were disappearing. Probably dying. What were my petty problems compared to that? I was still puzzling through the possibilities as Father herded us toward the carriage waiting to ferry us to the viceroy's villa.

The worst thing is that no one seemed to know anything that would have illuminated the unfortunate situation. Apparently, Juana had only just started working there and no one really knew her. Her death, while tragic, seemed to impact them so very little. All I know is that she was not the first. Three girls had gone missing from the brothel in the past three months. Missing, and most likely dead.

"Bad for business" was all Tati herself had said. She was a wizened old woman, as thin as a reed and as mean as a stray cat. "About as bad as you coming 'round here to ask about it. Unless you plan on dropping coin, get out."

I'd done as she asked, though I am left with more questions than answers. Rosalita had warned us about girls going missing (and, as we know, turning up dead). But none from Doña Esmeralda's so far. Tati's had been hardest hit. It's worth noting perhaps that Tati's is directly across the square from Esmeralda's. They are rival brothels. Perhaps there is something to that. But I can't sort out what.

These are the thoughts that I focus on as the carriage rolls us uncomfortably to the viceroy's villa. Uncomfortable because the roads are so wretched, and doubly so because, despite being crammed into a carriage together, Ana still stubbornly refuses to look at me.

My stomach lurches with every jolt of the wheels. There is nothing in it for my body to expel, but that does nothing to keep my nausea at bay. I press my temple to the cool glass of the carriage window, even though doing so makes the lurching gait of our ride tremble through my entire body.

I close my eyes, squeezing them shut tightly. Maybe that'll make it better.

It doesn't.

My father has brought along a sheaf of papers, delivered to him by the captain of some ship he owns. Trading negotiations or records of things sold and purchased, I'm guessing. Or maybe negotiations for more trade routes. I've never paid much attention to my father's business dealings. They seemed incredibly dull to me as a child, and even duller as I grew up and found my own interests. His cane rests at his side, the silver lion's head that tops it rattling against the side of the carriage door with every jolt.

Meanwhile, Ana has her nose buried in a book. It's the copy of *Don Quixote* I gave her years ago. Unlike the softened paper of my own well-loved copy, hers is practically pristine. It does not escape my notice that she hasn't turned a page in at least ten minutes. She isn't reading. She's just using the book to have some kind of physical barrier between us. At least it spares me from having to look at her face. Normally, I find her face quite pleasing. But she showed up at breakfast the other morning looking like she'd been trampled under a herd of cattle. My first inclination had been concern. I don't like seeing her hurt. I don't like not knowing how she got hurt. I really don't like knowing I could have—*should* have—been there to watch her back in the midst of whatever brawl led to that face.

I glance at the book in which she's buried her nose. All I see is her auburn hair and a hint of forehead. I turn back to the window, tightening my arms around my empty, roiling stomach.

Beside me, Alejandro nudges me with his elbow. "Are you all right?"

My eyes open to slits, just wide enough for my glare to get through. A wry smile touches his lips. He checks to make sure my father's face is still buried in a stack of papers before reaching into his pocket. When his hand emerges, it's holding a small silver flask. He wiggles it in my direction in a wordless offer of liquid courage.

I shake my head.

"Suit yourself." He unscrews the cap and takes a swig.

My father chooses the moment to look up. He sets the papers down on his lap with a disapproving huff. Shaking his head, he removes his spectacles and rubs at the bridge of his nose. "Honestly, Alejandro."

Smiling, my brother wipes at his lips with the back of his hand. "What?" He holds the flask out to our father. "You want a sip?"

My father snorts, setting the spectacles back on his nose. "From the way you lot act you'd think I was raising a traveling carnival."

The horses slow as we climb up the path leading to the viceroy's villa. It's the grandest in all of Potosí. It also sits at the highest elevation of all the noble residences. He's not a subtle man, the viceroy.

The carriage rolls to a shuddering stop. I don't know if it's just me or if the air is actually thinner up here, the way it's said to be high up on the mountain, but suddenly, I find it terribly hard to breathe.

Ana drops the book onto her seat and spills out of the carriage before the coachman can even get a hand on the door. She moves so fast that all I see is the fabric of her gown fluttering after her like a peacock's dragging tail.

My father blinks after her, his graying brows furrowing slowly. He's a quiet man by nature, but now there's an astute quality to his silence that worries me. When his gaze slides to me, it's a little too knowing for comfort.

"I know you think I never notice what happens in my own home."

As one, Alejandro and I tense. We aren't *bad* children, per se. Well, we aren't the best, but we love our father. We respect him. At society gatherings, our behavior is beyond reproach. But we aren't exactly what my father envisioned, I am sure.

"But be honest with me, mija." My father wipes his spectacles with a square of fabric that perfectly matches the black and golden tones of his chosen outfit for the evening. "Should I worry about tonight?"

The question is worded vaguely enough that I don't have to lie to respond to it. "Whatever do you mean, Papa?"

The look he levels me with would be withering were it not tempered with genuine affection, albeit exasperated. "The two of you have been in a snit. Don't think I didn't notice. I'm not the doddering old man you children seem to think I am."

My lips clamps shut. Silence generally can't get me into trouble. I learned that at a very young age.

"I don't know what happened between the two of you but I expect you to be on your very best behavior tonight."

I shift in my seat, though the elaborate nature of my dress makes even that simple gesture harder than it should be. The coachman waits at the open door, his eyes studiously forward, his expression artfully blank. He will wait, however long he must. He will radiate the illusion that he sees and hears nothing unusual.

"I promise I won't embarrass you in front of the viceroy, Papa." Disdain trickles into my voice. If my father notices it, he refrains from commenting upon it. "As for Ana . . . well, I cannot make promises on her behalf."

My father sighs. "Of course not. Ana will do what Ana will do. Part of her charm, I suppose." He awkwardly reaches over to pat my knee, or rather, to pat what might be a knee hidden under approximately seventy-eight thousand layers of fabric. I hardly feel it underneath the mounds of silk. "You could never embarrass me."

"Quite right," Alejandro chirps. "That's my job."

Just like that, the tension breaks as my father chuckles despite himself. "Try not to bring disgrace upon our family, Alejandro."

"I make no promises." My brother gestures toward the open door.

"After you, Father. I sense the line of coaches behind us growing ever longer."

My father bundles himself out of the coach. "Far be it from the humble Sonzas to keep a viceroy waiting."

"Humble." Alejandro knocks a jovial elbow into my ribs; my corset acts like armor. "That's us, eh?"

He climbs out of the coach after my father. Suddenly, it's just me. I make no move to disembark. My hands curl into loose fists in the silk of my skirt. My skin looks oddly pale against the midnight-blue silk. When I look down at my fists, it feels as though I'm looking at someone else's appendages. It's like I'm not quite in my body.

The sound of a throat clearing draws my eye to the still-open door.

Alejandro holds out a hand to me. The permanent rakish grin on his face has faded into something softer, something realer. "You'll be all right."

It's not what I expected him to say. But it is perhaps what I needed him to say.

"How do you know?" My voice is so soft it hardly carries outside the coach to where Ale is standing.

"Because you're Eustaquia de Sonza, and no man will ever get the best of you."

The corners of my lips twitch. It's not quite a smile, but it's the closest I've come all week. "Thank you. You know, you're a halfway decent brother when you want to be."

Alejandro shrugs. "I try. Now get out. I'm thirsty, and I heard the viceroy's cracked open his oldest cask of wine for the festivities."

With a roll of my eyes, I begin the arduous task of unseating myself. "Never change."

I gather up my miles of silk and exit the coach with as much grace as they will allow, which is not that much at all. Now that I'm standing outside, I can see the viceroy's villa. Its white stone walls glimmer almost silver in the moonlight, with pools of gold spilling forth from the torches mounted on the walls in regular intervals. The entire edifice looks like a giant pile of coins.

*Appropriate*, I muse. *Considering what this city's been built on.*

Alejandro offers me his arm to escort me into the ball. I take it, glad to have something to hold on to as I navigate the steps leading up to the wide, wooden doors. They look like a darkened maw, waiting to swallow me whole.

Alejandro tucks my arm under his and gently pats the back of my hand. "If that ass Sebastian gives you any grief, you let me know. I'll set him right."

I snort as we begin to climb the stairs. "That's one fight I'd pay to see."

Once we reach the doors, all talk of violence upon the heir to this lavish estate ceases. A servant ushers us inside. The still, hot air is suffocating. I focus on breathing, in and out, in and out, barely hearing the introductions made on our behalf as we enter the ballroom. And what a ballroom it is.

The interior of the viceroy's villa is every bit the gilded monstrosity one might expect from the richest man in the New World.

Fat cherubs perch in the corners, fingers poised over the strings of their golden lyres. An elaborate mural dominates the ceiling, painted in deeply pigmented jewel tones. I squint, trying to make sense of the scattered imagery. When I figure it out, I laugh.

It's Midas, the fabled king of the house of Phrygia, whose hand turned everything he touched to gold. A distinguished figure, draped in ermine robes, head topped with an elaborate jeweled crown, stands in the midst of a vast horde of golden treasure. His hand is raised as if to say, *Look upon me and despair, see what I have wrought, see the riches I have made.*

That the viceroy thinks of himself in such grandiose terms comes as no surprise. That he had his artist leave out what is arguably the most important part of Midas's mythos is even less surprising. My eyes scour the mural for the doomed figure of Midas's daughter, herself turned to a lifeless golden statue when her father's greed proved more powerful than his love. She is nowhere to be seen. The viceroy has hand-picked the mythology to serve his purposes while learning absolutely nothing from it.

*Men*, I think. A fitting summation.

My father touches my elbow, pulling me away from what surely must be one the world's most ironic bastardizations of Greek mythology. I turn to find the viceroy, resplendent in his frock coat and lace, standing before me. And beside him is his son. The man I am to marry.

Sebastian is handsome. To call him anything less would be a lie. Hair the color of burnished gold sweeps away from his brow, pulled away from his face by a length of crimson ribbon, exposing perfectly chiseled cheekbones and a jaw straight enough to cut through steel. But his beauty floats on the surface. The second he opens his mouth, the illusion falters.

He sweeps a low, courtly bow before me. The gesture is grand. As grand as the opulent house in which he lives, in which *I* will live, whether I want to or not.

When he stands, a smile that's more of a smirk flits across his face like a stray cloud obscuring the sun. He extends a gloved hand toward me, palm up. "May I have this dance?"

A group of girls off to the side swoon like a gaggle of fainting maidens.

*Honestly.*

"No."

My father chuckles. It's as fake a sound as I've ever heard him make. "Take no heed of her, Sebastian. She's just shy."

"I most certainly am not."

My father nudges me, none too subtly. "Mija, is that any way to treat your future husband?"

The stays of my corset dig into my tender flesh as I sigh. "I suppose not."

My father nudges me again, this time right into Sebastian's waiting arms.

The band of musicians picks up a lively saraband, and we're whisked into the center of the crowd. The grouping splits into duos as dancers pair themselves off. Sebastian executes the little hops with such perfunctory efficiency it hardly looks like dancing at all. It isn't *bad*. It's just utterly soulless.

When the steps of the dance bring us close enough to speak, he asks, "Are you enjoying yourself?"

"I'm not particularly fond of the saraband." This is a lie. I love a good saraband. As a matter of fact, I love anything Jesuit priests consider indecent. "Did you know that Cervantes wrote an entremés in which hell is described as the birthplace of the saraband?"

I'm rambling. I *know* I'm rambling, which makes it worse somehow. But filling the air between us with nonsense seems preferable to passing the length of this dance staring into one another's eyes.

"Is that the charlatan who wrote that dreadful tale about a man and his donkey?"

To slander *Don Quixote* in my presence. The nerve. The audacity. The absolute gall.

"One and the same." I glissade away from him, twirling in the air, glad that for at least a few seconds, I can pretend that he doesn't exist. That he doesn't symbolize the end of my life as I know it.

But eventually, we are facing each other. I don't like the feel of his eyes on me. So I decide to do what I do best. Hurt him.

"What happened to your face?"

It's quite possibly the worst thing I could have said to a boy as vain as Sebastian.

Those lovely lips twist into something close enough to a sneer that for a fleeting moment, his beauty is eclipsed by the venom running just under his skin.

He—or likely, a maid in his household—has done a decent job covering up the bruises on his fair flesh, but my eye is too knowing. Lord knows I've spent many a morning covering up the remnants of my own fights in a similar manner. But all the paint and powder in the world can't hide that telltale sallow stain from me.

"Nothing." The word is hard and clipped. He clenches his jaw so hard that I can see the muscle just underneath twitch with the force of his repressed fury.

"Is that so?" I cannot help myself. If I am to be shackled to this man until my dying day, I want to make sure I am not the only one who lives in misery. "Because it looks like someone bested you in combat."

Now perhaps *that* is the worst thing I could say to him.

"It was a lucky hit," Sebastian says through gritted teeth. "Nothing more."

"If you say so." The dance calls for me to twirl away from him, and I have never felt more blessed by a bit of choreography.

When I twirl back, his gaze is measuring. His hands on mine are oddly gentle. "It doesn't have to be like this, you know. All barbs and jabs."

"It looks like someone else got to the jab before I did."

Petty, I know. But I couldn't help myself. It was right there.

Sebastian's lips twitch, but he only sighs. "I know what marriage must seem like to a girl like you."

"A girl like me?"

"Spirited."

I huff, swishing my skirts in time with the music. "That's what men call women they can't control."

Sebastian captures my waist, his blue eyes piercing. "And who says I want to control you?"

My breath stutters. "That's what marriage is. A woman swearing obedience to a man, is it not?"

Sebastian guides me into the next step of this cursedly long saraband. "It doesn't have to be. Quite frankly, I have no interest in curbing your spirit. I rather think it could serve us both well."

"What do you mean?"

A smile ticks at his lips. "Imagine us, ruling Potosí from the top of the hill. Our two families joined, their power pooled. We could make a fine team, if you only give me a chance."

My stomach feels like lead. It would be easier to hate him. "Why are you saying this?"

"I didn't ask for this marriage either," Sebastian says. "But it's happening. We might as well make the best of it."

The song comes to its crescendo as the lines of men and women twirl to a stop, facing one another. The men bow at the waist while the women dip into curtsies, their heads inclined coquettishly.

The musicians take a breath, readying for the next piece. The silence is my chance.

I turn my back on Sebastian, ducking into the crowd before he can stop me. I don't think he'll try. To chase after me would look foolish, and whatever his flaws, he is not a fool. Already, whispers rise up about my behavior, but I can't bring myself to care about how bad my fleeing the dance floor looks.

I don't want to have that conversation with him. I need a moment to myself, away from him. Away from his hands and his eyes and the words that don't sound nearly as unreasonable as I want them to.

# CHAPTER 10

*Ana*

I hate balls.

I hate the frilly dresses.

I hate the fake smiles and the barbed words.

But most of all, I hate the people who go to them.

Specifically, Sebastian. If I had a sword, I would run it through the soft skin of his belly as if I were disemboweling wild game. I bet he'd barely put up a fight. Murdering him would hardly be sporting. Satisfying, probably, but hardly sporting. He wouldn't be much of a challenge on his own. Not now when I am sober. I imagine cornering him in a dark alley when it's just the two of us. No friends to deliver his punches for him. Just him and me and a nice, sharp blade. He wouldn't be so pretty after that.

But alas, I don't have a sword. Apparently, it clashed with the emerald silk of this absurd dress. The coarse fabric of my undergarments scrapes against my skin, reminding me that I'm wearing something I have no business wearing. My lack of sword, however, doesn't mean I'm unarmed. I slip my free hand into the pocket I cut into the dress and feel for the solid grip on the knife I have strapped to my thigh. The feel of it against my skin grounds me. That is who I am. Cold, hard steel. Not soft, delicate silk.

With my other hand, I clutch the cup of wine I've been nursing for the past fifteen minutes and glare at the crowd of people milling about the viceroy's ballroom. The villa is quite possibly the grandest building in all of Potosí, second perhaps only to the bank built on the orders of the king of Spain himself.

No one approaches me. Not that anyone ever does at these things. Certain segments of society consider me fashionable but in the way a curiosity can be fashionable. Something to ooh and aah over to make them forget how miserable they all are. I'm an honest-to-God street urchin, something the vast majority of these people have only ever read about. To them, I am a cheap thrill.

But now, with the bruises still livid on my face, people keep a wide berth. I take a very generous swig of my wine—how indecent, a *swig* of wine and not a sip—and settle deeper into my corner. Out of respect for Kiki's poor father, I keep to the shadows, trying to draw as little attention to myself as possible.

I wish Rosalita were here. She'd know exactly what to say to these well-dressed buffoons. She can smile with one side of her mouth and insult you with the other without you even knowing it. It's a skill I desperately wished I'd picked up. I'm good with my fists. Not so good with my words. Usually, my fists serve me just fine, but I have the sneaking suspicion that if I started throwing punches in the middle of the viceroy's ball, Don Carlos de Sonza would be somewhat miffed.

The wine sours in my mouth as I watch Sebastian twirl Kiki around the dance floor. She smiles at him, but I see it for what it is. A mask. A lie. He probably does too. But everyone around them is fooled.

"What a beautiful couple," sighs the woman beside me. Her face is so heavily powdered that she barely looks human.

I snort into my nearly empty cup before knocking the dregs of it back. I will need another one and soon if I am to survive this night without murdering one or two people. At the very least. Or maybe something harder.

Alejandro. That's who I need in my corner right now. He's a riot at these things—and he usually sneaks in the top-shelf stuff from his father's cellar. And he never leaves me to my own devices unless I want to be left alone. Right now, I don't. But he isn't occupying his usual haunts.

One of his friends—Rodrigo—passes by. I grab his sleeve. Rodrigo turns to me, an affronted look on his face before he sees who it is.

"Oh, Ana. Hello." He smooths out the wrinkle that formed right above his elbow when I grabbed him. He's a fastidious one. A little odd, but an offenseless quirk. "Forgive me, I didn't see you there."

I shrug. "I'm good at becoming invisible at these things."

When he finally looks at me—really looks at me—his brow crumples with concern. "Oh, Ana, what happened to your face?"

I have a sneaking suspicion I will be fielding this question from everyone who isn't too good to speak to me tonight. I shrug again and reach for the most convenient lie. "Lost a bet. Didn't want to pay it. You know how it goes."

A soft pink flush crawls across Rodrigo's cheeks.

Oh, he knows. He knows very well. The reason Rodrigo is so nice to me isn't because he's Alejandro's friend and I am Alejandro's sort-of-sister and by the laws of polite society that means he's required to treat me with at least a modicum of kindness. No, Rodrigo is nice to me because he once lost a bet of his own and was short the coin to pay it. Fortuna must have smiled on him because she saw fit to arrange for Kiki and me to be at the same gambling parlor that night. We handled it. Not with silver but with steel. He's been gratuitously nice to me ever since.

I spare him the embarrassment of reliving that particular moment of his life. "Have you seen Alejandro?"

He shakes his head, frowning. "No. Not since you arrived."

I grunt, releasing him. He scampers away, perhaps to avoid being seen with me. Can't say I blame him. I probably wouldn't want to be seen with me right about now. My mood is as ugly as my face is with its bruises and scars.

My eyes roam over the crowd. It's hard to distinguish one overly dressed fop from the next. A male voice rises almost loud enough to be heard over the music. No one else seems to mind, but it's out of place enough to catch my attention. Inside voices only at these parties, or so one wrinkled old dowager saw fit to inform me when I had the nerve to laugh too loudly at one of these things. I was twelve. She's dead now, so really, who's laughing now, you rotten old tramp?

A quartet of men has gathered in the corner opposite me. Three of them look vaguely distressed, but the one in the middle appears unbothered. His perfectly aquiline nose is high in the air as he fixes the man who raised his voice—another of Alejandro's friends, a man named Santos who mostly pretends I don't exist—with a look cold enough to freeze this dreadfully warm wine.

I grab a fresh cup of wine off the nearest table and head over to the group. I don't much care for the look of some of them, but they might know where Alejandro is.

The man at the center of the group watches me as I approach. He's new here. I don't often pay attention to the people who attend these balls, but I'm pretty good with faces and his is one I haven't seen before.

He tilts his head to me as I approach in a polite little bow. "My lady."

I can't help it. I snort. "Hardly."

The man remains unruffled, his face stoic, but there's a hint of a smile in his gray eyes. "I do not believe I have had the pleasure of making your acquaintance." He reaches for my hand—the one not holding the wine—and brings it to his lips.

Santos clears his throat as the man's eyes cut to him. "It is my honor to introduce Cristobal Téllez-Girón, Marquis of Peñafiel."

The Marquis of Peñafiel stands, releasing my hand. I fight the urge to wipe my palm on my skirts. I hate it when men do that. Keep your lips to yourselves, please and thank you.

"Ana," I introduce myself. "No fancy title. Nice to meet you." It's not. I don't care about him or his rank or Peñafiel, wherever the hell that is. I turn to Santos. "Have you seen Alejandro?"

Santos blinks at me once. Twice. Something passes across his face, like he can't quite believe I'm speaking to him, and in public no less. "I—No. I have not."

"Alejandro de Sonza?" The man who is apparently a very important son of a bitch in Peñafiel asks. "Are you an acquaintance of his?"

I shrug, taking another drink of my wine. It's not bad stuff. "If you want to call it that, sure."

Cristobal makes a considering sound low in his throat. "Is he the Baron de Sonza's son?"

I nod. "That's what they say."

"Then I do believe I saw him make his way to the garden. Perhaps he was in need of some fresh air." His brow furrows. "Though he did seem to be in a terrible rush. Perhaps something was troubling him."

Odd.

I shove my cup at Santos, splashing a bit on his fancy doublet. With an indignant gasp, he clutches the cup before more can spill.

"Take that. I'm done with it."

The way the Marquis of I've-Already-Forgotten described Alejandro doesn't quite sit right. He was in a fine enough mood when he arrived. Something must have set him off.

"Thanks," I say over my shoulder as I turn to find my way to the garden.

"I do hope the boy is well," Cristobal offers, but I'm already gone, his voice half-lost to the rising instrumental as the musicians pick up some new dance.

* * *

The scent of flowers whose names I don't know fills the air. Gardenias, maybe. Or lilies. Florals were never really my thing. They're cloying, and they make my nose tingle. I regret coming out here, but I want to find Alejandro. Unfortunately, the garden is a maze.

Not in a poetic sort of way, but in a very real way. There are all sorts of nooks and crannies, every other one I come across occupied by people doing naughty things. Normally, I would find this amusing. But now, it just reminds me of the things I cannot have.

My skirts slither across the ground. I spare a thought for the poor maid who's going to have to get the dirt out of them. I can never not think about those things. The people who wait on the rich hand and foot are so often invisible to them, but they never are to me.

"Alejandro," I call out softly. "Where are you?"

From a little alcove in the garden, a man laughs. There's a woman sitting on his lap, but that doesn't seem to stop him. "I can be an Alejandro. I can be whoever you want me to be."

"Oh, get stuffed." I pick up my skirts and flick a rude gesture at the man. The woman in his lap laughs so hard she nearly topples to the ground.

I follow the twists and turns until I reach an area that spreads out. It is a grove, much like the one at the Sonza estate, but the trees are different. Taller. Stronger. Oaks, perhaps.

Their canopies hide the light of the moon while their dark leaves seem to absorb the illumination from the party's lanterns. My shoe—an impractical thing that matches this impractical dress—catches on a rock on the ground, and I trip. My knees hit the dirt with a dull thud. The fabric of the dress absorbs most of the shock, but it also makes it harder for me to find my footing. Cursing, I grab up fistfuls of silk and lace. A cool breeze toys at the fabric in my hands, making it even harder to gather. The wind blows my hair into my face just as it blows the clouds away from the moon.

I brush my hair away and look up, now that I have at least some light by which to see.

And immediately wish I hadn't.

Before me stands a tree.

From that tree, a thick branch protrudes.

From that thick branch hangs a rope.

And from that rope hangs a body.

It sways in the evening wind, booted feet twirling ever so slightly in place. Dark hair hangs over the face, obscuring the poor soul's identity from view. From the build and clothing, obviously a man. From the quality of those clothes—I saw them, I swear, at some point tonight, but where I cannot recall—he is likely a nobleman. His hands hang limply at his sides. Something—blood, perhaps—stands out against the skin of one hand. A scrap of paper sticks out from his pocket, as if shoved there in haste. Beneath the lanky hair, the man's chin is just barely visible, square and strong and familiar.

Gathering my skirts, I force myself to stand. The night has gone eerily quiet. Were there birds singing just now? And have they stopped? The wind dies down. The soft soles of my shoes crunch over dead leaves and dry twigs.

I do not want to get a better look, but something drives me forward, some dark, invisible force.

*I know that jawline.*

Voices rise low in the darkness, coming from behind me. I am rooted to the ground as if I had become one of these very trees.

A woman's voice. The one from earlier. And the man, the one who said he could be—

She screams, the woman. The sound doesn't pierce me. I hear it, but as if it were coming from very far away instead of right behind me.

*I know that jawline.*

I don't know how long I stand there, staring up at the tree and its branch and its rope and its—

People flood the garden, following the sound of that scream. Another person yells. Someone else shouts. A man pushes past me, a man with a familiar gait, unbalanced because of some ailment (gout), a cane (topped with a silver lion's head) clattering to the ground. He doesn't seem to see me. I see him but I cannot make sense of what I am looking at, even as he collapses to his knees, his cane forgotten. A sound comes out of him that I have never heard come from a human before. A low and terrible wail.

The wailing cracks as the wailer's voice breaks, stricken clean through with sharp-edged despair.

"My son," cries that broken voice. "My son, my son . . ."

*I know that voice.*

I don't want to look back. But of course, I do.

Kneeling beneath those swinging boots is Don Carlos de Sonza, my guardian and father of Eustaquia.

And Alejandro.

Alejandro, who is now hanging from a tree.

Dead.

# CHAPTER 11

*Kiki*

Like everyone else, I followed the scream. I'd heard it, clear as day, from my hiding spot on the balcony just outside the grand hall where I'd been dancing with Sebastian. A crowd had already formed by the time I reached the garden.

Something had caught my eye. Red hair, billowing in the breeze. An emerald dress, vivid even against the soft dark of night.

She—Ana—was standing rigidly still even as the people all around her fell to hysterics or, worse, desperate gossiping. Her eyes were riveted to something before her.

I shouldn't have looked.

I shouldn't have come out here.

I shouldn't have followed the scream.

My eyes see, but my mind refuses to make sense of it. Any of it.

Time stands still.

No.

It freezes.

It solidifies into something hard and incomprehensible.

I forget how to breathe.

My lungs fail to fill themselves with air.

My vision goes pink at the edges, the way your eyelids look from the inside when you close them against the sun.

There's something cold and unyielding beneath me, bruising my knees.

It's the ground. I have fallen. I do not remember it. I do not remember pushing through the crowd though I must have. I am closer now.

Closer to the thing I wish I could not see.

"Kiki. Kiki, get up."

My eyes blink, and my head moves to the source of the voice, but they're not working in tandem.

My eyes. My eyes are the problem.

They refuse to move. To detach themselves from the sight before them.

Boots, swinging slowly in the wind.

Moonlight dances across the leather. It's been polished. Recently. Just last night when he—

He wouldn't do this—

He wouldn't—

No.

It's not a he, that thing swinging there, jostled with nauseating tenderness by the wind.

It's not a he. It's not *him*.

It's not.

It can't be.

Because if it was that would mean—

*No.*

"Kiki!"

Someone grabs my face and turns it away.

I'm not looking at the boots anymore, but every time I blink, I see them. It's like someone has taken an iron brand and held it to the inside of my skull, burning that image there for all eternity.

But when I open my eyes, all I see is Ana kneeling before me, her face so close to mine it eclipses all else.

There's something wrong with her face though. She looks . . . scared?

The expression is so unfamiliar on her face, I struggle to place it. I have never seen it there before. It is foreign. Unwelcome.

I reach out to touch her, to make her face do something different.

My hand floats between us, disconnected from my body. It doesn't feel like my hand. It feels incidental that it's attached to my body.

My body.

Body.

The body.

*No.*

The tips of my fingers brush Ana's cheek. They come away wet.

"You're crying." My voice sounds distant to my own ears, like I'm listening to someone speak in a room on the other side of a large, empty house.

"Kiki, you have to get up."

I shake my head. "No."

I try to turn back to the swinging boots, but a strong hand grabs my chin. There are callouses on those fingers, from years of learning to wield a sword.

*We used to watch his lessons,* I think.

He always made sure to speak louder than was strictly necessary so we could hear, learning the nuances of swordplay by subter-fuge.

When his tutor cottoned on to the presence of two little girls hiding behind the hedges in the courtyard, he started speaking louder too. The way they moved was so graceful. It looked like dancing.

"Kiki. Come on."

Ana's on her feet now, tugging on my arm to get me to stand. I keep shaking my head.

Did I stop? I can't remember. My body is operating entirely of its own accord, each segment of it acting independently of the next.

"No," I say again. "No."

"Kiki."

"I can't leave him."

The tugging stops.

She kneels down again. Her face is wetter than before. I don't even need to touch it to tell. Her tears catch the flickering torchlight of the sconces on the garden wall.

"Kiki, you must."

I shake my head again, too hard, too vigorously. It hurts, like my brain is slamming into the walls of my skull.

"No. No. No, no, no."

Once I release that single word into the night, I cannot stop it. It repeats, falling off my tongue over and over.

It is all I can think. All I can focus on.

I keep muttering it as Ana pulls me to my feet, her fingers digging into the muscles of my upper arms. Such force, those hands have. They will leave bruises later.

I keep muttering it as she pulls me away, even though I fight. I don't know where she's taking me. I don't care. All I know is that I cannot leave this place. I am needed here. *He* needs me here.

But my body refuses to cooperate. My feet are clumsy, like they belong to someone else. My vision blurs, stealing the sight of those swinging boots from me.

"No," I say. Over and over and over and over.

And every time I blink, those boots swing, back and forth, back and forth, with nothing there to stop them.

# CHAPTER 12

*Ana*

I am no stranger to grief.

You don't get to live as I did without learning what it feels like to lose someone. The city has its way of teaching you how cruel and ugly the world is. It chips away at you, smoothing down all your jagged edges until all that's left is something as hard and as callous as the hard and callous things that made you.

Grief—my own—is something I know how to deal with. But handling someone else's? That is beyond me. All I can do now is watch Kiki and hope that I can catch her before she hits the ground and shatters.

I should be sad.

Alejandro was my family. Not by blood, no, but he was family all the same.

So, I *should* be sad. But strangely, I'm not.

All I feel is anger.

No, not anger.

Rage.

It feels as though it's bubbling right under my skin, a building pressure that never finds release.

The problem is that I have no one to be angry at. No place to direct my rage, to funnel it out of my body. It just builds and builds and builds. Soon, there will be nothing left in my body but fury. No blood, no bones, no bile. Just pure, unadulterated wrath.

The anger follows me everywhere.

It follows me to the stables, where I consider jumping on Tornado and riding until his dark flank lathers with sweat, until we both collapse, until I cannot run any farther away.

It follows me to my bedroom, where I scream into a pillow for lack of anything better to scream at.

It follows me to the basilica, where I stand now, listening to some shit-for-brains priest tell Don Carlos that his son cannot be buried in hallowed ground.

Outside, the sun beats down on the stone plaza surrounding the church. The heat of it bounces off the stones. It's a beautiful day, which at this point just sort of feels like an insult. Beneath my skirts, I am sweating. I wasn't going to wear a dress, but I didn't want to upset Kiki's father. The poor man has been through enough. Kiki didn't even rouse herself from her grief-stricken state to accompany him to the church on this doomed, last-ditch effort to see his son be granted the dignity in death he wasn't in the final moments of his life.

The bishopric had been kind enough to send someone to the villa to spit on Alejandro's grave. Or rather, to tell us he couldn't have one in their goddamn cemetery.

"He's a suicide, you must understand." The priest holds up his hands, palms open, begging for a grieving father to make sense of something violently senseless.

Don Carlos's hand shakes on the head of his cane. He shouldn't be here. He shouldn't have to do this. I place a gentle hand on his arm. Through the fabric of his coat, his arm feels frailer than it should.

With his free hand, he pats the back of mine absently, like a reflex. His skin is so sallow, he looks like he might be a ghost himself. He shakes his head, his jowls trembling as he prepares to speak.

"He was not—my son would not—"

"To take one's own life is to spit in the face of God."

I do it without thinking.

I spit.

The three of us stand frozen, watching my spittle arc through the air like a well-shot musket ball. It lands on the priest's cheek with a satisfying plop.

And there endeth the discussion.

Don Carlos doesn't even tell me off for it. That might be the worst part. Once we are unceremoniously hustled out of the church and back into the carriage, he hands me his kerchief to wipe a stray bit of my own spittle off my chin. For the ride home, he is quiet, staring forlornly out the carriage window. I do not acknowledge the tears falling down the sides of his face. He does not acknowledge mine either. We sit there, two souls broken and trying to pretend not to be.

I don't know what to say to him. There is nothing I can say. Other people's grief is too strange, too big, too wild for me to handle. Part of me wishes Kiki was here. If this were happening to another family, she would know what to say, what to do. But it isn't happening to another family. It's happened to us. To her. She hasn't left her room since that night. No one's tried to force her to do so either. Maybe it would be better if they did.

She won't eat. She barely sleeps. When she does, it's fitful. She tosses and turns.

And through it all, she does not cry. I don't think she's holding it in either. I know what Kiki looks like when she's trying not to cry. Her lower lip gets creased from how hard she's digging her teeth into it. A tiny wrinkle forms between her brows as she furrows them. Her cheeks hollow with the effort of clenching her jaw tightly enough to keep everything inside.

But this . . . this is different.

This is silent. Still. There is no turmoil lurking beneath the surface of calm waters. There is simply . . . nothing. And that nothing is the most terrifying thing of all.

I can't do it. I can't sit by and watch her waste away. The resolve hardens in me as I alight from the carriage. Don Carlos looks so small as he makes his slow, painful way up the villa's steps. The building seems to swallow him whole, just as it has consumed all of its inhabitants in their sorrow.

I will not let it consume me.

And I will not let Alejandro be violated a second time.

He was not a suicide. And I will prove it if it's the last goddamn thing I do.

* ● ●

I have to bide my time until the sun falls. I don't want anyone to know where I'm going or why. I don't even know if I'll be able to find anything. The only thing I do know is that I have to do something.

When I make my way out of the villa, I hardly have to sneak. Everyone is too wrapped up in their own mourning to take much notice of me. The horses, at least, are glad to see me. They've never gone this long without exercise. I pat Rocinante's pale flank as I walk past his stall.

"She'll come see you soon. I promise."

He neighs, tossing his head back like he knows I'm spouting bull-shit. I always have believed that horses are smarter than people.

Tornado knocks his head into my side as I saddle him up, pawing at the ground like the restless beast he is. "Calm down. We'll be on the road before you know it."

Once I'm on his back, he tears out of villa's grounds as if shot from a cannon.

Potosí is both different and the same during the day. From a distance, it's a beautiful city. The Spanish do so love their colors; they've seen fit to paint rows and rows of houses in vivid hues borrowed from landscapes more robust than ours. But when you're in the muck and the mire of the streets, it's far less pretty. The smell of the city is worse during the day, or at least it feels worse. There is no other way to describe the stench other than *oppressive*. It's never great, but with the heat of the sun beating against the cobblestones and seeping into the mud and clay of the houses, the stench is more powerful than ever.

Day or night, the poverty doesn't change. Children still scamper, their bare feet dark with dirt and dust, nimble fingers seeking out unprotected pockets and poorly guarded purses. Vendors hawk their wares—beads strung together by local wise women, various roasted meats stabbed through with skewers, half-burnt but still oddly tasty. Black-robed priests harangue the poor women working the brothel district, assuring them that their souls can be saved if only they repent, repent, repent.

All of this action—all this bustling life—fades away as I near my destination. This particular street is quiet. There are regular patrols that march to and fro, as close to the magistrate's offices as we are, but their presence is hardly needed around here. No one's keen to visit the place where they keep the bodies of the dead and dying. It's a terrible location for a day trip.

My hand slips into the pocket sewn inside my coat. I've checked its contents more than once on my way here, but I like the feeling of the coin in my pocket. The heft of it. All these years living in the lap of luxury, and it has yet to grow old. This silver isn't Don Carlos's though. It's mine. Won in a card game at one of the seedier gambling halls Potosí has to offer. I don't want to spend his money on this.

In this city, a bit of silver will buy you anything. A house. A horse. A title.

A glimpse at the dead.

Against an arching doorway leans a single guard, his hat pulled low over his brow, hiding his eyes from the meager torchlight spilling on to this dark, merciless street. He barely looks up as I approach, but I can sense the moment his awareness alights on me. It's subtle, the way his body tenses, but I've spent years studying all the slight ways in which people signal their movements. He shifts, like he's readying for a fight, but, for once in my life, I'm not interested in a brawl.

The exchange is silent. My hard-won coin slips from my hand to the guard's without a single word traded between us. He studies the silver, turning it over in his palm.

I'm not offended, but I *am* impatient. I don't want to be here. I really, truly do not. But I'm here and I have a task I aim to complete. "It's real, I assure you."

The man's only response to that is to hold my gaze as he brings the coin to his mouth and sets it between his teeth. Satisfied, he grunts, slipping the coin into his pocket. It's more than what he makes in a month, but he seems unsurprised and underwhelmed. I wonder how often he takes this sort of bribe. Who comes here to gawk at the dead? And why? Are they doing more than just looking?

A chill steals through me. That is a thought best left alone.

The guard moves aside, removing a large ring of brass keys from a hook by the door. He slides one into the lock and turns it. "You have ten minutes."

I don't thank him as I step through that heavy door. I don't want to be doing this. I don't want to be here at all. But I have to be. I have a limited window in which to work before I lose my chance to find some answers. And in the absence of answers—any answers, no matter how flimsy—I fear I might go completely fucking mad.

The door closes behind me, plunging me into darkness.

Panic seizes me, tightening my muscles, clogging my throat. In the moments it takes for my eyes to adjust to the dim, barely there light of the candle on the table by the door, a primal urge takes hold of my body. I want to run, to pound at the heavy wooden bulk of the door until the guard lets me out. I have known death before, but never this intimately. I wish I had never made its acquaintance.

I rest my back against the door and breathe.

*In and out. In and out. In and out.*

My heart hammers at the walls of my chest while I force air into my lungs and out again. In the quiet, each ragged breath seems louder than it ought to. After a moment, my pulse begins to slow. My eyes adjust to the dim. And I see, finally, what awaits in this room.

A body lying stretched out on a table.

*Alejandro*, my mind supplies. *That is Alejandro.*

But I push the thought away. I cannot think of *it* as Alejandro. It isn't him. Not anymore. It is just a body. A lifeless sack of meat and bones. Whatever it was that made that body Alejandro is gone.

To be perfectly honest, I don't know if I believe in souls. Frankly, I don't know if I believe in much, but what I do believe is this: We are more than flesh and bone. There is something undefined, something unknowable, that makes us who we are. Something that makes us people. It is the thing that makes us smile, makes us laugh, makes us cry, and makes us grieve. It was what makes us love and hate. It makes us human. And whatever that was for Alejandro is no longer there. I don't know where it's gone. I just know that it's not here.

What lies on that table is just a body. Nothing more.

My hand trembles the tiniest bit as I pick up the heavy brass candleholder. The light flickers, casting dancing shadows against the bare brick walls.

I force one foot in front of the other until I draw up beside the table. A white blanket covers his nude form, as if the dead have any dignity to be spared. His eyes are glossy and open. Unseeing. My hand twitches toward his face to close them, but I know better. They won't stay closed without the muscle cooperating. That's not how dead bodies work, no matter how many plays and novels try to convince us otherwise.

My hands curl into fists at my sides. The desire to touch him wars with the part of me that knows I'll regret it if I do. He won't be warm. He'll be cold and weirdly soft. He won't be what I remember him to be at all.

It takes every inch of my will to guide my eyes away from his.

I came here to find something. Anything. A single clue that would tell me where to start looking for the truth of what happened to him.

Alejandro did not kill himself. This, I know. He was murdered. It's the only thing that makes sense, if a senseless, cruel, violent death can be forced to make any sense at all.

But my brain refuses to be clever when confronted with the awful truth of his dead body lying on a wooden slab like so much meat.

"Come on," I say out loud to no one but myself. "There has to be something."

The last thing I want is to reach out and pull the blanket back. It's not that his nude form is a mystery to me. I'd seen him naked before, in the lake by the Sonza estate, with its crisp, cool waters. He wasn't ashamed, and I grew up in a brothel. Neither one of us were overly bothered by it. But that was when he was alive. Now, he's not. But I do what I must.

Breathing a prayer I don't quite feel in my heart, I reach for the sheet. Bile rises in my throat as my fingertips brush against his cool skin.

*It's not him. It's not Alejandro. It's just a body.*

The thought isn't as comforting as I want it to be.

I squeeze my eyes shut as his—as the corpse is revealed. But I have to open them eventually. Otherwise, this whole trip was a monumental waste of both time and money.

He looks smaller, lying there. Lifeless. Still.

There is no tension, no strength, in those corded muscles lying beneath his mottled skin. There is no pumping blood to warm the pale skin of his cheeks. No air in his lungs to make his chest rise and fall. There is nothing. Just . . . nothing.

I drag my eyes across his body, looking for something. I don't know what. I'll know it when I see it, I suppose.

My gaze stutters and stops when it hits his neck. Bile rises, sharp and acidic, in my throat. I want to look away but I can't.

His skin is still indented slightly where the rope dug in. The flesh is mottled purple and black. It's a bruise that will never heal.

Warmth floods my body, but it isn't the pleasant kind. It's hot and vicious and angry. It is rage, pure and undiluted.

"Who did this to you?" I ask softly, knowing I will never receive an answer.

I force my eyes to wander further south, down the curve of his shoulder and his arm. My brow furrows as my gaze reaches his wrist.

There is a mark carved on the back of his hand. That was what I saw the night in the garden. At the viceroy's ball. There had been too much happening around me to notice the finer details but I see them now. The blood's been cleared away and the mark stands out bright and lurid against the pale skin of his hand.

It looks a bit like a *P*, but the loop is too large, and something resembling a tail wraps around the stem of the symbol like a snake coiled around the trunk of a tree. A circle surrounds the—I don't know, sigil, perhaps—containing it. Marking it as deliberate.

This is no accidental scar.

My eyes follow its swooping lines, committing its shape to memory. There might be something in Kiki's library that can give it meaning. It's one of the more extensive collections in all of Potosí. Perhaps even in all of New Spain. It's somewhere to start at the very least.

I'm about to pull the sheet back up when an overwhelming urge stills my hand.

*Don't touch him.*

But I cannot help myself.

My hand approaches his, as if guided by some unseen force that isn't me. When my fingers brush the sallow skin of his knuckles, it isn't revulsion I feel.

It is sadness.

"I'm sorry." There is no one to hear the words but me, but it feels important to say them. "I'm sorry this was done to you."

I watch his face, as if a part of me is expecting his lips to tick up into that wry grin of his and tell me that it's okay. That everything will be fine. But that face will never smile again.

"I don't know what happened, or who did this . . ."

I hold his hand even though he cannot hold mine back.

"But I swear to you, on all that is holy, on all that I love . . ."

I tangle my fingers with his one last time.

"I will find out who did it. And I will make them pay."

# CHAPTER 13

*Kiki*

Something lands on my bed with a heavy thump.

"Get up."

Ana's voice is hard. Harder than it's been in quite some time. For days, she's been soft, soothing whispers in the dark, a gentle hand brushing the hair off my brow, a calming presence by my side.

But not now.

"Get. Up," she says again, enunciating each word with enough force to punch a hole through the wall, as if there was even the slightest possibility I—in the absolute silence of my bedroom—hadn't heard her the first time.

"No."

I burrow deeper into my pile of blankets. The goose feathers in my pillow tickle my nose. It will need fresh stuffing soon.

"That wasn't a request." More hard consonants. More clipped vowels.

Before I can muster a suitable retort, my armor is stripped away. Ana yanks the blankets off me all at once, exposing my legs to the frigid morning air.

"What are you—?" I scramble up to sit, pulling my nightgown

over my bare knees. It's not modesty that compels me to cover up. Ana has seen everything and then some. But I feel naked without the weight of those blankets on me. Naked and vulnerable.

"Come on." Ana is already dressed, a rarity for her so early in the morning.

The breeches she's wearing are tight enough to drive a nun to sin. They're a nice contrast to the flounce in her loose white shirtsleeves. Her copper hair tumbles over one shoulder in a sloppy braid. She did it herself, then. She can never get the plaits quite right. It's not incompetence on her part. It's impatience.

Frowning, I glance down to see what the thing was that she tossed on my bed.

A sword, nestled comfortably in its scabbard. My sword, to be exact. My sword, that I haven't touched in ages. My sword, that I have absolutely no interest in picking up. What good will a sword do me now, when I already know I cannot use it to protect the people I love?

"No," I say, flopping back down onto my bed, blankets be damned.

A hand—small and strong—closes around my ankle.

"I said, that wasn't a request."

And then, with all her might, she pulls.

Goose down muffles the sound of my shriek as Ana manhandles me out of bed and into a set of clean clothes.

If I had the heart for vengeance, I would make it long and painful. But I have the heart for very little. And that, I know, is why Ana is so keen to make me suffer.

●  ●  ●

"Hit me."

"I don't want to."

The tip of my sword hangs listlessly inches above the ground. I am not so careless as to let it drag, damaging the good and very expensive steel, but it's heavy. Heavier now than it's ever been.

Ana puffs out a frustrated breath, her bottom lip directing the exhalation upward to blow an errant lock of hair off her face.

The solarium is hot. Unseasonably so. Normally, this high up on the hills, we are blessed with crisp winds and cool air. But today, even the sky seems listless. Heat clings to the painted stone walls, trapping it in here with us. Beads of sweat form at my temples, at the nape of my neck, trapping my unkempt hair against my skin.

Ana knocks her sword into mine. Gently, but the impact still reverberates up the blade. "Attack me."

I begin to step away. "Ana—"

"You need to hit something!"

I freeze, my weight half transferred to the ball of my left foot as I cease stepping away. "Is that how you solve all your problems? By hitting things?"

"Not all my problems." Ana shrugs. "Just most of them."

It's almost enough to make me smile. *Almost.*

Instead of smiling, I sigh.

"If I refuse, will you continue pestering me like this?"

With a grin sharp enough to slice through stone, Ana says, "Yes."

I stare at her, longing to feel the spark of recognition that razor-sharp grin should incite within me. But all I feel is a stodgy dullness. It's like the sensation you get in your mouth after a long, hard night of drinking catches up to you in the morning. Except it's not just in my mouth. It's everywhere. In the center of my chest, in my heavy legs, in my leaden arms.

"Why?" I ask her.

*Why are you doing this?*

*Why are you making me do this?*

*Why does any of it matter anymore?*

The grin fades. Ana's eyebrows shift, ever so slightly, toward each other. Not quite a furrow, but something close to it.

"Because I need you to be yourself again."

I stare at her for a beat. I don't know what to say, so I go with honesty. "I don't know if that girl exists anymore."

The words sound hollow to my own ears. Again, those copper brows twitch.

"She does. And I need her to wake up."

That is the last thing Ana says before she charges me.

Alejandro was the first to let us handle these particular swords. That's the reason I've chosen them for this little exercise. We were too young, too small, too weak to be able to properly use any of these blades then. But we grew. And now, we can wield them as good as any man. Better, even.

Kiki is not quite herself yet. Her arms are sluggish, but that's to be expected. Spending several days straight in bed without eating a single bite of food isn't the best way to build muscle and maintain agility. Her footwork is a goddamn mess. I'd point it out to her, but I can tell from every grimace, every bitten-back curse, every trembling exhalation that she knows.

Eustaquia de Sonza has lost her edge.

And I, Ana Lezama de Urinza, am here to help her get it back.

She is going to need it.

*We* are going to need it.

If we are ever going to find justice for our fallen brother, then she will need all her strength and then some. She will need to remember who she is. What she is capable of.

I lunge. She parries. I thrust. She dances out of the way. Or at least, she tries to.

The seconds tick by into minutes. Minutes into hours. Her strength should be depleting, but I can see it returning, inch by fragile inch. Her shirt clings to her chest with sweat. Her muscles quiver with exertion. I can see the moment she stops thinking about the past few weeks—about the ball and Alejandro and the great and terrible hole left at the heart of this family—and starts thinking only about the fight. About the movement of her body through space. About the sword in her hand and the sword in mine.

Slowly, her feet remember how to move. How to sidestep an oncoming blow. How to trick my eye into thinking she's going one way when she's actually going the other.

She is not herself. Not yet. She's getting there though. She's trying. And that counts for everything.

But all it takes to bring down an opponent is one small misstep.

It happens too fast for a sluggish Kiki to counter. My blade connects with hers at just the right angle. The hilt slips from her hand. My heel hooks around her ankle and I pull.

"Ana—!"

Kiki tumbles to the ground, her rear end smashing into hard stone. I almost feel bad about it. Almost.

But life is going to hit us a lot harder than that if we follow the path I know we must.

She strikes out with her legs, but she's still slow. I dodge her feet with ease, extending the hand holding the sword until the tip is inches from her bare, vulnerable throat.

"Yield," I say.

It's the word that does it. Not the loss of her weapon or the tumble to the ground.

A spark flashes through those dark eyes.

*And there she is.*

With trembling arms, she pushes herself to stand, keeping wisely just out of reach of my blade. I watch her stand, our eyes connected.

She needs this. Needs to stand on her own two feet, under her own power. She needs to know that she can.

"Yield," I say again, stepping forward. The blade of my sword presses against her throat. Not hard enough to draw blood. (I would never hurt her, not like this, not ever.)

She stares me down, that spark building and building until I see that flame ignite.

"Never."

## Kiki

· · ·

If it were possible for me to hate Ana, even a little bit, I would hate her. But it is not. And so, I don't. Not even a little bit.

It hurts to breathe. It hurts to stand. It hurts to exist. But it's a good kind of hurt. Not the bad kind. Not the kind that has laid over me like a shroud for days. Since the ball. Since Alejandro. Since my world fractured into a million tiny pieces that I fear I will never be able to pick up and reconfigure into something approaching normalcy.

Sweat drips down my brow. I wipe at it with my shirtsleeve, feeling the fabric pull away from my sticky skin with the motion. I don't know how long we sparred. All I know is that I needed it. I needed to move. To fight. To feel, even if only for a fleeting moment, like myself once more.

I watch as Ana hangs up both our swords—my arms are too shattered to even try to pick up mine—and fills a cup of water from the jug on the table by the rack. Only then do I realize that my throat is absolutely parched.

"Thank you," I say as she hands me the cup. I down it in a rapid succession of unladylike gulps.

I am not talking about the water. Judging by the knowing look that flits across her face, she is well aware.

"Don't thank me yet." Her expression is carefully guarded. It is so unlike her, it nearly makes me forget that I am so thirsty that I have half a mind to pour the entire jug of water down my gullet in one go.

"What is it?" My hands tighten around the cup. I do not know if I can handle one more morsel of bad news. My cup is already overfull.

"There's something I have to tell you," Ana begins. Again, so unlike her to hedge her words. Normally, she wears her feelings on her sleeve, for anyone to see. She is not careful or circumspect. It is not in her nature.

"Whatever it is, just spit it out, Ana."

"Alejandro didn't kill himself."

The mention of his name, breathed aloud into the air, feels like another blow, this one right below the sternum. I have not spoken his name out loud myself. I could not bear to do so. Not when I knew it would go unanswered forever more.

I stumble over the name to the meat of what Ana has just said. The words are out of my mouth before my conscious mind truly has time to process both her statement and my response. "I know."

Her brow furrows. "I—Wait. How?"

*How?* It's a ridiculous question. Absurd. Truly. I know it the same way I know that water is wet and the sun rises in the east and sets in the west. I just know.

"He wouldn't."

Ana nods, slowly, as if to herself. "I saw him."

If the mere mentioning of his name was like a blow, this particular collection of words is like being run through with a blade, like being gutted, left to hold my own, still warm innards in my trembling hands.

I see him then too. I blink and I am there. In the viceroy's garden with the smell of flowers in the air and the muffled sounds of lovers rustling together, hidden behind a wall of hedges. Boots swinging in the wind. Hands, limp, pale, bloodied.

"Kiki."

Something warm lands on my shoulder. I blink. It is Ana's hand. Again, her brow is pinched, but more severely this time.

"Stay with me."

I breathe in through my nose. A mistake. I can smell it still. Flowers and blood.

"There was something on his hand."

Limp, pale, bloodied.

"Someone carved a sign. Or a crest. Something. I don't know."

My racing thoughts come to an abrupt stop. His hands. They'd been bloodied. But why?

I stand there, silent and dumb, as Ana takes a piece of parchment out of her pocket. It's folded, and the ink is smudged, but the image is clear enough. A circular sigil, inscribed around the edges with letters and symbols. What they mean, I do not know.

My hand extends toward Ana, toward the paper. She places it on my palm. I stare at it, and the memories of that night slough off like half-dried mud.

"What is this?"

"I don't know." She gives a helpless shake of her head. "I checked every book I could think of in your library—"

"You did research?"

"Try not to sound too shocked. But yes, I tried to look it up, but I couldn't find a damn thing. All I know is that a man who is about to hang himself—"

"He wouldn't."

"I know." She breathes in deeply. Rubs the bridge of her freckled nose. "I know. But what I'm saying is, someone else carved that onto his skin. It was on his left hand."

Our eyes meet, and I frown. It takes a moment for the significance of that statement to sink in.

"Ale is left-handed."

We both hear it the moment I say it. *Is.*

It's *was*, isn't it? But my lips refuse to form that conjugation. Ana lets it pass, unnoticed, or at least unremarked upon.

"Yes. And he couldn't write shit with his right, much less draw anything with precision." She places her finger on the center of the parchment, in the middle of the sigil. "Somebody else did this to him. And I think they were signing their work."

"Who?" Everyone loves—loved—Ale. Everyone. He had no enemies. Only friends and admirers. He would never harm a soul. "Who would want to hurt him?"

"I don't know," Ana says kindly. "But if we're going to find out, I think I know where we have to start."

# CHAPTER 14

*Ana*

Alejandro's room is exactly as he left it.

A pair of riding boots sits by the door, one standing upright, the other knocked sideways to the carpet. The mud on their soles is dry and cracked. But that there is mud at all makes something inside of me seize.

He wore those boots a few days ago. He tramped through the mud and muck of the stalls in the yard, heedless of the fine leather and the expensive craftsmanship. He probably left a trail of footprints in his wake as he strolled into the villa. He toed them off as he stood here, his mind—as restless as Kiki's even if he never really bothered to use it as much as she did—probably already wandering to the next thing to occupy his attention after his horse.

Oddly, this is worse than seeing his dead body. There was no mistaking what it was. A corpse. An empty shell.

But this—his room. It feels so very alive in a way I had not expected. The space was lived in, truly. I could feel his presence. Hell, the bed still holds the indent of his body.

Heat stings at the corners of my eyes. I blink once, twice. Squeeze my eyes shut until it passes. I'm under no illusion that it's gone for good. It'll come back. It always does. Grief cannot be put down, abandoned, or erased. It will beat at the doors until it has worn itself out. Until then, all I can do is push it back. Ignore its call.

Kiki stands frozen on the threshold, her fists clenched in the folds of her skirt. She looks at me, her eyes unblinking. Shiny.

"Do you smell that?" she asks.

I don't. Not until she asks.

Scented oil, fragrant with the crushed herbs I knew were distilled in it before it was bottled. Alejandro likes to smooth it over his hands and then run them through his hair. To keep it soft, he says.

No.

He *said*.

He cannot say it now. He will never say it again. Words have been stolen from him along with his life.

That heat comes back, summoned by that smell.

This time, I don't try to force it back. I let it simmer on my eyelashes.

"Come." I extend my hand to Kiki to help her across that threshold.

The desk is mostly hidden by scattered papers strewn across its surface with seemingly little care.

I pick one up, holding it up to the light drifting through the closed windows.

It's stifling in here. Someone should open them. But then, I think, to what end?

"'I could spill a river of ink describing your beauty and still, I would not come close to charting the depths of your . . .'" A glob of ink blots out the rest of the sentence. The next line is scratched out so vehemently, there's a small hole in the paper, like the poetic scrawl had so infuriated Alejandro, he'd given up on it in a fit of pique. I set down the note. The dry, coarse feel of the paper clings to my skin, a reminder that Alejandro was the last soul to touch this letter. "A bit wordy for my tastes . . ."

"Ana," Kiki says, shooting me a sharp look.

"What? Alejandro wouldn't want me to lie." Her eyes tighten as she goes back to shuffling through the papers. My teeth dig into the tender flesh inside my cheek.

*Shit.*

Being flippant is my thing. It helps me navigate the horrors of this unjust world. It soothes me when I would much rather throw myself on the ground and begin wailing like some kind of keening penitent.

But it's not Kiki's thing. Her pain is too raw, the wound too open. I'm just the ass cracking jokes about her dead brother's romantic scribblings.

*Shit, shit, shit.*

"Ana . . . look at this." Kiki saves me from further self-flagellation— what I wouldn't give for one of those many-tailed flogs the priests at the basilica residence use. She hands me a note, this one more complete than the last.

"'My love, it's almost time. We will be together soon, no matter the cost to me. I don't care about the villa or the estate or the lands in Spain I have never even seen. All I care about is you.'" I frown as I look up at Kiki. "Who was he going to send this to?"

She shrugs. "I don't know. A bunch of these letters are addressed to someone he calls mi corazón, but . . ."

"But Alejandro . . ." I shake my head. "That doesn't sound like him. He was . . ."

I bite my tongue so I don't say something insensitive again. But then Kiki huffs a soft, humorless laugh.

"You can say it." She shuffles a few of the papers around, looking for a key perhaps to unlock the secrets Alejandro took with him. "He was a cad."

"That's one way of putting it," I mutter.

Alejandro had a girl for every day of the week. He never treated them poorly, as far as I could tell. Never led them astray with false promises of love and constancy. But he'd always seemed to be the type to delight in variety. Not the type to pen romantic missives full of such great and terrible longing.

Kiki picks another letter out of the pile. "'Please, be careful,'" she reads. "'Stick close to Esmeralda's. Wolves prowl the streets. Wolves always do, but these are worse. Protect yourself. If anything were to happen to you, I would never survive it.'"

We share a look.

"Esmeralda's?" My voice lilts up at the end of the name, but it's not a question. We both know exactly what that one name implies. "Does that mean . . . ?"

"My brother was in love with a whore?"

The word sounds so vulgar falling from Kiki's lips. She's staring at the letter, her brow pinched in disbelief. But then, her eyes dart to me, remembering perhaps that I grew up there. For better or worse. Even if I myself had not turned to their trade. I could have. My fate had balanced on that razor's edge before I tumbled to the side with Kiki and Alejandro and this massive home, grander than anything I ever could have imagined.

"I didn't mean . . ."

For a brief delirious moment, I'm glad I'm not the only one who's taken a misstep in this conversation. "It's all right."

Kiki sets the note down on the table, fingertips tracing over the blank space where Ale would have signed his name had he ever finished writing it. "I knew he'd been to such places. Most of his circle frequents them regularly."

"Half of his friends are probably Rosalita's clients."

She glances at me. "You don't think . . . ?"

"No, of course no—" But then, I *do* think. I think about that night on the rooftop, when Rosalita held my breaking heart in her hands and did her best to help me mend it. The way her face lit from within when she told me about her new love. How she couldn't share any details about him. Not his name, not even what he looked like. How she said he was different from all the rest.

I paw at the papers on his desk, looking for—something. I don't know what. But I'll know it when I see it. And soon enough, I do.

A letter, written in the soft, curling hand of a woman in love. The creases are still sharp. Not worn down like the others. It must have been received very recently. It hadn't been pored over and treasured. Hands had not smoothed the places here the paper had been folded in on itself.

I bring the paper close to my nose. Closing my eyes, I take a deep breath. Memory strikes me, deep and true. A perfume I know well. I smelled it the other night on the rooftop, when I tried to use its wearer to drown my own sorrows. Opening my eyes, I exhale. "Shit."

"What?" Kiki asks. "What is it?"

"It was Rosalita."

She frowns. "How can you be sure?"

"It's her perfume." I hold the letter out for Kiki. She inclines her head, her hair brushing against the page. She sniffs, but there is no sense of recognition on her face. She doesn't know Rosalita the way I do.

"Alejandro was seeing Rosalita?"

"I'm almost certain." But I shake my head. "Something doesn't add up. What about the sigil? What does that have to do with her? With him? With anything?"

"I don't know." There is a weight to Kiki's voice. A determination I have not heard since before the viceroy's ball. "But there have to be answers here somewhere."

She brushes me aside to yank the drawers nearly clean off the desk, searching for some shred of proof. Some further evidence.

We turn the desk inside out. Then the room upside down. His bedding is pulled off the bed, the mattress is overturned. Heaps of clothing are removed—gently, mind you—from the wardrobe as we search for whatever it is that will lead us somewhere, anywhere. So long as it's out of this room and this house and toward something. Anything.

And then, I find it.

A small box of ebony wood, so polished it feels like tumbled stone. Enamel inlay decorating the top in shades of blue and green and white, swirling together to create some kind of ocean scene. And a simple silver lock holding it together.

"Give me that." Kiki snatches the box from my hands. Before I can stop her, she slams the lock down on the hard floor once, twice, three times until its hinges give and it falls off.

The box cracks open. Nestled inside it, cradled by a mound of plush silk, sits a ring.

It is stunning, and I have been told more than once that I have no eyes for jewels. But this ring impresses even me. It is a hefty emerald, glittering in the warm light of the candelabra, such a deep, clear shade of green that it seems like it contains fire in its depth. Or maybe water. Maybe that's what the ocean looks like, deep, deep down, where the rays of the sun barely penetrate.

Kiki's hand trembles as she reaches for the ring, her brow pinched, her eyes blinking far too rapidly.

"Kiki, what is it? What's wrong?"

She plucks the ring from its berth and holds it gently in the palm of her hand, as if it is something precious. Something worth far more than the value of its stone.

"This was my mother's ring."

And then it clicks into place. The letters. The hope etched on Rosalita's face. The knowledge that her days of working under Doña Esmeralda's roof were numbered.

"Alejandro was going to propose."

Kiki responds with only a wordless nod.

"But someone made sure he didn't." With tremendous reverence, she places the ring back in its box. And then, with one final look, she closes the lid, shutting her eyes as if the enormity of it is too much to bear.

It wasn't just one life cut short that night. It was two. Rosalita will never walk the path Alejandro wanted for her. She will never take his hand in marriage. She will never live under this roof, in this home. She will never know the future she dreamed of.

And we know who is to blame.

"The wolves," I say.

Kiki opens her eyes. She nods.

"But who are they?" She places the box down on the desk, surrounded by the letters its intended wearer sent and the one Alejandro never had the chance to. "And why did they want my brother dead?"

# CHAPTER 15

*Ana*

This is a mistake.

As I sit in Don Carlos de Sonza's study, watching his sallow face read the letters Kiki has laid out on his desk, I cannot help but think those words over and over and over.

This is a mistake. A great, big, terrible mistake that is going to bite us in the ass.

He shakes his head in jerky starts, his jowls quivering with the motion. He has never been a healthy man, but now, after the loss of his only son, he isn't even a shadow of his former self. It's like someone has scooped out his insides and left him completely empty. Not a man, but a husk. The firelight from the hearth in his study casts dreadful shadows in his wrinkled face, making him look like something half-dead already.

He removes his spectacles and pinches the bridge of his nose. Chaotic stacks of paper flank him from all sides. They were already there when we entered, piling up and up and up during the family's period of mourning. There is no respect for the dead, not where money is concerned. The Sonza family's wealth is old, but Kiki explained to me once how it continues to grow, stacks of gold and silver multiplying like fertile beasts. They control several very important shipping routes between Spain and the New World, and people apparently pay for the right to use them. How a man can control great big chunks of ocean is not something I will ever understand. The sea is not property, and yet they have carved it up like a prize pig being led to slaughter.

Don Carlos hasn't paid me much attention since the night Alejandro died, but I've been watching him, same as I've been watching Kiki. She is my family, and so is he. I've watched him attempt to sift through the reports of shipping routes and supply manifests. His eyes hardly move. A single page will remain atop a pile for days with nary a signature in sight.

"What am I looking at?" His voice is as hollow as the rest of him. He's looking at the papers, but he isn't really seeing them. When Kiki first slammed the stack of letters onto his desk, he'd reached for them, instinctively. But his fingers had barely grazed the one on top when his brain seemingly caught up. His son's handwriting, slashed across the page. A sign of a life no more.

"We found these in Alejandro's room," Kiki explains. "They were love letters, some of them, but there was also other correspondence with the same person. We think he knew something, was trying to warn her—"

"Warn who? Of what? Kiki, this is nonsense—"

"It's proof, Papa!"

Her shout bounces off the dark wooden walls.

He looks up, eyes blinking slowly, like he's trying to see us through a great fog. "Proof? Of what?"

Kiki leans forward, bracing her hands on his desk, looming over the old man in a way that makes my stomach hurt. He is suffering. I know despair when I see it. He's too deep into his own pain to be able to see outside of it.

This is a mistake. I reach out to Kiki, laying a hand on her arm, but she surges forth like she doesn't even feel it.

"Alejandro didn't commit suicide."

Each word makes her father flinch as if she had reached across the desk to strike him.

"Eustaquia—"

"He was killed, Papa."

He stares at her for a moment. Then he shakes his head, sighing long and weary, as if every passing second of this conversation is taking something out of him that he cannot spare. Her father can barely hold himself upright in his grief. I cannot blame him for not wanting to hear it.

With a trembling hand, he grips the silver head of his cane and pushes himself—painfully, slowly—to his feet. He shuffles the letters together into a neater pile gingerly, as if they were coated in poison that stung with every touch. "I know you're hurting, Eustaquia, but this is no time for your fictions. This isn't one of your novels."

"But—"

"Enough!" His hands tighten on the letters, now more of a wad than a pile.

I flinch. Never have I heard this man raise his voice to his children. Not Alejandro. Not Kiki. Not even me. He is a temperate man, slow to anger and quick to forgive.

But now—now, he is different.

Dark smudges stain the skin beneath his eyes. His hair falls limply around his face, striped with grays that have multiplied since his son's death. A sallow tint colors his skin. But the worst are his eyes, bloodshot and fatigued.

They are the eyes of a broken man.

Tugging on Kiki's arm, I lean in to speak softly in her ear. "Kiki, let's go. This isn't helping—"

But my words go unheard. From her pocket, Kiki retrieves the ring she'd removed from Alejandro's room. Slams it onto the desk.

"Look at this."

"Eustaquia—"

"Look!"

And he does. He squints at first, like he doesn't recognize it. But then, the shape triggers something in him, a memory. "Is this—"

"It was my mother's ring. Your wife's ring. He was going to give it to the girl he loved. He was going to marry her. That is not the action of a man who wants to take his own life."

The breath leaves Don Carlos in a weak sputter. Those wizened jowls quiver. He opens his mouth. Closes it. Says nothing. Only shakes his head. "Eustaquia, mija—"

"Somebody murdered my brother. Your son. Don't you care?"

I suck in a breath through my teeth. Everything goes still, as if the room itself was holding its breath. I thought he looked broken before, but now he is shattered. Utterly and completely.

"Alejandro is gone, mija." His shoulders sag forward. He presses his fist against his forehead. "We have to let him go."

He tightens his hand around the papers, crumpling them even further in his fist. His arm juts out toward the hearth and before I can understand what's happening, Kiki shouts.

The fire.

Kiki lunges around the desk, knocking her hip into its sharp corner. A stack of Don Carlos's papers flutter to the ground in her wake. She falls to her knees in front of the fire and I realize what she's going to do a second before she does it.

"Kiki, don't—"

She thrusts her hand into the fire, grasping for the papers. I lurch forward, grabbing her shoulder and hauling her back. We tumble backwards onto the floor.

"What are you doing?" Kiki tries to wrestle free of my hold. "We have to—That's all we have!"

"Kiki, stop." I press my face into the crown of her head, squeezing my eyes shut. "You have to stop."

The corners of the paper blacken and curl as the note catches fire. I hold her as we watch our last hope burn.

"We'll find something else," I whisper into her hair so only she can hear. Her father need not listen to this. His pain is too great and terrible. It has consumed him so thoroughly he cannot see past it. But I can. I must. For her sake. And mine. "We'll find something else."

And then I do something else, make another, even greater mistake than coming into this room in the first place. I make a promise I don't know if I can keep.

"We'll find out who did this, Kiki. I swear it."

*Kiki*

• • •

"Are you sure you're ready for this?"

I pause, the boot halfway up my calf. The leather is so soft from wear that I know I should probably invest in a new pair soon. But I like my boots. They're perfectly broken in, molded to my feet as if the Almighty himself had crafted them just for me. My thumbs rub into the grain, feeling the ridges and bumps of old wrinkles.

It's easier to focus on the boots and not Ana's question.

*Am I ready?*

I'm not. But I need to be. I want answers. And I am not going to find them here, quivering under my blankets like some helpless, grief-stricken maiden. I need to do something to shake the sight of my father casting Alejandro's letters into the fire. Of the look on his face when I hurled the very worst words I could into his face. Of the stench of burning paper. The acrid smoke. The crackling flame.

"Yes," I lie.

It had been easier to feel the fiery resolve of intention earlier in the day, when my father's refusal to accept what was right in front of him was still raw. But now I feel that resolve beginning to crack and splinter. It's not that I don't want to do this. I just don't know if I *can*. Not the way I want to. Not the way Alejandro deserves.

Ana makes a noise that's too polite to really be called a scoff, but I know in my heart that's what it is. "You're a terrible liar, Kiki."

I say nothing more as I pull the boot all the way on. My eyes fall to the patterned rug at my feet. Ana is so silent on her feet, I see the tips of her own boots land in front of me before I even realize she's approached. Her hand finds its way to my chin, tilting my head up.

I look up at her. She is a hair shorter than me, but from this angle, she looks like a goddess, rising tall and strong above a mere mortal penitent. Auburn waves fall about her face softly. It always feels a little bit like a loss when she ties her hair back. It is difficult to argue with the utility of it. I don't like it when my hair falls in front of my face either but . . .

*Stop it.*

The thought is so reflexive, I obey without even pausing to consider what it means.

I don't have to stop.

There is nothing stopping me from admiring the way her hair falls when it's loose. It's a more comfortable thought than any I've had since—

I would rather think of this than anything else.

Ana gazes down at me, her fingers warm against my chin. Her eyes go soft when mine finally find hers.

"I'm with you," says Ana. "Every step of the way."

"I know." And that is not a lie.

Her fingers trail from my chin to my cheek as she holds my gaze with hers. I know her so well, but in this moment, I cannot read what I see in her eyes. They are guarded in a way I'm not used to seeing. That Ana can build a wall inside her is not news to me. But that she would build one now, in this particular moment is troubling in a way I'm not sure I can articulate.

"What is it?" I ask.

She merely shakes her head.

I lean into her touch, her palm moving so that my cheek is cupped in her hand. Then, I stand. She begins to move back, but I still her with a hand on her elbow.

"Thank you," I say.

She smiles, and for the slimmest of moments I feel whole.

We finish getting ready, donning coats and daggers and hats. The leather belt is heavy and warm in my hands, weighted down with the heft of the sheathed blade attached to it. I wrap it around my waist with practiced ease. I've done this so many times, I could probably do it in my sleep.

With the heavy, comfortable weight of the sword at my hip, I feel almost like myself again.

Ana peeks her head outside the door to make sure there are no curious eyes about. She turns to me and nods before slipping through the door, trusting that I will follow. And I do. The hallway is dark, barely lit by the fading torchlight on the walls. It's just enough for the servants to find their way through the villa's corridors as their nightly routines draw to an end.

But the dark doesn't bother me. I could navigate any part of my home blindfolded. I know every step, every corner, every doorway and dead end. Every statue and alcove.

Memory twists at the muscles of my heart as we tiptoe past Alejandro's door, closed once again.

I pause a few steps beyond the door. "Wait."

Ana shoots me a quizzical look.

"There's something I need."

Her eyes drift from mine to the closed door. The corners of her lips twitch downward, as if words were tickled at her tongue to get out. She wants to say something to make me not do whatever it is I'm about to do. I cannot blame her. I was crazed earlier. I thrust my hand into a fire, for God's sake. But having a plan of action has given me a sense of clarity I had briefly lost. I have a mission. I am more than my despair. But Ana says nothing. She only nods, short and sharp.

The door swings open under my hand. The air is stifling inside.

Ana stays at the threshold, just outside the room. Waiting for me. Keeping watch.

His clothes are still strewn on the bench at the foot of his bed. A wild urge strikes me so suddenly it nearly knocks me off my feet. I want to pick up that pile of clothes and hug it.

*Stop it.* I cannot allow myself to go there now. My mission. Our mission.

That is where my thoughts must lie for now.

I trail my fingers along the desk's edge. It's bare, the polished wood gleaming in the faint moonlight drifting through the window.

"I came back," Ana says quietly from the doorway. "After we talked to Don Carlos. I took the rest of the papers and hid them. They're safe. I don't know if they're helpful or not but—I got them."

The tension in my chest releases, just a bit but enough for me to breathe.

"Thank you," I offer her.

She nods again.

I find what I'm looking for in the second drawer from the bottom. A sad smile touches my lips as I hold up my prize. The ornate silver barrel of the flintlock pistol gleams beautifully in the moonlight. It's a work of art, truly. The ebony handle fits my palm like it was always meant to be there.

The pistol seems to hum with power as I slip it into my belt. I know it's in my head, but I feel better with it. More whole, somehow. Like the chunk that was carved out of my heart with Alejandro's death is just a little bit smaller.

I turn back to Ana, a true smile on my face. I am not the quivering, crying thing crumpled on the floor of my father's study.

I am Eustaquia de Sonza, and I know what I must do.

"*Now* I'm ready."

# CHAPTER 16

*Ana*

Our first stop is Esmeralda's, but for the first time since I was a child, I find myself unable to just waltz right in.

I stand on the threshold of the main door, staring down the burly man blocking our path. Kiki hovers behind me, a silent shadow. Around us, the Potosí night is alive as it ever is, but the sounds of drunken revelry—and drunken despair—seem distant. Like they exist outside the small bubble formed on this one brothel doorstep.

"Move." My voice is strong. Steady. It's the kind of voice that usually results in me getting my way. It's a voice people don't want to fuck with. And yet, he doesn't move.

Rude.

"Customers only." He leans his shoulder against the frame of the door, filling up the space in a way he probably thinks intimidates me.

I've stared down bigger men than him. Scarier men. And I wasn't afraid of single goddamn one.

"Move," I say again.

His only response is to clear his throat and spit on the ground at my feet. Not quite at me, but close enough. I step toward him, ready to show him just how much of a mistake that was, but a hand on my arm stills me.

"Please, sir," Kiki says, her voice as sweet as honey. The amber glow from the sconces bracketing the door gilds the strong lines of her face, softening them so she looks as sweet as she sounds. It's a mask but a good one. "We're here to see Rosalita. She's a friend of ours. Doña Esmeralda can vouch for us. All you need do is ask."

He chuckles, low and dark, the way men do when they're thinking something that would make a nun blush. Not that it takes much. I would know. "Here to see Rosalita? You and half of Potosí."

The way he says it makes me bristle. I know who she is and what she does. There is no shame in it. But he makes it sound like there should be.

"Where's Esmeralda?"

Before he can open his mouth to respond, a voice comes from behind him. "Miguel, who in the world are you talking to—?"

Esmeralda's hand is the first part of her I see, reaching up to sink her nails into Miguel's too wide shoulders as if she were sinking her claws into a hunk of meat. He stiffens, standing just a little bit straighter. His size dwarfs her, but her stature has never been an obstacle before. She directs him out of the way, away from the door. When her eyes land on me, they seem to shutter. It's a quick thing, gone in a moment before her usual mask of cheerfulness drops into place.

"Ah, Ana. Mija. What are you doing here?"

She's never asked me that before. It's enough to startle me into a baldly honest answer. "I'm here to see Rosalita."

"Oh, my dear, I'm afraid that won't be possible." Shouldering Miguel aside as if he were nothing, she folds her hands primly in front of her, looking for all the world like one of the governesses

Kiki and I ran off when her father was still trying to convince us we needed one. "We have a very important client in at the moment, and I'm afraid he's insisted on the utmost discretion." She gestures as if to usher us away, like we were children begging at her door for scraps. "Surely, you understand."

Kiki and I share a look. We're good at that. Communicating with nothing but our eyebrows.

*Something feels off,* I think at her.

*Agreed,* she thinks back.

But what Kiki actually says out loud is, "Of course. We wouldn't dream of troubling you. It's only, I have something very important to ask her and—"

Esmeralda cuts her off. "I'm afraid she is otherwise engaged."

*Otherwise engaged.* That's a very nice way of putting it.

"But—"

Esmeralda smiles at us, tight-lipped like she's losing patience with us. Now, that is a look I'm more than familiar with. "Girls, I will inform Rosalita that you called upon her. I'll make sure she gets word that you were here. Now if you'll excuse me."

She doesn't wait for us to excuse her. She does that thing with her hands that people do when a gnat is flying by their faces, annoying the ever-loving shit out of them. She shoos us away like two buzzing flies.

"Fine, we'll get out of your hair," I say, allowing myself to be shooed. In the stables around the corner of the building, I can hear Tornado's distinctive neigh, as if he can sense that I'll be coming back to him sooner than anticipated. "But we'll be back later."

"Of course, of course, no need to be dramatic." Esmeralda is already turning toward the entryway, her back to us. I shoot her one last glance, but she isn't looking at me. Instead, Miguel catches my eye. Holding my gaze, he spits one final time on the ground and slams the door closed behind them, sealing away, for the moment at least, any answers we might have found within those walls.

## *Kiki*

• ● •

I hold myself together just long enough to be out of shouting distance of Esmeralda's. My legs carry me into the night, away from the brothel, away from the only person who might have answers for me.

"Goddammit!"

I kick the nearest thing, which happens to be a stack of empty crates lining the alley en route to Santiago's.

The wood cracks under the force of the blow, buckling inward.

I don't know why I did it.

I don't know why I let Esmeralda close the door in our faces.

I don't know why I didn't fight.

*Because that's not what ladies do.*

The voice in my head isn't mine. It isn't anyone's. It's an amalgam of every tutor, every governess, every person who had ever tried to shove me into a box in which I would never fit. The voice is always there, always lurking in the shadows of my mind. Usually, I'm so good at ignoring it I forget it ever existed.

But not now. Not when I need it to be silent more than anything.

"What the hell is wrong with me?" I whip the hat off my head. I'm too hot all of a sudden. Beneath my frock coat, my shirt sticks to my skin with a fresh sheen of sickly sweat.

*I'm not ready for this.*

That's what's wrong with me.

"Hey." Ana has to jog to catch up to me. Had I been walking that fast? I don't recall. My body moves as if of its own accord. I am merely a passenger, going where my limbs take me.

"Kiki, what the hell was that?"

*That was me, not knowing what I'm doing. I am not ready.*

But all I do is shake my head. "I don't know. *I don't know.* I just—"

"Hey, it's all right. You're all right."

I don't even realize I'm still mumbling until Ana lays a gentle finger against my lips.

"Come on. We'll wait it out. Rosalita won't be *otherwise engaged* forever. We'll go, get something to drink, and then head back. And we can ask Santiago if he or his little urchins have heard anything unusual about the death of a certain nobleman."

She doesn't say his name. A small kindness for my benefit. The sound of it is still raw. An open wound.

It's not a bad idea. And a familiar setting might give me the chance to marshal my thoughts, to pick up the pieces of myself that were left scattered in the wake of Esmeralda's obstinance.

"I—Yes, all right." I draw in a shaky breath. I cannot afford to fall apart at the first—and incredibly slight—obstacle we encounter. My brother deserves better than that. "Maybe some wine is precisely what I need."

"Wine. Or something stronger?"

She offers me a half smile. An easy grin. She seems to have those in endless supply. I hold on to it, grateful for its attempt at normalcy.

"Lead the way, and we'll find out."

• ● •

We don't have far to go. Only to Santiago's. If I were to cut all the thoughts out of my head, this would feel like any other night. But, of course, it isn't.

The tavern looks the same as it always does. Patrons packed in around tables, playing cards flying from hand to hand, copious amounts of wine and chicha flowing like water. The rich scent of a stew bubbling in a massive iron pot in the hearth.

But what isn't the same is the way people peer at me as I enter.

It takes a moment to understand why.

The look Santiago offers me is full of the last thing in this world I want: pity.

I pause so suddenly, Ana collides with my back.

"What—" But then she looks around. "Oh."

Some people turn away, back to their cards and their drink. One man I half recognize—the drunk who stuck to the bar despite Ana and I wreaking all manner of havoc in this tavern during that fight—lifts his cup and nods at me.

Ana presses close to my side, her body—and mane of loose hair—blocking my view of half the room. She catches me eye, her expression soft and steady. There is sympathy there, but sympathy I can bear. Pity . . . that is another beast entirely.

"We can leave if you want."

In that moment, I love her as much as I ever have.

"Thank you." I reach for her hand and give it a quick squeeze. "But no. I can stay. I want to stay."

She studies me for a moment, eyes raking over my countenance like a bloodhound scenting for a lie. But then, she nods. "All right."

And that's it.

We settle at our usual table, nestled in the corner with the best view of the entrance and the rest of the bar. Ana raises her hand, beckoning Santiago over.

He comes, tossing a rag over his shoulder. "What brings you here?"

"The same thing that always bring us here," Ana says. "We need information. And ale. Definitely ale."

With a wry smile (infinitely better than the pity he was serving when I walked in), Santiago says, "And here I was thinking it was my devilishly good looks that kept you coming back."

Ana leans back in her chair, her arm coming to rest on the back of mine. Her fingers tangle with my hair, tugging gently on the ends. She glances at me, a fond smirk on her face. "Sorry, Santiago. You're not really my type."

For a moment, I feel like myself again. But only for a moment.

"Well, what do you want to know?" There's a tension to Santiago's voice that I don't quite like. He knows what I'm going to ask. He just doesn't want me to ask it, for whatever reason. Curious.

Ana's gaze slides toward me. There's a question in her eyes.

*Which one of us should take point?*

A part of me knows Ana should lead this dance. She is not unaffected by our loss, but she has held herself together far better than I. But a different, louder part of my brain screams that I need answers, and I need them now, and I cannot allow anyone or anything to stand in my way. Not even reason.

Lifting my chin, I meet Santiago's eyes. My voice is steady when I speak, steadier by far than how I feel.

"I want to know who killed my brother."

Heaving a sigh, Santiago says, "I'm afraid I don't know anything."

And there it goes again. A tightness to his words I don't trust.

I narrow my eyes. "Are you sure?"

His brow pinches. "Of course. If I knew something, I would tell you. I wouldn't lie to you. Not about this."

Interesting phrasing. "Do you mean to say you've lied to us about other things?"

"Kiki." Ana places a hand on my elbow. I wrench my arm out of her grasp almost on instinct, my body tensing up. But when I glance at her face and see the worry etched on her expression, something deep in my chest loosens.

*You're being an ass*, supplies a helpful little voice at the back of my head.

"Fine," I say, turning away from him so I don't have to look at his face. Trust is a fickle thing. Before any of this bullshit happened, I would have said I trusted Santiago, as much as I trust anyone, but now, I am not so sure. I am not so sure of anything. Since that night at the viceroy's ball, it feels like the world—my world, at least—has shifted on its axis. Up is down. Left is right. Nothing is what I thought it was. Nothing is as it should be.

"Bring us some ale," Ana tells Santiago, mostly just to get him away from me and whatever aura I am radiating. I am sure it is far from pleasant.

Santiago nods, and with a last glance at me, he turns away and retreats back to the bar.

"I hate ale," I say.

"I know," Ana replies.

"Then why did you order it?"

"Because I'm selfish like that."

Santiago returns with two large cups, filled to the brim with the vile brew. I bring it close enough to sniff. Make a face. Ana smiles. It's disgusting but drinkable. It'll do for now.

"I had another reason for ordering the ale," Ana starts, tentatively, as if she's uncertain of my response. "I happen to know that Ale preferred the taste of ale to the taste of wine."

She pauses for a beat, studying my reaction. When I don't scream or cry or hurl invectives at her, she holds up her cup and says, "To Alejandro."

The snake that had been coiling around my rib cage since the night of his murder constricts, stealing my breath. But then, it loosens. I have spent every waking moment agonizing over his death without sparing a single thought for his life.

He would hate my grief. He would loathe my self-indulgent suffering. He would despise my torment.

I lift my own cup, tapping it against the rim of Ana's. "To Alejandro. And to justice."

With that, I knock back the ale, relishing the way it burns all the way down.

# CHAPTER 17

*Ana*

Why in the nine circles of hell did I think this was a good idea?

A swirling combination of horror and awe fills my gut as I watch Kiki down her fifth—or sixth?—cup of ale. Her cheeks are rosy, the way they always get when she's had a bit too much to drink, but it's not mirth filling her eyes tonight. It's something different, something darker. A manic, unfocused energy that's so unlike her, I don't quite know how to handle it.

Grief, as it turns out, is a terrible drinking companion. Some part of me knew this. I had drowned my own sorrows for days, but it was sobering to see it happening to someone else.

She slams the heavy metal cup down on the table, the sound ringing in my ears, loud even in the bustling chaos of the tavern. "Another! Santiago!"

From across the room, the man in question shoots me a look. *Get ahold of her*, that look says. Normally, I would tell any man suggesting we rein it in to go fuck himself, but Santiago isn't just any man. And he has a point.

"Kiki," I say softly, like I'm trying to corral a wild horse. "Maybe you should slow down."

She turns her unfocused gaze toward me, swaying slightly in her seat. The ale shouldn't have hit her this hard, this fast.

*She hasn't been eating.*

I squeeze my eyes shut, the realization hitting me like a fist. Of course. I hadn't thought about that. I hadn't been thinking much at all.

*Typical Ana*, a sober Kiki would say. Rushing headlong into things, guided by instinct and blessed by luck.

But this Kiki is anything but sober.

"What?" Somehow, she manages to stretch the word into three distinct syllables. With her eyes on me, she reaches for her discarded cup. Gazing into its depths, she frowns when she notices its empty. "Someone drank my ale." She chucks the cup over her shoulder and thrusts her hand out to steal mine, the back of her knuckles rapping the rim, knocking it straight to the floor. "Dammit." She waves her arms in the air and shouts, "Santiago! More ale!"

I grab her hands and yank her arms down. "No. No more ale for you."

Anger flashes through her eyes, but it's not her usual sort. This anger is messy. Unfocused. It's the rage of an animal being backed into a corner, knowing it's going to have to fight to get what it wants. "What crawled up your ass?"

It's something I would say. Not Kiki.

"We have to go back to Esmeralda's, remember? To talk to Rosalita?"

"Fuck Esmeralda. And fuck Rosalita."

I flinch, dropping her hand as if burned. Kiki doesn't seem to notice my reaction.

"Maybe if my brother hadn't met her, he'd still be alive. Maybe he was killed because—because—"

"Don't." I have heard enough. Misery makes you unwise. I know that. But I will not allow Kiki to walk—or stumble—down this road. "You know this isn't her fault."

Kiki shrugs, a sloppy version of her normal, artful gesture. "Don't know anything. Couldn't talk to her." She glances around as if wondering where all the ale has gone.

"And at the rate you're drinking," I say, "you'll pass out before we get the chance."

"Never pegged you for a . . . for a . . ."

Whatever insult she seems to want to lob at me hovers just out of her reach. Works for me. It would be nice if she didn't say anything we'd both regret.

She shakes herself, waves a hand as if batting away the words that won't obey her slurred speech. "Seems awfully hicoprytic—hicorotici—hypocritical. Of you, specifal—specifically."

Lord have mercy. I never should have brought her here. I stand, reaching for her arm. "We're going back home. It was a mistake coming out tonight."

She jerks her arm out of my grasp. "You drink all the time. You think I didn't notice?" The anger makes her words sharper, more lucid. "You think I didn't hear you skulking about to drown your own sorrows? Why must mine be made to swim?"

I don't know if the metaphor makes sense—literary bullshit is Kiki's thing, not mine—but I don't much care. "Yeah, well, that was different. We came out for a reason, Kiki. To get answers. Or have you decided you don't care anymore?"

I don't know if it's the right thing to say or very, very wrong, but either way, it gets her out of her chair and onto her feet. "How dare you?"

"Yeah, how dare I? How dare I try to keep you from drinking

yourself into an early grave before we've even had a chance to speak to the one person who might be able to give us ans—"

I don't get to finish my sentence because all of a sudden, a fist—Kiki's fist—is hurtling right toward my face.

## *Kiki*

• • •

I don't know what comes over me in that moment. There is no reason good enough to justify it. It happens, as if some demon harpy is piloting my body.

I do what I have never done outside of our sparring sessions.

I take a swing at her.

The moment seems to slow as time goes oddly lugubrious. Ana's eyes widen, then narrow.

She steps to the side, as deft as ever.

The edge of her coat brushes against my fist as I fall forward, pulled along by the force of my own sloppy punch.

*Well, shit.*

My hand hits the ground first, followed quickly by my cheek. The rough wood scrapes my skin, drawing blood. Something bubbles up inside me. For a moment, I fear I am going to be sick. That Ana will leave me here and I will drown in a puddle of my own vomit. But what comes out of my mouth isn't the regurgitated sins of my very recent past. No. It is laughter.

I laugh into the floor, aggravating the scrapes on my face. I laugh and laugh and laugh.

At some point, the laughter changes. It morphs into something darker, something uglier.

My face is sticky, probably with the remnants of decades of ale and spit and whatever else has soaked into these floorboards. But tears, too. My own.

A strong arm wraps around my middle, pulling me up to my feet. I sag against the chest of whoever is holding me. Ana, I presume. But the part of me that cared is soaking into those floorboards too, left behind after seeping through the cracks of whatever has broken in me.

"Come on." Ana's words are a balm against my ear as she steers my useless form out of the tavern. "Let's go home. You're no good to anyone like this. We'll try again tomorrow when you're sober."

This time, I don't argue. There isn't much fight left in me even if I wanted to. All I want is to forget any of this ever happened.

We've almost made it to the door of the tavern when the night goes from bad to worse.

A gaggle of finely dressed gentlemen saunter in like they own the place. That's how they enter any room, really. I know this well enough because I know that between the lot of them, their families own more than three-quarters of the land this fair city sits upon.

"Wha—?" Kiki mumbles into my shoulder. She looks up to see why I've stopped moving, and I feel the moment she recognizes the man blocking our path.

"Sebastian," I say by way of greeting.

He blinks at us for a moment before he sees beyond the breeches and boots and coats. Men's clothing. The lot of it. Tailored for us but still. His gaze slides from me to the woman holding on to me for stability. "Eustaquia?"

He doesn't even address me. It's as if I'm a mere servant, unworthy of his attention. Normally, I wouldn't give half a rotten shit about a snub from some high-society prick, but this particular high-society prick is standing between me and the door. And worse yet, he's the one who's trying to take *my* Kiki from me through the holy sacrament of marriage. Fuck this guy. What the hell is he doing in Santiago's anyway? This is *our* place. Mine and Kiki's. Not his.

He tilts his head, trying to get a good look at Kiki through the veil of her unbound hair. "Are you quite all right?"

She goes curiously still as she angles her head to look at him. "'m fine."

Sebastian's scoff is oddly gentle. "Clearly not."

One of his companions approaches us. A man with storm-gray eyes, a little older than the rest. He peers at Kiki with a look of concern. "Lady de Sonza? Would you like us to escort you home?"

I angle Kiki away from him. "You're not escorting anyone anywhere. Who the hell are you anyway?"

His pale eyebrows inch upward. "I am merely a concerned spectator, nothing more."

"Yeah, well, we don't need your help."

Sebastian's gaze shoots to me, something flashing through his eyes that I can't quite read. "You're a fool. You do realize that, don't you?"

"And you're a prick," I say. "Get over yourself. And get out of our way."

Shaking his head, Sebastian waves his friends off, shooing them away to engage in whatever drunken debauchery they have planned. The gray-eyed man is the last to leave. His gaze lingers on us as he walks away. Then, he shakes his head and turns toward the bar with the others. Sebastian huffs in disapproval.

"I want to say I'm disappointed you'd bring a mourning woman into a den of iniquity, Ana, but that would hardly be the truth."

"Said I'm fine," Kiki slurs. That last ale must be hitting her hard right about now. And on an empty stomach to boot.

"You are very clearly not fine," Sebastian quips, sounding for all the world like a prim and proper governess. Where's the boy who had his friends smash my face in? Hidden away, where Kiki can't see him. "Come along. I'll take you home." He sneers in my direction. "Seeing as how your present company doesn't seem to have your best interests at heart."

He moves forward, as if to take Kiki from me. I tighten my hold on her arm, but the second he touches her, she reacts as if her blood hadn't almost entirely fermented. She whips her coat out of the way to retrieve something from her hip. Steel glints in the warm firelight of the tavern.

Before my brain can even register what's happening, the barrel of Alejandro's gun is pressed to Sebastian's chin. Kiki drew it so fast, I didn't even see her do it. Sebastian goes very, very still. Kiki's hand trembles just so slightly as her finger curls around the trigger.

But when she speaks, her voice is clearer than it should be. "You keep your hands off me."

If I didn't know any better, I would say that she sounded sober. Maybe it's her fury, drying the drink right out of her blood, even if only for a scant few moments. I approach her, slowly and deliberately, keeping my steps audible so as not to spook her. The last thing any of us need is for her to pull the trigger because she is surprised. If she's going to kill the viceroy's son, I'd rather she did it on purpose.

Sebastian swallows thickly. "Eustaquia."

The pistol quavers. "Keep my name out of your mouth."

Sebastian catches my eye over Kiki's shoulder. I shake my head at him, hoping he understands that to provoke her would mean certain death. For them both, no doubt. There is no way Kiki would survive whatever the viceroy would do to her if she were to slay his oldest son and heir in a fit of pique.

"Kiki," I say, closer to her now. Close enough that I know she must hear me, even over whatever darkness is roaring through her head. "Let him go."

"Why?" Her voice is oddly soft. Distant. "Why should he live when better men have died?"

The pistol quivers. Sebastian's eyes slide toward it, his nostrils flared, breathing hard. But he doesn't say anything to piss her off.

I suppose he's smarter than I give him credit for.

With unparalleled care, I reach for Kiki's hand. The one holding the pistol. Sebastian squeezes his eyes shut, bracing himself.

My fingers brush Kiki's wrist. Softly. Slowly. When she doesn't flinch, I slide my palm across the back of her hand, wrapping my own around her white-knuckled grip on the pistol.

Gently, I lower our joined hands.

"It's all right," I say, even though it isn't. Nothing is.

Sebastian skirts away from us, shrugging his frock coat back into place. He meets my eyes. Something passes over his face, but whatever thought is running through his head goes unvoiced.

"For what it's worth," Sebastian says, "I am sorry for what happened to Alejandro."

Kiki doesn't move. She remains where she is, swaying slightly, staring at the wall where Sebastian's head had been.

"You keep his name out of your mouth." I wrap an arm around Kiki's shoulders and walk her out of the tavern.

I've got one foot over the threshold when a hand falls on my shoulder.

I turn, ready to bite the face off whoever dares stop me, Kiki's weight growing heavier by the second.

Sebastian stands behind me, his face pale beyond the limits of the tavern's firelight.

"There may be no love lost between us—"

"That's putting it mildly."

Sebastian's brow furrows. If I had any faith in him as a human being, I would say that was concern etched into his features. "All I want is for Eustaquia to be safe."

"Why do you care? Worried that your precious fortune will take a hit if you don't get to leech off hers through marriage?"

He cants his head to the side, fixing me with an inscrutable look. "Whatever you think of me, know that there are far worse men out there."

With that, he turns away, joining his friends in the tavern.

I don't like the way he said that. If life has taught me anything, it's what a man's voice sounds like when he's trying to hide something.

But I can't follow him back inside. Not now. Not with Kiki half out of her mind on piss-poor ale.

"Ana . . . ," Kiki mumbles into my throat. "I think I'm going to be sick."

"If you have to vomit, don't do it on me," I tell her, angling her chin in the opposite direction.

* ● *

It isn't easy getting Kiki—and the horses—home in her condition, but somehow I manage by having her sit in front me on Tornado while Rocinante follows us like a white shadow. I prop her up on a bale of hay once we get to the stables as I put the horses up. They're happy to be home and docilely chomp on their hay as I remove their tack and give them a cursory brush. I can make them pretty in the morning.

Hauling Kiki up the stairs and into her room is an ordeal in and of itself, but we make it in one piece. As a unit, we collapse onto the bed. Breathing heavily, I lay beside her, not bothering with my own clothes and boots, mud-stained though they are. She shouldn't be alone. Also, I'm tired as hell, and my own scattered thoughts will be poor company. Sebastian's words chew at me, long into the night.

*There are far worse men out there.*

# CHAPTER 18

*Kiki*

When I wake—if you can call clawing myself from the edge of a pained oblivion waking—my mouth is filled with the sour taste of vomit and the even sourer taste of regret. I roll over, burying my face in my pillow. Squinting one eye open, I check to see if I am alone. I have the vaguest recollection of Ana carrying me home, hauling me through the front door, not even caring if the servants saw. What propriety is there to save in a family marked by suicide and scandal?

My bed is empty, but there is a lone strand of red hair lying on the pillow next to me. So, she did spend the night. I haven't the foggiest clue where she's gone off to, but the sight of that single strand warms something within me, even if I do still feel like I've been trampled by a herd of very angry cattle.

I don't know how much I drank—a bad sign, to be sure—but if my body had decided to expel its contents during the night, it must have been far more than I could safely hold. My memory is pocked with gaps. Did we talk to Rosalita? Did she know anything? I remember having the plan to return to Esmeralda's but a low, sinking feeling in my gut suggests that my behavior scuttled those plans.

A knock sounds at the door—far too loud for my liking—before I can put together the broken pieces of my memories.

The door opens a scant few inches, allowing Magdalena to slink in between the narrow gap. She moves as if everything hurts. Her face is pinched, her hair—normally so tidy—is dull and lank. Her eyes rove over the room, touching each item of the mess I'd left behind. My muddied boots, dropped where Ana must have pulled them off my feet. A woolen frock coat stained with a bit of sick. A white shirt crumpled by the bed like so much garbage. She closes the door behind her and stands just inside the threshold, her face drawn.

"You're up." Magdalena's voice is thin and reedy, as if it had gone unused for quite some time. "I'm sorry to disturb you but . . ."

A pang of selfish shame hits me, sudden and sharp. Not one thought have I spared for her loss since the night of the viceroy's ball, so wrapped up was I in my own.

Death has visited this house far too often, kissing each and every soul beneath its roof.

"Magdalena, your cousin—"

Magdalena clears her throat, cutting me off. "Now is not the time to discuss such things. You have a caller."

Frowning, I glance at the window. The sun is nearly setting behind the great hulking ridge of Cerro Rico. It's getting late. Far too late for a social call. "Who?"

"Your betrothed."

*Sebastian.*

The mere thought of his name tickles something at the back of my mind. The sour taste in my throat intensifies as bile rises up. I grit my teeth and will it back down. Though my body protests, rather vociferously, I fling the sheets back and force myself out of bed.

"Did he say what he wanted?"

"Only to see you."

My feet hit the cool wooden floor, a jolt to my senses. "Then I suppose we must not keep him waiting."

·  ·  ·

My mourning dress is beautiful, and I want nothing more than to set it aflame. Preferably along with the seamstress who refuses to cease her meddlesome fussing with the lace dripping from the sleeves.

The lace is fine. The finest, perhaps, that I've ever worn. It's so soft, it reminds me of spider silk. So soft, I can barely feel it brushing against my skin. Rich dark velvet cascades around my frame like the loveliest of shrouds. Black beads dot the seams, tracing lines across my bodice. It's almost spiteful how well they catch the sunlight. It glitters off them as if they were jewels.

The dark fabric makes my already pale skin look monstrously paler. The light dripping through my window burns my eyes. My skull pounds as the sins of the previous night catch up to me. I want to wrap myself in shadows and disappear into a veil of darkness.

But not like this. Not in this lovely, godforsaken gown.

It is beautiful, truly, but I do not want to look beautiful.

I do not want to be looked at while wearing a mourning dress. I do not want to be found beautiful somehow in my grief.

I do not want to be looked at full stop.

But what I want is of no consequence.

Though I am in mourning, my grief does not belong to me alone. It hardly feels like it belongs to me at all. All of us—me, my father, even Ana—must perform our grief for others to see.

And right now, I must perform mine for Sebastian.

He is waiting in the library. My library. He cuts a striking figure as he stands there, his sharp chin angled upward as he studies the spines lined up neatly on the shelves nearest the window. There, he will find Spenser and Shakespeare and Marlowe. Faerie queens and star-crossed lovers and passionate shepherds.

The thought of him in my inner sanctum makes something in me rebel. This is not a space for him. Not a space for the part of my life that he represents. This space is mine and mine alone. I shared it with Ana, opened the door to allow her in. This place was safe in her hands. She knew—knows—what it means to me. These books, these wonderful tomes, were my windows into other worlds, other lives. Their fiction was a comfort. Sebastian's presence is a cold, sharp stab of reality.

He isn't wearing black, but his clothing is suitably mournful. A deep blue so dark it reminds me vaguely of the night sky when there's only the moon and stars to give it hue. The dark velvet of his frock coat is interrupted only by a spill of white lace at his collar. It isn't too much. Just enough to be in fashion but not enough to come across as frippery.

For the first time, I am grateful for my mourning dress. It is so elaborate, so adorned, so heavy that it feels like armor. Several thick layers of silk and whalebone separating me from the rest of the world. With that thought, I step over the threshold.

The floorboards creak under my feet as I approach. He turns to look at me, expression careful, pleasant, guarded.

"Eustaquia." With an arm across his stomach, he cuts me a shallow, graceful bow. "I rather hope you're unarmed today."

I blink at him. And then I remember.

The noise of the tavern.

The caustic burn of the ale.

The cold handle of the pistol.

I open my mouth—to say what, I don't know—but then I close it again. What do you say when you realize you've threatened the son of the most powerful man in New Spain with death?

"Sebastian, I—"

He holds up a hand, cutting me off. "Speak nothing of it. You were not in your right mind." He smooths a hand over his golden hair, an almost self-conscious gesture. "Grief can make us behave in irrational ways, wouldn't you agree?"

He's giving me an out. Why, I haven't the foggiest. But I am grateful for it nonetheless.

Magdalena bustles in behind me, laden with a silver tray bearing what smells like coffee. Sebastian's eyes don't even register her existence. It is that way, I suppose, with people like him. People like me. Ana told me I used to do that too, in the early days of her living here.

I graciously accept a delicate porcelain cup, wrapping my hands around it for warmth. "What brings you here, Sebastian?"

He looks at me as if I've grown an extra head. "To offer my condolences, of course." Only now do his eyes track Magdalena as she departs, waiting for the door to close behind her before he continues. "And to check up on you. You were in quite a state last night."

"Yes, well . . ." I take a sip of the coffee. It's too hot, and it burns my tongue ever so slightly. "I must apologize for my behavior. It was unseemly."

Sebastian shakes his head again. "No need. I lay the blame not at your feet."

There's something about the way he says it that doesn't sit quite right. "Then at whose?"

"The company you keep, of course."

I open my mouth to protest, but he barrels onward.

"Now, I know the girl is like family to you, but I worry about you, Eustaquia. Kiki."

The girl. Like Ana isn't even worthy of her name gracing his lips. And the sound of my name—the one that's always felt more real—feels obscene coming from his mouth.

"Her name is Ana. And she is not responsible for my actions." I stand, brushing invisible dust from my skirts. "I have no one to blame but myself." White-hot pain cuts through my temples. It must show on my face because Sebastian rises, concern etched into his.

"Kiki, are you—?"

"I'm fine."

I am absolutely not fine.

His brow crinkles.

"I'm sorry." Sebastian actually has the nerve to look abashed. "I'm afraid I'm bungling this terribly." He places the delicate cup back on the tray. The clink of porcelain against silver feels like a dagger straight through my skull. "I was worried about you. With the loss of your brother, I cannot imagine your suffering."

That I believe. I do not think Sebastian has ever suffered a single day in his life. He has always lived a thoroughly blessed experience. And until recently, so had I.

"I merely wanted to make sure that you were all right." He reaches out to take my hand. "I knew him," Sebastian says. "Your brother. Not well, but I did know him."

"We all know each other. It's a small circle in which we all move."

"He was a good man."

Those were not the words I was expecting him to say. They are true but . . . unexpected is all.

"I . . . thank you."

"Please. Condolences are the least I can offer." He looks around at the library. "An impressive collection. I take it your father has been collecting books for quite some time."

"Actually, the books are mine."

Sebastian blinks at me. "All of them?"

"Women are perfectly capable of basic literacy, I assure you."

"I meant no offense." He holds his hands in a gesture of surrender. "I would be glad to add to your collection. When the time is right, naturally."

Now it's my turn to blink stupidly. "What are you talking about?"

"When we are wed, obviously." He offers me a polite smile. An expectant one even. "I will make sure that you shall want for nothing."

I haven't spared a single thought for the wedding. The fact that it would still happen, even after everything, feels wrong.

A strangled little laugh works its way up my throat. "I want for nothing now." I spread my arms wide, indicating the riches that surround us. The gilded molding on the ceiling, the paintings set between the shelves imported from the most desired European masters of the arts. Trophies from my father's travels scattered about on every surface that isn't occupied by a book. Ivory from the deepest reaches of the African continent. A collection of jeweled scarabs from some pharaoh's tomb. Tapestries woven from Chinese silk. And, of course, the books. So many books. More than any other household on the hill. First editions and folios and illuminated manuscripts so beautiful it breaks the heart to look upon them. "What else could you possibly offer me?"

"Power." He says it like it's so obvious. "Protection."

"And what, pray tell do I need protecting from?"

Sebastian scoffs softly. "People like us are always in danger." His eyes rove to the portrait set against the far wall. It is a portrait. A large one. I have tried very hard not to look at it since entering the room. The artist was one of the finest money could commission. He did a lovely job rendering the faces of our family—me, my father, Ana, and Alejandro. So much so that if I look at it, if I glance upon my brother's visage, I might just crack. "What happened to Alejandro should have proven that."

Time seems to dilate, as if we were standing underwater, suspended and slow. "What do you mean?"

Sebastian looks back at me, and I cannot read what's on his face. "All I meant was that I do not wish to see you hurt. In any fashion. You are to be my wife, and as your husband, it will be my solemn duty to protect you from all harm."

"Losing my brother is not the sort of thing anyone could protect me from."

"Perhaps not."

"Perhaps nothing. My brother killed himself." The words sit heavy on my tongue, clinging thick and viscous like the foulest of oils. I do not believe them to be true. I know that they are not. And yet, that is the prevailing wisdom. It would not do to blare my theories aloud to anyone with ears. "Haven't you heard?"

Sebastian cants his head to the side, his gaze measured. "That is what they're saying, yes."

The curiosity those words arouse in me is far too powerful to fight. "And yet you do not believe it?"

"Far be it from me to mistrust the wisdom of our holy mother church."

Something must show on my face because Sebastian reaches for me. His hand hovers in my peripheral vision, almost touching me but not quite.

I turn away from him. I do not want his sympathy or his doubts or anything that he has to offer. There is no room in my life right now for Sebastian and all the accoutrements that he brings. Weddings and dresses and a future that seems more fictional than it is.

"I'm sorry. I've upset you. That was never my intention."

I can't help myself. I whip around to face him. "No, your intention was to pick at my wounds and blame someone I love for my own sins."

Sebastian's eyes tighten. A small flinch, but a flinch all the same. "She poured liquor down your gullet to drown your grief."

"She tried to get me to stop." That much I remember.

He gazes at me for a beat longer. Then, with a brisk nod, he straightens the lapels of his coat. "I want what's best for you. That is all. And I do not believe Ana is what's best for you."

I scoff. "And you are?"

His face hardens, those beautiful lips pressing into an unhappy line. "Whether or not either of us likes it, we are to be wed. I do not wish for our marriage to be unhappy, but I would have thought that you of all people would understand the significance of our union. Especially now."

"What do you mean?" The second the words are out of my mouth, I realize how short-sighted they are.

"News that Don Carlos de Sonza has lost his only male heir has already spread to Spain. The vultures are already circling his fortune, his trade routes. And from what I hear, he's been in no state to safeguard his business or his legacy."

I breathe sharply through my nose. He isn't wrong. "And you want to help me with that endeavor?"

"It is my duty to do so. And I have never shied away from my duty." With a sigh, he rakes a hand through his hair, disturbing his pristine locks. "I do not believe you would either. We can help each other, you and I. If only you could see it."

With that, he makes his way to the door. He pauses at the threshold, one hand resting on the brass doorknob. That inscrutable expression returns to his face. "Think about what I've said, Kiki. I am not your enemy."

He leaves, the door clicking shut behind him.

I am left standing alone in the library, with naught but a sea of books and a painted ghost for company.

He may not be my enemy. But I am not quite sure he is my friend.

# CHAPTER 19

*Ana*

Last night was a complete and utter mess. It's partly my fault for thinking it was a good idea to bring Kiki to the tavern. Hell, she wasn't ready to go back out. I should have known.

But even if I had, it wouldn't have made a damn bit of difference. We need answers. And we're going to get them. Tonight. A second stab at talking to Rosalita. I wonder if she knows about Ale. I wonder if anyone has told her. If I had known, if I had even suspected that she and Ale—

But then, of course she would know. That sort of gossip would never remain contained. The death of one of Potosí's most eligible bachelors at the viceroy's ball of all places would be too salacious— that's one of Kiki's favorite words, *salacious*—to remain silent.

But maybe Rosalita will know something. Maybe she will be the one to help us find justice.

Kiki seems to be in a mood as we make our way through the streets of Potosí. Her bad mood glows brighter than the lamps that illuminate the way to Esmeralda's. Even the beggars who routinely dog our steps for spare change give us a wide berth.

"What crawled up your ass?" I ask because I am not a poet and never will be.

"Sebastian."

A pang of emotion sings through me. Or really, a mix of emotions. My own anger. A little bit of hate. A great, big load of jealousy.

"Yeah," I say, trying to keep my voice even. "I heard he stopped by today." I'd been busy in the stables, grooming Tornado, but word had trickled down. The servants had looser tongues around me. "What did he want?"

"To remind me of my duty."

I pause. We're nearly at Esmeralda's, but I don't like the sound of that.

"What duty? You mean—"

"Marriage."

I grab her arm. "You can't possibly mean you're going through with it."

She stares at me for a beat before her features arrange themselves into mild surprise. "Did you think I wouldn't?"

"But your brother just died. Alejandro—"

"I don't need reminding of that, Ana. That's why we're out here."

"I know. I'm sorry. I just—"

*Got used to the idea that it would be the two of us against the world forever.*

"Look, I don't want to talk about this right now." There is a note of soft desperation in Kiki's voice. "All I want to do—all I can do right now—is talk to Rosalita and try to find answers."

"But—"

"Leave it, Ana." She turns on her heel and strides toward Esmeralda's. I watch her walk away from me, the tails of her frock coat billowing with every step.

"Fuck," I say to no one but myself. And I force myself to jog to catch up with her.

* ● *

"Rosalita's not here."

There's a different man at the door tonight. Where does Esmeralda find these clowns?

"Bullshit," I say.

He shrugs, taking a bite of an apple. The crunch echoes against the walls of the alleyway around us.

"Where's Esmeralda?"

He shrugs again, wiping stray bits off apple off his stubbly beard. "Don't know. Didn't ask."

Kiki steps forward. "Look, we just need to talk to Rosalita,"

That line works about as well as it did last night. A third shrug. "Can't help you there."

"Why are you even here?" I shove Kiki out of the way, ignoring her little yelp of indignation. "Why is Esmeralda keeping me out?"

A fourth shrug. "Don't get paid to ask questions."

None of this is right. There's something rotten here. But I don't know what. And I'm getting sick and tired of being left in the dark.

Rosalita and Alejandro. They'd been carrying on an affair right under our noses with no one being the wiser.

Well, not no one. *Someone* knew. I can feel it in my bones. Someone knew—the same someone who left Alejandro hanging from a tree in the viceroy's garden—and that someone might be coming after Rosalita next.

I cannot let that happen. I will not. I have lost too much. I will not lose her too.

"Fine," I say through gritted teeth. "We'll come back later." I grab Kiki's arm and storm off, doing my best to give the impression of righteous indignation.

What he doesn't know is that later is sooner than he might think.

"Ana, what are you—"

Once we've turned the corner, I break into a silent run, rounding the building. Heading toward the back. Kiki falls silent, her stride matching mine. We share a look, and it says everything we need. She'll follow my lead.

The door is open as it always is. The kitchen gets punishingly hot, even during these cool autumn nights. The only way to survive in there without boiling alive is to prop the door open to let the breeze in.

Tonight, though, there will be more than a breeze slipping through. I put a finger to my lips signaling for Kiki to keep quiet. She nods, short and sharp.

No one takes notice of us as we enter. Our presence in the brothel is so commonplace that it's not weird for me to be in the kitchen. Not weird at all. I stop as I get to the open doorway connecting the kitchen to the more public areas of Esmeralda's establishment.

I peek around the corner. Esmeralda is at her usual post by the door to the parlor, her back to us. The lace ties of her dress look like they're holding on for dear life in the back. The parlor is mostly full. Working girls perch fetchingly on velvet sofas while mildly inebriated men hang on their every word like lapdogs looking for a treat. Good. They're all well distracted. I tuck my hair up under my hat. Kiki does the same. That's about as incognito as we're going to get.

Pulling my hat down low, I slip through the doorway. No one looks at us twice. Well, no one but a girl by the fireplace. She's vaguely familiar. Maria or something. Half the girls in here use fake names, so who's to say if it really is Maria or not. She frowns at me as Kiki and I pass. I put a finger to my lips, and though she looks confused, she nods subtly enough for no one else to notice. I've done more than one favor for the girls under Esmeralda's roof since I left. At this point, I'm probably owed one or two myself.

Sneaking past Esmeralda herself is trickier than swanning through her parlor undetected. No one makes it upstairs without the lady of the house noticing. I pause, back pressed against the upholstered wall. Kiki draws up beside me, her shoulder pressed to mine. She asks the question with her eyes.

*Now what?*

But then, God himself smiles down on us, providing exactly the answer we need.

"Hey! Get back here!"

A commotion on the street outside draws Esmeralda's attention. She shuffles from her post at the foot of the stairs to peek outside. Without wasting another second, I tiptoe around the banister and up the stairs, grateful my boots are worn enough to whisper silently over the plush carpeting.

With long strides, I take the stairs in twos until we reach the landing. The hallway stretches out before us, then curves to the right at the end. It's empty save for a girl I don't recognizing leaning against the open door next to Rosalita's room. Rosalita's door is closed. Not unusual in and of itself but the sight of it triggers something inside me, a thick coiling dread snaking around my ribs like an anaconda. Usually, when she's in with a man, she leaves a red ribbon tied around the doorknob, signaling to anyone who might come calling that she's otherwise preoccupied. The doorknob is bare. No ribbon to be seen.

I stride right past the girl, who studies me with barely a passing glance. Kiki keeps an eye on the stairs behind us, just in case Esmeralda or anyone else sees fit to follow us up.

"Rosa," I call, knocking on the door also as loudly as I dare.

No answer.

I knock again. Wait.

"Rosalita?"

Nothing.

"Maybe she stepped out?" Kiki ventures. "Could be the man downstairs was actually telling the truth."

But I shake my head. She knows as well as I do how unlikely that is. "Today's one of her busiest nights. She wouldn't."

I try the doorknob, but it rattles uselessly in my hand.

Locked.

Biting back a curse, I turn to the girl in the doorway. Her blond hair falls in loose curls down her back. She looks very European. Not a trace of native blood in her, at least on the surface. Esmeralda's more aristocratic clients would pay a pretty penny for a night with her. The more European the outside, the heftier price they can command. She never said it outright, but I'm fairly certain my hair was one of the reasons Esmeralda took me in. It was the only gift my father ever gave me. He was a Dutch merchant who passed through town only long enough to sire me with a local prostitute. Esmeralda probably thought I'd grow up to be one of her moneymakers. Red hair was rare enough in Europe, but even rarer here. A contrast to my complexion, Esmeralda once called it. She said it like she was eyeing up a prize sow. Unlike this girl here, my skin is the sun-kissed color most people in the city share. She's pale. Very pale. Like she'd crisp up if she even thought about the sun. Her eyes—a grassy green—meet mine. There's a hard look in them. She's seen things. No one who winds up working in this part of town reaches adulthood without that very same hardening.

"Where's Rosalita?" I ask.

The girl shrugs, crossing her arms under her bosom. It's a bit small for Esmeralda's, but I suppose there's a market for all types. "Don't know. Don't much care."

"You're an insouciant little thing, aren't you?" Kiki asks.

Another shrug, this one somehow even more *insouciant* than the last. The girl analyzes her nails as if she could divine the secrets of the universe in their ridges. "Don't know what that means."

Kiki and I share a look. Her eyebrows inch ever so slightly upward before she shrugs a single shoulder.

*Your call*, says that shrug.

With a grin that's more than a little feral, I move closer, disrupting her study of her own damn nails. "Where. Is. Rosalita?"

The girl may be a tiny little shit, but to her credit, she isn't the least bit cowed. Lip curled, she sneers up at me. "Don't. Know. Don't. Care."

"Well, can't say I didn't try asking nicely."

Kiki steps back, giving me space to operate.

I step into the girl's space. She's really very short, now that we're toe to toe. I'm not terrifically tall but she still has to crane her neck to hold my gaze. And hold it she does.

"Try anything and I'll scream," she hisses.

I nod. And then my arm snaps up and presses against her throat, not hard enough to do damage but with just enough pressure to keep her from following through on her threat.

"Do I need to ask again, or do you already know what I'm about to say?"

The girl struggles against my grasp, her cheeks reddening with anger. When my only response is to cock an eyebrow at her, she sags a bit, rolling her eyes. I ease up the pressure, just a bit. Enough for her to speak, but I keep my arm up, just in case.

"I don't know where your Rosalita is," she chokes out. "Don't even know who she is. I just got here yesterday." I lower my arm fully as the girl shrugs her corset back into place, yanking the neckline up and to the side. "Heard there was an opening at Doña Esmeralda's and threw my hat into the ring."

"An opening?"

Kiki and I share a look.

"I don't like the sound of that," she says.

"Neither do I." I release my hold on the girl and step back. She rubs her neck—dramatically, at that.

Rosalita's door is the same as any other on this floor. Sturdy, but not overly so. I step back and draw in a breath. The sounds coming from downstairs are loud but not quite loud enough for what I plan to do.

"Hey, Kiki?"

"Yes?"

"What time is it?"

Frowning slightly, she pulls the watch out of her inner pocket. The gold chain connecting it to her coat glimmers in the light from the sconces on the walls. The girl's eyes widen a bit when she sees it. Our clothes are fine but this watch is finer. It was a gift from Don Carlos two summers ago, when Kiki had begged and pleaded for one just like his.

Kiki glances at the watch face. "Nearly ten."

"How nearly?"

"Five, four, three . . ." She looks up at me, realization dawning on her face. "Two . . ."

On one, I rear back and bring up my foot as hard as I can, kicking the flat of my boot against the side of the door near the lock just as the bells from the cathedral down the road begin to toll, marking out the hours.

The door splinters open. The sound of the bells is just loud enough to cover the noise, though I am under no illusions it went entirely unheard. I just need time, is all. Time enough to—

I freeze just over the threshold, my blood running cold.

The room is trashed.

The mattress has been torn off the bed, turned over, and slashed open. Feathers drift in the air, floating about on the breeze coming in from the open window. Shattered glass litters the floor around Rosalita's vanity, peppered with smears of rouge and dusty powders. The doors of the wardrobe stand wide open, one ripped nearly off its hinges. Her dresses—the beautiful, delicate, flowing gowns Rosalita so loved—lie on the floor, shredded like discarded ribbon.

Kiki steps around me, tiptoeing over a broken vase. "What the hell happened here?"

I shake my head. "Nothing good." Fear and worry and confusion bubble up inside me like champagne that's gone sour.

The girl is still standing in the hallway, her curiosity evidently more powerful than her sense of self-preservation.

"Who was here last night?"

The girl frowns at me. "Some old rich man. I don't know. Think he might have been a magistrate or something."

"Do you remember his name?" Kiki asks.

The girl crosses her arms, as belligerently stubborn as she was before. "Can't say I recall. My memory might need some jogging."

I take a step toward her, ready to give her memory all the jogging it needs, when Kiki inserts herself between us. A shiny gold coin appears in her hand. "How about now?"

The girl snags the coin from Kiki's hand. "De la Vega. That's what Doña Esmeralda called him."

Kiki's brows draw together. "Magistrate de la Vega? He's a friend of my father's. I didn't think he was the type to—"

The sound of boots pounding up the stairs steals the rest of her thought.

Two of Esmeralda's goons appear at the top of the stairs. The one from yesterday and the one from tonight. They're each twice my size, easy. But oh well. I have toppled greater mountains.

But then, Esmeralda comes up behind them, her eyes gone storm gray with righteous fury. At the sight of her, doors slam shut behind me, as all her precious "jewels" tuck themselves away from what I am certain is about to be a hell of a fray.

"I put a roof over your head. Food in your belly. And this is how you repay me? By damaging my property?" She shakes her head. "You can leave here quietly or not so quietly. The choice is yours, ladies."

I chance a quick look at Kiki. Her eyes are trained on Esmeralda's and her minions, but she must feel me staring because she nods her head just once, almost imperceptibly.

"Doña Esmeralda," I say, drawing a dagger from its scabbard. "I have never done anything quietly. And I do not intend to start now."

# CHAPTER 20

*Kiki*

I should have stopped her.

I should have told Ana to sheathe her blade so we could all carry on with our lives.

I should have placated Esmeralda.

I should have done all those things, but I didn't. Once the promise of a fight sang through the air with the clarity of the finest choir, I couldn't help myself. All the pent-up energy, the useless anger, the righteous fury, came pouring out.

What can I say? It feels good to punch something.

I just don't really want to be the thing that gets punched. A fist—roughly the size of a whole roasted ham—hurtles toward my face with alarming speed.

"Kiki, duck!" Ana shouts, as if it wasn't obvious.

I duck. The man's fist lodges itself in the wooden slats of the wall behind me.

"Mother of God, where do you find these ruffians?" I pop up, brushing the dust off my sleeves as if I hadn't a care in the world. Which isn't true. I have a great many cares. But now's not the time to entertain those. "More muscle than brains, and that's putting it politely."

"Kiki, less quipping." Ana spins away from the second man as he lunges at her, arms extended as if to grab her. As if she'd make it that easy. "More fighting."

"As you wish." I slip the dagger from my sleeve and fall into a crouch as the first overly muscled barbarian lumbers back toward me. Around his bulk, I spy Esmeralda walking downstairs, her hair flouncing with each step.

Doesn't want to get her hands dirty, I see.

The lout takes one step toward me. His first mistake. Well, his first mistake was starting the fight in the first place, but I can certainly finish it.

And I do, by thrusting my dagger through the top of his boot, straight through the meatier bits of his foot and into the wooden floor below.

He *howls*.

Doors farther down the hallway open as girls and worried men peek their heads out to see what all the commotion is, but those very same doors slam shut when they find Ana and me elbows-deep in some truly cathartic violence.

It isn't the way it was yesterday. My grief and my anger and my fear are not riding me like some prize show pony, not wielding me like a weapon. They are there. They might always be there, but I am in control. I am issuing the orders. My fists and my feet and my blades all follow, going exactly where I want them to go.

The man falls to his knees, which probably only makes the blade tug more on his poor, beleaguered foot, but the folly of my plan becomes evident immediately. The knife is his now. Pulling it free of meat and bone and wood would take more time than I have in the moment. More time than Ana has right now.

She shouts, and I turn away from my own foe to find her locked in a vicious hold with hers. His arm is pressing against her neck as he pins her against the wall. Her face is beginning to redden as she grapples with him, but he's simply too strong for her to outmaneuver in this instance.

Fuck it.

I grab the hilt of the blade protruding from the first man's boot and, with all my might, I pull.

His scream accompanies me as I throw myself bodily across the hallway, bloodied blade splashing droplets of crimson against the walls.

My hand snakes around the man's throat, yanking his chin up. The dagger flies up toward his throat, right under his generous growth of stubble. The blade is sharp. All my blades are sharp. It's a point of pride how sharp I keep them. But right now, I'm not considering that. The only thing that exists is his hold on Ana and my blade at his neck.

I don't think.

I don't hesitate.

I just pull.

Blood spurts from the wound, spattering the side of Ana's face. Her hair gets the worst of it. He slumps to the ground, his hands flying up toward his throat as if they alone can stem the bleeding. But it's too late for him.

Ana slides down the wall, gasping for air. She kicks at the man, but weakly, like her limbs aren't quite up to the task of cooperating just yet.

"Ana, are you all right?" I fall to my knees, reaching for her. She grabs my hand with one of her own while the other massages her neck.

Her breath comes in harsh, belabored pants. "That . . . son of a . . . bitch . . ."

The first man is moaning on the floor, but he's pushing himself to stand. Slowly, but he'll get there. One stab wound isn't enough to keep a gargoyle like that down. I loop my arm around Ana's waist and help her stumble to her feet.

"Come on. We have to get out of here."

It isn't easy, but I manage to get us to the top of the stairs. But then, when I see what's waiting for us below, I stop.

Two members of the city guard, wearing the viceroy's colors, glare at us from the landing. The feathers in their hats bob gently, as if in tutting disapproval of our little brawl.

"You won't be going anywhere."

Ana coughs once. Twice. Then, she manages a faint, but still clearly audible, "Shit."

• ● •

"Unhand me, you lout!"

The guard merely laughs in response as he half tugs, half drags me out of the brothel. My feet tangle with each other as he propels me down the short flight of stairs by the entryway, but he keeps me upright with an unkind, steel grip on my upper arm.

"Why on earth would I unhand you?" He yanks me closer. His lip curls into a sneer as his foul breath wafts over my face. "Do you think a pretty face will get you anything you want?"

"From the looks of you, beauty is the least of your concerns. But I take it money is more to your liking. Whatever Esmeralda paid you, I'll double it if you let us go."

The man snorts.

"I have no need of your money, girl. Save your change."

I scoff, purposefully dragging my boots over the uneven cobblestones just to make this unpleasant man's life marginally more difficult. "Do you have any idea who my father is?"

Ana makes a terrible retching noise. She's also being dragged out but she stops putting up much of a fight just for the sake of shooting me an incredulous, slightly disappointed look. "I cannot believe you just said that."

"I'm not proud of it either but"—I struggle to pull my arm from the man's grasp, but he's far too strong, and I've expended far too much energy battling those brutes at Esmeralda's—"needs must."

Ana snorts. "Yes, well, how is that working out for us?"

"Not excellently."

The city guard bundles us into a carriage. Ana strikes out with her foot before they can close the door, catching one right on his chin and forcing him to stumble away. The victory is short-lived. The man's cohort slams the door shut and locks it. From the outside. The sound of the bolt sliding into place feels abysmally loud in the sudden silence of the carriage. It's not even so much a carriage as a rolling cage, with heavy iron bars on the windows and nothing to sit on besides cold hard floor.

Ana huffs as she plops down on the floor. "Well, this is a piss-poor turn of events."

"Where do you think they're taking us?" I ask.

She looks at me as if I'd just said something incredibly daft. "To prison, you dolt."

"Yes but . . ." But there's something else that's bothering me. "Why?"

Ana shrugs, picking at the dried blood crusting under her fingernails. Not hers. Probably from the man who nearly choked her to death. "Because we got in a fight in one of the most well-connected brothels in town?"

I shake my head. "If they arrested everyone who rumbled at a brothel, the entire population of Potosí would be behind bars. There's something else. Some other reason."

Ana arches an eyebrow. It's hard to tell in the near dark of the coach's interior, but the flickering lights from the city illuminate just enough of her face for me to be able read it. "This makes me think someone *really* didn't want anyone poking around Rosalita's room. Or asking questions about her whereabouts."

"Then," I say, smiling even though I know nothing good will meet us on the other end of this journey, "that means we're on the right track."

Ana pushes up to her knees to glance through the barred window of our rolling cage. I lean over to follow her gaze. The dark, ominous bulk of the city jail rises up against the velvet blue of the night sky.

"I hope that thought keeps you warm," Ana says as the coach begins to slow to a stop. "Because we're here."

# CHAPTER 21

*Ana*

The jail in which we are unceremoniously tossed is the finest in Potosí.

Which means it's a single rusting rung above one of Dante's circles of hell.

*See, Kiki,* I wish to say, *I do read the books you tell me to.*

But now hardly feels like the time to gloat over my literacy.

"I refuse to die here, Ana," Kiki says as she toes at a pile of dirty hay in the corner. "What *is* this?"

Her bravado faded the moment they tossed us in this cell.

"I suppose that's our bed for the evening." It's cruel that I said so just to get a rise out of her, but this cell is tiny, and if we're going to be here all night, I'm going to have to find a way to make my own fun.

Kiki hops away from the hay when something moves beneath its depths. I catch the briefest glimpse of a thin hairless tail as the thing disappears into the shadows of the cells.

"What the *hell* was that?"

"Our new bedmate."

She retches as if she's going to be sick.

Sometimes I forget how delicate she is. Not delicate as in fragile but . . .

Kiki is not as comfortable with rats as I am. As I had to be. She stands in the middle of the room, looking desperately uncomfortable.

"You should try to relax." I stretch my legs, then cross them at the ankles. "We might be here for a while."

The look she shoots me is cold enough to freeze the bars of this cell brittle enough to snap. "I will *not* be touching anything."

I close my eyes and sigh. "Let's see how long that lasts."

● ● ●

An hour.

That's how long she lasts not touching anything. I'm almost impressed.

But it's been a long night. And day. A long couple of days, actually.

She settles next to me, as far away from the filthy bedding and its rat inhabitant as possible.

"Magdalena will notice that we're missing sooner or later," I say.

With a groan, Kiki slumps, dropping her head on my shoulder. "Jesus."

I pat her head gently. "I don't think he's listening."

She snickers. But then, she frowns. "Why would a magistrate be involved with any of this? With Alejandro? With Rosalita?"

"Honestly, Kiki, I don't know. I feel like we're only seeing a tiny corner of a puzzle but we're missing all the pieces."

Letting my eyes drift shut—the left one is truly swollen now, I'll be lucky if I can see come morning—I lean my head back against the stones. They're damp and disgusting, but my exhaustion wins out.

I've slept in worse places. Slept in far better places too, but in this case, prisoners cannot be choosers.

"We'll figure it out," Kiki says. "I know we will." She pats my knee gently. "And for now, soothe yourself with the thought of what the warden's face is going to look like when he realizes he's jailed the children of one of the most powerful men in Potosí."

I crack my good eye open to look at Kiki. She's barely more than a dark blur in the penumbra of torchlight. Her expression is lost to me in the gloaming. "I am not his child."

"No, but you are his ward," Kiki insists. "You live under his roof. You eat at his table. He provides for you, just as he provides for me. You are a part of this family. You count."

The fact that her words create an odd little lump in my throat has nothing to do with anything. Nothing at all. Pure coincidence.

"Thank you," I say softly.

"No need to thank me for stating the truth," Kiki says. She opens her mouth as if to say more, but a yawn cracks her jaw. It may be damp and disgusting, but it is pleasantly dark down here in this cesspool of human suffering.

"Get some rest," I say. "I'll wake you up if the rat comes back."

Was it a mean thing to say? Yes. Of course.

Would I say it again just for the amusement her disgruntled face provides me? Absolutely.

But eventually, Kiki dozes off, head resting against my shoulder. It feels lovely, having her so close to me. Lovelier than it should, considering the circumstances. I try to stay awake, honestly, I do. It's a valiant effort, but slumber comes for me too. I am only human, after all.

· ● ·

I am awoken by the sound of footfalls against stone.

It takes my eyes a moment to adjust to the darkness, punctuated now only by the weak light of a single torch mounted on the wall opposite our cell.

Boots click against the floor, oddly loud in the silence.

I glance at Kiki, but she's still out. At some point, she curled over to her side, her head resting on her folded arms. Gingerly, I rise to stand, my aching joints protesting with every movement.

The sound of those boots draws closer still.

A man emerges from the darkened entryway, his face half-hidden in shadow. It takes me a second to place him. He steps closer to the bars, just close enough for the light to catch his face.

That face. I have seen it before. Hair of gold and eyes like flint.

"I know you."

He inclines his head in a little bow. "Cristobal Téllez-Girón, Marquis of Peñafiel. But my friends simply call me Cristobal."

"I don't think we'll be friends," I say. "You were at the tavern with Sebastian."

A mirthless smile stretches across his lips. "Ah, yes. Not your proudest moment, I take it."

I shrug, trying to look more nonchalant than I feel. "Just business as usual for us. Kiki loves her pints."

He approaches the bars of the cell and stops just outside of arm's reach. "They didn't seem to love her back." His voice marches across my skin like ants.

I weigh a number of responses before settling on, "What do you want?"

The man tilts his head to the side. The torchlight casts shadows in the hollows of his cheeks, making him look gaunter perhaps than he truly is. His pale eyes blink slowly at me, his lip curling into a knowing smile.

"I'm here to see you. Well, her, really." He dips his head in Kiki's direction.

I shake my head, my fingers clutching the bars. I want to make a quip, to say something smart that would likely earn me more than my fair share of lashings from the guard, but there's something about him that holds my tongue. Something lurking beneath the veneer of civility. All I manage to say is, "Why?"

He pulls his gloves off, finger by finger. Slowly. Deliberately. So slowly and so goddamn deliberately that it makes me want to scream. "Let's just say I have an interest in your friend's well-being. The viceroy is a dear family friend, after all."

"And you're here out of the goodness of your heart, huh?"

He nods, a small, humorless smile playing at his lips. "I must admit it was as much curiosity as generosity that compelled me to come. When I heard the two of you had been taken into custody, I had to come see for myself."

"And are we everything you hoped for?" I do sometimes try not to be a smart-ass, but I can't help myself.

"Quite. Two girls from a fine house, cutting a path of destruction and depravity through the city. Hard not to take notice of something like that." He steps closer to the bars. Close enough for me to reach out and grab, but I don't. It wouldn't gain me anything, and mostly, I don't want to. Every fiber of my being screams at me to retreat, to hide deeper into the cell, to get away from him, but I stay where I am. I do not cower. Not before him. Not before any man. I don't plan on starting now.

"But you're not from a fine house, are you?" He's so close now, I can smell him. Perfumed. Completely out of place in this rotten jail.

"You live in one now, but you come from humbler stock, do you not?" He reaches out, his hand slowly approaching the bars. I want to flinch. I don't. But it is a near thing, especially when his fingers graze my hair. "Such a beautiful girl. It's a shame you insist on running amok and getting yourself into trouble."

"I don't go looking for trouble," I say, grinding my teeth. His hand retreats, but the phantom sensation of it against my hair lingers. "It just has a habit of finding me."

He makes a sound that's almost a laugh. "Of course it does."

"Why did you really come here? Not just to gawk, surely."

"Not to gawk, no. To help, I assure you."

"Help? Why the hell would you do that?"

"What can I say? I find your escapades riveting. Young women, taking on dangerous men. It's the stuff of fiction, surely. And yet here you are. As real as anything."

I lean in. The bars are cold against my cheeks and probably filthy with God knows what but I don't care. I want him to know who I am.

"They may be dangerous men," I say, low and vicious. "But *we* are dangerous women. And *that* is worth so much more."

That mirthless, icy smile returns.

"Oh, you have not disappointed me, Ana." I hate the way he says my name. Hate the way it sounds falling from his lips. "You have not disappointed me at all."

He turns to leave, boots clicking against the stone floor with every step. But before he reaches the door, he tosses a handful of words carelessly over his shoulder, "I've paid your bail. No need to thank me."

And with that, he's gone.

The slamming of the door behind him is loud enough to finally rouse Kiki. She sits upright, the skin of her cheek indented with the pattern of the filthy hay. She probably has fleas now. We probably both do.

"What happened? What was that?"

I rest my forehead against the bars and groan.

"Honestly, Kiki? I have no goddamn clue."

# CHAPTER 22

*Kiki*

When Ana fills me in on what I missed, I'm so angry I could spit. I wish I could spit, right here on the street, with the merciless light of the sun bearing down on me and the eyes of merchants on me. But I can't. That breach of etiquette is a bridge too far, even for me.

"How could I have slept through that?" I ask as we trudge through sun-drenched streets. The prison is a long way away from where we left the horses last night. A trustworthy stable, close enough to Esmeralda's to get us there quickly but far enough away that we had some kind of plausible deniability. Fat lot of good that did us. "Why didn't you wake me?"

Ana shakes her head, looking at me askance. "Have *you* ever tried to wake you? You sleep like a damn log."

"I most certainly do not."

"You most certainly do." Ana mimics my accent, butchering it atrociously. I suspect that might be entirely purposeful on her part.

"Be that as it may—" I sidestep the splash of a bucket emptied out of a window as we pass, holding my breath so I don't have to think too hard about what it may have contained. My clothes are filthy enough as it is. Despite what Ana may sometimes claim, I am not so precious about my things that the mere thought of getting a little dirty is enough to send me into a tizzy. But prison filth? That was an entirely new and horrific realm I wish to never again visit. The heat of the morning sun only exacerbates the stench that emanates from us both in waves. The woolen coat might be a complete loss. Unless Magdalena—

Oh.

*Oh.*

I never told Ana.

We're nearly to the stables when I grab her arm. She skids to a stop, eyebrow arching upward. Morning light kisses her freckles in a way that I would find charming any other day. Any other time. But not now.

"I forgot to tell you."

Ana's face turns to puzzlement. "Tell me what?"

"Magdalena's cousin. Juana. She was killed."

Ana blinks and then her face crumples. "Oh." And then, the slightest look of consternation. "How?"

No words of horror. We have seen too much of that recently to let it stop us dead in our tracks. "Murdered. Like the girl we saw in the brothel district that night. I was looking into it before the ball, when we—before—"

Before you kissed me. Before my brother died. Before I let my own suffering distract me.

"There's a killer on the loose," Ana says softly. Not to me. Her eyes drift downward. She breathes in deeply. When she looks at me, worry creases her brow. "Rosalita—do you think?"

"She's alive," I say, far too hastily. But the alternative is not something I am willing to consider just yet. "If they were just going to kill her, they would have dumped her body like the others."

Ana draws in a shaky breath. I can see it on her face as plain as day. She wants to believe me. She doesn't. But oh, how she wants to.

"We'll find her." There is more confidence in my voice now. This, I can swear to. Alive or dead, we will find her.

Ana nods as if she hears the words I do not say.

"And the first place we need to look," I say, "is the magistrate's villa."

• ● •

We wait for night to fall before we make our move. The darkness will provide excellent cover for sneaking into a place we're not meant to be.

Magdalena helpfully draws baths for us when we get back to the villa. She scrubs the jail grime from my hair with nary a grimace.

"What did my father say about us being gone?" I ask as she works at a particularly stubborn bit of I-don't-even-want-to-contemplate-what on my hands.

"He didn't even notice," she says, shaking her head. "He's taken to his rooms with a fit of gout."

"How bad is it?"

She purses her lips. "I think it's less the gout than it is his heart. It's broken, my lady."

I bite my bottom lip hard enough for it to hurt. "Yeah. Mine too."

We fall silent as we prepare for the night's activity. Soft, quiet boots. Dark breeches and coats to make sure we don't draw attention to ourselves. And, of course, our weapons. I sincerely hope we do not need them. Inciting violence on a government official's property is never a good thing.

My father does not emerge even once.

Soon enough, night falls and we are gone, Rocinante's and Tornado's hooves the only sound to pierce the still dark.

Magistrate de la Vega is no stranger to me. The man is a frequent visitor to my father's estate, especially fond of popping by when word spreads of a new shipment of art arriving. His expensive tastes are known far and wide, much to the detriment of his financial situation. He has a list of creditors a mile long, but he somehow manages to live a lifestyle considered extravagant even amongst the aristocracy which, honestly, is saying something.

From the outside, his villa looks like any other. Marble fountains pepper the property, each one more erotically charged than the last. They look more lurid by moonlight somehow, their forms outlined as if in silver. There is a grouping of figures at the center of the gardens contorted into an elaborate tangle of limbs that I'm not certain is even physically possible.

Beside me, Ana whispers, "Money can't buy taste, can it?"

I peer through the hedges, searching for any sight of guards. "It most certainly cannot."

"So, how are we getting in?" Ana asks. "Doesn't the magistrate have guards?"

I pat the satchel I brought with me for precisely this purpose. "I have a secret weapon." Putting two fingers into my mouth, I let out a whistle.

It takes no more than a few seconds before I hear them approach. Steps trotting toward us, breath heavy.

"Ozzy," I say softly. Too softly for human ears.

"Who?"

I shush Ana just as a massive shepherd with jaws big enough to snap a grown man's femur in half comes into view. From my satchel, I extract said secret weapon and unwrap the paper that envelops it. Once the scent hits the air, the hound takes a generous snuff.

"Come here, boy."

Ana tenses beside me, her arm twitching toward her sword, but I still her hand with my own on her elbow.

The dog trots up to us, tongue lolling. I toss the seared meat to the ground.

"It's fine." I crouch as the dog approaches, his large paws indenting the flower beds. "Ozzy knows me."

Ana looks at me skeptically. "Ozzy?"

The dog sniffs my hand once before flopping onto his back and exposing his belly. Smiling, I scratch his belly. The charm of dogs is irresistible. His back leg twitches happily. "He used to accompany the magistrate when he came by Father's house. You would have befriended him, too, if you hadn't been so busy hiding every time Father had guests over."

Ana shifts a little uncomfortably where she stands, scratching at her hip the way she does whenever she's feeling a bit out of place. "Well, it's not like any of those high-society friends ever wanted to make my acquaintance."

It's true. She was more often than not met with curious glances at best and thinly veiled derision at worst. When Father's business contacts were at the villa, Ana would disappear into the orchard or go into town from sunup until sundown. She was rather a champion at making herself scarce when she wanted to be.

I give the dog's belly a good and thorough scratch. "Well, Ozzy and I took a liking to each other quickly, but that might be because I bribed him with my table scraps. His full and proper name is Ozymandias."

"God bless you."

I roll my eyes. "It was what the Greeks of antiquity called Ramses II. He was a pharaoh, one of Egypt's most noteworthy."

"I know who Ramses is," Ana grumbles.

"Terribly sorry. I didn't mean to condescend."

"And yet, you manage to condescend so often."

"It's part of my charm." I stand.

Ozzy whines as if to say, *How dare you stop rubbing my belly and also I love you and also please never stop rubbing my belly.*

But alas, I must.

With Ozzy occupied, we head toward a darkened bank of windows to the rear of the house. If the layout is as I remember it—I've been to one or two events here—then that is where the magistrate's office will be. We just have to get inside without getting caught.

I pause when we reach a low balcony. Pressing a finger to my lips, I listen. The sound of nighttime insects is all that fills my ears. When no other noise comes, I jerk my head toward the balcony, signaling Ana to go on. Cupping my hands together, I kneel so she can vault over. Her boot is rough against my palm but I pay it no mind. I heave upward as she half leaps over the balustrade. Once over, she extends a hand and pulls me up behind her.

Inside, the house is ugly as sin. The walls are covered with massive oil paintings, each so big I feel like I could step inside them. I recognize most of the myths depicted in the paintings. There is Leda and the swan. A bathing Diana and her coterie of nymphs. Narcissus gazing at his own lovely reflection in a pond, cheeks just the right amount of flushed, golden hair curled delicately around his angelic face, his lithe body mostly nude save for a very strategically placed silken veil, its transparency somehow more revealing than if there had been nothing there at all.

Ana scoffs as we take in the truly unbearable decor. She fingers the petals of an elaborately blooming orchid, seated in a vase as tacky as the rest of the place. It's burnished gold, with a complex scene etched into the side in a sort of bastardization of a Greek amphora. The details are a bit muddled, but I am fairly certain it's some kind of orgiastic frenzy. There are plenty of limbs, all tangled up together in a jumbled mess. The scene depicts either sex or murder. Hard to tell.

"I'm beginning to think the magistrate might be a pervert," Ana says, scrunching her nose as if she's smelled something distasteful.

I tug on her sleeve, pulling her away from the pungent florals and shamefully bad art. "Let's have a look around. See what we can find. If there's a record of malfeasance lying around, I doubt he's left it out in the open where just anyone could find it."

And so, we begin our search. A large portrait behind the magistrate's desk draws my eye. It depicts the man himself, albeit in extraordinarily generous fashion. His double chin has been singled and his ruddy skin has the exquisite sheen normally reserved for artistic representations of kings and cherubs. His legs stretch for miles compared to what I know they look like in real life. Likewise, his shoulders are broad to the point of heroic.

Ana follows my gaze. "Pathetic, isn't it?"

"It is certainly eye-catching," I say as I approach the painting. There's something about it that tickles my curiosity.

I run my fingers along the gilded frame. About halfway down the right side, the pads of my fingers brush against something anomalous.

A latch.

"Got you," I say softly.

I pull the latch open and the painting swings outward.

"Christ," Ana says as she draws up beside me. She's clutching a newly found erotic figurine in her hand. How many of those did this man have? "Could he have been more obvious?"

"The arrogance of the affluent. They think they can get away with anything. Admittedly, they usually do."

"*They?*" Ana quirks an eyebrow at me. "Don't you mean *we?*"

"Fair enough." I shrug. "At least I'm aware of it."

Behind the painting is a safe. Ana lets out a low whistle because it is entirely gold. The metal has been carved with nude figures tangled together in debauched ecstasy.

"Well, at least he's consistent," I say.

Ana shakes her head, disgust written across her face. "This amount of gold could feed every hungry child in Potosí for a year," Ana says.

She isn't wrong. I lean closer to get a better look at the safe. The lock is a simple mechanism, meant more for show than security.

From the inside pocket of my frock coat, I pull out a leather roll. "I was hoping I'd get a chance to use these."

I unroll the leather parcel, revealing a set of iron picks of varying size.

Ana peers at me. "How did you learn to pick locks?"

"I read about it in a book once."

"Of course."

I gently slide the appropriate-size picks from their leather pockets. "I practiced on every door in the villa when no one was looking." I shoot her a small smile. "I thought I'd have a chance to impress you someday with a new skill."

She chuckles, soft and low. "Consider me impressed."

I make quick work of the lock. It's honestly shameful how easy it is to get into the safe. All the money the magistrate must have spent on this went into the form over the function. The door swings open silently, revealing a tall stack of books, mainly large ones.

"Shall we?" I ask.

Ana sighs and starts taking the books out of the safe. "We shall."

The two of us comb through the stack of books, spreading them out on the floor of the magistrate's office, then putting them back as we finish. Some are journals, others are account books detailing his expenditures on art and food and wine. The numbers are astronomically high. How the man hasn't developed severe gout at this point is a mystery.

"Look at this." Ana holds out one of the larger volumes, pointing to an open page. Numbers and letters are scribbled down in neat rows and columns, but they don't appear to be actual words.

I frown at the page. "Is it in code?"

Ana hefts the book onto the table, laying it flat. "Yes and no."

"Oh, well, that clears it all up."

"Hush you."

"Did you just actually say hush to me?" I feign clutching at a set of nonexistent pearls.

"Yes, I did, now shut up." She points to one of the columns, tracing her finger down its length. "It's a ledger. These values are for money coming in." She points to another column. "This is for money going out. And these are dates. And this"—she taps her finger against the first row, the one with the illegible word scramble—"is for what exactly the keeper of this ledger is moving."

"How do you figure?"

Ana shrugs, her shoulders tight. "Esmeralda had one just like it."

"But I thought—" I cut off said thought before I can speak it aloud. It seems too rude to point it out.

"What? That I couldn't read before I met you?" Another shrug. "I couldn't, not really. No one bothered teaching me the alphabet, but I could make sense out of shapes and patterns. I saw more than that old bag probably wanted me to. She assumed my ignorance meant I didn't understand what was going on. But I did."

There's something lurking beneath her words, some dark thread woven throughout. I shouldn't grasp for the end and tug but . . .

"What was she tracking?"

"People, mostly. Girls coming in. Girls going out. What they were pulling in every night and what they were costing her."

"I suppose it's a business like any other . . ." But still, the thought sits uneasy.

Ana cants her head to the side as she studies the page.

"Can you make sense of it?" I ask, crowding beside her. She doesn't move, though her arm is pressed flush to my stomach. "We know it's a ledger, but for what exactly?"

She shakes her head. "No. Maybe if I look it over, compare it to other pages, other records but . . ." Her voice trails off. "What did you say Magdalena's cousin's name was?"

"Juana. Juana Garcia Lorca. She and Magdalena shared a family name. But why—"

Ana waves me silent, bending over the page with the same look on her face as when she's working her way through one of the many puzzles my father gifted me with as a child. He'd returned with one for us—for me and Alejandro—after each of his travels.

"These are initials." She indicates one of the entries. "JGL 210958. Juana Garcia Lorca. Did Magdalena say when she disappeared?"

I think. The realization flows into me like molten lead. "She came to me on the twenty-third of September."

Two days after the date on this ledger.

"Shit," Ana says softly, leaning back in the magistrate's own chair.

Leaning over her, I take a closer look at the entry in the ledger. There is another smaller notation in the margins. "O, S, H. What do you think that means?"

Ana frowns, her lips pursing in concentration. Then, her eyes widen. "No. It can't be."

"Can't be what?"

"Like I said, Esmeralda had a ledger just like this." She taps the OSH notation. "When a girl was in trouble, she marked their name in the ledger with these letters so she would know that they weren't earning for that period of time."

"In trouble? What period of time?"

She looks at me as if I've just said something hopelessly naive. "Pregnant, Kiki. And roughly nine months. OSH is the name for the Ordo Sancti Hieronymi. When one of her girls got with child, she'd send them there. But why would—"

A noise captures my attention. My head swivels toward the door of the study. It is closed, but not locked.

"Did you hear that?" I ask.

Before Ana can reply, I hear it again. The distinct sound of a door opening and closing. The dull thud of footfalls approaching the study. I think about taking the ledger but it's too big. Its absence would be noted. Instead, I opt for ripping out the final page and putting it back in the safe as quietly as I can.

"Kiki, what are you—?"

I clap a hand over Ana's mouth and drag her behind the heavy curtains, praying there is space enough for both of us between them and the windows. There is. A padded bench provides ample room for us to perch—albeit precariously—and pull our feet up so our boots aren't sticking out from beneath the thick velvet drapes. That's the last thing we need. Starring roles in some kind of operatic farce.

The sound comes again, a heavy thud, following a distinctly male voice swearing with alacrity. The door bangs open as a man enters. But there are too many stomping boots for just one person.

"It's your own impulsiveness that got you into this situation," a gruff voice barks. I recognize it as the magistrate's, though I've never heard him this angry. Whenever he was in my father's presence, he was always obsequious, always sniveling after my father's good graces.

"Regardless of that, I do expect you to do what you've been paid to do and make it go away."

Beside me, Ana stiffens.

She knows that voice. We both do.

*Sebastian.*

"Make it go away?" The magistrate scoffs. The feet of his chair scrape at the floorboards as the leather shifts under his weight. "This isn't one of your youthful indiscretions that can be so easily wiped clean."

Sebastian's voice is so different than the softer tone he took with me in the library. "You needn't be so dramatic. I have everything well in hand now. Or I will, once you do your part."

Ana and I share a look in the half-light of the moon filtering in through the window.

*What part? And what is Sebastian trying to erase?*

"I have done my part. No one will find the girl. Nuns know how to keep a secret."

Ana and I share a look. *What girl?* she mouths at me. I shrug, wishing I could hear them more clearly.

"They'd better," says Sebastian, a slight note of what sounds an awful lot like worry in his voice. "If anyone knows what we've done, we're dead men."

With that, one set of feet leaves, boots pounding through the corridor until their exit is punctuated by the sound of a slamming door.

Leather creaks. A man curses softly. The magistrate leaning back in his chair perhaps.

"Rotten boy."

Ana cocks her head at me. All I can offer in response is a shallow shake of my head. There is so much I want to say. So much we need to know. But now all we can do is wait.

# CHAPTER 23

*Ana*

The only good thing about being stuck in a tight spot for the hours it took for the magistrate to angrily down an entire carafe of wine and then pass out thoroughly enough for us to slip out the window without him noticing is that it gave us both plenty of time to think.

By the time our aching legs are stumbling away from the property— with Kiki dispensing one last goodbye belly rub to Ozymandias—a theory has formed in my head.

"Sebastian is involved," I say bending down to rub at my sore calves. "The nuns they were talking about—they had to be from the convent. Maybe the girl is Rosalita. Or maybe even Juana. Maybe she's not actually dead."

Kiki bites her lip. "We don't know that yet. We don't have enough information to know anything for sure. There are likelier reasons for a well-born young man to want to hide a girl away at a nunnery."

"You think Sebastian knocked someone up?"

"Not how I would have phrased it, but it's entirely possible. The magistrate might be facilitating hiding away all manner of sins at that convent for the members of Potosí high society."

I shake my head. "No. I don't think that's it. Sebastian has something to do with Rosalita going missing. I know it. I feel it in my bones."

Kiki's gaze softens. "Ana, I know you want that to be true but . . ."

It is only through the grace of God that I don't yell loud enough to summon the hounds even this far from the magistrate's grounds. "I saw him! At Esmeralda's. He was being a prick."

"You always think he's being a prick."

"Because he always is a prick." I kick a rock as we get close to where we tied the horses up. Tornado huffs at me. "Don't be pissy," I tell him. I stroke the side of his neck to quell his irritation at having been left outside for so long. Rocinante nuzzles at Kiki's shoulder, ever the sweetheart.

I adjust Tornado's girth strap as Kiki does her own survey of Rocinante's tack. "Look, this is the only lead we have. We might as well follow it."

Kiki motions me over to help her onto Rocinante's saddle. I kneel, cupping my palms. She leverages the toe of her boot against my hands and hauls herself up. "On that, we are in agreement. We need to know everything we can before we make any accusations. Maybe Sebastian is involved with Rosalita's disappearance somehow. Maybe he's hiding a secret bastard child. Either way, we need to find out what's going on. If he and the magistrate have something to do with Rosalita or Juana, then we need proof."

"We have the paper from the ledger," I say, though even as the words leave my mouth I know how weak they are. How flimsy.

Kiki shakes her head. "It's not enough. Not for men like this. Men rich enough to live outside the limits of justice. And de la Vega is a magistrate. Do you think the law is going to touch him? Do you think the word of two girls and a single sheaf of paper is going to convince anyone that there's some kind of conspiracy afoot?"

My teeth sink into the tender flesh on the inside of my cheek. I don't want to say it, but I do. "No."

Kiki's nostrils flare as she turns Rocinante's head in the direction of the Sonza estate. I pull myself up onto Tornado's saddle, placing more weight on the stirrups than I ought to. Tornado whinnies a protest. So fussy. The horses begin their homeward trek at a happy trot. They aren't bothered by the thought of a conspiracy possibly taking place in the heart of Potosí society. They just want fresh hay and clean water. Poor things must be tired and hungry. We were stuck in the magistrate's study so long, dawn is beginning to pinken the farthest edge of the horizon.

I should be tired. Exhausted even. But I'm too angry, too curious, too determined to feel anything of the sort.

"We need answers," Kiki says, "And you're right. The convent is our only lead." She turns to me, expression grim. "There's *something* happening there. And I want to know what it is."

## Kiki

• ◉ •

As much as I want to head straight to the convent, the horses need rest for the remainder of the day. And to be honest, so do I. I tumble into my bed, not bothering to change. I'll just be wearing the same riding clothes tomorrow anyway. I doze for a few fitful hours before I arise and begin preparations. The nunnery is a long ride away, and we'll have to make sure we have everything we need. None of the stable hands ask us why we need provisions for a longer than usual ride, but I suppose that's none of their business.

Magdalena slips an extra-large hunk of cheese into my saddlebag, along with a loaf of crusty bread and apples for the horses. The stables are quieter than normal. We have had no guests for days. The only people coming and going are Ana and myself.

"How is my father?" I ask.

She shakes her head, concern pinching her features. "He's hardly left his room. It's all I can do to convince him to eat."

My heart squeezes in my chest. I should be home, taking care of him. Being a dutiful daughter. But the lives of these missing girls are more important than my grief or his. "If he asks for me . . ."

"I'll come up with something," Magdalena says. "I'll tell him you're sequestered in prayer for your brother's soul."

I don't say anything to that. I don't want to approve, but I cannot reasonably disapprove of her lie either. It's a good one. Believable. But the thought of using Alejandro's death like that makes me feel flush with shame.

"Ready?" Ana asks as she strides back into the stable, her own saddlebags slung over her shoulder. "We're burning daylight."

I nod. We mount our steeds, and together, we ride.

Leaving Potosí is like stepping into another world. The chaos of the city falls away to reveal a sweeping landscape, expanding as far as the eye can see. Mountains thrust up into the sky, puncturing slate gray clouds far in the distance.

The heat of the sun beats down on the dusty roads as if personally offended by their existence. Sweat trickles down the back of my neck, trailing a long unpleasant line down the ridge of my spine. Clouds gather in the distance but they're far enough away that I don't think we have to worry about them. Not yet at least. Though the weather here is often unpredictable. The sky can sometimes spit out a storm faster than you can find shelter. I mumble a quick prayer that this particular storm keeps its distance. I am miserable enough as it is without being caught in that nonsense.

Rather a long ride was putting it mildly.

"My ass hurts," Ana whines. Her earlier anger has gone out of her. It was too strong to maintain for the hours we've been on the road. And honestly, I think what she needed was a purpose. A goal. She can be like a musket, my Ana. Full of gunpowder lying dormant, waiting for the right spark, waiting to be aimed at the rich target.

"You should ride more," I say. "You're sore because you don't work those muscles enough."

Ana affects an irritatingly high-pitched voice to parrot my words back at me. "You're sore because you don't work those muscles enough."

"And yet, I'm still right." I frown as the horizon behind Ana darkens. "That doesn't look good."

Ana follows my gaze and likewise frowns.

The clouds that I was fairly confident were far enough away are now alarmingly not far enough away at all. They're far too close for comfort.

"Oh." Ana's hands tighten on her reins. Tornado whinnies, high and afraid, as if he can sense the change in the air. "I don't like that at all."

Rocinante tosses his mane, pawing at the ground.

I lean down, stroking his neck.

"Hush, my sweet." I glance up at Ana. "He doesn't like it either."

My poor horse whinnies and neighs, shuffling in place as the sky darkens.

Ana tosses me a smirk over her shoulder. "For a horse named Rocinante, he's awfully skittish."

Normally, I'd rise to her bait. No one speaks ill of my baby. But right now, we have bigger problems.

"What can I say? He's governed by his passions." And right now, he is passionately afraid of thunder and, in the way only animals can, he can sense it brewing in the air. I pat his neck again. He leans into the touch, comforted.

"Steady on, Rocinante," I say. "We'll find shelter." A quick glance at our surroundings is less promising. "Somewhere . . ."

A sudden crack of thunder rends the sky, booming so loudly it makes my bones shake.

Rocinante rears back, nearly dislodging me from the saddle. My hand tangles in his mane, holding on for dear life. As soon as his front hooves pound against the ground, he's off, streaking forward as fast as his powerful legs can carry him.

As it turns out, that is extremely fast.

I flatten myself against his body, my hair whipping around my face, the wind stinging my eyes. Distantly, I hear something that might be the sound of Ana shouting but we're already too far for the sound to carry.

"Rocinante, slow down, you buffoon."

For some reason, the horse does not listen to me.

He runs and runs and runs, trying to outpace the storm that's about to break out.

I'd pull on the reins but it would do no good. He will slow when he's good and ready. Fear is not logical, whether in humans or in horses. All I can do is my level best to guide him toward what I desperately hope is a viable shelter. There's an outcropping of rocks in the distance, the kind you find low on mountains that usually has caves large enough to spend a night in.

If we can get there . . .

Pounding hooves—of a different cadence than Rocinante's—come up behind me, strong and fast. I chance a look backward and find Ana and Tornado nearly caught up with us. Tornado's top speed is nowhere near Rocinante's, but Ana is pushing the horse with everything she's got.

Tornado pulls up beside Rocinante, eyes wild. There is no higher thought there. The beast's eyes are filled with pure terror.

"Kiki!" Ana's scream is nearly whipped away by the wind, but I hear the panic in her voice. She can ride well enough, but not like this. She didn't grow up in a saddle as I did. For ages, she was too terrified of the horses in our stable to get too close to them. It took months before she was willing to even brush one, much less ride.

If she falls at this speed, on this unforgiving earth, if Tornado trips and breaks a leg, they could both die.

Squeezing my knees against Rocinante's sides, I guide him as close to Tornado as we can get. Their hooves pound against the dirt and stone, louder even than the storm on our tails. Ana's boot bumps into mine and she nearly startles right out of the saddle.

"Hold on!"

Red hair whips across her face. "I'm trying!"

I pull Rocinante level with Tornado's head. Tornado's eye rolls wildly in its socket as a flash of lightning cracks open the sky. He tosses his head, fearful beyond all logic.

I reach across the small gap between the two horses and I grab his mane. I make sure his head is pointed where it needs to be. I need the horses to see each other. I need Tornado to see Rocinante. To see me. To know there is nothing to fear.

"What are you doing?" Ana's shout is nearly as fearful as Tornado's eyes. I ignore her. If this works, all will be explained.

I can feel the moment the horses connect. The moment when Tornado realizes he isn't alone, running like a demon out of hell. He is in his herd. He is as safe as we can make him.

"Come on, Roci," I whisper into my own horse's mane.

Gentle pressure on the reins and adjustment of my weight in the saddle slows Rocinante down incrementally. The fear has left him. He trusts my lead, and he will follow.

And then, Tornado begins to slow.

His stride shortens to match Rocinante's. His heaving breath starts to steady. The wild froth of fear begins to quell.

And he finally lets Ana use her reins.

She catches my eye as we canter on, far slower than the unrestrained gallop, but much, much safer.

"Thank you." Her words are swallowed up by a peal of thunder but I know the shapes those lips make and I hear it all the same.

The rain comes before we reach the caves. It's sudden and hard and unrelenting. In mere seconds, I am soaked through to the bone, my coat clinging to me, my boots sliding against the leathers of the saddle.

But the horses steady on. Rain is less scary than the crack of thunder, and that holds off, as if the gods of sky and storm have decided to be blissfully generous.

The weather continues its relentless assault as we finally—finally—reach the outcropping. And, as I had wished, there is a network of caves just tall enough to allow a horse through.

I slide off the saddle and lead Rocinante into the nearest one. It won't be a comfortable night but it might be a dry one.

Ana follows behind, Tornado's reins in hand. Their iron shoes clomp against the stone, echoing loudly into the cave. It's slightly larger on the inside than I expected. There are paintings on the walls, crude things, made from mud or blood. Hard to say, but what is clear is that we are not the only ones to seek shelter in this place.

"Well, this is less than ideal," I grumble. I only half mean it. Any shelter is good shelter right now. But I wouldn't be Eustaquia de Sonza if I didn't grumble at least a little at our rather rustic accommodations. Rocinante grumpily paws at the ground, as if annoyed that it's stone and not grass.

"I, for one, have never been gladder to be out of the goddamn rain." Ana puts up Tornado's reins and slips a cube of sugar—precious stuff, even in the richest city in the New World—out of her pocket. It's more than a little soggy. Half-melted, to be honest. But Tornado laps it out of her palm all the same. "That's my boy. Thank you for not getting me killed."

She turns to me, a soft, shaken smile on her face. "And thank you."

The sight of her smile warms something inside me even though I, like the horses, am drenched through to my skin. I feel my skin flush and I hastily look away. "Now, come on, let's get this tack off the horses and dry them before they get sores."

Still smiling, Ana follows my lead, but there's a knowing glint in her eyes that tells me my blush was not the least bit subtle.

# CHAPTER 24

*Kiki*

To say I am not comfortable would be a vast understatement.

Wool is not a fabric that should ever be wet. The heft of my sodden coat weighs me down. The horses, at least, have been tended to—as well as they can considering the circumstances—and now it's time to tend to ourselves.

A renegade lock of hair falls across my face as I huff out an exasperated breath. Rainwater trickles from my forehead, cresting the ridge of my eyebrows, tangling with sweat from our hard ride. The salt stings my eyes. I don't know what's worse. That or the feeling of hours of dust drying out my eyeballs.

"I am not built for life on the road, Ana."

She sniggers into her arm, but not even the thick wool of her coat can quiet the sound of it.

"Go on. Laugh at my torment."

"I can't help it. You look like a drenched cat. A drenched angry cat."

I whip my coat off and chuck it at her head. She dodges. The wet fabric slaps against the stone floor with a loud squelch.

"That was a delightful noise," Ana says, chuckling.

"We just got waylaid by a storm, why are you so goddamn cheerful?" I don't like being wet. In that regard, I suppose I am rather feline, but I refuse to admit it out loud. At least not with Ana chortling at my pain.

"I'm sorry, Kiki."

"No, you're not."

"No, I'm not. But I do hate to see you suffer."

"Sometimes you enjoy it."

"Only when it's amusing."

"Why don't you stop amusing yourself at my expense and help me find the candles? I know I packed them somewhere."

Ana raises an incredulous eyebrow. "You brought candles?"

I shrug. "You never know when you might need a reading light."

Her eyebrows raise even further. "You brought books?"

"You never know when you might get bored!"

This back-and-forth between us—God, I've missed it. After the orange grove and then the ball, I never thought I would feel normal with her again. And I don't, not fully. But we are at least performing a respectable facsimile of normalcy. It is comforting, and in our circumstances, I think we *both* need the comfort of the familiar.

The candles and flint were buried far enough in my saddlebags that they managed to stay mostly dry. I strike them into action, filling the cave with a soft, amber glow. It isn't much, but it's enough to see by. And the light might help keep the horses calm.

For the moment, they are happy to be out of the rain. They are snuggled together on the far side of the cave, as far away from the entrance and the storm raging outside as they can get. In the dim light, Tornado's black coat blends with the shadows. Rocinante is so white he almost radiates his own light. A particularly nasty clap of thunder makes Rocinante neigh loudly in objection. Tornado moves to press himself tighter against Rocinante's side. Rocinante calms at the touch, huffing out what sounds like the equine equivalent of a sigh.

"That's a good boy, Tornado. Keep that hothead calm."

"That hothead saved your skin." With my back to Ana, I don't see her undress, but I can hear it. Wet clothing peeling off skin and dropping to the floor. "You should be thanking him."

"Thank you, Rocinante." From the corner of my eye, I see her cut the horse a truly sloppy curtsy.

I snort as I begin to peel off my sodden clothes. "You know, I—"

My sentence fizzles out because I choose that moment to turn around, and I'm struck dumb by the sight that greets me.

Ana, stripped down to nothing but her small clothes.

She catches me staring and frowns. "What?" Her hands tighten on the wet shirt she's still holding. It begins to come up, to cover up her exposed torso.

By the light of the candles, I can barely see her scars, but they're there. Flickering shadows catch the ridges of uneven skin.

Her scars. It's been so long since I last saw them that I nearly forgot they were there.

Hastily, she begins to pull on her wet shirt.

"No, Ana, you don't have to . . ."

But it's not my place to tell her what she should and should not do. It's her body. Her history. Her past written across her skin in a network of scars, the stories of which I have not been trusted with. Not yet. Not even after all these years.

I reach for her, but it's not the smartest thing I've ever done.

Ana recoils from my touch, holding her sodden shirt between us like a shield. "Don't."

My hands hover uselessly between us. "Ana, it's okay . . ."

She shakes her head, short, brusque. "No, it's not."

And just like that, a wall slams down between us. That brief flash of vulnerability was too much. Our facsimile of normalcy was just that. A pale imitation of the easy way we used to exist with each other. A shell, easily cracked. The languid grace Ana usually possesses is gone, replaced by a stiff, jerky set of movements that move her farther away from me in more ways than physical. She begins to turn away, but there's nowhere for her to go. She was right. We are trapped in here until morning. "Ana, please . . ."

She pauses, her face angled toward me just enough for me to appreciate the way the candlelight loves her features. The sharp line of her nose is gilded by the honeyed glow emanating from the candles. But still, she radiates ice and not fire. She sighs, her eyes drifting shut, as if sealing out the sight of something only she can see. "Just . . . don't."

Ana's scars are a thing we do not discuss. I know they're there. I've known for years. The first time I saw them was when we went swimming in the pond near the villa. I had stared, like an uncouth child, and she had kicked me so hard in the shin, I knew that to ask about their provenance would be to risk even greater bodily harm.

"You don't have to hide from me," I say.

She opens her eyes to meet mine. But almost immediately, she turns to the side, as if holding my gaze is too painful in that moment. "I bared myself to you before. In the orange grove. And you made your stance perfectly clear."

I don't know what to say to that. My own gaze drifts down to my hands. The reins have thoroughly abraded my skin, despite the callouses already formed from years of riding. Water and leather is a bad combination, no matter how good you are on a horse. "I am sorry. I never wanted to hurt you."

"Are you really going to marry him?"

I look up to find her staring at me. Hard.

"Ana . . ."

"Best-case scenario, we get to the convent and find a girl he's impregnated. Worst-case scenario, he's involved with a kidnapping, maybe even murder." She shakes her head in disbelief. "Would you honestly marry a man like that?"

"Find me a man who's any different."

"Your father."

Touché.

I heave a deep, tired breath. "You wouldn't understand."

"Why?" She spits to the side. "Because I wasn't born rich?"

Well, yes, but I wisely don't say exactly that. "Things are different now."

"How?"

My broken laugh makes the horses start. Ana rears back as if cut. I slam my teeth together, suppressing it. It surprised even me. "Because, Ana . . . my brother is dead. My brother. My father's only heir."

When she just stares at me, I continue, "I have to think about more than just my own wants."

Silence hangs between us after I say that. I do not elaborate any further on what it is that I want. That would only pour salt in our open wounds.

Ana shakes her head ruefully. "You're fooling yourself if you think you can hide all that you are just to be some asshole's wife."

"I'm not saying I'm going to marry Sebastian." As soon as the words are out of my mouth, they feel suddenly more possible. Ana's eyes cut to mine. Her expression is carefully guarded, as if she is afraid to let anything slip through. Like hope. With the next statement,

I crush any there might have been. "But I must consider marrying someone."

"But I don't understand why!" Her raised voice echoes against the cave's walls. Tornado huffs in his corner, responding to his mistress's anguish.

"I have responsibilities, Ana." My voice is sharper than she deserves, but I am tired. So very tired. "I have people to care for. People like Magdalena. Everyone who lives on and works the Sonza lands. It's not only my future I have to think about securing."

She looks away, fiddling with the laces of her shirt. "I didn't really think about that."

That much is obvious. But saying so out loud wouldn't accomplish anything.

"Please, just . . ." I squeeze my eyes shut, praying for even the slightest drop of grace from the Almighty. "Can we not talk about this? I can only focus on one crisis at a time, and right now, all I can think about is getting the answers we need to find Rosalita. And to get justice for my brother."

That seems to mollify her. After a tense moment that seems to stretch on infinitely, Ana nods. "Fine. Truce."

She's quiet as she unearths her bedroll. I am quieter still as I retrieve my own bedroll. It was protected from the worst of the rain by the saddlebags but it's still a bit damp around the edges. But it's still better than the alternative, which is cold, unforgiving stone.

The silence between us is as uncomfortable as an iron spike through the eye. From the corner of my eye, I see her plop down, curling into a ball on her side with her back to me. With a soft sigh, I lie down on my own bedroll, staring up at the stone ceiling and its strange, wild paintings, praying for sleep to come. If I'm unconscious, at least I won't be able to experience this horrible, awkward silence.

## *Ana*

• • •

Sleep proves elusive. Even through the bedroll, I can feel every stone, every pebble, every twig.

I have no idea how much time passes before Kiki's voice cuts through the darkness. "Ana, are you awake?"

"Yes."

She's silent for another moment longer. And then, "I'm sorry. I really am. I don't want to fight with you. I can't."

My instinct is to stay where I am. To say nothing. To hold myself back. But her voice is thick with suppressed tears. The weight she's been carrying must be so heavy. And here I am, being a selfish ass. I can't stay angry at her. Or whatever it is I'm feeling. Not anger. Anger keeps me warm. This is something different. Something cold that I don't like.

The candles have mostly dimmed, so I make my way to her side mostly by feel. A startled laugh escapes me as my hand collides with hers, the two of us groping for each other in the darkness.

Before I can think of what to say or do, her fingers tangle with mine and she pulls me down onto her bedroll.

The bones of her legs dig into mine.

She's thinner now than she was before. Of course she is. She wasn't eating properly after Alejandro died.

"I'm sorry," she says again. "For everything."

My hand finds her cheek, my fingers trailing along its curve. "Shut up."

A startled laugh escapes her. Then she slaps a hand over her mouth. "Sorry. I mean—"

"I've never told you about the scars."

It is an abrupt change of subject, but I would rather talk about that than go back and forth about Sebastian or marriage or what lies ahead for her. For us. Sometimes the past, no matter how painful, is safer than the future.

She falls silent. Somber. And then: "No. You haven't. And you don't have to."

I shake my head, my hair rucking up against our makeshift bedding. "I want to."

And I do. But everything seizes up inside me when I think about forming the words. I haven't spoken to anyone about the night I got them. Not since it happened.

"My mother was a prostitute. She worked at Esmeralda's."

Kiki nods, her chin hooking onto my shoulder. "That much I know."

I draw in another breath, fortifying myself. "I don't really remember her much, but I don't—I don't think she was well."

The candlelight flickers, nearly dead.

"I knew she didn't want me. I was a nuisance. A bother. A burden. There was some debate about how the fire started."

Kiki tenses, comprehending perhaps where this tale of woe is going.

"I was in my bed. Though calling it a bed was generous. It was more of a pile of old rags, dresses too threadbare to even try to salvage. Cast-offs from the older girls."

A lump begins to form in my throat. I stumble over the next words. Kiki's hand seeks mine out, clutches it almost tight enough to hurt.

"They went up like kindling. I remember seeing someone through the flames. My mother, I think. She was just standing there. Watching. I rolled out quickly, but my shirt was on fire. I couldn't put it out."

"Ana . . ."

"Then somebody else ran in and threw a bucket of water on me. It was Esmeralda. She grabbed my mother by the throat and pulled her out of the room while the women tended to me. Paid for the physician out of her own pocket. I never saw my mother again. I don't know what Esmeralda did to her or what she said, but the woman never came back. And Esmeralda let me stay. I wasn't much good to her. I never would be. Not looking the way I did. Nobody wants a scarred whore. But she let me stay."

"She saved your life," Kiki says softly.

I nod, eyes riveted on the darkness. And then, I add, "I don't want to believe she has anything to do with Rosalita going missing. She's a bit of an asshole—"

"She did have us arrested," Kiki mutters.

"But she cares about her girls. She wouldn't do anything to hurt us. Them. She wouldn't hurt them. Especially not Rosalita. She always was her favorite."

"I'm sure she isn't involved," Kiki says. "And whoever it is, we'll get to the bottom of it. I promise you."

Kiki's hand rises to brush the hair off my face.

I close my eyes, leaning into her touch. She sighs, inching closer to me. It's cold in the cave, so, so cold. When her ankle hooks around mine I shiver for more reasons than that.

"We should rest," Kiki says, her voice so soft I can hardly hear her. "Heavens knows what we're going to find tomorrow."

I nod, burrowing into her side.

With the storm raging outside, sleep doesn't come easy, but eventually it does come. Kiki is right. We don't know what tomorrow will hold. All we can do is keep looking until we find the answers we need.

# CHAPTER 25

*Ana*

We move at first light.

The convent is nestled in the treacherous mountains outside of Potosí, protected by natural dangers provided by God's own hand. The ground grows more perilous the higher we climb. Tornado huffs as rocks slide under his hooves. We walk in a single line for the path is too narrow to ride side by side. Behind me, Kiki swears, angry and colorful as only she can be with her learned vocabulary.

After several hours, the convent rises from the barren landscape like a mirage.

The first thing I see is trees. Tall, green trees, bursting through the ground as if their growth in this unkind terrain was the will of God. They surround a building that balances on the knife's edge between humble and grand. The walls are a crisp, clean white, punctuated by stained glass that probably costs more than what the average inhabitant of Potosí will ever see in the lifetime.

The horses whinny as we get closer. They are tired and filthy, and they know that buildings are good. Buildings mean fresh water and clean hay. Hopefully. Will the nuns have hay? Only time will tell.

"I almost joined a convent," I say. It's an old story, but not one I have ever shared. It was a fleeting desire, from before we ever met. Before I learned to pick pockets with the best of them and fill my belly with the fruits of my thievery.

An unladylike cackle erupts from Kiki unbidden. To say I am glad to hear it after last night's argument—if you can call it that—would be an understatement. But our fragile truce seems to be holding. Kiki shakes her head in disbelief.

"You could have told me you'd sauntered through the gates of the garden of Eden itself and I would have sooner believed that."

"It's true," I insist, laughing. "A roof over my head and three square meals a day? There were worse ways to live, trust me. But I couldn't afford the dowry."

"Oh, you poor thing. You should have said. I would have gladly sold some of my jewels to cover the cost of your heart's desire."

I dip my head in a courtly bow of gratitude. "My lady is too kind." Then, I shrug. "As it turns out, virtue is expensive. That's why I never bother with it."

"Yes," Kiki says, as our horses draw up to this unlikely speck of civilization. How strange, to have a convent all the way out here, in the middle of nowhere. Maybe the vast nothingness makes them feel closer to God. That sounds like exactly the sort of nonsense the type of believers who seek shelter under its roof might think.

No sooner have we dismounted our horses does the door swing open, its hinges squealing in the otherwise silent courtyard.

A nun steps over the threshold, the hem of her black habit sweeping against the uneven, dusty cobbles. Her skin is weathered with age, the wrinkles particularly deep around the eyes. But those eyes are as sharp as any I have ever seen. They are not the eyes of someone with whom one ought to trifle. Even so, they soften when they catch sight of us.

"Welcome," she says, her voice surprisingly warm. Her gaze slides from Kiki to me and then back again. "Which one of you is it?"

Kiki blinks. "Excuse me?"

"Which one of you is pregnant?"

I nearly choke to death on my own spit. Through my bout of coughing, I hear Kiki stammer through an explanation that no, neither one of us is pregnant and that we would only like to talk.

The nun's brow furrows as she takes in our garb. "You don't look like acolytes."

Even after what I confessed to Kiki, I still find this thought almost as funny as the notion of either one of us falling pregnant. I may have considered taking the habit once, but I'm fairly certain I have sinned far too much and enjoyed it far too well to ever be pure enough for God.

"We're not here for that either."

The nun's eyes narrow. That sharpness is back. Even sharper now.

Kiki and I share a look.

"We are searching for answers," Kiki ventures.

The nun seems to consider this. "So are many who come knocking at our door." She takes in our garb. Our weapons. "But you two don't look like penitents, seeking answers from the Almighty."

"It's not God's help we're looking for." Kiki reaches into her satchel and retrieves the paper she tore from Magistrate de la Vega's ledger. The nun's eyes widen as she takes it in.

She takes a step back, clutching her black skirts as if readying to run back through the open door and slam it shut behind her. "Who sent you?"

"We mean you no harm," Kiki says in a rush.

The nun shakes her head, gathering up her long wool skirt. She turns to leave us standing there. "I cannot help you. Leave. And never return. Tell no one you set foot here."

"Please." There is a plaintive quality to Kiki's voice that pains me. "We need your help. A woman's life is in danger, and this is the only clue we have."

It's a bit of a stretch to call the ledger page a clue. Kiki herself said that. But she's proficient at talking her way into situations even if that means stretching the truth just enough to accommodate our needs.

The nun studies Kiki, as if she could discern what lies deep within her heart with nothing but a good, long stare. "And if I do help you, if I provide you the answers you seek, what will you do with that knowledge?"

"I will find the men who took her and make them pay."

The nun shakes her head. "Vengeance is not yours to dispense. It belongs to the Almighty and no other. To enact it would be a sin most grave."

"Then let that be between me and God."

"I'm sorry." The nun is already stepping through the door, one hand on the iron ring to pull it closed behind her. "I cannot help you."

I lunge forward, grabbing the side of the heavy wooden door. "Her name is Rosalita."

The nun tries to tug the door anyway, but I'm stronger than she is. I hold my ground. "Her favorite color is green, and she loves the way dirt smells just after it rains."

The nun's eyes narrow. "Why are you telling me this?"

"When she was a little girl, she dreamed of marrying a prince. She would draw pictures on the floorboards beneath her bed with bits of charcoal she took from the fire. She made up whole stories about wondrous lands, full of good things happening to good people, just so I would stop crying at night when I was scared. She would hold me when I cried and taught me how to throw a punch when boys got fresh."

Something in the nun's face begins to thaw.

"Rosalita is a good person." That is inadequate, but it is true. "She prays to the Virgin every night, not for herself but for all the girls like her who were born into a world that shows them only unkindness and cruelty. If I were missing, she would knock down every door looking for me. And I can do no less for her. Please." Slowly, I let go of the door. The nun does not try to pull it closed. "I'm begging you. Let us in. Talk to us. You're not helping us. You're helping *her*."

After a long, silent moment, the nun sighs. "Fine. Come inside. But knock the dust off your boots. We try to keep things clean here."

•   •   •

The nun, as it turns out, is the prioress of this entire establishment. After directing a young nun to lead our horses to the stables for water and feed, she leads us to what I assume is her office. It is more of a cell really. The tiny space can barely be called a room. A modest closet, is what I would call it. The Lord craves not the comfort of nuns.

The prioress bustles to a small table in the corner of the room. A silver pitcher stands on a tray, flanked by two glass cups. Glancing over her shoulder, she asks, "You girls must have had a long ride to reach us. Are you thirsty?"

"Parched," Kiki says.

The prioress nods. She pours water from the pitcher into the two cups.

The water is like a blessing from God himself. I close my eyes, savoring the cool slide of it down my throat. The waterskins we'd packed ran dry about an hour before we reached the convent.

"Now," the prioress's penetrating gaze rests on us. "How did you know to come here?"

Kiki and I share a look.

"Sister . . ."

"Mother," the prioress says. "Mother Ines."

"Of course." Kiki ducks her head. "My apologies."

"Don't try to sweet-talk me, girl. I will ask again and not once more: How did you know to come here?"

"Magistrate de la Vega," I say before Kiki can stop me. She is always too cautious. The look she shoots me isn't angry, but it is annoyed. But playing our cards close to the chest won't get us anywhere with Mother Ines here. I know her type. No-nonsense. Best to be honest and see where that gets us.

And besides, my ass hurts from all the riding, and the sooner we get our answers the better.

"We found his books," I continue, handing her the page from the ledger. "He had this convent marked off in his ledger next to what we believe is the name of a woman who was murdered. We want to know why."

Mother Ines's eyebrows inch upward to the white border of her veil as she looks closer at the torn page. Then, she shakes her head, biting back what I am sure is an unholy curse. "That damn fool. Putting everything in writing."

"Why would he care about the convent?" Kiki asks. "What are you to him?"

"A place to hide the indiscretions of the rich and powerful."

Mother Ines snorts. "They like to feign piety, but you'll never find a bigger group of sinners."

"I thought judgment was reserved for God alone."

Mother Ines barks a wry laugh. "I'm far too old to pretend I am without my own sins, girl."

She seems to consider something. Then, she sighs. "Wait here. There is someone you ought to meet."

We wait.

"What do you think?" I ask Kiki.

She just shrugs, sipping at her water. "I don't know what to think. But I think we're about to find out."

Mother Ines returns, but she is not alone. A younger nun follows behind, eyes bowed, hands clasped demurely in front of her. She looks like a frightened animal, ready to run.

"Hello," Kiki says, voice soft and kind. "What's your name?"

The girl looks from me to Kiki and back again. Her head lowers, her face hidden by the stiff, voluminous fabric of her veil.

The prioress places a hand on the girl's shoulder. The gesture is so maternal in nature, it makes me wonder if she had always been a nun. Perhaps she led a different life once, long ago. Perhaps she had children of her own.

"Sister Catalina is the name she uses now. The name she was born with she has cast aside. It brought her nothing but pain and grief and sin."

I peer at the girl's face. As if she can sense my gaze on her, she lifts her face, just enough for our eyes to meet. "Was that name Juana?"

A slow, shallow nod is her only response.

"She is part of the reason Magistrate de la Vega donates so generously to us," Mother Ines says. "It is to pay for her care."

The girl looks up at the prioress. The elder woman sighs. Then nods. Her gaze hardens as she looks back toward me. "If what she shows you ever leaves these walls, it will bring Satan himself to our door."

"It won't," I promise. "No one knows we're here."

"And no one will ever know," Kiki adds.

Juana's hands rise to the edge of her wimple but then she pauses. She looks at the prioress again, her brow furrowed in question.

The prioress nods. "Show them."

With trembling hands, the girl removes her many layers. First the heavy woolen veil, then the cloth that covers her hair and neck beneath it.

Her throat has been slit.

The gash is healed but not prettily. The skin is marred with the remnants of its tearing. The lines of the wound are as clear as they probably were when the blade first dragged along her flesh.

"Christ."

"Mind your tongue," the prioress chides. But there is no heat to the chastisement.

How else can any sane person be expected to react when faced with such horror?

"Mind my tongue?" My voice rises an octave higher than normal on the question. "Look at her."

"I am well aware of what the wound looks like. I sewed it together myself."

Kiki approaches the girl, her hand rising as if to touch the wound. The girl flinches, and Kiki's hand drops. "I'm sorry. I wasn't—I shouldn't—" She gives up, shaking her head. "Who did this to you?"

The novice shakes her head, her eyes pleading with me . . . for what?

"You have no idea?" Kiki presses. "None?"

Again, the girl shakes her head, seeming to grow frustrated with Kiki's line of questioning.

"You didn't see his face?" I ask. "His eyes? Any scar or markings on his skin?"

Juana—or rather, Catalina—makes a strangled sound. God, it must pain her to do even that. But she gestures with her hand, as if miming the act of writing something down.

"Are you sure?" asks Ines.

The girl nods.

Lips pursed, Ines shakes her head. "Fine."

She fetches paper and a quill from her desk and settles Catalina in at her chair. With trembling hands, the novice reaches for the quill, nearly upsetting the glass tub of ink by its side.

Kiki's hand shoots out to steady it. She offers the girl her best comforting smile. "It's quite all right. Take your time."

It takes everything I have not to fidget in my seat like an impatient child. Rosalita is out there, probably being held prisoner by the very same men who cut out Catalina's goddamn tongue. The last thing we have to spare is time.

But rushing the girl wouldn't accomplish much of anything. Her hand shakes as she presses the nib to the parchment and draws.

"They plucked her right off the street," Mother Ines said. "She was blindfolded and brought to a nobleman's estate on the outskirts of the city. He . . . defiled her."

The lines are shaky, uneven. But they gain confidence as she draws. Abstract shapes become a chin, a nose, an aristocratic forehead. Sharp cheekbones. Hollow cheeks. Empty eyes, as if she couldn't bear to draw them.

I lean over her shoulder. Kiki does the same, brow furrowing.

A nobleman with long hair and regal bearing. That description covers half the sycophants who crowd the viceroy's halls, sniffing around like dogs for scraps for even the slightest chance of garnering favor with the man. But there is something to the curve of his lips, the angle of his jaw.

"It's him," I say, the moment it dawns on me. "Cristobal."

Catalina presses the quill to the parchment with such force it breaks.

"You know him?" Mother Ines asks.

"Not really. He bailed us out of jail."

Kiki looks from me to Catalina and to Mother Ines, searching for answers that none of us have, not yet anyway. "This doesn't make any sense. He's a close friend of the viceroy's. Surely, Sebastian's father wouldn't associate with someone who could do this."

"What do we really know about him?" I ask. "One day he's a nobody, the next day he's the Viceroy of Peru. Maybe he had help from a certain marquis."

Kiki releases a shaky breath. "What happened next?"

"When he finished with her," Mother Ines continues, her hand coming to rest on the poor girl's shoulder, "he released her into the woods. Chased her down with his dogs."

"He hunted her like game." I can't keep the horror out of my voice.

Catalina nods, her eyes fixed to the portrait. She makes a pained noise, her hand rising up to graze her scar.

"A young man on horseback found her. He must have been on the property. He brought her to us." Sadness and fury war in Mother Ines's voice. "Asked me to save her. Green around the gills, he was."

"Sebastian. The viceroy's son," Kiki says. "He was with the marquis at the stables. Our stables."

"I saw them together at Santiago's. Cristobal and Sebastian. That night you got blisteringly drunk."

I tear my eyes away from the drawing, away from Catalina's scar to meet Kiki's gaze.

"So he was involved," I say. "Just not how I thought. But why would the magistrate be involved?"

"The man is hungry for power and wealth," the prioress says. "If that boy was the son of a viceroy, doing him a favor would be a boon. I assume the young man did not want his name tracked back to us or her."

I turn back to Catalina. Her eyes are haunted but there is something else in them, something I understand quite well. "Is there anything else?"

Catalina looks to Mother Ines for approval. After a long moment, the older woman nods. "It is your choice, Sister."

The girl stands, pushing the chair back. Slowly, as if the movements pain her, she disrobes. Beneath all that heavy wool, she is thin and frail, like a little bird. When her torso is bared, she wraps her arms around her chest and turns around.

When I see the scar carved into her back, my blood runs cold.

Kiki draws in a short, sharp breath when she sees what I do. "That's—"

"The mark that was carved into Alejandro's hand the night he was killed."

"Who is Alejandro?" Mother Ines asks.

"My brother," Kiki says softly. "He was strung up from a tree. Made to look like a suicide."

"But he did not take his own life." It is not a question, but a statement from Mother Ines.

Kiki shakes her head. "No. Someone killed him."

"The same someone who hurt Sister Catalina," Mother Ines offers. "We did our own research after Catalina came to us. After she finally opened up." She rests a firm hand on the girl's shoulder. Unshed tears balance on the girl's eyelashes. "From what we could gather, the symbol is related to a demon."

"A demon?" My question is almost a sputter. "You're joking."

Mother Ines fixes me with a hard stare. "Do I look like the kind of woman who jokes?"

"No, ma'am."

"What demon?" Kiki asks.

"A prince of hell named Asmodeus." She turns to a shelf of books but instead of plucking one off the shelves, she presses her palm flat against the side of it and pushes. The shelf swings open under her touch, revealing a recessed alcove in the wall. Within it lie even more books, stacked one on top of the other. When she sees our stunned faces, her mouth makes a shape that's almost a smile. "I trust this will remain between us. The Church would not approve of nuns possessing such books."

"No," Kiki says, "they most certainly would not."

"Yeah," I add. "I hear they had a whole Inquisition about that sort of thing."

Kiki elbows me in the ribs.

With a sound that is half scoff, half chuckle, Mother Ines hands Kiki the book. "This is the only book we have that mentions the demon by name. He is a creature of lust and desire, a being who craves power."

Catalina makes a soft little noise. Mother Ines nods, understanding some language only they share.

"We believe Sister Catalina fell prey to a man who is transfixed by this figure. If he is carving the symbol onto his other victims, I would wager it is something of an obsession for him."

"Or like some kind of signature," I say. "Like he's signing his work."

Kiki rubs at her temples. "But why kill my brother? He didn't hunt him for sport or pluck him off the street."

"Maybe Alejandro knew," I say. "Maybe he heard or saw something he wasn't supposed to and was going to expose Cristobal. Hell, maybe he even heard something from Sebastian."

"Anyone your brother might have mentioned this to is in equal danger," the prioress says.

"Shit." Kiki glances at me, brow furrowed. "The letters he wrote. The warnings."

"Rosalita." I am already striding toward the door. "We need to find her before Cristobal does."

Both Kiki and Mother Ines are too kind to state the obvious. That he already has.

# CHAPTER 26

*Kiki*

Everything we learned at the convent swirls inside my skull as we head back to town. The weather holds, so the journey is, at the very least, mercifully shorter.

The man who slit that poor girl's throat.

The man who killed a young woman and left her dead body in the street like garbage.

The man who killed my brother.

One and the same. How many lives has he stolen? How many families destroyed? And what does the viceroy know? And Sebastian?

How deep does this rot run?

• ◦ •

The same question is still running through my mind as I trudge up the front steps to the villa, tugging the dusty gloves from my fingers. The leather will need to be conditioned. Thoroughly. My entire body feels like it needs a good conditioning. I am utterly encrusted with the dirt from the roads. I can feel it caking in my pores. Seeping through my scalp. Casting a thin, thoroughly vile film over my teeth and tongue.

Naturally, this is the state in which I find myself when I skid to a halt in the entry hall.

Ana collides with my back, kicking up a fresh cloud of dust. "Kiki, watch ou—"

"Hello, Eustaquia."

Standing not six feet from me is Sebastian. To his right is my father, a man I have not seen in days. Not since he chucked the only evidence we had for my brother's murder into the fire. He meets my gaze but only fleetingly. His skin looks sallow in the twilight, and his frame looks smaller. Like he's lost weight. Magdalena did say he wasn't eating.

"Sebastian. Father."

That is all the greeting either one will get from me. I know I should be kinder to my father. I lost a brother, but he lost a son. And I know better than anyone that sorrow can addle the mind as well as—no, better than—any poison. But I do not have it in me to be so kind. Not yet. Not when my own pain is still so raw. Not when I am on the cusp of finding his killer.

My eyes slide from my father to Sebastian. His own gaze is carefully guarded. Undeniably pleasant. It tells me nothing. It is the perfect mask to wear around his future father-in-law. Sinking my teeth into my tongue—hard—I bite back all the things I want to say to him.

*What were you doing at the magistrate's in the middle of the night?*

*What do you know about my brother's death?*

*Were you involved?*

*Did you bring the rope?*

Ana, bless her heart, has no such filter. "What the hell are you doing here?"

"Ana," my father hisses sharply. It would have been a yell, but I suspect he no longer has the strength for that.

Sebastian holds up a mollifying hand. "It's quite all right. I find I'm rather fond of our Ana's verbal eccentricities."

Our Ana? Beside me, she bristles.

My father finally seems to take in the truly wretched state of our clothing. "Why in heaven's name do the two of you look like you've ridden halfway across New Spain? Magdalena said you were sequestered in prayer."

"Change of plans." I set my gloves—the poor things might be too ruined to save, honestly—down on a nearby table. "We were out for a ride instead."

Well, it isn't a lie. It simply isn't the whole truth.

I want this conversation to be short. Rosalita is still out there somewhere, and Lord knows how long she has left. If she has any time left at all.

"I can see that," Sebastian says with a fond smile. But it doesn't reach his eyes. It's a painted-on look, one for show. It lies on the surface, like oil on water. "Well, I hope you haven't worn yourselves out." He shares a look with my father who offers him a shallow nod. "Cristobal Téllez-Girón, Marquis of Peñafiel, is hosting a masked ball this evening, and I would like for you to join me. As a guest and as my beloved."

My brain handily skips right over the invocation of Cristobal's name and Sebastian's flagrant use of a word he has not earned. I shoot my own look at my father. "A ball? After what happened at the last one?"

The poor man actually flinches. "Eustaquia—"

"Kiki."

My father's glare at least is almost a return to form. "As a family, we are still in mourning. But life must go on."

I shake my head, bile inching its way up my throat. With Sebastian here, I cannot say what I honestly think. What has happened to my father? Did Alejandro's death break him utterly and completely? Has he completely taken leave of his senses. "How dare—"

"Your father's words are sound, Eustaquia." He smiles fleetingly. "Kiki. Now more than ever it's imperative we show a united front."

Ana snorts, but to her credit, she bites her tongue.

"These people," he says, as if he wasn't among their number, "they can smell blood in the water. They bide their time, waiting to strike, but we can show them that even in the wake of tragedy the Sonza family is not one to be trifled with. That you have the protection of the viceroy himself." He steps closer to me. From his vantage, my father cannot see how Sebastian's nose crinkles ever so subtly at my stench. But the gesture, however involuntary, is not lost on me. "And that any slight against your family, any infraction, is a slight against me."

"What slights?" I ask. Oh, how I long for him to say something incriminating in front of my father.

"There have been movements against our interests," my father says quietly. "Efforts to usurp the contracts we have with the throne." He draws in a breath, as if steeling himself to make some great gesture. "I know you are angry with me, and I will not argue with your right to be so, but please, Kiki"—he looks at me plaintively; he is not the man I once thought could topple mountains with a mere glance— "put in an appearance. Make a show of it."

Sebastian reaches for me. He takes my hand in his and cuts a courtly bow. "I will be by your side, every step of the way." His eyes roll up to meet mine, and even now I cannot read what lies within them. He brings my hand—filthy as it is—to his mouth and brushes his lips against my knuckles. "Will you join us? It's a masked ball. I remember how fond you are of those."

I have attended several at the viceroy's villa over the years. I did love them. The pageantry. The costumes. The air of mystery. But now I have real mysteries of my own to solve.

With my hand still in Sebastian's grasp, I glance back at Ana. I expect to see anger on her face. Or maybe jealousy. But instead, I find something approaching curiosity. Eagerness. She offers me an almost imperceptible nod.

This is an opportunity. We know Sebastian found one of Cristobal's victims. But what else does he know? And is his father involved?

All the men we suspect, located conveniently under one roof. Cristobal, delivering himself to us on a silver platter? It's almost too good to be true.

"I'll go." I turn back to Sebastian. "But only if I can bring Ana."

A vaguely pained expression flits across Sebastian's face. But to his credit, he nods. "Of course. She is dear to you, and now, to me. When our families are joined, she will be like a sister to me as well."

Ana opens her mouth, no doubt to say something truly insulting, but I yank my hand out of Sebastian's and wrap it tightly around Ana's arm. "And what a happy family we will be."

It almost breaks my heart to see how those words make my father seem a little lighter. A little less broken.

If only he knew.

I have no intention of marrying this man. Not if he is any way affiliated with the man who killed my brother.

But I will use him. Oh, I will use the ever-loving hell out of him if it means I get my way.

Sebastian straightens. "I'll send a carriage for you."

I'm already tugging Ana toward the stairs. "Much obliged," I call over my shoulder. I don't have time to waste on pleasantries. I have a masked ball for which I must prepare. And it's such a hassle hiding weapons in an evening gown.

# CHAPTER 27

*Kiki*

I am a creature of words.

I live them. I breathe them. They were my saving grace when I needed them most. Wrapping myself in stories of faraway places and fantastical lands was sometimes all that kept me afloat in my darkest hours, when I was alone and afraid and too terribly small to make a difference in my own life.

But now, as I stand at the base of the stairs watching Ana descend, words have failed me entirely.

She is resplendent.

That is the only term that can possibly encapsulate her in this moment.

The dress is perfectly suited to her. Soft gold details curl around the edges of rich cinnamon velvet. The silk of her bodice has been painted to look as soft and touchable as fur. My hands twitch with the urge to reach out and do just that. My whole body feels pulled toward her. I want to rise to meet her, to burn myself on that fire like Icarus with his wings of wax and dreams. I know doing so will hurt but I absolutely cannot bring myself to care.

A smile tugs at the corners of her lips as she sees me staring.

"Like what you see?"

The vixen. She knows that I do.

She comes to a halt a few steps above me, so she's peering down at me through the mask that obscures the top half of her face. It is a delicate thing, like gilded gossamer. The filigree twists and twines about her features, rising up into two foxlike ears.

A perfect costume choice, really. What is a fox if not clever and cunning? Sleek and beautiful. Soft to the touch but with fangs as ferocious as any predator.

In other words, my Ana.

"The gold suits you." It is the purest of my thoughts in this moment and therefore, the only one I unleash into the air.

A smirk alights on her mouth, as if she knows how much I'm holding back.

But the gold does suit her. She's borrowed a few pieces from my collection, and I decide, in this moment, that I am never asking for them back. They are hers now, in thought and in deed. My skin does not do them the justice hers does with its sun-kissed warmth. I am too cold a beast to make gold glow the way she does.

I raise my hand to touch the thin chain of her necklace. She goes utterly still. Silent. Waiting. My fingers trace the fragile length of gold from the bend of her neck down and down and down, skirting over the crest of her collarbone. Her breath hitches, loud enough to reach my ears. I allow my fingers to descend that final inch, to rest on the topaz teardrop cradled in her décolleté.

"Keep it," I say.

She has to swallow thickly before speaking. "The necklace?"

I nod, curling my fingers around the pendant, knowing exactly how the slide of my skin on hers must be affecting her. Because it's affecting me the same way.

"You wear it better."

I release the jewel, stepping away from her lest I do something rash, like push her up against the iron banister and devour every single inch of her the way I want to. That simply wouldn't do. We have places to be. A masked ball to crash. Lives to ruin.

I offer her my arm, cutting my very best, most chivalrous bow.

"My lady." I roll my eyes up, catching her gaze with my own. What I see in her face lights an ember low in my gut.

"Not a lady," Ana says as she slips her hand under my arm. "But yours. Always."

I lean in. I want to kiss her. I want to kiss her so badly that if I do not, I fear I might burst. And no one wants that.

"Do you mean that?" I ask softly. I am afraid to hear her answer. I am afraid I may have pushed her away so far that I have lost her.

But she holds my gaze, lifting her chin. "I do."

Equal parts fear and courage sing through my body, heady enough for me to forget why we are here, dressed in such finery. I forget what awaits us at the ball. That there is a very real chance this night will end in bloodshed. But if it does, I do not want to meet it with regret. Not after everything.

I lick my lips, extremely aware of the way Ana's eyes follow the motion. My whole mouth feels suddenly very dry. "There is something I would like to ask you."

"Go on."

I have to swallow twice before I manage to choke out the words. "May I kiss you?"

Ana goes still. So still. She is stone. Ice. A statue carved in marble.

Panic floods through me. This is what she must have felt in the orange grove. How horrible. How utterly wretched. How—

"Yes." That one word is quiet but firm. "Yes, you may. But only if you do not plan on marrying Sebastian. Or any man for that matter."

I swallow again, unable to speak.

Ana's lips part as she exhales, waiting for me with a patience she shows nothing else in life. My mouth brushes hers, so softly it may as well be an illusion.

It wasn't hell, I think. The phantom sensation of her skin against mine that tormented me so after she kissed me in the orange grove. It was heaven all along.

Her mouth parts against mine, and oh, that is a whole new world of sensation, the likes of which I have never dared to dream. Her tongue slides against mine and I think I might actually die. Right there. On the spot. Struck dead where I stand.

Suddenly, a thought occurs to me. I pull away from that exquisite pleasure, completely addled.

I have two great loves in my life: Ana. And swords. I have one, but I cannot forget the other.

"Weapons!" I say, far too loudly, considering how close our faces are to each other.

"Ow." Ana frowns at me as she steps away, rubbing at the ear I just unceremoniously shouted in.

"I'm so sorry," I say in a rush. "I just . . ." And although stepping away from her causes me physical pain, I do so. "Stay here. I have something for you."

A smile flirts with the edges of Ana's mouth. Even after all these years, she still isn't quite accustomed to be showered with gifts or the ease with which my family and I can acquire them. "Is it a weapon?"

I pick up fistfuls of my dress and begin walking toward the drawing room at a brisk pace. Over my shoulder, I call, "It's a present."

Ana follows right behind me, a subtle skip in her step. Impressive considering how many layers she's wearing under that magnificent gown. "A weapon-shaped present?"

"Oh, hush, you'll ruin the surprise."

"You just shouted the word *weapons* directly into my face, Kiki."

Rolling my eyes, I push open the drawing room doors.

"Fine! It's a weapon," I say. Ana absolutely *beams*. "And I think you're really going to love this one."

## *Ana*

• ● •

I try not to quiver with anticipation as I watch Kiki dig through an old chest for whatever this most definitely weapon-shaped gift is, but I fail.

Look, I like presents. A lot. Who among us does not? Fucking nobody, that's who.

Or maybe I'm still quivering at the feeling of Kiki's lips against mine. The softness of her skin. The little hitch in her breath when we kissed. I have oh so many reasons to quiver.

After what feels like an eternity but is probably less than the full rotation of the minute hand of a clock, Kiki stands, a long wooden box in her hands.

"Give me." I extend my hands toward her, curling my fingers rhythmically.

With another roll of her eyes—honestly, she excels at that—Kiki thrusts the box into my eagerly waiting hands.

"Happy birthday," she says as I fumble with the latch on the box.

"But my birthday isn't for weeks."

"I know. I had this commissioned ages ago. I was going to give it to you then, but . . ."

Her voice trails off, soft and sad. But then our lives crumbled down around us, all our plans and dreams foiled in the most violent manner. I pause in my fumbling and reach out to take her hand in mine. "I know. It's all right."

She nods, a bit too briskly, but then she's smiling and it's not entirely forced. "Go on. Open it."

I do. And when I see what lies inside, my breath catches.

"Oh, Kiki. It's beautiful."

The dagger lays in a bed of deep green velvet, all the better to display the flawless gleaming steel. Vines dance along the center line of the blade—roses and thorns, twining their way from the handle almost to the very tip. The hilt itself is a work of art. Two iron branches form the quillons, shaped to look as though they are wrapped in the very same vines on the blade. The handle itself is finely etched with a flurry of leaves, culminating in a rounded pommel in the shape of a rose.

"There's a matching scabbard, too." Kiki reaches around me to trigger some sort of mechanism on the underside of the box. A hidden drawer shoots out, revealing said scabbard. It's green leather, embossed with more roses, more vines.

"Kiki, this is too much," I say, unable to keep the awe I feel out of my voice. She has bestowed upon me far more than my fair share of gifts over the years, from gowns and horses to swords, but nothing as fine or as personal as this.

"Nonsense. It's just right." She lifts the dagger from its berth and slides it into the scabbard. The steel whispers softly against the leather. "May I?"

I don't know what she's asking but, honestly, at this point I'd agree to anything she wanted.

What she wants is to kneel at my feet and lift the hem of my voluminous skirts, a gesture which makes every last bit of sense left rattling around in my brain flee with tremendous haste. My mouth goes curiously dry. My tongue feels too thick for the space allotted to it.

"Kiki . . ."

She glances up, a smile on her face that probably isn't too far off from the one Satan must have worn as he wrapped his serpentine form around the Tree of Knowledge and offered Eve a single juicy apple. "Yes, Ana?"

Her voice is low and deep, and it makes me forget that I am a higher form of life, capable of language.

I watch, struck dumb, as she unearths a soft leather belt—from where, I don't know—to hold the scabbard and wraps it around my thigh, right beneath the top of my stocking. She pulls it tight, and I almost pass out.

Then, she does the worst thing she has ever done to me. She gently lowers my skirts, covering the dagger and my exposed legs and all my other bits.

"There," she says as she smooths the skirts back into place. "Now you're armed."

"I love you," I say because my brain in its current state has the mental capacity of a lizard, and that's all I can manage in this moment.

She stands, hands fussing with her own skirts. "I know."

Before I can add anything, she steps away. "Now to gather my own . . . accessories. I'll only be a moment."

As sad as I am to not have her within touching distance, it's probably for the best. We are preparing to enter the lions' den. I need my wits about me if we're going to survive the night.

As much as I hate to admit it, formal gowns may be terrible for maneuverability but, as it turns out, they're excellent for hiding all manner of weaponry.

I twirl in the mirror, admiring my reflection. "Who knew all these miles of fabric were good for something besides being a pain in my ass?"

Kiki looks up from where she's strapping a holster to her thigh. I try not to stare at the inches of exposed skin above her stocking or how nicely that skin contrasts with the dark brown of the leather belt she's securing around the upper portion of her leg. I fail, quite spectacularly.

"I've been trying to convince you of that for several years now." She pulls the belt tighter so it doesn't fall, and I have to look away. I am not made of stone.

My eyes are firmly fixed to my own reflection once more as I tug at my sleeves for no other reason than to give my hands something to do. "Yes, but you know I hardly ever listen to anything you say."

Kiki snorts as she lowers her skirts. I watch as she slides Alejandro's silver pistol into her pocket. I expect it to pull the fabric down, but the line of the dress remains undisturbed.

When she sees me watching, she smiles. "I cut a hole in the pocket so that I can reach for the gun."

"Won't the dress slow you down anyway?"

Kiki shrugs. "That's why I have you to cover me while I draw." Her smile widens. She places her hands on my shoulders and turns me around to face the large mirror that inexplicably lives in the drawing room. The wealthy are a vain lot, but looking at our shared reflection, I'm finding it hard to complain.

Alone, we are stunning. Together, we are a vision.

Me, the sly vixen. Kiki, the elegant black swan.

She smiles, her rouged lips curling in satisfaction. "We do make the most splendid team, don't we?"

"We do." I turn to her, catching her eyes with mine. I lean in to brush a phantom of a kiss against the seam of her lips. Not enough to sidetrack us, but enough to remind her of all the things I lack the words to say. "Now, let's get out of here. We have a hell of a night ahead us. And I would so hate to be late to the party."

# CHAPTER 28

*Kiki*

We are late to the party.

It's not entirely surprising. Being on time is never fashionable, and I do so care for fashion. And besides, our tardy arrival makes it far easier to slip into the crowd milling about the entrance to Cristobal's villa relatively unnoticed. Though we've arrived in Sebastian's carriage, I would like to avoid him for as long as I can.

The masks help. It seems like all of New Spain is waiting to be introduced to the glittering throng within. Ana presses in against my side. For all her savvy on the unforgiving streets of Potosí, this is where she is most uncomfortable. Milling about with the aristocracy, especially when they are out in full force, each jockeying to best the person beside them, each vying for even the tiniest elevation in their own standings. Balls like this are never mere social events. There is always an angle. Always an opportunity. And I am hoping that this is where we find ours.

As we approach, the footman by the door glances at us. It is his duty to announce visitors as they enter so that everyone inside knows exactly how much deference new arrivals are owed. But with our masks, I assume he is having a rather difficult time discerning who we are.

Taking pity on the poor man, I smile. And then I loop Ana's arm through mine and pull her against my side. She makes a sound that I would call a squeak, if I were cruel enough to ever point out that she was capable of making such an undignified noise. I lean in to whisper in his ear. Ana tugs on my arm, a question clear on her face even through the mask. The footman arches a single eyebrow, as if to ask if I am absolutely certain of what I have asked him to do. I offer him a single nod in confirmation.

With a look that's far too incredulous considering his rank, he straightens up to announce our presence in a booming voice:

"Ana Lezama de Urinza, escorted by the Lady Eustaquia de Sonza."

One of the musicians inside the ballroom misses a beat as his hands fumble on the strings of his instrument. All movement around the entryway ceases as people turn and stare, nearly identical looks of shock and dismay on their faces.

Ana's hand tightens on my arm as she leans in to whisper, "What the hell do you think you're doing?"

I turn to her. Our faces are so close, our noses nearly brush. "What I've always wanted to do."

With that, I lead her down the grand staircase into the ballroom. The eyes of every noble in the Viceroyalty of Peru are on us. Judging. Analyzing. Measuring. And I cannot find it in me to care. I am here with a purpose with my partner on my arm. She is my equal in all things, regardless of the circumstances of either of our births, and I want them to all to know. She is no less than I and most assuredly better than all of them.

"I thought the idea was to lay low and see what we could find out,"

Ana whispers again. And though I may be mistaken, I am fairly certain I detect the slightest hint of pleasure in her voice.

"It was." I shrug. "But then I had a better idea."

By the time we reach the base of the steps, another set of nobles have taken our place for the footman to announce. Already, the fickle attention span of the surrounding crowd is hunting for new targets, but there are a few glances that linger, a few whispers behind masks and fans and silk gloves. I smile sweetly at those brave enough to meet my eyes. Few are brave enough to hold them.

"So . . ." Ana begins. "Now what?"

I swipe two gilded cups from a table absolutely heaving with wine and offer Ana one. I take a sip of my own as I survey Cristobal's kingdom. The masks do complicate things, but where there is a will, there is a way.

"Now," I say, "we wait. Wine will loosen their tongues." I smile at Ana over the rim of this ostentatious golden cup. "And then, we strike."

*Ana*

We have to wait until the wine has been flowing and tongues loosened and guards dropped. Then, we move in.

But until that point, we must bide our time. Enjoy the evening. Pretend we're doing something other than biding that time.

The host of the evening has so far remained as elusive as he's always been. Nobles mill about in their finery, casting silent judgments on one another as they engage in the sort of one-upmanship at which Kiki excels and at which I am a complete failure.

"Any sign of Cristobal yet?" Kiki asks. She nibbles on one of the small bites of food displayed like tiny works of art. I cannot for the life of me deduce what any of it is made of, so far removed is it from its natural state.

Rich people are ridiculous when it comes to this sort of thing.

Kiki spots me staring and holds out the whatever it is—some kind of creamed meat atop a piece of toasted bread—and offers it to me. "Care for a bite?"

I lean away. "You couldn't pay me to eat anything that man put on his table. It's probably poisoned."

Kiki merely shrugs as she takes another bite. "It would be awfully foolish of him to poison every single aristocrat in Potosí. I'd wager half of this room is in his pocket and the other half is clamoring to be there."

I snort, taking a sip of my wine. That, at least, I feel comfortable ingesting. I have a standing policy to not eat anything I don't recognize, regardless of who's serving it.

A rather large woman bumps into me from behind, nearly upending my entire cup onto Kiki's lovely frock. She dances out of the way just in time to avoid getting splashed. I am not so lucky. A few stray droplets of wine splash onto the pale silk of my bodice, as vivid as blood.

"Oh, how clumsy of me." The woman's voice warbles, thick with drink. The color is high in her cheeks and not just from rouge. "My dear, I am terribly sorry."

It takes some doing but she fishes a handkerchief out of her ample bosom and tries to blot away the spilled wine. I dodge her as I would dodge a man charging me down with a sword.

"That's quite all right," I say, doing my best to channel my inner Kiki. "No need to worry yourself over a bit of spilled wine. There's more than enough to go around."

This seems to be enough to mollify the woman. I meet Kiki's eyes. From the way she nods, it's clear the same idea has occurred to us both.

"I'll just go find someplace to wash up."

I begin to turn away, but Kiki grabs my hand.

She leans in close "I'll do my part here. See what I can find out. You do yours. But be careful."

I nod. "I always am."

"Now, *that*," Kiki says, smiling softly, "is a lie."

She releases me, stepping backward and into the crowd. I am on my own now. The two of us wandering about Cristobal's villa would be too much of a red flag. One of us is easier to explain away.

Even with the gown and the mask, I feel oddly naked as I work my way through the crowd, evading the attention of men craning for a dance and women angling for an introduction to my—or rather, Kiki's—dressmaker.

It takes some doing but eventually, I break through the throng of people clustered by one of the double doors leading away from the ballroom. I glance around to make sure no one's watching as I open the door just enough to slide through. I am fairly certain no one saw, but there are so many people, it's hard to tell. Oh well. If I wind up with a guard's blade in my belly then I'll know I wasn't nearly as subtle as I was attempting to be.

Cristobal's villa is huge. Well, all of these villas seem huge to me, but this one feels particularly labyrinthine. As I make my way through halls, I try to keep the twists and turns straight. Rooms jut off from corridors with seemingly little logic. In one there is nothing but a harpsichord and a divan. In another there are rows of Hellenistic statuary draped in the thinnest of gauzy fabric. Yet another boasts an impressive collection of Bronze Age weaponry, arranged with meticulous care on wall-to-wall displays.

"If I were an evil mastermind," I whisper to myself, "where would I hide my goodies?"

The music from the ballroom fades to a soft melody, distant but present, to silence. I am nearly well and truly lost by the time I stumble upon a room with a locked door.

Strange, that there has been only one. A man like Cristobal surely has his secrets, but so far, his home has been something of an open book. A confusing one, governed by no logic I can determine, but not a place that screams that the owner has something to hide.

But a locked door? That is a nice juicy secret I would love to sink my teeth into.

Plucking one of the many pins stuck through my hair, I kneel down. My skirts poof up around me. I must look ridiculous but thankfully, you don't need to look glamorous to pick a lock. You just have to know what you're doing. And I most definitely do.

My hands work on memory alone. This is not the first lock I've picked. Oh, far from it. It isn't even the hundredth. Maybe not the thousandth. I press my ear to the door to listen for the sound of the tumblers moving, sliding into place as the pin toggles them.

*Click, click. Click.*

The door swings open under my hand. I smile.

Perhaps this night will not be a waste after all.

It's more trouble than it ought to be, struggling up from my knees in this godforsaken dress. But needs must, I suppose. We could have probably slipped into the villa some other way, but Kiki did always like to make a grand entrance.

Inside, the room looks more utilitarian than any other I have thus far encountered. A desk made of dark polished wood sits toward the rear of the room, flanked by a set of massive bookshelves. A chair upholstered in red leather so rich it looks much like the wine spilled across my bodice sits pushed back from the desk as if someone had stood up and left it where it was, perhaps to return to soon.

There are no windows. Peculiar, since every other room on this floor had them. Tall ones, too. The kind that go all the way from floor to ceiling and are largely impractical considering the mountain chill that plagues us for several months out of the year.

I waste no time. I'm not nearly as good with this sort of thing—record-keeping, dreary as it is—as Kiki, but I make do. All I need to do is find something suspicious. Anything will do. A man like Cristobal must have the bodies buried somewhere, literally and metaphorically. Although I'd much rather unearth a metaphorical one made of paper than a real one made of flesh and bone.

Trying to leave as little disturbed as possible, I begin to shuffle through his papers. Most of the books are records of accounts, nothing that seems overly suspicious in and of itself. Wages paid to the household staff. Titles for land inherited from dead relatives. Deeds to property the man has probably never even seen. Accounts settled with businesses both local and abroad. Correspondences with family members and acquaintances back in Spain, covering topics that seem utterly mundane. How the livestock is faring. The condition of the olive groves back on the continent. Rolled maps of shipping routes across the New World, Europe, and Africa, stretching all the way to the isle of Madagascar. I put those aside with all the rest.

But—wait.

The map. There is something familiar about it.

I retrieve it from the pile and unroll it across the expanse of Cristobal's desk.

And yes, it is very familiar. I trace my fingers along the routes. I know them. I've spent years looking at them, my eyes wandering to those very same lines every time they wanted a break from whatever tome Kiki was forcing me to slog through.

There is another version of this map, nearly identical but slightly more elaborate, hanging above the double doors leading into the Sonza library.

These are the shipping routes Don Carlos controls. These are the pathways that made him one of the wealthiest men in the Viceroyalty of Peru.

I riffle through the papers, looking for something else, something damning. It takes me half a second to find it. It's right there, under the maps.

Transfers of title. Unsigned, but plain as day. Orders to switch ownership of the routes from Don Carlos de Sonza and his heirs to Cristobal Téllez-Girón, the Marquis of Peñafiel. If these documents were filed, they would give him everything and leave Kiki's family with nothing. There's no way in hell Kiki's father would sign these.

"What the hell are you planning, Cristobal?" I ask the silent room.

No answer comes. But the silence is broken by the sound of footsteps approaching the room.

"Shit." My hands fumble as I hastily roll the map back up and slot it onto the precarious pile of similarly rolled documents. The pile teeters dangerously. Both of my hands fly up to keep the mountain in place, but one of the smaller maps slides off the top, hitting the carpeted floor with more noise than a piece of parchment—no matter how heavy—has any right to.

"For God's sake." With the toe of my boot—a pair I'm surprised Kiki allowed me to leave the house wearing but I suppose the light brown leather was fine enough to go with the dress—I kick the roll of parchment under the nearest bookshelf.

Hopefully, that will suffice.

A glance cast over the room tells me everything is in place, or as good as it was when I entered. I wipe my sweaty palms on my heavy skirts. But before I can leave, the sound of the incredibly well-oiled and nearly silent door hinges makes me freeze, booted feet rooted in place, my back to the door.

"Are you lost, little fox?"

The skin on the back of my neck prickles with gooseflesh.

*Shit. Shit, shit, shit.*

I know exactly who the speaker is. And I know that I am royally fucked.

# CHAPTER 29

*Kiki*

My chest tightens as I watch Ana go. I do not like the thought of her alone in this house. Especially since I have yet to lay eyes on the man who owns it.

Golden cup in hand, I make my way through the throng of revelers, skirting the edge of the dance floor. I make a point of sticking to the sides of the grand ballroom, where people cluster in groups and bend their heads together to have conversations in hushed voices they think no one can overhear.

"That Lorenzo boy ran off with the haberdasher's daughter! Can you believe such a thing?"

"And him a firstborn son! If I were his mother, I'd never show my face in public again."

"That she came here tonight is even more shocking. Has she no—"

"The price of grain is plummeting. At this rate, the market will—"

"This is such a fine vintage. My sweet, we absolutely must find out where—"

Heaving a sigh, I come to a stop in a corner of the room. I hope Ana is having more luck than I am. The conversations in this room are as dull as they ever are. Gossip and industry and frivolity, all of it.

From behind me comes the distinctively male sound of a throat clearing. "You know, I was half expecting you not to show."

My hand tightens on the stem of the cup. "Sebastian."

He takes my utterance of his name as an invitation to step into my line of sight. If I were a lesser woman, I would be moved by the vision he presents. His frock coat is a gold only a shade or two darker than his hair. A touchable soft fur ruff adorns the coat's collar, sinfully plush. I weep for whatever poor animal had to die.

"A lion, I see." I take an unimpressed sip of my wine. It is, in fact, a fine vintage, but it tastes sour on my tongue. The very notion that the man before me might have been involved in my brother's death in any way makes me to want to grab him and scream until he tells me what he knows, what he's done.

Sebastian's lips stretch into a wry grin. The delicate gold filigree of his mask does little to hide the blue of his eyes.

"And you are a swan. A black one. Fitting, I suppose." He sips his own wine. "You are a vision, Kiki. Truly."

Now, my hand tightens so hard, I can feel the indentations of the cup's etchings press into my skin, nearly hard enough to draw blood. "There are only three people allowed to call me that. And one of them is dead."

Something I never thought I'd see occurs. A faint blush crawls across Sebastian's exposed cheeks, interrupted by the filigree of his mask.

"Ki—Eustaquia. I—" He heaves a sigh, waving over a footman to take his glass. The liveried man does so without batting a single eyelash, disappearing back into the crowd as efficiently as he appeared. "I'm sorry."

A chill runs through me. It is a battle to keep my voice measured. "For what?"

"I just thought . . ." He trails off, turning away from me. Perhaps it's a strategic move, feigned humility. But it oddly doesn't seem so. His profile is rather divine from this angle. Strong jaw. Straight, aquiline nose. Cheekbones I could have used to saw our way through the iron bars on our jail cell. "I thought that since we are to be wed that you would perhaps allow for some greater . . . intimacy between us."

I had half expected a confession. That he would tell me that he roped my brother into Cristobal's murderous delights somehow. That he was responsible. That I could blame him. But of course, it wouldn't be that easy.

"Why do you want to marry me?" The question is bluntly delivered but gracefully received. He doesn't balk. He merely takes a sip of his wine, scanning the milling crowd.

"Would it please you to hear that I don't?" Sebastian says. "That our union is one of mutual benefit. A sound decision for both your fortune and mine. Is that what you want to hear?"

I follow his gaze, eyes roving over the crowd. I hope Ana is all right. I hope we can get out of here in one piece. And I hope the truth outs.

"What do you know about my brother's death?"

Maybe it's unwise to ask. Maybe I'm showing my hand. But I need to know. I need him to tell me. I need to study his face to see if he's lying.

"As I already told you, nothing. Though I'm glad you're not waving a pistol in my face this time."

His voice is too even. Too measured.

I capture his eyes and hold that gaze for a long moment.

"I think you're lying."

I don't know what response I expect from him. Honestly. We stare at each other for a long moment before his gaze slides from mine. He spots something over my shoulder and frowns.

The musicians change their pace to a saraband I'm rather fond of. He extends a hand to me, palm up, arm stiff. "Shall we dance?"

My cup halts its progression halfway to my lips. "What?" Now, that I was not expecting.

"Please." There is something to the quality of his voice that gives me pause. I study his eyes—or what I can see of them through his mask—and find a matching flavor of concern there.

"Fine." I set my cup down on a nearby plinth and accept Sebastian's hand. "Let's dance."

His soft sigh of relief is not lost on me.

The saraband carries us onto the dance floor as we enmesh ourselves with the other dancers. The steps bring us apart, and then together, Sebastian's hand raising to flatten his palm to mine. He dips his head to whisper in my ear, his expression arranged to make it seem that he's about to say something scandalous meant for my attentions alone.

"Smile," he says.

"Why?"

"Because we are being watched."

I stiffen, but Sebastian's hand on my waist tightens in warning. With painstaking care, I relax, settling into the familiar rhythm of the dance. When the steps bring us back together again, both hands raised this time as we circle each other, I whisper, "By whom?"

Cristobal is the obvious answer, but I haven't spied him here yet. Surely, he's around. This is his house after all. I spare a thought for Ana, hoping she's nowhere in his vicinity. I spot the magistrate in the corner, by a table piled high with a pyramid of golden goblets, full to the brim with wine. But who else is there? Who else is part of this conspiracy? Who else partakes in the murder of innocents?

Sebastian twirls, his golden coat catching the light off the chandeliers. "Men who matter."

I pirouette into his space, too close for what the dance actually entails. "Be less vague or I walk away right now."

"Wouldn't recommend it."

As much as I hate to admit it, he is probably right.

"I offered you protection once," he continues. The saraband carries him away from me as we each rotate partners with the person next to us. My steps are stiff and awkward until we meet again. "You are better off with me than without."

"Oh, Sebastian," I say, allowing him to lead me into the next step of the dance. "If only that were true."

## Ana

I would never mistake the sound of that voice. It is both as smooth as silk and as hard as steel. I heard it last in the cold, dank shadows of a jail cell.

*Breathe*, I remind myself. *You are a guest in his home. And you have a shiny new dagger to try if he attempts anything unsavory.*

My skirts tangle in my legs as I whirl around, the silliest smile I can muster plastered on my face as I purposefully sway as if my unsteady feet are not to be trusted.

"Oh, if it isn't the man of the—*hic*—hour."

Was the hiccup too much? Quite possibly.

Cristobal stands in the open doorway to his study, hands clasped behind his back, his face arranged into a pleasantly bland mask of curiosity.

I bow down at the waist, sketching out a flamboyant and wildly inappropriate bow.

My hair tumbles in front of my face. It is foolish to take my eyes off him, but that is what I want him to think me in this moment. Just another wine-soggy little fool.

"Are you quite all right?"

The concern in his tone makes me want to gag.

I jerk upright, and my stumble isn't even that feigned this time. The blood rushes back to my head. Two strong hands clasp my shoulders to keep me upright and steady.

For a brief moment, my body tenses as I raise my eyes to meet his. They are the same cold gray they were before, but now, one golden eyebrow is arched. The corners of his lips tilt upward in amusement.

His gaze lowers. It rakes across my throat, my décolleté, my chest and lands squarely on my bodice.

"Had a bit too much to drink, have we?"

His finger digs into the meat of my arms as I fight to offer him a wobbly smile.

"What—*hic*—gave it away?"

Kiki is by far the better actress. She would be doing much better in my place, but I would never wish that cold gray gaze on her. I would serve myself up to Cristobal a thousand times over to prevent him from every sullying her life any more than he already has. Probably.

He is not innocent. I know that much. For all my many flaws, I am an excellent judge of character.

"The wine all over your lovely dress," he says. "Though I can't say I blame you. Freedom is a heady thing, is it not?" And then, the son of a bitch winks at me. "I hear the masked balls in the Potosí jail aren't nearly as nice as this one."

"I was just..." I glance around like a puzzled gazelle. Frown. "This isn't the washroom."

A delicate chuckle tumbles from Cristobal's lips. "Indeed. It is not." He releases my shoulders, allowing me to sway in space. "Shall I perhaps escort you back to the ballroom?"

I twirl, hands out to my sides, arms undulating to music only I can hear. "Oh, a ball. How lovely. I do so love to—*hic*—dance."

Cristobal offers me his arm. After the thinnest moment of hesitation, I take it. It is tense and quiet as he guides me back through the twisting corridors to the ballroom. Something inside me loosens when I hear the sound of a lively saraband.

When we get to the doors, he pauses. A footman waits for his signal to open them. "It was my pleasure to accompany you, but I am afraid this is as far as I go." He releases my hand. "Do be mindful of where you go sniffing around. You never know what you might find." His smile is thin and mirthless. "I would so hate to see harm befall a girl as lovely as yourself."

He reaches out to brush a lock of hair over my shoulder. It takes everything I have not to yank up my skirt and grab my shiny new dagger and bury it in his throat.

My smile is more of a grimace, but it'll do for now. I offer him my very worst curtsy. "Thank you, kind sir. I shall—*hic*—bear that in mind."

I don't wait for him to say anything else, or worse, to try to touch me again. I make my retreat, as hastily as propriety will allow. Even so, I can feel his gaze burning a hole in my back as I go.

# CHAPTER 30

*Ana*

I have to tell Kiki what's happened. Her family is a target. Alejandro's death—his murder—was part of something larger than we could have anticipated. It wasn't just about whatever damning knowledge he must have come across. It wasn't about Alejandro alone. Her family—the Sonza fortune—is a target. *Kiki* is a target. I don't know how exactly, but the fact that Cristobal has his eyes on her family's source of income makes worry clog my throat. He seems like a man who will stop at nothing to get what he wants.

And yet, all these dire warnings sputter out when I reach the ballroom.

In the center of the ballroom dance a swan and a lion. Feathers and fur, parting and colliding with the grace of the animals to which their costumes harken.

Sebastian dancing with Kiki. *My* Kiki.

Something toxic and thick sludges through my gut.

Once, I stood by and watched her dance with a man she does not love. A man she can never love. And I let it happen.

I will not let it happen this time.

Once was enough.

There are things I have to tell her. Maps and deeds and shipping routes. But all of that can wait. Right now, I have something to prove.

I make my way through the crowd of swirling silks and fluttering feathers. Perhaps it is the determination in my stride or the murderous look I can only assume is on my face, but people get out of my way.

I like that. I like it very, very much.

People part before me like the sea before Moses, but it is not God's power propelling them to the side. It is mine.

When I reach the edge of the dance floor, I pause.

*Now or never, Ana.*

The dance brings Kiki closer to me, close enough for her to meet my eyes and frown, a silent question written in the downturn of her lips.

I smile, sharp and half-feral.

A dark, elegant eyebrow lifts. Partly question. Partly challenge.

Oh, little does she know.

When Sebastian's lead brings her within my orbit, I clear my throat. Loudly. Obnoxiously.

He turns to me, confusion clear even through the mask. "Ana?"

I step into their path, stilling their twirling progression.

"May I cut in?"

The goal was not to make Kiki sputter like a broken wagon wheel, but it is a delightful side effect of my brazen question. It would be a lie to say I don't enjoy the way her mouth opens and closes, dumbstruck for once in her unbearably clever life.

"Have you gone mad?" Sebastian asks.

I smile at him because if I don't, I might spit in his face—again—
and that will absolutely get me kicked out of this party. "Quite possibly."

Without waiting for a response, I insert myself into his space, forcing him to the side. He could put up a fight but that would make a
scene and, unlike me, Sebastian prizes the social niceties of the upper
classes. He would *never* make a scene, especially not one as spectacularly scandalous as this.

One hand settles on Kiki's waist while the other twines with hers.

She blinks at me through the black lace of her mask. "Are you sure
you want to do this?"

"I am." I shake my head, ignoring the musical cue lifting the feet
of the dancers around us. We are a stone in a river, unmoved by the
tides. "That is . . . if you are."

For a second, she is silent. It is a terrible second. Truly, one of the
worst.

But then, she smiles.

"I am." She steps closer to me, our gowns flush against each other.
"I don't want to hide. Not from you. Not from them. Not anymore."

There is no word in any language that can encapsulate what I feel
in that moment. But I have always relied more on actions than words.
And now, I let mine speak for me.

I take Kiki's hands in mine and pull her close.

"Let us show them, then. Let us show them all."

# *Kiki*

• • •

I have danced with Ana many times—for instruction at first, tripping over each other's toes and laughing so loudly we couldn't hear the music, and then for practice—but never before has it felt like this.

Even through the layers upon layers of silk and velvet separating us, I can feel her warmth radiating against me. It burns me nearly as hot as the shocked and appalled gazes of every single soul in this ballroom, but it's the only heat that matters to me.

"Everyone is staring," Ana says. To anyone but me, she would sound like her normal self. All hard edges and bravado and courage, but I can hear the things she wants to hide from others. The note of uncertainty woven through every word.

"Let them," I reply, twirling away from Ana with extra relish. When our bodies come together once more, my blood bubbles in my veins, effervescent.

The saraband has long since passed us by. We've entered into musical territory that is slower, more intimate. If I stopped and thought about it, I know I would be able to identify the exact tempo and style of dance but I don't want to stop. I don't want to think. I want only to be here with Ana in this moment, suspended like two twirling motes of dust on a sunbeam.

Ana's smile shifts from feigned bravado to something softer. Something more genuine. I want to bottle that smile and carry it with my always, to hang it from a glass vial around my neck, to keep it always near my heart.

"You look happy," I say because it is true. She does. And I feel so, in a way I haven't since before the viceroy's ball, before talk of my marriage, before any of this mess began.

But then her smile falters. She blinks, and a shroud falls over her eyes, as if someone has pulled a veil of darkness over this perfect, glorious moment. "I shouldn't be." Her lips do that thing they do when she's worried. A slight twitch downward. Not quite a frown, but a near thing. "I found something. We need to—"

I place a finger over the seam of her lips, holding back whatever she was going to say next.

"Whatever it was, it can wait until the end of the song, can it not? Will the sky fall if you don't tell me right now?" I shake my head. "This is the first time I've felt anything but horrible in weeks. Please, I just . . ."

Her arm tightens around my waist, pulling me closer to her body, as if she could shield me from all harm. It is an illusion, and a silly one at that, but it is an illusion I welcome all the same.

"Of course."

There are steps to this dance but we are not performing them. We have long since disrupted whatever the natural order is for this particular piece of music. We are simply two bodies moving in time.

I go where she follows, content for once to simply allow another soul to lead. To take the burden off my own for a few stolen minutes. I wish I could rest my head against her shoulder, bury my face in her neck, and simply breathe.

I settle for meeting her eyes. They pierce me, even through the mask on her face.

We are so close. Close enough nearly to kiss. Her lips hover mere inches from my own. Reddened by rouge. Plush. Inviting. Her hand is so unbearably warm against my waist. It's almost as though I can feel its heat searing straight through the layers of my gown, burning a brand into my flesh. She breathes, her chest brushing against mine as the delicate beadwork of our gowns scrapes together.

It would take so little effort to close the distance between us.

Wouldn't that be the most delicious scandal to rock Potosí?

But then, of course, the universe has other ideas.

Over Ana's shoulder, I spot a cluster of men gathering near the far doors. My body goes stiff in her arms.

She notices immediately. "What is it?"

"Cristobal," I say into her hair, my lips moving by the curve of her ear. "And our old friend, the magistrate. He looks like he's about to shit his pants."

Ana begins to angle her head in the direction in which I am looking but I still her with a warning hand on her shoulder.

"Don't. Not yet. I don't want to arouse their suspicion. They seem . . . distracted."

"Kiki, we're hardly inconspicuous."

She's not wrong. We are two women, dressed in the finest gowns this ballroom has likely ever seen, proudly screaming that we are utterly enamored with one another through the language of dance.

"Fair point," I say. "But I think they're taking the opportunity we've provided them with to discuss something they want no one else to overhear."

Ana snorts. "We do make one hell of a distraction, don't we?"

"We do indeed." As I watch—as subtly as I possibly can considering the circumstances—Cristobal storms out of the room, followed quickly by Magistrate de la Vega. A stern-faced footman closes the door behind them, moving to stand in front of it so that no one else can follow them through. "And it would appear they wish to take advantage. It seems they've a better party to attend to than this one."

"Are we following them?" Ana asks, no longer bothering to hide her lips against my hair. What a shame. It felt so terribly nice.

I nod. "We are. And who knows? Your brand-new blade might see action before the night is through."

"Oh, good." Ana's smirk makes something twist low and tight in my gut. "I was hoping I'd get to play with my new toy sooner rather than later."

## *Ana*

• • •

Slinking about a nobleman's villa late at night in a ball gown without drawing attention to oneself is harder than it sounds. Or maybe it's exactly as hard as it sounds because it sounds goddamn difficult. Following Cristobal and the magistrate as they departed the ball has proven more of a challenge than anticipated.

Now, Kiki and I are huddled against a wall outside the stables, the hems of our skirts absolutely destroyed by mud and other substances I would rather not think about.

The men are around the corner, whispering in hushed tones too quiet to hear. At one point, the magistrate gives a startled shout before he is silenced by a harsh but indecipherable word from Cristobal.

That we have made it this far is impressive.

That we have not been detected despite my clumsiness in a dress is a minor miracle.

"Shit," I whisper. Again, I have trod on Kiki's skirts. And again she shushes me.

"I'm sorry, I just hate—"

A hand claps over my mouth as Kiki pulls us both back behind the corner.

Cristobal's voice comes low and clear, resonating through the dark, silent night. "You do not know with whom you are dealing, Magistrate de la Vega. I am not a man to be trifled with."

"I assure you, I will draw up the contracts with enthusiastic haste."

"See that you do. I want those routes before I set foot back on the ship to Spain."

I catch Kiki's eyes.

There is a minor commotion as horses are summoned and saddled. My muscles twitch with the urge to peer around the corner, to see what's going on, but Kiki's hand on my arm holds me still. It would be far too risky to chance detection like that.

A horse neighs. Then hoofbeats pound the stable floor as one, two, three—no, four—horses ride out into the night.

With a curse under her breath, Kiki gathers up her skirts. And runs.

"Kiki!" A half whisper, half shout is all I dare. There could still be grooms about. Stable hands. Prying eyes that would be best not seeing us. "What are you doing?"

But it's clear what she's doing. She is peering over the stall doors, looking for a mount.

"Are you completely mad?" With only slightly more caution than she exhibited, I ease out from our hiding spot. God must be smiling down on us because the stables are largely empty. The sounds of activity drift over from another end of the barn, but for right now, we are safely ensconced by shadow and solitude.

One of the horses—a dappled gray—seems to satisfy Kiki. She holds her hand out for the horse to sniff. It does before butting its snout against her hand. A friendship forged. Delightful. But shortsighted. So very, very shortsighted.

"You can't possibly be considering going after them," I say, but Kiki's already reaching for a bridle. She can ride bareback just fine—I can't—but she still needs a set of reins.

"I most certainly am." She examines a bit before deeming it sufficient. Her hands are rising, reaching to loop the bridle around the horse's head when I grab her by the wrist.

Impatience—seasoned with not a small bit of anger—flashes through her eyes. "Let me go. If I don't leave now, I'll lose the trail."

"Kiki, this isn't what we came here for."

"Ana—" She tries to wrest her arm from my grip, but I hold on tight. If I let her go now, I might lose her for good. And that is something I refuse to do.

"No, you listen to me. We're here for Rosalita, not revenge."

"He killed my brother," Kiki presses. "He killed Alejandro."

I don't want to say it, but I must. "Alejandro is dead, Kiki. Rosalita may still be alive."

Her face hardens, as if turning to stone. Like the men in those Greek tragedies she likes to read me. The one with the cursed woman with the snakes for hair. I never did like that one.

But what I'm saying needs to be said.

"You can't save him now. But we can save Rosalita."

She shakes her head. "You don't understand." And then she hits me with her finest blow. "He wasn't your brother."

I rear back, stung. Her wrist drops from my hand.

She wastes no time slipping the bridle over the horse's head. The mare paws at the ground, seemingly excited to get out of her stall and run. Kiki swings herself—gown and all—up onto the horse's back.

"I'm sorry, Ana." But she doesn't look at me when she says it. Her heels dig into the horse's flank and she's off.

"Kiki, wait!"

My whispered shout goes unanswered.

She's already gone. And now, I am alone.

# CHAPTER 31

*Kiki*

The wind flies through my hair, whipping it about my face with a fury that keeps me warm despite the brisk night air and the impracticalities of my gown.

*You shouldn't have left her behind.*

I push the thought away. Ana will be fine.

*You left her all alone in a viper's den.*

But the viper left. I saw it with my own eyes.

*Did you? Or did you just hear it?*

That is the thought that gives me pause.

I seat myself more firmly on the mare's back. She is a good mount, fast but with a nice steady gait. At the canter, there's hardly a shred of discomfort despite the fact that I am riding a horse astride while wearing approximately seven thousand layers of skirts and their underlying architecture.

I did not see Cristobal leave. I just assumed he had.

The horse slows as she feels my indecision emanate through my seat. Horses are clever. They can tell when their rider is unsettled, often before the rider does. They know when you aren't secure in your seat, when your balance is off even if just a hair.

She slows, as if giving me time to appreciate what a tremendous fool I have been.

I glance behind, but already, the villa is but a speck of light in the darkness. The windows are all ablaze for the ball, but I have ridden so far and so fast that I can hardly see it. Trees obscure the faraway illumination and clouds all but block whatever scant starlight penetrates them.

*Go back.*

But the same feelings war within me.

Cristobal killed my brother. That, or he knows who did. Of that much I am certain.

And for that, he must pay.

Clicking my tongue, I urge the mare forward. She tosses her head, fighting the bit as if arguing with me.

A sharp breeze cuts through the urgency pumping through my veins that had kept me warm until now, propelling me forward with nary a backward glance.

Until now.

I don't know what I'm doing. I am chasing ghosts. When Ana is trying to save a life.

*Fool. You are a wretched fool.*

I dig my left heel into the horse's side. She whinnies, as if pleased with the decision I've made.

Together, we turn back around, her sure steps carrying me back toward the villa and Ana and whatever else lies in wait there.

Cristobal will wait.

*Vengeance* will wait.

Now, Ana needs me. Rosalita needs me. And I am failing them both.

# *Ana*

• ◉ •

I have never felt this way toward Kiki before. Have never entertained this simmering rage, this sense of betrayal.

*She left you. She chose revenge—not even revenge, just a chance at it—over you. Over Rosalita. She chose vengeance for the dead over saving the living.*

Watching her ride off into the night was like being run through with a sword. A rusty one will a dull edge and a serrated blade.

*She will always follow her heart. But her heart will not always lead to you.*

"Oh, shut the hell up," I tell my own traitorous brain. I don't have time for this. *Rosalita* doesn't have time for this.

*She could be hurt. She could be scared or worse. And you're here nursing old wounds and tearing open new ones.*

I didn't find anything about her in Cristobal's study, but that doesn't mean there isn't anything to find. If he's involved with her, maybe he's hiding his secrets deeper in the belly of his home than that. Maybe he's hiding things where no one would dare to look.

Gathering up my skirts, I leave the stables the way we came, tiptoeing as quietly as I dare—and as quietly as this gown will allow.

I should have worn my breeches and coat. It was a masked ball, for God's sake. I could have worn anything and it wouldn't have mattered, but no, I had to wear the damn gown, and I had to relish the way Kiki looked at me in it and—

*Stop it.*

My steps lead me away from the stables and into a dark corner of the villa.

The air is cool but dry. Beneath my feet, wooden slats creak softly. The faint smell of oak drifts to my nose.

*I know that smell.*

When I first moved into Kiki's home, I found the high ceilings and lofty windows overwhelming. They frightened me in a way I couldn't articulate then and probably couldn't now. Part of it was that it was all too grand, too foreign. But another part was that it felt unprotected. Exposed. Everything was there to be displayed, to show off the family's wealth and power and position.

The one place in the whole building that didn't make me feel like that was the wine cellar. It was cool and dark and quiet. The ceilings were vaulted but relatively low. The bottles gleamed like warm glass by the light flickering in the sconces on the walls. It was like a cocoon, sheltered from the overwhelming, overpowering house above.

A wine cellar. The perfect place to hide.

The light is too low to see much of anything here, but I feel along the walls for a door or a latch or something. My palms trail over cold stone for an agonizing moment before my fingers butt against something metal and hard.

A lock.

I try the door but the heavy wooden bulk refuses to budge. Strange. On a night like tonight, where wine is flowing like water, one would think that access to the wine cellar would be something of a necessity.

I run the pads of my fingers over the lock, feeling its shape. The mechanism is of solid construction but not complex. A simple and straightforward design.

I may not have Kiki's delicate instruments to pick the lock, but then, I never needed them. My education on the streets of Potosí had less to do with books and more to do with practical experience. I slip two pins from my hair and kneel before the door, regretting for once in my life that I am ruining a dress. Then, I get to work.

Even now, this far from the action of the party, I can hear servants rustling about in the rooms upstairs. Sorting out food and drinks. Cleaning up the detritus of the wealthy and the privileged as they gorge themselves on roast duck and the finest wines in the New World.

A cold breeze dances along my spine as I work the lock. I can feel the tumblers resisting the push of the pins. One of them snaps in my hand, and I bite back a curse. At least my thick mane is host to many, many more. I slide another pin free, further mussing my hair. Oh well. The ensemble looked good while it lasted. Seconds tick by as I maneuver the pins in the lock, working as quickly as I dare. Locks do not like to be rushed. Two more broken pins later, the lock tumbles open.

Finally.

The door swings open, blessedly quiet, the hinges well oiled.

A set of winding stone stairs leads downward into a darkness so complete, I can practically taste it. When I reach the last step, I stumble. Before me, all I can see is pure, undiluted black.

In those impenetrable shadows, someone whimpers.

With shaking hands, I fumble at the walls until I find a torch. Kiki will absolutely hate me for it, but I strike the dagger against the stone wall to create a spark. The torch catches, and I jerk it out of its holder on the wall.

The whimper comes again, louder this time. More pitiable.

Bottles of wine and spirits line the walls and aisles and aisles of shelves.

Cristobal's collection must be one of the most extensive in all of Peru. If he wasn't so loathsome, I'd almost be impressed.

Quietly, I inch forward, torch held aloft.

At the end of the far row, I see her.

"Rosalita."

In my haste to reach her, I nearly trip over my gown no fewer than three times. I also nearly light my own hair on fire twice. I fall to my knees beside her, grateful for the gown for once. It's thick enough to absorb the impact of my bony kneecaps hitting hard stone.

I place the torch on the ground beside us and reach for Rosalita. Her eyes are squeezed shut, and her face is angled away from me, turned nearly into a bare shoulder. Scraps of fabric cling to her form. The remnants of the shift she would have worn under a dress. She must be freezing.

Heavy iron chains cut into her wrists. The flesh around them is raw and torn, the blood dried and crusted around the metal.

Someone will die for this. Probably many someones. But not right now.

"Rosalita?" I keep my voice soft.

She doesn't move. The only sign that she's even alive is the shallow, broken rasp of her breathing.

*Her ribs.* They must be cracked.

Her voice wavers. "No more . . . please."

"Hush," I whisper, cradling her face as quickly as I dare. I need to get her out of those shackles but she needs at least this one moment of comfort. "It's me. Ana. I'm here to save you. No one is going to hurt you again."

Rosalita raises her head, blinking owlishly at me through the tangled, greasy mess of her hair. "Ana?"

Her voice is hoarse. Broken.

*What have they been doing to her down here?*

I shake my head, dislodging the thought. Can't dwell on that now. I have to get us both out of here. And fast.

A loud bang from upstairs makes us both jump.

"Someone's coming," Rosalita says through her cracked and bleeding lips.

"If they want to get to you, they're going to have to go through me."

I wish I felt as confident as I sounded as I get to work on her manacles. But I cannot unchain her and defend us both at the same time, especially if I have to carry her out of here. From the looks of it, her legs will hardly be able to hold her up. And I am only one person. It will take a miracle to save us now.

## *Kiki*

· ● ·

The mare carries me with an alacrity that makes me love her just a little. Not that I would ever turn my back on my good and loyal Rocinante, but this horse deserves a better master than the one she's got.

I pat her neck as she trots back to the stable with little to no direction from me. She knows where her home is, after all.

"Once I slay your owner," I whisper in her ear. "I'll come back for you."

She makes a happy whinny, as if pleased by this arrangement.

I dismount in a swirl of silk and lace. Slipping her bridle off, I lead her back into the stables. Luckily for me, no one's around to see me return a stolen horse.

My luck doesn't hold out as long as I want it to though.

Voices from the corridor leading into the main building ricochet off the wall.

"I'm telling you, I heard something."

"Don't see why you have to go sniffing out trouble where there is none."

I press myself to the wall of the mare's stall, ducking my head out of sight. She noses at the shoulder of my gown affectionately.

"You ain't been working for the master longer than fortnight. You don't know what he's like when he's angry."

"Fine, fine. Where was this banging or clanging or what-have-you coming from?"

"Wine cellar, I think."

Banging. Clanging. Wine cellars. Sounds like Ana.

Lifting my skirts, I step out of the stall and shut the door behind me as softly as humanly possible.

The men aren't quiet, which makes them delightfully easy to follow. And they don't hear me coming, which is even better.

When they reach the door to what I assume is the wine cellar, I clear my throat.

They turn, nigh identical looks of surprise on their faces. It's almost comical.

The shorter of the two peers at me, bushy eyebrows furrowed. "You're not supposed to be down here."

I nod. "Very true."

Reaching into my pockets, I smile as my fingers brush up against what I am looking for: Cold, hard steel.

My grin must be feral indeed.

The shorter man pauses. "Who the hell are you?"

I draw my knife, savoring the whisper of the steel against the sheath as it slides free. I could go for the pistol, but I am far more confident with a blade. Gunpowder is far too impersonal for what I want these men to experience. "The last woman you will ever see."

The taller one laughs. "Big words coming from such a small thing." His lip curls into a sneer. "Bet you don't even know how to use that thing."

I smile. From the looks on their faces, it's as ferocious as I hope it is. "Oh, you have no idea."

And then, they charge.

I rattle off a silent prayer for Ana and the fight begins.

The two men are more competent than I gave them credit for. The quarters are close and they know them better than I do. And of course they would. They are Cristobal's guards. Of course they know the house and all its nooks and crannies and twists and turns.

And they have swords. All I have is a knife. And a pistol, but I dare not use it now. Not when there is a house full of people upstairs who would most assuredly hear a gunshot.

The taller man is easier to dodge. His body is too cumbersome to move efficiently but he's strong, and I'm shackled by a skirt and corset. Hardly at my best.

The shorter one is the bigger problem. He's fast and agile, getting under my guard more times than he should.

I dance away from them, keeping myself between them and the door. The larger one charges at me, a low growl on his lips. I hold my ground for three . . . two . . . one. Stepping to the side, I kick out the hem of my gown, praying for a miracle.

And God sees fit to bestow one upon me. The heavy tulle catches on the man's boot, tripping him up. With my elbow, I smash him in the back of the neck as hard as I can. He tumbles down the stairs with a series of dull thuds. He groans at first, and then, there is silence.

My victory is short-lived.

"You shouldn't have done that."

I shouldn't have done a lot of things.

Shouldn't have left Ana's side.

Shouldn't have let myself crow over the taller man's head-first descent into the wine cellar.

Shouldn't have worn this dress.

And I never should have taken my eyes off the shorter man. Not even for a second.

Because a second is all it takes.

I turn but I'm too slow. Too weighted down by pounds and pounds of silk and velvet. The pain in my side is sharp and immediate. It's like being punched but so much worse. Dark eyes meet mine as the shorter man pulls his blade free from my side. My hand flies up to touch the wound. Even through the gloves, I can feel the wet, sticky sensation of my own blood.

"Got you," he says, right in my face, breath acrid and powerful.

"No," I say. "You don't."

I grab him by the lapels and smash my skull into his.

Or more specifically, my skull into the bridge of his nose.

There are plenty of things I shouldn't have done. But what *he* shouldn't have done is taken a mere stab wound as a victory.

Bone and cartilage crack on impact. He goes limp immediately, sagging out of my hands and onto the floor.

The angle was just right to send a shard of cartilage into his brain. Or so I hope. I don't stick around to find out. I turn, ready to charge down the stairs but I'm stopped by someone in the doorway.

My knife is coming up before I see that it is not just someone in the doorway. It is two someones.

Ana looks at me, one arm looped around a very injured Rosalita's waist, the other holding the girl's wrist over her own shoulder.

"Jesus Christ, Kiki." She hoists Rosalita higher as the other girl sags with a pained groan. "Took you long enough."

# CHAPTER 32

*Ana*

Kiki handles the logistics of our departure from Cristobal's estate. She slips a generous amount of coin to one of the stable boys to bring a carriage around—specifically *not* Sebastian's—after sending its driver off on a false errand. She tosses in an extra coin for the boy's silence. Some poor sod is going to find himself without a ride home, but that is no concern of mine. I follow behind, emerging only when the stable boy has cleared off, praying Rosalita stays conscious long enough to get to someone who can help. With every slow, pained step, her weight sags against me more and more.

It takes both of us to bundle her into the carriage. She whimpers as we maneuver her bruised limbs onto the bench. At least it has cushions. We cannot take her home, that much is certain. The Sonza villa is the first place anyone would look for us. So we take her to the next best spot: Santiago's. He may always have the best gossip but the man knows how to keep his mouth shut when it really counts.

"You stay with Rosalita." Kiki steps through the carriage's small door, her skirts barely fitting through the opening. "I'll drive."

The journey is a blur. Rosalita slips in and out of consciousness, and I am terrified in a way I do not think I have ever felt. Every bump in the road makes me wince in sympathy with the pain Rosalita must be feeling.

"Please don't die," I whisper as I brush damp hair off her sweaty forehead.

Her only response is an incoherent mumble against my shoulder.

When we arrive, Kiki pays off one of the orphans who hangs around Santiago's tavern to take the carriage somewhere else, far from here, and abandon it. We can't have our mode of escape parked right in front of the place we plan to hide Rosalita. If Cristobal wants to track her down, I don't want to make it easy for him. Another coin is slipped to another orphan.

"Go to the Sonza estate. Knock on the kitchen door and ask for Magdalena. Tell her we are here and to send clothes." The orphan nods, eyes widening as he holds the coin up to see if it gleams in the moonlight. "They'll feed you when you get there."

His eyes widen even further at the promise of good food. With that, he runs like the fires of hell are licking at his feet, taking off in the direction of the estates.

I call out to Santiago as we head inside. He turns to me, a scowl on his face that disappears as soon as he lays eyes on Rosalita. "Christ, what happened to her?"

Santiago grabs the unconscious girl's other arm as we heave her up the stairway to the rooms on the second floor.

"End of the hall," he says. "It's the most secure."

Kiki gets the doors, leading us inside.

In that moment, I love Santiago as if he were my own kin. No *What the hell, Ana?* Or *Why have you brought her here?* Just simple concern, right out to the gate.

"A very bad man," I say. The less he knows, the better probably.

But it is enough. Fury blazes in his eyes. Everyone in this part of town knows Rosalita. And they all love her. "Lay her down on the bed."

Kiki tosses the bedcovers back. They're a clean, light linen. They won't stay that way much longer, not with the amount of blood on Rosalita's skin. Much of it is dry, but some is fresh, and that is most worrisome of all.

Together, Kiki and I hoist Rosalita's limp body onto the bed, as gently as we can.

"There's cold water in the basin," Santiago says. "And fresh linens beside it."

Kiki grabs both, tucking the towels beneath her arm and grasping the heavy brass basin with both hands.

"I'll fetch hot water." Santiago stands, wiping his bloodied hands on his apron. "And some rum for the wounds."

He leaves, his stride purposeful and firm, but closes the door gently behind him.

Kiki perches next to Rosalita, wiping her brow down.

"You're all right," she intones in a soft, soothing voice. "You're safe."

Rosalita whimpers in her slumber, leaning into Kiki's touch.

I watch, arms wrapped around my stomach. I am good in a fight, but comfort was never my strong suit.

But when Rosalita's hand twitches in my direction, something inside me cracks. I fall to my knees beside the bed, taking her hand in mine.

"I'm here." I wrap both my hands around hers. Were her fingers always this thin? This bony? "You're going to be fine."

Rosalita opens her mouth but all that comes out is a hoarse croak.

"Water," I tell Kiki. She bustles from the bedside to pour a cup from the jug on a nearby table.

Her hand trembles as she passes it to me. I glance up to find her pale as a sheet, but maybe it's just the black gown.

Carefully, I cradle Rosalita's head as she raises herself up just enough to soothe her parched throat. After she drinks half of the cup, she pushes it away with one hand. The other she wraps around mine.

"He told me Ale was dead, but that cannot be true." Rosalita's weak grip on my hand pulses. "Tell me it isn't. Tell me he was lying."

I glance back at Kiki. Her face has gone still, her shoulders rigid. All emotion has bled from her eyes, leaving them as cold as a winter sea.

When I look back at Rosalita, there is such raw pleading on her face that I cannot speak. How could I form the words that will break her?

"He's dead." Kiki's voice is devoid of inflection. Perfectly flat. Perfectly informative, as if she were conveying the price of grain.

Shaking her head, Rosalita squeezes her eyes shut. Tears well up on her lashes. "No. No, no, no."

Without another word, Kiki turns, fisting up her skirts and walks out of the room. I watch her go. There's an uneven quality to her steps that makes me worry, but I have only so much worry to give. And right now, Rosalita is soaking it all up.

Santiago returns with a large copper basin of hot water. Together, we clean Rosalita up as best we can. All the while, she cries softly, from pain both within and without.

Once the blood has been washed away, Santiago reaches into his pocket and pulls out a small glass vial. "I have a dram I can give her." He pitches his voice so low I doubt Rosalita can hear. "It'll put her to sleep."

I nod.

Rosalita doesn't even put up a fight when Santiago sets the vial against her lips and tips its contents into her mouth.

"How did you get so good at this?" I ask.

Santiago snorts. "I had a life before I became the keeper of a tavern, Ana." He glances at me. "I was a soldier once, a long, long time ago. The life wasn't for me. I am not fond of violence."

"And yet I keep bringing it to your door."

"Nobody's perfect." Santiago begins to unwind linen for Rosalita's bandages. Already, the poor girl is going loose-limbed. "Go. Find your girl. There's something off about her." He spares me one last glance before turning his attention fully to Rosalita. "I think she's hurt."

I shake my head as I stroke my fingers down the back of Rosalita's hand. She doesn't flinch. Not one bit.

"Aren't we all?" I say.

But I do what Santiago suggests. I go and I find my girl.

●　◉　●

I find Kiki in the next room over, being a complete, fiery imbecile.

Her dress is halfway off. And there's blood all over her underthings. She's trying to unhook the holster around her thigh, but she's entirely too pale and swaying on her feet.

My breath leaves me in a rush. "Mother of God, Kiki."

She looks at me, brow drawn and hands even more covered in blood than mine. "It's just a flesh wound."

"Yes, flesh. That protective layer meant to keep your blood on the inside." I snatch up another clean rag by the basin beside my own vanity. We're going to go through more than our fair share of these tonight.

"Will you stop being so stubborn and let me help you?"

Kiki glares at the holster in her hands. She says nothing. Her chest rises and falls in stilted little hitches.

"Oh, for Christ's sake." I don't quite stomp over to her, but it's close. I should be quieter for Rosalita's sake, but after what Santiago gave her, she'd probably be able to sleep through a horde of the Sun King's elephants stampeding through the house.

I unhook the holster and snatch it out of Kiki's hands. She grabs for it, but she's too slow. That alone conveys how bad her wound must be. Her reflexes should be as sharp as her saber. But now, her arms spasm when she reaches for the gun, her breath stuttering through a pained hiss of an inhalation.

"I don't know why you're being such an ass about this." I set the holster gently aside. The ornate gun glimmers in the warm light of the fire, looking out of place against the plain wood of the table. When I turn around, Kiki is glaring but thankfully not at me.

A streak of crimson—still wet, still fresh—stains the left half of her shift. The blood stands out so starkly against the white fabric that I almost feel dizzy on her behalf. The edges of the material have frayed around the long, jagged cut, revealing only glimpses of the wound beneath.

Kiki hums thoughtfully. "I honestly don't remember it being that bad."

And then, she falls.

My feet work faster than my brain.

*Thank God for small miracles.*

They dash toward her—a small distance, but one that feels monumental in the moment—and she collides with my chest as I half catch her before she can crack her skull open against the heavy wooden bedpost.

That makes two maidens swooning into my arms tonight. I really could do without it, honestly.

I help her undress before seating her on the bed to tend to the wound. Judging from the nick in her corset, she was saved by the trappings of femininity. The blade must have skittered over the whalebone stay.

"Why didn't you say anything?" I dab at the gash, grimacing when she hisses in pain.

"It didn't feel that bad. Honestly."

My eyes find hers. Whatever she sees in them make her look away.

I probably don't need to say it but I do anyway. "I find that very hard to believe."

"Believe what you want," she says. Her voice strained. Her teeth gritted. "It is of no concern to me."

Because I am a rotten person, I dab an extra generous serving of alcohol on the edge of the wound. The muscles of her abdomen jump under her touch as she lets loose a string of rapid curses.

"God doesn't like liars," I say, smiling beatifically.

It was an asshole move, but it works. She's focused on being mad at me and not on being in pain.

Truly, I am selfless all the way to my very core.

But she doesn't hold my gaze as she would normally. Her eyes skitter away from mine, down and to the side.

She goes quiet while I work. After a handful of minutes that feels like an hour, she says, "I shouldn't have left you."

My hands pause in their application of the gauze I am using as bandages. But then, I resume my work.

"No," I say. "You shouldn't have."

I wrap the gauze around her waist, nice and firm, before tying it off.

"But you're here now. We all are. And that's all that matters."

But she shakes her head, teeth worrying at her lower lip.

"I deserved it."

Those three words break something inside of me. I grab her face in my hands, turning her to look at me. She tries to turn her head away, tries to void my gaze, but I will not allow it.

"Look at me," I say in a tone that brooks absolutely no argument.

She does. Her skin is sallow and her eyes are strained and tired but she looks at me.

"Don't you ever say anything like that again."

"But I—"

"But nothing. You came back. For me. For us." Now it's my turn to shake my head. "That is what matters. That is all that matters."

She opens her mouth, as if to argue, so I don't give her the chance.

I slot my mouth over hers, stealing whatever excuses or self-loathing diatribes are about to pour free.

She goes tense, but after a second, she relaxes, moving her lips against mine.

It is not a sweet kiss. It is hard and a little sad, but it is no less precious to me for it. When I pull away, I rest my forehead against hers.

"I love you," I say softly, brushing my bloody fingers against her cheek. We are, both of us, such a goddamn mess. "Even when you're being a fool."

The sound she makes isn't quite a laugh, but it is a near thing.

"You're too good for me," Kiki says, sniffling.

I nod solemnly. "Yes, I am."

Now that pulls an honest laugh out of her. It's followed immediately by a pained hiss, but that's fine. After all, it's just a flesh wound. And if she can laugh after tonight, after everything, then we're going to be all right.

# CHAPTER 33

*Kiki*

"To the valiant ladies of Potosí."

Santiago clinks his cup against mine, and then Ana's. He tosses back the wine, downing the entire contents of the cup in a single, practiced move. A patron from the other side of the tavern beckons for his attention and he leaves us to fend for ourselves. I lean against the bar, slouching uncomfortably. At least we're out of the dresses. Not only were they ruined, but they were conspicuous as all hell. Magdalena arrived two hours after the orphan had run off, coin in hand. She had dutifully delivered a wrapped parcel of clothes—and menswear, God bless her—but not even duty could keep her from scrunching her nose at the sight of the tavern's clientele.

"Stay for a drink?" I asked.

"I'm afraid I'll have to refrain." Magdalena sniffed haughtily as she sidestepped around a swaying drunken man. "Someone will have to make excuses to your father for your absence."

She left immediately after that exchange to do just that. At this point, I doubt my father was believing Magdalena's excuses. That is, if he was even noticing we were gone. After Sebastian's visit, he had shuffled back into his rooms, a broken man.

After we dressed, Rosalita roused just long enough for us to pepper her with questions, though they proved fruitless.

What did you see? Nothing. What did you hear? Nothing.

"I'm sorry," she'd said, shaking her head sadly. Then, wincing. "Someone struck me from behind and I woke up in that cellar. A man asked me all sorts of questions about Alejandro, but I didn't know anything of use."

I told her it was fine. It wasn't her fault. It wasn't. But that leaves us with no more information than we had earlier.

"Does this wine taste sour to you?" Frowning, I swirl the thick, red liquid around the cup. It does smell a touch foul. And considering how generally low my standards for drinkable wine are, that's saying something.

"It tastes fine to me," Ana says, taking another hearty swig. But I can see the moment the faintly peaty aftertaste hits. Her lips curl in a grimace. "Well . . . maybe fine is a bit of an exaggeration. It's drinkable." Another sip. Another grimace. "Mostly."

I smile fondly at her. This scenario has played over many times. I complain about the quality of the booze. She mocks me for my aristocratic palate. So on and so forth.

Her cup comes to rest on the table with a dull thud. She cants her head to the side as she studies me.

The soft smile fades from my lips.

I hate it when she looks at me like that. Like she can read all the thoughts marching through my head as joyfully as I can read what she lovingly calls *that damn Cervantes novel* for the fiftieth time. Heat rises in my cheeks though the warmth of the tavern and the dim lighting is probably enough to mask it. Probably.

"I don't think it's the wine that's the problem," Ana says.

I let my eyebrows ask the question: "Then what is?"

She blinks. A long moment passes between us. The group of patrons clustered around the table by the hearth breaks out into a bawdy drinking song, mangling the lyrics something terrible in their drunken state. Somewhere, someone drops a glass bottle, shattering it against the floor. Ana opens her mouth once. Then closes it. Opens it again. Closes it again.

She shakes her head as her gaze slides away from mine. Her copper waves fall across the side of her face I can see, hiding her eyes from view. She is an expert in this move. Using her features to hide when she does not wish to be seen. Normally, this skill isn't directed at me.

"Nothing," she says. "I'm being silly."

Wordlessly, I sip at my own foul wine. It tastes even worse this time around.

"No." I force myself to swallow the wretched brew. "It's definitely the wine."

"Do you feel," Ana begins, her eyes roaming over the crowd of drunks and gamblers, "that we've won a battle but maybe . . ."

"We're not winning the war?"

She turns back to me. Nods.

"Perhaps," I say. "But I'm glad we won this round."

Ana shakes her head. "It was too easy."

I let out a breath. "It was. But . . ."

But I don't want to think about that right now.

I reach across the table and settle my hand on Ana's. She looks up at me, one copper eyebrow arched.

"But we're alive," I continue. "Rosalita is alive. And for one night . . ." My thumb strokes across the ridge of Ana's knuckles, committing each bump, each divot, to memory. "I would like for that to be enough."

My thigh inches across the bench, closer and closer to her.

"What are you doing?" Ana asks, though she must know damn well what I'm doing.

The corners of my lips twitch with a repressed grin. "Something I've wanted to do for a very long time."

I lean over the table and, with the entire tavern as my witness, I kiss her.

Distantly, I'm aware of someone shouting. Applause. But none of that matters. All that matters is that I am here and so is she. That this is not my father's house. That there are no ghosts to haunt me here. That I am with her. And I am not ashamed. I am alive. More alive than I have ever been.

And for today, that will have to be enough.

●  ●  ●

I am very good at pretending I know what I'm doing. Feigning confidence is a skill I have mastered with the proficiency of a virtuoso. No one does it better than me.

But for all my skill, pretending to know what I am doing does not actually help me when it comes to the actual doing of a thing.

Then, the artifice is stripped away and all that is left is my own ignorance.

This is the thought that plagues me as I climb the stairs, Ana's hand warm in mine and just a tiny bit clammy. Perhaps she's as nervous as I am. Perhaps she also has no idea what she's doing. Hard to believe considering she grew up in a brothel but stranger things have happened I suppose.

The toe of my boot catches on the top stair, and I stumble. Ana's hand keeps me from pitching forward onto my face. She yanks me upright. My heart hammers in my chest with the force of a war drum.

*This was a mistake. An error in judgment. You don't know what you're doing.*
*You can't fake it. Turn around. Claim a cramp. Anything. Save yourself.*

"You all right, Kiki?" Ana asks. A small crease forms between her brows as she looks at me, puzzled. Her hair is tied hastily away from her face and somehow, that makes her even more charming to me. My hands automatically go up to adjust the slightly off-kilter angle of her hat. It must have slipped when I fell, making her lurch along after me.

For years, I've made her believe I am more competent than I am. More knowledgeable. More worldly.

The truth is, everything I know about the art of making love I learned in books. And, shockingly enough, books are a rotten substitute for the real thing. In most things, it's true, but *especially* in this.

"'Course I am," I say. "Why wouldn't I be?"

"Because you're acting like a loon," Ana says, but there is no heat to the words. She has never said an unkind word to me. Well, that's not entirely true. She has—she's only human, after all—but she has never meant those unkind words.

My palms have gone suddenly clammy. I rub them on the thighs of my breeches and turn away. Step one: Get to the damn room. Everything else will come later. Inside, there is already a fire crackling in the room's modest hearth. Good old Santiago. Ready for anything.

Ana has slept in my bed a thousand times. When we were younger, it was nearly habitual. She was given her own room as soon as my father welcomed her into our home, but she claimed it was too big. Too grand. She couldn't fall asleep surrounded by the high ceilings or the tall windows or the fine furnishings she was terrified to break. And so, she slept with me, slipping under the ample covers and burying herself amid my jungle of pillows.

I never minded. I don't think I even realized how lonely I was until then.

But now . . . Things are different now.

"I've just . . ." I turn back to her, not bothering to hide the embarrassment I feel. "I've never done this before."

Ana giggles before clapping a hand over her mouth. "I know that, silly."

"Please don't laugh at me," I say, though I'm fighting back one of my own. "I'm trying very hard to be suave."

Another giggle. Well, more of a chuckle. And at my expense. Smiling, she says, "It's not going very well."

"Oh, for heaven's sake—"

Ana crosses to me with a single stride and slots her mouth over mine, her hands coming up to cup my cheeks. She holds me in place with such aching gentleness as she kisses me that I almost want to scream right into her mouth. I don't, but the urge is there, and it is powerful.

When we break away, I forget to be embarrassed by anything at all, least of which how much I want her.

I reach for her coat and push it off her shoulders. It slides to the floor in a heap of thick green wool. Ana tenses as my hands rest on her shoulders.

*Her scars*, I think.

"If you don't want me to see, that's fine. We can even snuff out the candles if you like . . ."

The barest trace of a sad little smile toys with the corners of Ana's lips. "But I want to see *you*."

Her fingers lace with mine, a pleasant warmth spreading from our connected palms, all the way up my arm, dispersing through my chest and into every part of my body. It's a bit like drinking a cup of milk that's just this side of too hot. It's soothing when it doesn't burn. And even when it does, you don't quite mind.

"I want to see you too." I don't know if it's the right thing to say, but I know that I have to say it. It is the truth, after all. And we have promised each other that at least. The truth, always.

Ana's gaze turns downward, as if the study of our joined hands is far more interesting than anything she would find on my face. "You don't mean that."

A flicker of indignation cuts through me, sharp and hot, but I swallow it down before it can pick my words for me. This isn't about me. "I do. I absolutely do."

The little hum under her breath is anything but convinced.

"But more than that, I want you to feel comfortable," I go on. "I want you to be safe and happy. Always, but especially right now."

Her eyes rise, slowly, to meet mine. A little wrinkle forms between her brows as she furrows them. "Why?"

I can't help it. A small laugh bubbles from my lips before I clamp them down tight. Her frown deepens. Her fingers loosen their hold on my hand and start to slip away. My other hand comes down, sandwiching her hand between both of mine, holding her close. "You're lucky you're beautiful because sometimes you can be rather daft."

She shakes her head again. "I'm not."

"You are."

"Am not."

"Are too."

*This is ridiculous.*

"Am no—"

I cut her off with a kiss.

It is every bit as heady and overwhelming as every kiss that has come before. I wonder if I'll ever get used to it. I sincerely hope that I do not.

When I pull away, I make sure to meet her eyes. I want her to look into mine when I ask what I am about to next. I want her to see what I'm feeling. My hands hover in the air between us, awaiting permission.

"May I . . . ?"

After a moment, she offers me a single, slow nod.

She's so still under my hands. If not for the warmth radiating from her skin, one might mistake her for a statue. Her breathing is almost too measured as I reach for the ties at the throat of her shirt, as if she's counting each inhalation and timing it to match every exhale in perfectly even beats.

It's quiet, the only sound in the room the pop and crackle of the fire.

The shirt slides over her skin, baring a single shoulder to my gaze. A light cluster of freckles dapples her skin right up until the scars begin. My hands are as gentle as I can make them as I drag the shirt away from her shoulder, exposing more of her to the light. And to me.

I lay my hand against her stomach, against the scars there. She stills under my touch, but she's still the way a jittery horse is when it's not quite sure of its rider. Her muscles twitch almost imperceptibly under my palm.

"You're beautiful," I say. And she is. She's the most beautiful creature I have ever seen.

Ana stiffens. "Am not."

"Are too," I say, swallowing thickly.

My body moves of its own accord, following the steps to a dance I have never learned but somehow know by heart. My hands are on her shoulders, pressing her back against the mattress. My knees are sliding along the coarse sheets to bracket her thighs as I crawl over her. My hair falls around her face, a dark curtain shielding us from the world outside this fragile, perfect bubble.

It is a sin to want anyone this much.

And I absolutely do not care. If this desire condemns me to the pit, then I shall burn with pleasure.

"I love you," I say.

"I know."

Such a very Ana thing to say.

My mouth descends upon her. I put everything I feel, everything I am, into that kiss.

I am a creature of words, it is true. But sometimes, only actions will do.

# CHAPTER 34

*Ana*

My limbs feel oddly loose when I wake up, like my joints have been well oiled and my muscles thoroughly liquified.

I don't hate the feeling.

Kiki rolls over, burying her face in the crook of my neck. We have shared a bed countless times before, but it has never felt like this.

I don't hate this feeling either.

Her arm tightens around my waist. The sheets are tangled around my hips, giving me an unfettered view of the way her skin looks against my darker flesh.

Don't hate that either.

"I'm hungry," she mumbles, her lips tickling my neck.

I poke her in the arm, eliciting a soft grumble. "Well, maybe you should eat."

Somehow (and I do not know how exactly such a thing is possible) she burrows even deeper into my side. "But I don't have any food."

Her leg comes to wrap around mine.

Really don't hate that. But . . . "If you want me to get you food, you'll have to let me go."

Another grumble, this one decidedly less pleased, but she loosens her hold on me. It's cold suddenly, without Kiki's warmth wrapped around me like a snake on a branch.

Pressing a kiss to her temple, I say, "I'll be right back. Don't go anywhere."

"I'm naked and content." Kiki pulls the blankets up to her chin as she fills in the empty space I leave as I rise. "Why would I go anywhere?"

I shrug as I pull on my shirt and breeches. "Stranger things have happened. Where are my boots?"

She flings a useless arm in the direction of the entire room. Rolling my eyes, I resign myself to finding them on my own.

One of them is under the bed. The other is across the room, curled up in a corner. Don't really remember how that happened.

"I'll be right back," I say as I tug on my boots. All I get in response is a sleepy little grumble from the mound of blankets that used to be Kiki.

So spoiled. But then, here I am, enabling that.

The noise of the inn overwhelms me the second I step outside of the warm little cocoon Kiki and I created for ourselves.

There is an undeniable skip in my step as I head downstairs. It's still night, but the party is beginning to slow. Dawn must be pushing at the horizon, but right now, I don't really care for anything except for the joy bubbling through my whole body and the girl waiting for me upstairs.

"Working up an appetite, are you?" Santiago says, a knowing smile gracing his lips. There's a small scar on the upper right corner I'd never noticed before. I was probably too drunk to notice or to care, but right now, I am alarmingly, splendidly sober. I have been in this tavern a thousand times but now, it feels new. *Everything* feels new and fresh and wonderful.

"I have indeed." I slide a coin across the bar toward Santiago. "Your finest meats and cheeses, please."

With that, he disappears into the kitchen, hopefully to procure his finest meats and cheeses.

"You deserve no less than the finest. Thank you for saving me."

I turn to find Rosalita nursing a cup of wine, her arms crossed tightly over her abdomen. The ring of bruises around her wrists stands out starkly, even in the gloomy half-light of the tavern. She's wearing clothes supplied by Santiago. A pair of breeches and a loose blouse, so different from her normal attire. It makes her look smaller somehow than those ridiculous gowns she always wears.

"Are you all right?" I regret it the moment I say it.

But Rosalita merely shrugs. "No. But I will be." She cants her head to the side, studying me. "You seem happy."

Warmth floods me, as intoxicating as any spirit. I smile at her, knowing full well how silly I probably look in that moment. But I don't care. Because she's right. "I am."

"Then, I'm happy for you." She smiles, but I see the tightness in her eyes. I hear the sorrow she dares not speak.

And just like that, the furiously burning joy within me fades to little more than a smoldering ember. It isn't gone, not entirely, but it is drowned in a wash of guilt.

Here I am, emanating my own happiness while Rosalita is trying to quell her own despair.

I have the surviving de Sonza child upstairs. The one she loved is gone forever.

"Rosalita . . ."

She must hear the things I lack the capacity to verbalize because she shakes her head. Vehemently. "Don't."

"Don't what? I haven't done anything."

Other than be an insensitive jerk, but that's to be expected from me at this point if we're being perfectly honest.

"He would have wanted you to be happy." There's a certainty in Rosalita's voice that I'm not sure I'd feel if our positions were reversed. "He would have wanted *her* to be happy."

And it is true. I know it. Alejandro was a good person. A better one than I am, that much is certain.

"I'm glad you two have each other." Rosalita's eyes drop as she stares into her cup. I don't think I've ever seen her drunk, and while she doesn't seem inebriated, I know that look. It's the look that screams of hurt that wants nothing more than to be silenced by the sweet bliss of oblivion.

"I miss him, too."

Her smile is watery. Wobbly. But real. And still good. She reaches for the locket at her throat, wrapping reverent fingers around it. "He was one of the good ones, wasn't he?"

I nod, blinking past a sudden heat in the corners of my eyes. "He was."

She nods, more to herself than to me. Then, she tilts her head in the direction of the stairs and the bedrooms and the person waiting for me behind one of those doors. "Go. Don't keep her waiting." She exhales a soft, wistful sigh. "Time is precious. You never know how much you have. Cherish every second."

"I will." It doesn't feel like enough, but it's all I have. "I promise."

She nods, a little too rapidly. "Good. Now get out of here and let me drown my sorrows in peace."

I hesitate. She fixes me with a hard stare.

"I'll be fine."

"Are you sure? Because usually when someone says they need to drown their sorrows, they're anything but fine."

A weary smile tugs at her lips.

"True enough, but . . ." She jerks her head toward the stairs again. "Go. It'll warm my heart to know one of us is content."

* ● *

With Rosalita's words lingering in my head, I head back upstairs, arms laden with a heavy wooden tray, heaped high with meat and cheeses and grapes and generous hunks of bread. The good kind, all soft and warm and delightful. Not the shitty kind that's more suited to blunt force trauma to the head than anything else. And then there's the wine. That I took when he wasn't looking. A fresh jug from Santiago's secret stash. He thinks I don't know about it, but, oh, I do. Of course I do. How could I not?

"Kiki, get the door," I call out as I near the threshold. "It'll be a bitch to get it open myself."

The door doesn't budge. Not even an inch.

It's probably too loud. She can't hear me.

It takes some juggling but I manage to free one hand enough to grasp the handle and push the door inward.

But Kiki is not waiting for me inside, body half-hidden by a threadbare sheet, skin warmed by the fire crackling merrily in the hearth.

Said sheet has been discarded, draped across the floor as if abandoned. It's crumpled, as if someone's legs had gotten tangled in its length. The rickety chair that had been sitting by the fire is now lying on its side, one of it legs shattered into two pieces. The window stands open, drapes fluttering gently in the cool night air.

And on the window's lintel is a streak of something dark and liquid. Something I can mistake for nothing other than what it is.

Blood.

The tray tumbles from my hands. The handle of the jug slips from my fingers. Grapes bounce away from the place where I am rooted. Chunks of cheese land with dull thuds against the wood. Wine splashes against the toes of my boots, seeping into the cracks between the floorboards, soaking into the fallen bread.

Kiki is gone.

And she did not go willingly.

I turn to run, to grab my weapons, but something smashes into me from behind.

"What the fu—"

Another something hits the back of my head, and my world goes dark.

# CHAPTER 35

*Kiki*

Everything happens so fast.

I am lying in bed, my limbs heavy. Slow. Sated. I feel more comfortable in my own skin than I have in quite some time. It's almost as though some great and burdensome carapace has been removed, one that I believed had been protecting me but had, in fact, only been shielding me from my true self. This is who I am. This is the real me. The me I am with Ana. That is the truth I had tried so hard to deny.

These thoughts are joyous. Loud. So loud, I don't hear the window open. So loud I don't hear the first footfall on the ground. I don't see them until it was too late.

The sound of a weapon being drawn is what finally breaks my warm, soft stupor. My head whips around. Two men, too close. I try to stand, but my bare legs tangle in the sheets and I fall, doing their work for them. One of them even has the gall to snicker as he wraps his burly arms around me, scooping me up as if I weigh nothing. I open my mouth to scream, to call for Ana, but a blade at my throat silences me.

"One peep out of you and it'll be your blood staining these sheets."

"Fu—"

A rag—not a clean one—is shoved into my mouth, halting the string of invectives I was ready to hurl at them, knife be damned. My hands are wrenched behind my back with such force I'm fairly certain one is nearly dislocated, and a rope tied around my wrists with far too much alacrity. The man holding me hauls me over his shoulder as if I am a sack of grain and descends from the window with more ease than a lout of his size should be able to accomplish. There is a small outcropping to the rear of the tavern that provides a suitable landing between our room on the second floor and the cold, hard ground. It isn't far to jump, but my body still jolts with the impact, the man's shoulder digging painfully into my belly.

*You son of a bitch, put me down.*

I try to scream but my voice is too muffled.

Ana. They're going to hurt Ana. I know this with the same certainty I know my own name. They're treating me like precious cargo, but I don't think they will do Ana the same courtesy.

A carriage waits a short jaunt down the road. The street is curiously empty as I am carried toward it. The streets of this neighborhood are never this empty, never. Someone has gone to a great deal of trouble to make sure my kidnapping has no witnesses.

The door to the carriage swings open. I glimpse only a sleeve—dark blue, velvet, gold embroidery around the cuff—before I am hauled over the lout's shoulder and into the belly of the carriage. My tailbone hits the floor and the door is slammed shut before I can even attempt to scramble to freedom. The force of it knocks the dirty rag out of my mouth, so that's something to be thankful for at the very least.

"Hello, Kiki."

The sound of that voice makes the skin at the nape of my neck pucker into gooseflesh. I turn, slowly, to see a man sitting there, clad in a fine velvet frock coat of deep blue with a spill of white lace at his throat.

"Hello, Sebastian."

I should have killed him when I had the chance. I should have pulled the trigger when I had Alejandro's pistol pressed to his temple. I would have saved myself so much trouble.

But now, all I can do is sit as upright as I possibly can considering my circumstances. "Would you be a dear and explain to me why I'm being kidnapped?"

It wouldn't do to get spitting mad just yet. I am wearing nothing but a bedsheet and my hands are tied behind my back. And the bedsheet is perilously close to covering more of the carriage floor than my body. To say I lack the upper hand would be an understatement of epic proportions.

Contempt radiates out of Sebastian's eyes. Contempt and perhaps even disappointment? Resentment? Hard to tell.

"You had no plans on following through with the marriage, did you?" He huffs out a breath that is almost a mirthless laugh. "It didn't have to come to this, you know. You could have just done what you were meant to."

I blink at him. "Is that what this is about?" A laugh bubbles up from deep within me, jostling the bedsheet into an even more precarious position. Sebastian will get more than an eyeful soon at this rate. "Sebastian, you're the viceroy's son. You can have any girl you wanted. Why go to the trouble of kidnapping me?"

He shakes his head ruefully, rubbing at his jaw with impatience. "It was never about you, Eustaquia. Trust me, you weren't my pick either."

"Then whose pick was I?"

He seems to have realized that he's walked into an area of conversation that is somehow verboten. A knock on the carriage door spares him from having to answer.

Sebastian grabs me under the arms and yanks me out of the way of another body being unceremoniously tossed into the carriage. Red hair cascades against the floor as a head thunks against the boards.

"Ana!"

Now, *she* is spitting mad. She spares me enough of a glance to ascertain that I am in one piece before she lashes out, kicking at the delicate bits of the man who chucked her in here. He crawls in after her, grabbing her ankles with his too big meaty hands.

"Get your goddamn hands off me," she shouts.

Something cold and sharp presses into the skin of my throat. I don't see the knife, but Ana does. She goes still, as still as stone.

"Don't you fucking dare."

"I won't." Sebastian's voice is infuriatingly calm. "So long as you both behave."

Then, like a gentleman, he tugs the bedsheet higher over my nearly exposed chest with the hand that isn't holding the knife to my throat.

Ana's nostrils flare, but she behaves.

"Are you hurt?" Ana asks softly, not daring to draw her eyes away from the blade.

"Only my pride," I say.

"Good thing you have more than your fair share, then."

"Indeed."

Sebastian huffs. "One more word out of either one of you, and I'll slit your throat on principle."

Ana's jaw ticks with the force of her clenching it.

"Sebastian," I venture, trusting that his threat runs only so deep.

He wouldn't go through all the trouble of kidnapping me just to slay me in the carriage. "I think you'd make a really shitty husband."

He digs the knife in a little deeper, just deep enough to ever so slightly nick the skin, and that is the last thing I say as the carriage begins to trundle on into the night.

# CHAPTER 36

*Ana*

*Don't get Kiki hurt.*

I repeat those words over and over in my head as the carriage jumps and jerks over uneven terrain. The prick who grabbed me at the tavern has a musket on his lap, its barrel pointed in my direction. He knows I'd be trouble if given the chance.

But I wouldn't do anything to hurt Kiki. And hurting him would hurt Kiki. Because Sebastian—that smug bastard I knew was no good from the goddamn start—still has that knife in his hand. His arm is around Kiki's shoulders, the knife held nonchalantly by her neck. With her hands tied behind her back, there's not much she can do. They have us arrayed against each other. If I try anything, Kiki gets hurt. If Kiki tries anything, I get killed.

I'd hate to call any of these assholes smart, but they are. They know us well enough to understand that our first priority has always been each other.

The carriage hits a divot in the road and lurches to one side. The curtains sway open, giving me my first glance outside since we left. A dusky blue sky, brighter toward the horizon as if it has been dipped in honey, lit up by the lights of the bustling city below. So we're leaving Potosí. Not a good sign.

Kiki must see it too. "Ana—"

Her words are stolen by the tightening of Sebastian's arm around her neck. The dagger presses against her skin, not quite hard enough to draw blood, but hard enough to indent.

*I am going to kill him.*

The thought sings through me with the clarity of lightning scarring the night sky. It is not an abstraction. It is not hyperbole. It is a certainty. He has put his hands on her, and now, he will die.

"Where are you taking us?" Kiki asks. Softly. Cautiously.

"You'll see," Sebastian replies.

I want to punch him in the face so badly, my knuckles are tingling with anticipation. But not yet. Not yet.

Kiki catches my gaze and holds it. *We'll get through this* those eyes say. *We just need to bide our time, but we will get through this.*

Drawing in a steadying breath, I offer her the shallowest of nods back.

I don't have faith in much, but I do have faith in her. And that will make all the difference. They may think they have us right where they want us, but soon enough, they will learn that they don't. Not even a little bit.

• ● •

Eventually, the carriage rolls to a bumpy stop on what feels like a dirt road.

"Oh, good," I say. "I was just about to ask if we could stop for a piss break."

Kiki sighs. "Ana."

Musket man holds said musket up, looking for all the world like he really, really, really wants to use it.

"Right. Silence or death. Got it."

"Christ, you really are something else, aren't you?" Sebastian asks.

"Took you this long to figure that out?"

Rolling his eyes, Sebastian slips his knife back into the holster it emerged from, hidden beneath the depths of his coat. He wraps a hand around Kiki's bare arm and fixes her with a hard stare. "Try anything and she dies."

Kiki's breath stutters on the exhale, but she nods.

Sebastian turns to me. "Try anything and—"

"You're not going to kill Kiki." Yeah, yeah, silence or death. But I know he won't. Why go through all this trouble just to murder his fiancée by the side of the road?

"No. Her death would be a tragedy. Yours would be collateral." The corner of his lip ticks upward, as if considering a smile. "But how do you think our poor Eustaquia would feel if she had to watch a musket ball blow half your skull into the dirt?"

A dirty tactic, but an effective one. "Fuck you, Sebastian."

"You will never know the pleasure. Come on."

With that, he pounds on the side of the carriage. A coachman is there to open the door, and Sebastian yanks Kiki through it, heedless of her undressed—and unshod—state.

Musket man grunts at me. "Move."

"Fuck you too." But I do as he says, and I move.

I'm going to figure something out. We're going to get out of this. Just—not yet.

• ◉ •

We are marched through the woods. Kiki maintains a steady stream of complaining about her poor delicate lady feet. Sebastian grits his teeth and bears it because there's really nothing else he can do about it.

I love this woman more than I can say. Here we are, trudging on to some unknown doom, and she's finding any way she can to make the lives of the men forcing us into it as miserable as possible. That's my girl.

Musket man stays close behind me, weapon trained at my back. If shot from this angle, a good chunk of my body would paint the earth with blood and bones. I would like to avoid that, if at all possible.

Eventually, a dark hulk of a building rises up over the tree line.

"What is that?" Kiki asks.

"An old church," Sebastian says, oddly helpful. I think he's just glad she stopped complaining. "Built by some of the first missionaries to set foot in Peru."

"It looks rather worse for wear, don't you think?"

The closer we get, the more accurate Kiki's assessment becomes. It is not a church so much as a ruin. There is no glass in the windows. Half the gables have collapsed at least partially. The faces of the stone saints carved into the alcoves above the door have been weathered by age and elements.

"The mission was abandoned soon after it was completed. Everything was left where it stood. Food was left to rot in bowls. They say it was natives."

"Of course they do," Kiki says. "When in doubt, blame the locals, isn't that right? That's how this works. We swan in, steal their land, and blame them for everything that goes wrong on it."

Those are my words coming out of Kiki's mouth.

Sebastian scoffs. "You say that as if you weren't living off that same land, eating its fruits, and luxuriating in its riches."

He's not wrong.

"It's had several uses over the years. The king's army used it as storeroom for their artillery but they abandoned it. Haunted, they said. They left all their things here, same as the missionaries. And now, it is ours."

When we reach the doors—their wooden planks rotting—Sebastian pauses. Then, he turns to Kiki, looking slightly less smug than he did in the carriage. "When we get inside, don't be smart."

"Impossible," Kiki says. "My intelligence knows no bounds."

I snort out an aborted laugh and am rewarded with the muzzle of a gun jammed into my back.

Sebastian's expression hardens. "You're no good to me dead."

"Truly selfless of you."

"And despite what you may think, you are not indispensable. Powerful men will find a way to take what they want, regardless of your willing participation." He cocks his head to the side, studying her. "Your consent is not required for what is about to happen."

My blood turns into molten lava in my veins.

"If you so much as touch her—"

The musket is rammed into my spine once more, harder this time. I stumble forward, saved from a fall by the meaty hand that wraps around my upper arm, holding me upright.

"And you." Sebastian shoots me a withering glare. "You'll find out just how useful you are soon enough."

With Kiki's arm in his grasp, he pulls her forward into the belly of this rotting mission. I follow after, vowing to cut his hands off at the wrist and shove them so far up his ass he'll be able to play his own teeth like a harpsichord.

❖ ◉ ❖

Heavy iron braziers hang from the vaulted ceiling, cold and unlit. Candles line the center aisle of the church, sitting in pools of wax that spill over broken stones. The shadows move, dancing in the flickering glow of the burning candles. Barrels of what smells an awful lot like gunpowder are stacked in the corner. Racks of rusting armaments line the walls, remnants of the old artillery storage.

"Dearly beloved," intones a voice as dark and deep as the shadows in the nave. "So nice of you to join us."

A man steps out of the darkness, his face half-lit by the lantern he holds.

*Cristobal.*

"What is a wedding without the bride and the groom?" His cold gaze moves from Sebastian and Kiki to settle on me. He smiles. "And a witness."

Now that we are close to the altar, I can make out what's on it. A dagger, long and wickedly curved at the end. There is a symbol carved into the hilt. Something cold and heavy settles in my gut.

It is the same symbol that had been carved into Alejandro's flesh. Into Juana's—I mean, Sister Catalina's back.

Cristobal caresses the handle of the dagger resting on the altar. The blade is clean, but I have a sneaking suspicion that sharp edge is for more than just show.

"This is my sacred space," Cristobal says. There is genuine reverence in this tone, and that is perhaps the scariest part of this all. He lights a brazier to the side of the altar, filling the room with warm light. "This is where I like to do my work."

"Work?" I try to scoff, but the sound comes out more strangled than incredulous. I am scared out of my goddamn mind. This man is insane. Well and truly insane. "Is that what you call your butchery?"

Cristobal huffs a small, mirthless laugh. Good. If I amuse him, maybe he won't use that dagger to slit my neck. Bile rises high in my throat. That we are standing in the place where he tortured those girls sends a chill up my spine.

"There is beauty in pain," he says. "There is ecstasy in death. Agony can be most exquisite when delivered by the right hands."

"Has anyone ever told you that you're one depraved son of a bitch?"

My fear is great, but, as it turns out, my horror is even greater.

The coachmen who ferried us here disappears through one of the shadowed alcoves. I crane my neck to see something, anything, but all I see is darkness.

"What is he doing?" Kiki asks. "Where is he going?"

"Will you shut up?" Sebastian hisses at her through clenched teeth.

"I will not."

A door opens somewhere deep in shadow. Light spills through the opening, piercing the black with a soft amber glow. The coachman enters, a lantern held high. Two figures trail behind him. One I recognize immediately as the goddamn archbishop of Peru, but the identity of the second person is obscured by a dark hooded cloak. I knew these assholes had friends in high places, but damn. The archbishop. That's almost impressive.

"You're late," Cristobal says, voice oddly flat. There is no emotion to it at all.

"You're lucky I'm here at all." The archbishop's gaze skitters across the motley group gathered before him. His tone is carefully sniping, but judging from the white-knuckled grip he has on the leather-bound books clutched to chest, he's as scared shitless as I am.

"And you're lucky I keep my mouth shut when it comes to your, shall we say, proclivities," Cristobal counters. "Though if you would rather have no part in these proceedings, I'm sure Rome would love to hear of your little . . . experiments."

Kiki pulls her eyes from Cristobal and glares at the archbishop. I'm pretty sure this is the same man who baptized her as an infant. And now, here he is, ready to marry her off under the watchful eye—and at the direction of—a sadistic murderer. "What experiments?"

His face blanches. Cristobal chuckles.

"Trust me," Cristobal says, "the less you know of that, the better. Such details are unfit for a lady's ears."

The cloaked figure, a woman by the shape of her, carries a bundle of white fabric in her arms. She approaches us, and there is something familiar about her gait.

She unties Kiki's hands so she can slip the bundle of cloth over her head. It's a white shift of delicate lace. "Isn't that better, dear?"

The ground feels like it cracks open beneath my feet. I know that voice. I know that woman.

She saved my life, once upon a time. I hated her, and I loved her in equal measure. I would be dead without her. And now, I might die because of her.

"Esmeralda?"

Hands rise up to push back the cloak, carefully negotiating the fabric around the elaborate curls of her hair. She smiles at me, the same as she ever did.

"Hello, mija."

It's that last word that breaks something inside of me. *Daughter.* She started calling me that after she pulled me from the flames. After she cast the woman who birthed me onto the street.

"Every wedding needs a woman's touch," Cristobal says lightly, as if this is all a game to him. She brought the dress, but that's not the only reason she's here, I realize. The thing that sick bastard loves most is pain. And this . . . this hurts.

"You have to be fucking kidding me."

She has the audacity to shrug. "We all do what we must to survive, mija."

"Don't call me that. You called us all that. You called Rosalita that and you—"

It all becomes clear to me in an excruciating moment.

"It was you, wasn't it? You handed her over to them"—I jerk my chin in the direction of Cristobal—"and for what? Money?" My voice rises with each word. "Power? What?"

"Silver is the language of this city," Esmeralda says. "Of this world."

I spit in her direction. Sadly, my spittle lands a few feet short. "You're a monster."

"I was a mother to that girl," Esmeralda hisses. "And how does she repay me? By running off to be some nobleman's whore?" She shakes her head. "That foolish girl should have known better than to aim so high. The Sonza boy would have dropped her the second he grew bored." \

I lunge at her, musket be damned.

"Don't shoot her, you fool!" Cristobal hollers, his voice bouncing off the mission's walls. Can't have that. He needs me alive. I am the only thing guaranteeing Kiki's obedience in this charade. Kill me, and he loses the best card in his hand.

Musket man hesitates. It's just for a second, but that's all I need. My hands may be tied but I've still got my feet. I rear up, kicking out. My boot collides with Esmeralda's chin, knocking her backward. The archbishop scampers to the rear of the church, Bible clutched tightly to his chest, eager to get out of the way of any contagious violence.

Esmeralda sags forward, moaning as she clutches her jaw. I press her against the wall, my forearm pinning her neck in place. When she tries to swallow, I press down harder.

"Please, mija—"

"Don't call me that. Don't you *fucking* dare."

"Enough!" Cristobal's voice ricochets like cannon fire. "Seize her!"

"Seize her?" I bark out a jagged laugh. "Who talks like that?"

They are not very clever words. They might also be my last.

Kiki's shout is the only warning I have before something slams into me from behind. My head throbs with the impact, and my vision goes dark.

# CHAPTER 37

*Kiki*

Sebastian holds me back as I watch Cristobal's hired muscle—the one with the musket—toss Ana's limp body over his shoulder. I fight with everything I have, but Sebastian has me beat on height and weight and sheer strength. Unarmed and barefoot, I do not stand much of a chance. But still I try, futile as my efforts are.

"The more you struggle," he says into my ear, "the worse this will be."

"Why are you doing this? Why are you helping him?" I angle my face to try to catch his gaze. His eyes dart away from mine, but not before I see something potent flash through them. Shame. "This isn't who you are, Sebastian."

"You don't know who I am."

What I am about to say is a risk, but now is the time for risks. "I know what you did. Mother Ines sends her regards."

His eyes widen. His breath goes shallow.

Cristobal watches us, flint gaze steady. "And who, pray tell, is Mother Ines?"

Sebastian opens his mouth—to say what, I don't know. What I do know is that if Cristobal learns that Sebastian left a loose end at a convent deep in the mountains, he will not survive the night. I don't want him dead. Not yet. Not until I know he is deserving of such a fate.

"A nun who taught us catechism when we were children." The lie rolls off my tongue with astonishing ease, cutting off whatever Sebastian was about to say. "He used to help her give alms to the poor, though I am fairly convinced he was forced to do so. She always thought Sebastian was capable of being a decent man, a fact of which I remain unconvinced."

Cristobal holds my gaze for a moment longer. But then, he shrugs. "Decency is overrated."

I can feel a sliver of tension bleed out of Sebastian. He doesn't quite sag against me, but it is a near thing. My only hope is that Cristobal does not notice.

"I have one question though, Marquis, if you would be so kind to answer it."

Cristobal looks at me, bemused, I think, at the politeness of my speech. It is as false as the tale I just spun about Mother Ines of course, but if my upbringing instilled in me one thing, it was how to remain calm in a crisis. "Go on."

"Why Alejandro? Why did you kill him? Why did he have to die?"

"Simple. He was in my way."

But there is something in the way he answers that seems too ready. Too rehearsed. The nonchalant shrug seems artificial.

I shake my head. Sebastian tightens his grip on me, hard enough for it to hurt. I don't care. I am this close to answers and I will have them. My pain is a small price to pay. "Maybe. You can get to the Sonza fortune through me so long as I am married to a spineless coward like Sebastian"—he stiffens against me—"but if it was just about that, you could have done it quietly. People, even the rich ones, fall afoul of the dark alleys of Potosí all the time. You could have made it look like a simple robbery turned tragically violent. But you made an example of him. Left his body there for anyone to see."

The skin around Cristobal's eyes tightens ever so subtly, but it's there. His tell.

"He found out about you, didn't he? He could—he would—expose you for the devil you are. And so you had to kill him."

Fury flashes across Cristobal's face like lightning across a storm-ridden sky. There and gone in a flash. There it is. A crack in the armor. Good. I want him off-balance. He is more likely to make a mistake I can use to my advantage that way.

"But," I continue because, at this point, I cannot stop myself, "how? How did he know?"

The smile that crawls across Cristobal's lips is laced with venom. "Why don't you ask your betrothed?"

The words crack through me like a musket ball. His grip on me loosens just enough for me to angle toward him. To look him in the eye. "Sebastian?"

He swallows thickly, shaking his head. "It doesn't matter now."

"It matters to me."

Cristobal paces around the altar, the heels of his boots clicking loudly against the cracked stone floor. "Our Sebastian learned a thing or two about loyalty on the night of the viceroy's ball."

Sebastian shakes his head, the movement too fast, too jerky. "I didn't mean to. I was drunk. I saw the girl, her body. There was so much blood. So much."

"Didn't mean to what?" My voice cracks halfway through the question.

When Sebastian fails to answer me, Cristobal does it for him. "It was an accident, of course, divulging what he knew about me. About my arrangement with the viceroy. But, you see, as with any accident, it had to be cleaned up."

"It was you." Of course. The picture crystallizes before me. The viceroy's astronomical rise from the second son of a minor noble house to the most powerful seat in New Spain. Cristobal put him there. And in exchange, the viceroy provided him with access. Hunting grounds. The protection that came with the title of Viceroy of Peru without any of the scrutiny.

"I made Sebastian's family." Cristobal looks past me, the cold steel of his gaze fixated on Sebastian. "And I can just as easily unmake them."

"You were scared." My own gaze is on Cristobal, but my words are for Sebastian. "You saw something you shouldn't have. You tried to forget, tried to drink it away, but you couldn't. You couldn't carry it alone. You had to tell someone."

And the person with whom he shared his burden was my brother. My Alejandro. Always ready with a kind word and a ready ear. Always there to listen when you needed it the most.

I rear my head back. Sebastian is not quite fast enough to avoid having my skull smash into his nose. His grip loosens but not enough. Before I can wriggle free, he tightens both arms around mine. Warm droplets of blood drop from his nose onto my shoulder.

"Younph binch," Sebastian says, or rather, attempts to say.

"Come again?" I inject so much sugary sweetness in my voice that my own teeth hurt. It is better than rage. More manageable than my fury. As angry as I am, I need to keep my wits about me. There will be a time later for mourning, for digesting these revelations. But Alejandro is dead. I cannot save him. Ana though. Ana is alive. And she needs me. "I couldn't understand you around that mouthful of blood."

Cristobal sighs. "I'm surrounded by fools and children."

"Need I remind you," I venture, never taking my eyes off of Ana's disturbingly prone form. "That not a single one of us wanted to be here. Not even Sebastian. He's only here because he's a coward and more afraid of you than he is of me." I angle my head back to catch Sebastian's eye, only for a brief moment. "A mistake he will come to regret."

The brute lays Ana out on the altar, stretching her hands and feet to the ends, where he loops heavy leather bindings around her wrists and ankles.

"Don't do this." I try to wrench myself free of Sebastian's hold, but all I manage to do is tear open the wound on my side. Blood seeps through the bandages Ana had so lovingly wrapped around me, staining the white shift they have the audacity to call a wedding dress crimson. "I will give you anything you want, just don't hurt her. Please."

"Anything I want?" Cristobal laughs as he rounds the altar, athame in hand. "I am on the precipice of all that I could want and more. The Sonza contracts will open trade to me—to us. We will have unmitigated access to the English, Dutch, and French colonies to the north. The west of Africa. The Mediterranean. All of it will be ours. And all you have to do is be a good girl and watch."

Of course. It makes sense. If he wants my father's shipping routes, he has to go through me. Or through my husband. If he controls them himself, it would be far too suspicious. But if they passed to my husband with me as nothing but a mere conduit, then no one would question a thing. Just as no one has questioned his place in society or indeed paid him any mind. That is his strategy, and it has worked for him thus far. He takes obliquely. Never drawing attention. Never stepping into the light. Remaining in the shadows, amassing wealth and power and satisfying his twisted cravings.

"You're sick," I spit out.

Cristobal shrugs. "Perhaps."

He sets a dagger down on the altar, right beside Ana's head as if to taunt her. He moves to the brazier by the altar. A set of iron pokers stand in a cage beside it, and he reaches for one. He holds it up to the light to examine it. Or rather, to let me examine it.

It is not a poker.

It is a brand. A crest. The very same one carved into my brother's flesh.

"It's beautiful, isn't it?" He caresses the end of the brand with such tenderness that I want to vomit. "It will leave the loveliest mark on that freckled skin of hers."

"Don't you dare!" I fight Sebastian with all my strength as Cristobal plunges the brand into the flames. When it emerges, the end of it is angry and red. My bare feet slip over the cold stone floor, slick now with blood, both mine and Sebastian's. "Don't you dare hurt her."

"Oh, I won't." Cristobal offers the brand to Sebastian. "But he will."

Sebastian swallows thickly as he reaches for the brand. It sits awkwardly in his hand, as if he's never held one before. He probably hasn't.

"Why?" I ask. I don't know what else to say. This is too much. Too vile. Too evil.

"Sebastian still has something left to prove to me," Cristobal says. "If he wants to reap the bountiful rewards I can offer, I need to know that he can be trusted." Cristobal traces a finger down the Ana's jawline. I may be hallucinating but I think I see her eyelashes flutter ever so slightly at the contact. "I need to know the boy has skin in the game."

Cristobal beckons Sebastian forward.

Sebastian transfers his hold on me to the man with the musket and approaches the altar. I wonder if that is hesitation in his gait or if I only hope it is.

But regardless, Sebastian wraps both hands around the brand. Raises it toward Ana's unprotected flesh.

Then, he stops.

"What are you waiting for?" Cristobal asks. "Are you a boy? Or a man? Do it."

I know what he is waiting for. Sebastian has never dirtied his own hands. Has never sullied them with someone else's blood. He has scuffled, like many a young man, but true violence? He is of the lot who pays other people to commit it for them.

Sebastian's Adam's apple bobs as he swallows thickly. The brand quivers in his hands.

"Oh, for Christ's sake—" Cristobal snatches the brand away from Sebastian, his lust for violence outweighing his patience.

On the altar, Ana groans as she begins to rouse. When she catches sight of the fire, and the brand, her eyes widen.

I thought I had seen Ana afraid before. As much as she denies it, she is deathly scared of spiders. She has nearly flown across a room when she sees one. I've always found it charming in its own way, that this girl with such a rough-and-tumble childhood would be so frightened of one of God's smallest creatures, but there is nothing charming about her fear now.

Now, her fear is raw and naked. Terror widens her eyes as she pulls at the leather bonds holding her to the altar. She shakes her head, mumbling *no* over and over and over again.

Until the brand touches her skin and that *no* becomes a scream.

The sound of that scream burns through me, leaving nothing but white-hot fury in its wake.

If I were to attempt to recount what happens next, I would surely fail. The experience happens as a series of sensations. The heel of my foot slamming into the musket man's instep with enough force that I am fairly certain bone cracks. My other foot catches his knee, shattering the bone. The sharp sting of his nails biting into my skin as his hands scrabble for purchase. Uselessly. I break free of him, diving for the man holding the brand. Cristobal. Nothing else matters outside of him and me and Ana, screaming in agony still as the scent of burning flesh fills the air.

I slam into Cristobal with all my weight. The brand clatters from his hand onto the floor skittering away from where we fall. Sebastian scuttles to the side, tripping over his own feet, as cowardly as I knew he would be. He is not a fighter. I am. And evidently, so is Cristobal. He thrashes against me, unleashing a barrage of curses, as we both scrabble for the brand. Except I get it first.

I swing the iron rod as hard as I can. It connects with the side of his face, the blow reverberating up through my arms. The sizzling stench of his freshly burned skin makes me gag.

He falls down like a sack of bricks. Finally, blessed quiet. The archbishop runs then, skittering into the shadows like the cockroach he is. The door slams shut in his wake. He is the least of my concerns now. When this is over, we will hunt him down. We will put an end to whatever nefarious acts he's committed that Cristobal has hidden from sight.

Movement in the corner catches my eye, pulling my attention away from Cristobal's still form. I whip my head around to find Sebastian pushing himself up against the wall. There is honest fear on his face now. He thought he knew me. He thought he had my measure. But he did not. Not even close. Now he knows what I am capable of. Now he knows what I will do.

I stand on trembling legs, flinging the iron brand as far away as it will go. My hands are still slick with blood as I work loose Ana's bonds. She is shaking even more than I, but the overwhelming terror has fled.

"Holy shit, Kiki." She says it over and over again. "You're incredible. Goddamn incredible."

When she is free, I help her slide off the altar, though I'm not sure how much help I truly am. Without the tide of rage flowing through me, my strength feels like it's rapidly depleting. It's like I've used up all the reserves God has allotted to me for several lifetimes. I don't much care. All that matters to me is that she is alive. Burnt and bloodied and bruised but alive.

Danger be damned. I press my lips to hers in a rough kiss. It is short, but no less sweet for its brevity.

A hysterical laugh rises from Sebastian where he's standing, staring at the chaos that surrounds us. "Unbelievable." He buries his face in his hands and laughs and laughs and laughs.

"What the hell do you find so funny?" Ana asks, and that's how I know she's going to be okay. She plucks one of the least rusted-looking swords from the nearest rack. Weapons are good. We like weapons.

"Is that why you hated me so much? Were you jealous? Is that it?" Laughter, low and manic, rumbles in his chest. He's cracking under the weight of all of this. "Wanted her all to yourself, did you?"

He is so focused on Ana that he doesn't notice me leaning down to pick up the dagger. The same one he threatened me with in the carriage. It had fallen in the scuffle, and now, it's mine.

But he sure as hell notices it when I brandish it right in his fucking face.

Shaking my head, I tell him what I should have said to him from the very beginning. "You could never have me, Sebastian. Not now. Not ever. Not if the sun rose in the west and Christ himself walked the earth and demanded it so."

I smile at him, bare blade burnished gold in the firelight. He flinches.

*Good.*

"Ana is mine." Each word rolls of my tongue. Slow. Deliberate. I don't take my eyes off him as I say them, though a part of me desperately wants to. But I don't need to look at Ana to know that the wicked grin on my face is matched on hers.

The tip of my blade traces the line of Sebastian's jaw. That perfect jaw. So perfect, it would make sculptors weep.

"Ana is mine." It's a phrase worth repeating. "And I am hers."

I bring the dagger down on Sebastian's perfect face.

Perfect no more.

He yowls like a cat that's just lost a fight, hands flying up to his bloodied face. He is lucky if all he leaves with today is a scar. I should kill him. I really ought to.

But already, there has been so much death.

And selfishly, I want him to live. I want him to know that he lost. That I won. That—

"Foolish girl."

I whirl in place, dagger coming up, but it's too late. Ana has crossed the room to get her sword back, and Cristobal had been left unwatched. Unattended. But not unarmed.

The iron poker slams into the side of my face so hard I know for certain something breaks.

My knees go out from under me. A boot connects with my side, right where the bloodied shift signals my weakest point. Gasping in agony, I fall backward, my head smacking into the stone floor.

A scream tears through me as Cristobal steps on my wrist. The pressure forces my fingers to twitch open, releasing my hold on the dagger. I am spared a collection of broken bones when Cristobal removes his boot from my arm long enough to go to one knee and pick up the blade.

"I was willing to let you live, you know," he says, staring down at me as he levels the dagger's point at my face. "Not her." He jerks his chin toward Ana. She is frozen on the other side of the altar, sword in hand but too far to use it. "Not after she served her purpose. But now, I'm afraid you've proven yourself entirely too troublesome to be allowed to live." He shakes his head, almost mournful. "You could have had it all, Eustaquia. It's always a shame to see potential squandered."

A mirthless smile stretches across his face. "I'll simply have to find another way to get what I want. I always do, in the end." And with that, he raises the blade.

# CHAPTER 38

*Ana*

"Wait!"

Cristobal actually does wait, quirking one eyebrow at me, dagger held aloft, ready to deliver a killing blow. The brand burned on the side of his cheek is lurid in the dim light.

"Wait?" Cristobal actually smiles. "Whatever for?"

God, this asshole really loves the sound of his own voice. But I can work with that.

"Wasn't this your grand plan?" I ask. "Marrying Kiki off to one of your sycophants to get your hands on her fortune? If that's the case, it seems a bit of a waste to kill her now, don't you think?"

With a pained groan, Kiki manages a short, "Thanks, Ana."

Cristobal snorts indelicately. "I have all the wealth a man could need. I could spend a mountain of it every day and never burn through to the end." He twirls the dagger around, admiring the way the blade catches the amber glow of torchlight. "I will find another girl. There's always another."

Cristobal punctuates this statement with a worrisome thrust of his dagger in Kiki's direction.

I don't like that. I don't like that one bit.

His attention needs diverting. Slowly, I get one foot under me and begin to raise myself to standing. I hold my sword out and away from my body to show that I do not mean to use it.

Not right now anyway.

"Drop it," he commands.

I don't like it, but I do. My sword clatters to hard stone.

"There's one thing I don't understand." I'm pushing my luck with him. I can feel it. But words are the only weapon I have right now. Deploying them wisely might be the only thing keeping me and Kiki alive. "Why invite us to the ball?"

"Isn't it obvious?" He sighs, as if disappointed I'm not following his brilliant strategy. "I was going to take sweet Eustaquia there, but the two of you proved more slippery than I expected."

I snicker. "Fucked up your plans, did we?"

Cristobal actually smiles like he's enjoying himself, as he stands to face me. "To your credit, you do keep things interesting."

I take another step forward. So does he. Our eyes are locked.

"One last question, if you'll indulge me."

Like I thought, he loves the sound of his own voice. Too much to deny my request. "I'll allow it."

"Why the brand?"

He shrugs one shoulder. The gesture is elegant, at odds with his depravity. "A great artist always signs his work."

I want to vomit. Instead, I take one final step toward Cristobal. He does the same.

Now, we are an arm's length apart. He raises the sword. I step forward, right into its path. The tip of the blade rests against the hollow of my throat. He could kill me now if he so chose.

But where would be the fun in that?

Men like him like it when you fight. They like it when you struggle. They like it best when you lose.

"This is my favorite part." He leans close, digging the knife's point into my flesh hard enough to cause a bead of blood to well up against it. "The start of the dance. I always like the ones with fire in their eyes the best. There's nothing quite like bleeding that fire out of one's toys."

I lean in, as close as I dare, heedless of the pain. Something flashes through his eyes. Anticipation. Pleasure, even. Little does he know that this is the last time he will ever feel such a thing. The last time he will ever feel anything. "I am not your plaything. And neither is *she*."

Cristobal turns but far too late.

By the time he spins, Kiki is standing behind him, the barrel of the musket aimed squarely at his chest.

"This," she says, voice low and dangerous, "is for my brother."

And with that, she pulls the trigger.

Blood blossoms crimson against the pure white of his shirt. He stares down at the expanding stain as if it offends him.

And it should.

Slowly, he collapses to his knees, his outstretched hands opening and closing into impotent fists as he slumps forward.

I step back to avoid the spreading pool of blood. It is oddly hypnotic to watch it grow larger and larger as his heart pumps out the last bits of his life's blood onto the cold stone floor.

The sound of metal clattering against that very same stone forces my eyes away from Cristobal's final labored breaths. It is the musket, dropped to the ground, as if its weight had simply become too great to bear.

Kiki's arm lowers by inches, slow, gradual. Where I expected to see triumph, there is only a blank sort of resignation.

"It's done," she says softly, more to herself than anyone else.

I nod, stepping over Cristobal's dying body to approach her. "Yes."

She nods dully. Her eyes are distant like she isn't seeing what's right in front of her. And when she speaks, her words are not meant for me.

"I did it, Ale." She squeezes her eyes shut. "He's dead. You can rest now."

I reach for Kiki. Nothing exists for me in this moment than her. Her pain. Her loss. And now, her triumph, if you can call it that.

That was my first mistake.

When Kiki opens her eyes, they settle on something behind me. Then, her eyes go wide.

I turn, but I can already tell I'm going to be too slow.

Sebastian is on his knees, his hand wrapped around a musket.

And it is pointed, not at me, but at Kiki.

His face twists into a panicked rictus. It takes less than a second for me to realize what he is doing and why.

What we know, what we have seen, will destroy him. It will destroy his father. His family.

"You should have just done what he wanted."

Time slows, passing thick and viscous, as if we were all suspended in deep water.

I lunge for him.

I am not faster than a speeding bullet.

But I just need to be faster than a wounded man's twitching finger.

But I am too slow. I put too much distance between us.

The thing about guns is that they're hard to control. Once that trigger is pulled, that's it. That particular mechanism of violence is a bell that cannot be unrung.

And so, the gun goes off, releasing a tiny steel ball of death into the room.

Directly at the stockpile of gunpowder in the corner.

I have a moment to comprehend just how fucked we are before the world erupts in hellfire.

# CHAPTER 39

*Kiki*

The funeral is an understated affair.

A simple mass in the church, a homily delivered by a priest who was always kind to all, be they poor and downtrodden or affluent and privileged. We are all God's children, saints and sinners alike. We are the only mourners in attendance. That was part of the deal. Too much attention being drawn to an event of this nature would invite far too many questions. Though a part of me rails at the injustice— this is a life that should be celebrated above all others—another part of me is shamefully grateful. I never wanted my mourning to be public. My grief is mine. These sorrows are ours. This hardship is not one I ever wanted to perform for the benefit of others.

But even then, I am not alone.

Ana's presence is a subtle, comforting weight at my side. Every touch still hurts, but I relish this pain. Every bruise, every scar, every still-angry wound is a reminder that I am alive. That we are alive. Despite the best efforts of evil men, we survived. The gunpowder went up in a conflagration of holy fire, as if the angels above had finally seen fit to lay waste to the corruption that had taken root in our city. Every time I close my eyes, I see it. The spark of gunpowder igniting. The searing flash of light as it went up so quickly my brain couldn't quite follow what was happening until it was too late. The ceiling collapsing inward. Thankfully, only a part of it. But in the seconds before I caught sight of Ana's shock of red hair among the rubble, before I knew she was okay, that she was alive, I had a revelation. A life without her is not a life worth living. She is more than my friend. She is a piece of my soul, lost for so long, until God saw fit to bring her back to me. And I think that is what I am to her. I hope that is what I am to her.

Cristobal's body was crushed under the debris. His face was left nearly unrecognizable, but one cold gray eye remained, open and unseeing. I watched them carry the body out of the wreckage as Ana held me up. My own injuries were far less severe, but they were enough to make standing a chore. But I had to know. I had to see it with my own eyes. The man who had brought so much evil to this city was dead. There would be other villains, other evils. But this one, at least, was vanquished. Sebastian was wounded too gravely to flee the scene, but Esmeralda, somehow, slipped through the cracks. She is out there somewhere, alive, but now that her protector is gone, she will not dare show her face in Potosí again. The archbishop has sailed back to Spain, reassigned to another diocese, or so the story goes. The Church protects its own, even if they're greedy, amoral scum.

"We'll hunt them down," Ana said. "And we will make them pay."

Of that, I have no doubt.

Now, a persistent drizzle bears down on us as we watch the pallbearers lower Alejandro's coffin into the ground. Finally, he can rest in consecrated ground. The thought doesn't bring nearly as much comfort as I wanted it to. He is still dead. His life was still cut far too short. There was so much good he could have done in the world. So much love he had left to give.

My father weeps silently as the first pile of dirt beats down on the lid of the coffin. He hadn't said much when Ana and I had stumbled back home, battered and burned but alive. He'd thrown his arms around me and held me with a strength I hadn't known his ailing body still possessed, whispering over and over and over, "Thank God. You are alive. Thank God."

God had nothing to do with it, but if the thought brought him comfort, then I would not begrudge him his faith.

Rosalita lays a hand on my father's shoulder. Her own face is pale and drawn, but no tears fall from her eyes. She looks at me and offers me a soft smile. My father pats her hand as he would a daughter. Her past, her life, her profession. None of it seems to matter anymore. At least to this family. If Alejandro could see them now, I know he would be smiling that rakish, beautiful grin of his.

We stand guard and watch until my brother is buried. Ana nudges me gently with her shoulder. "Are you all right?"

Her face is open, raw. Vulnerable. But strong still. Resilient. All the things I aspire to be. When I look at her, I know I cannot lie. "No. I'm not." I take her hand and give it a gentle squeeze. She squeezes back without hesitation. "But I will be."

She nods, but her gaze drifts away, over my shoulder. I follow the line of her sight to find Rosalita drifting away, her black dress—one I gave her for this occasion—stark against the gray light of day. "Do you mind if I talk to Rosalita for a moment?"

"Of course not."

She hesitates, as if weighing something in her mind. Then, she leans in and presses the gentlest of kisses to my cheek. Right here, in the light of day, on sacred ground, in front of God and his Church.

I watch as she follows Rosalita, lays a hand on her arm. They move to a nearby tree for a modicum of cover from the misting rain.

My father and I stand by the grave, the rich brown earth a contrast to the verdant grass beside it.

"I owe you an apology." His voice is low and quiet, but steady. His eyes are riveted to the grave still, as if through sheer force of will he could resurrect his son.

"Papa, you don't have—"

"I do." He turns to look at me then, grizzled brows drawn. There is a surety to his expression that I have not seen in quite some time. "I was wrong. I should have listened to you, and I didn't. If I had, perhaps—" He sighs, rubbing a hand against his closed eyelids. "I could have done more. I could have helped you. But I left you and Ana to fight alone against a pack of wolves."

"We handled them well enough, I should say."

"You nearly died."

I breathe steadily. "I know."

My father shakes his head, tightening one hand on the head of his cane. "I could not bear losing you, Eustaquia—"

"Kiki."

That earns me a small, tired smile. For the first time in weeks, he looks like my father again.

"Indeed. Kiki. You are exactly who you mean to be. And from now on, I will do better to honor that."

"I—thank you, Papa."

And, as if I were still a little girl, I throw my arms around him and we embrace. That pipe-smoke scent I always think of as his envelops me in its warmth.

"I'm so proud of you, Kiki. And I know Alejandro would be too."

For the first time today, it is not grief that makes tears well up in my eyes but love.

## Ana

Rosalita cuts a striking figure in her mourning gown. It is the finest in Kiki's collection, freshly dyed black to suit the occasion. When Kiki had presented it to her, Rosalita had attempted to demure, but it took a handful of words to accept.

"It was a gift," Kiki said. "From my brother. He picked it out himself the last time he was in Paris. And I want you to have it."

She meant every word, and I think she was right. And it seemed to comfort Rosalita, to have this one thing today that Alejandro's hands had touched.

We stand under the tree, a great big old one that has watched over these grounds long before the Catholics claimed it as their own. She clutches a kerchief in hand, a beautiful one edged in lace, but she has yet to use it. Her eyes have remained dry from the first word the priest spoke.

"What will you do now?" I ask her.

With a shaky little sigh, Rosalita folds up the kerchief with care. "Get back to it, I suppose."

"What do you mean? Back to Esmeralda's?"

At the mention of that rotten woman's name, Rosalita's face

hardens. Gone is the gentle grief and the stoic mourning, replaced by something harder and sharper. Anger, but more than that, strength. "It is Esmeralda's no longer. Haven't you heard? I've taken over."

"I had not." I lean against the trunk of the tree, caring little for how it rucks up the back of my frock coat. I hadn't worn a dress. I hadn't felt like myself in a black gown. Hadn't felt like the Ana that Alejandro knew. And that was who I wanted to be when I said good-bye to him. "You sure it's a good idea?"

Rosalita nods, resolute. "As sure of anything. If the recent past has taught me anything, it's that someone needs to protect those girls. That was Esmeralda's greatest failing. Not her greed or her selfishness or her pride. She had a duty to every soul in her care, and she failed them." She shakes her head, drawing herself upright, the stiff boning of the corset making her look as tall as a giant. "I will not do the same."

"You would never." I feel the corners of my lips twitch up at the thought of how fearsome Rosalita will be. "Any bastard who tries to start trouble under your roof won't know what hit 'em."

"That is my hope." Inclining her head toward the place where Kiki and her father still stand, she says, "Thank you for inviting me."

"I didn't." When she looks at me, perplexed, I add, "Don Carlos de Sonza did."

"What?"

"You heard me. His exact words were, 'My son loved her. Where else should she be if not by his side?'"

Only now do the tears begin to gather on her long lashes. "I—I don't know what to say. Alejandro and I—we had discussed what we would do. Where we would go. Never in a thousand years had either of us dreamed that we would be accepted. That his family—that yours—would allow us to be together."

"Well," I say with a soft snort, "they let me in. How picky could they be?"

It's enough to startle a tiny laugh out of her, which she quickly masks with the kerchief. "Ana!"

Warmth blossoms in my chest at the sound of that laughter, and the sight of her smile. We are family, Rosalita and I. And now, she is one of us. Part of our clan. Our little collection of lost souls has grown by one.

My limbs tingle in a weird but not a bad one. It's like my body is too full of emotion. Sadness, love, joy. It is all there, rumbling under the surface. I don't know what to do with it all, so I do the only thing I can think of.

I pull Rosalita into a tight hug. She stiffens for a moment, and I feel like a fool. Both of us are covered in bruises, but even so, she wraps her arms around me and holds me tight.

"I love you, Ana."

"Love you too, Rosa."

We stand like that for a long time, as the rain begins to ease and the clouds part. The sunlight warms us, washing away the cold, gray light of morning.

# CHAPTER 40

*Kiki*

Dawn is a harsh mistress.

She is not as harsh as the bruises on my ribs, each a different and alarming shade of purple. Nor is she as harsh as the powder burns on my hands or the abrasions on the side of my face, the existence of which I rediscover every time I have the audacity to rest my cheek against my pillow.

Sleep, therefore, has become problematic. And though fatigue has wormed its cruel way deep into my bones, I find that I don't mind quite so much when the view is so nice.

Ana's hair falls across her cheek, the strands rustled with every soft exhalation. Freckles dust the bridge of her nose, darker now than they were at the start of the season. She has spent every night of the past week in my bed, and no one has dared to say one word about it. Being apart from her was untenable. As tired as I am still, I am glad for the sleeplessness my injuries have blessed me with. I don't want to miss another moment of being with Ana. We wasted so much time. All I want is to savor every single second of every single day I get to call her mine.

"You're thinking too loud." Ana's sleepy grumble is soft but irritated. "I can hear it even with my eyes closed."

I rub my smile into my pillow. It hurts, but that tiny bit of pain keeps me from giggling like a madwoman.

"What on earth do your eyes have to do with your hearing?"

A clumsy hand fumbles for my face sleepily, though her fingers are delicate when they graze my lips. There is a tiny cut on the corner of my mouth that Ana has been nothing but solicitous toward. Even when she kisses it. Again and again and again.

"Don't bring your filthy logic into this. I'm sleeping."

"My logic is anything but filthy. It is pristine."

With a huff, Ana rolls over, presumably to escape any further applications of my logic, filthy or otherwise.

But I do not think I am interested in letting her go.

"Just where do you think you're going?"

I follow her deeper into the sheets, wrapping my arm around her waist. She puts up only a token protest, but judging from the grin flirting with her lips, she's not overly perturbed by my disruption of her slumber. Slowly, she unfurls into me, stretching her own arms up and around my neck. Her hands tangle with my hair. It's probably a godawful mess, but I don't care. Well, I might care a little, but I never said I wasn't vain.

"Good morning," she says when our eyes meet. In the wan morning sun, her eyes are a startling green. Like a cat's.

"Even better now that you're awake." I lean into press a kiss to the tip of her nose. She scrunches up her face.

"I hate it when you do that."

"Why?"

"It's too cute. We have a reputation to maintain."

But that doesn't stop her from nuzzling into my space, inserting her nose into the crook of my neck to press her own kiss to the juncture of my shoulder.

"Ah, yes," I say, carding my fingers through her hair. "The Valiant Ladies of Potosí. What a moniker."

"I can't believe that caught on," Ana mumbles into my neck. "Whose fault was that?"

"Santiago's." The feeling of Ana's hair sliding between my fingers is more fascinating than anything I can possibly imagine in this moment.

She nods, but she might also be using me as a scratching post for an itchy nose. I'll allow it.

"Remind me to thank him for it later."

I breathe in and out, allowing myself—*finally*—to relax. Having Ana pressed against me as a warm, pliant weight helps.

All of this feels right and good and true. This is as our lives were always meant to be. And always will be now. There is no marriage looming on the horizon. Sebastian survived the blast but his reputation didn't. Even if my father hadn't broken the betrothal as soon as he learned of what happened in the church, Sebastian himself had been shipped back to the continent in disgrace, removed from his own father's line of succession. It's too good a fate for him. I would much rather he were dead or rotting in a jail cell with all the best and brightest of Potosí, but money still talks louder than justice.

At least I made a lasting impression. He will think of me every time he looks in the mirror and sees his scarred visage staring back at him. It will be a warning for him. You have been marked, that scar will say. You are being watched. Put one foot wrong and not even an ocean between us will stop me from reacquainting you with my blade.

I know that this is what his reflection will say because that is exactly what I said to him when Ana and I showed up to see him off at the docks. Was it petty? Absolutely. But he is lucky to still be alive. He is the reason my brother was killed. The least he deserves is my pettiness.

"I'm hungry," Ana mumbles into my neck. Her lips tickle, making me squirm in her embrace.

As if summoned by some dark magic, Magdalena throws the door to my bedchamber open and sweeps into the room, arms laden with a silver tray. "Breakfast, my lady."

She doesn't bat an eye to see Ana and I curled up together. She's one of the few people who knows the full story. I trusted her with the truth, all of it. She and her cousin exchange letters weekly now. Juana—Sister Catalina, rather—even sends her drawings. Beautiful landscapes and towering cities full of silver and hope.

"Oh, food." Ana pushes away from me with an insulting amount of alacrity.

I push myself to rise with far more grace. "So is that where I stand with you? Second to a plate of eggs and a rasher of bacon?"

Ana's mouth is already full with a massive bite of buttered bread. "Yes, but"—she swallows thickly—"you're a very close second."

Rolling her eyes, Magdalena places the tray—minus the bread Ana swiped—on the bedside table. She brought everything. Bacon. Eggs. Freshly baked bread and butter. A glass bowl full of grapes. Even a carafe of the bitter bean juice Ana has taken a liking to. Coffee. It isn't for me, but it makes her happy, so I shall tolerate its pungency.

But there's something else on the tray far more interesting than anything else.

A scroll, sealed with a dark blue ribbon.

"What's this?" I ask Magdalena even as I reach for it.

She shrugs, but there's a hint of knowing to her expression that makes me believe she knows more than she's letting on.

"Your father asked me to bring it up to you. He said he wouldn't wish to disturb you so early in the morning with such trivial news."

Ana and I share a look. The scroll appears anything but trivial.

Magdalena bustles around the room for a bit, tying back the curtains and picking up the clothes I unceremoniously left scattered by the foot of the bed. Ana's are in a much neater pile seated on a chair by the vanity.

"What are you waiting for?" Ana crowds against me, peering at the still sealed scrolled. "Open it."

"I'll leave you to it," Magdalena offers, as if she could read my mind.

Once the door clicks shut behind her, I rip the ribbon from the scroll. Ana plasters herself against my side to read over my shoulder, but the missive is written in curling script, which I know she struggles with still.

"What does it say? And who writes like this?"

"My father," I say softly, eyes raking over the words again and again. I know what they mean individually but the significance of their totality is proving more difficult to digest.

"Kiki."

I can't tear my eyes away from the parchment.

This cannot be real.

"Kiki!"

Ana claps her hands right next to my ear, making me start. "Christ, Ana . . ."

She blinks at me as if I've lost my mind, every ounce of her being radiating eager curiosity. "What does it say?"

I set the parchment down on the blankets tenderly, as if a part of me expects it to disappear in a puff of smoke like some cruel cosmic joke.

"It is a notice," I say softly. "Of an amendment to my father's will."

"Oh." Ana falls silent at that.

The specter of Alejandro hangs above this house still. He was set to inherit it all.

I force myself to look away from the parchment, to trust that it'll still be there when I look back. When I meet Ana's eyes, I have to swallow twice before I can get the words out.

"He's named me his heir."

Ana's eyes go wide.

"His heir?"

"Yes."

"As in . . . the inheritor of his estate?"

"Yes."

"As in—" She waves her arms frantically at the expanse of the room, but it's clear she means more than the bedchamber itself. That gesture encompasses it all. This room and every room beyond it. Every corridor. Every marble balustrade. Every gilded frame. Every piece of priceless art, every precious artifact. Every orange in the grove outside. The grove where Ana kissed me for the first time. "All this?"

I nod, feeling more than a little numb. "Yes."

Ana howls, throwing her arms around my neck and knocking me back against the mattress.

But that isn't all the letter contains. I tap Ana's shoulder, gently extracting myself from her enthusiastic embrace.

"I haven't even told you the best part."

Ana rears back, lips stretched into a wide, pure grin. "How could it possibly get better than that? All of this is yours. Or, it will be, you know, when . . ."

She grimaces, realizing what she's nearly just said. But she isn't wrong. When my father dies, this will all be mine. All of it. Every inch.

And none of it matters to me. I don't need gold or jewels or all the oranges in the New World.

All I need is right before me.

"There's another clause in the will."

Ana cants her head to the side. It is such an endearing gesture that I cannot help but smile. "Oh?"

"Yes." I pick up the parchment and trace the curling lines of my father's handwriting. "Right here. Near the end." I look up at her. I want to see her face when I say what I am about to.

"I will never have to marry. All of my father's property will pass to me regardless. I do not need a husband and a title to own it all. I am my own woman."

Ana goes still. The only motion she makes is the rise and fall of her chest as she breathes in and out, seemingly very deliberately. Her voice comes in a hushed whisper as the import of that clause sinks in. "Then . . ."

"Then," I say, feeling a curious heat prick at the corners of my eyes. "We are free."

With a startled little laugh, Ana bends her head to press her forehead to mine. I close my eyes, basking in the scent of her. Leather and sword oil and oranges.

"Is this it?" Ana asks, still with that awestruck tone to her voice. I open my eyes to look at her, really look at her. She is so beautiful I could weep, but I do not. I have cried enough for a dozen lifetimes. The sun kisses the side of her face as a soft smile graces those lips I know so well. "Is this the end? It's all over?"

"No." I reach out to take her hand because to do anything else in this moment is unthinkable, unbearable, untenable. Her fingers wrap around mine without the slightest hint of hesitation. This is where I belong. This is where *we* belong. The Valiant Ladies of Potosí. Together against the world. I raise her hand to my lips and brush a kiss against the ridge of her knuckles. All the while, I hold her gaze with mine. I want to remember this moment for as long as I live.

"This is only the beginning."

# AUTHOR'S NOTE

· ◉ ·

While Ana Lezama de Urinza and Eustaquia de Sonza were real people, living in a real place, drinking real booze, and swinging real swords, this book is a work of fiction. After learning of their existence, I was tremendously inspired to write a story of two heroic girls falling in love and fighting the forces of evil. I have taken many liberties in the name of fiction; their appearances, manner of speaking (deliberately anachronistic, as I'm sure you'll have noticed), and the events that occur in their lives. Some things are inspired by fact, including but not limited to the death of Eustaquia's older brother (whose name I've fictionalized), the bond shared by these two extraordinary women, and the significance of the city of Potosí in the greater Spanish Empire. As a Latina, I have always been hungry for stories of rebels and warriors and fearless women in whom I could see myself, and I hope that you, the reader, have enjoyed this tale. To those eager to learn more about Potosí or the Valiant Ladies who lived in it, I offer the following selected sources to begin your journey.

Greenfield, Patrick. "Story of cities #6: how silver turned Potosí into 'the first city of capitalism.'" *Guardian*. March 21, 2016. https://

www.theguardian.com/cities/2016/mar/21/story-of-cities-6
-potosi-bolivia-peru-inca-first-city-capitalism

Lane, Kris. *Potosí: The Silver City That Changed the World.* University of
California Press, 2019.

Salmonson, Jessica Amanda. *The Encyclopedia of Amazons: Women
Warriors from Antiquity to the Modern Era.* Open Road Media, 2015.

Sarkeesian, Anita, and Ebony Adams. *History vs Women: The Defiant
Lives that They Don't Want You to Know.* Feiwel and Friends, 2018.

Thompson, Ben. "Ana Lezama de Urinza." Badass of the Week. June
26, 2015. Badassoftheweek.com/index.cgi?id=29009176046

Weatherford, Jack. *Indian Givers: How the Indians of America Transformed
the World.* Crown Publishing Group, 1988.

# ACKNOWLEDGMENTS

• ◉ •

Since its inception in 2019, this book has been a labor of love. It helped see me through the ghastly year of 2020 (and a good chunk of 2021), and I'm incredibly thankful to the people who helped me get it across the finish line.

My agent, Catherine Drayton, thank you for making my dream of writing about badass Latina warriors a reality. My editor, Holly West, thank you for your infinite patience and your overwhelming kindness. Lauren Scobell, Rachel Diebel, and Hana Tzou, thank you for your sharp eyes and words of wisdom. Clepz Arellano and Veronica Mang, thank you times a million for the beautiful cover. It's a stunner. Thank you to the wonderful team at Feiwel and Friends who turned this book into something real.

Most importantly, thank you, Ana Lezama de Urinza and Eustaquia de Sonza. I hope I have done you justice.

Thank you for reading this FEIWEL & FRIENDS book.

The friends who made

# VALIANT LADIES

possible are:

JEAN FEIWEL, Publisher

LIZ SZABLA, Associate Publisher

RICH DEAS, Senior Creative Director

HOLLY WEST, Senior Editor

ANNA ROBERTO, Senior Editor

KAT BRZOZOWSKI, Senior Editor

DAWN RYAN, Executive Managing Editor

CELESTE CASS, Assistant Production Manager

ERIN SIU, Associate Editor

EMILY SETTLE, Associate Editor

FOYINSI ADEGBONMIRE, Associate Editor

RACHEL DIEBEL, Assistant Editor

VERONICA MANG, Associate Designer

HELEN SEACHRIST, Senior Production Editor

Follow us on Facebook or visit us online at mackids.com.

Our books are friends for life.